I0586117

IMPERFECT CREATURES

THOMAS J. MAINE

Copyright © Thomas Barresi, 2022, All rights reserved

First published 2022

Published by Cell/Zero

The moral rights of the author have been asserted

Without limiting the rights under copyright reserved above,
no part of this publication may be reproduced, stored in or
introduced into a database and retrieval system or
transmitted in any form or any means (electronic,
mechanical, photocopying, recording or otherwise) without
the prior written permission of both the owner of copyright
and the above publisher.

A catalogue record for this
book is available from the
National Library of Australia

Barresi, Thomas, 1998-

Imperfect Creatures

ISBN: 978-0-6455180-7-8

To my grandmother Stella and my friend Dilhan.

Stella, no one has believed in my as much as you have, always telling me I could make this book. It was your encouragement and love that has helped me bring my ideas to life.

And without you Dilhan, those ideas were a bit out there, strange, or sometimes absurd. Your cold judgmental criticism helped shape this story into something that makes sense and isn't lost in my pretentious nonsense.

So without one, this work may not exist. Without the other, it might have been better that way.

Midfight, she paused for only a second, a girl in the crowd catching her gaze. Her eyes were dull, her hair a dirty blonde. *Utterly ordinary.* Except for her stare. It was the type she hadn't seen in years, not since leaving her childhood home. It was a look they all had once, drilled into them through every day of training. Intense, fierce, and concentrated. The type that felt like daggers pressed into the skull. For a split second, she stared, and in that instant, a gloved fist broke her nose.

Blood leaked from her left nostril and dripped just off the centre of her broken lip. Pain throbbed in mounting waves against her skull. Years of training became instinct, and without thought, her mind reached for her hallowed icon. One second of attention, one second wasted. Another blow landed, stealing the air from her lungs. It felt almost nostalgic.

Of course it didn't work. Just as bullets need a gun to be fired and a windmill requires wind to spin, a spell demanded the possession of a hallowed icon. Simply having the mana was not enough to actually cast one. A spell could only become real once channelled through an icon, rendering her attempt useless, and even harmful.

Relinquishing precious ground, she retreated three steps away from Rose, a girl as far apart from her as the division would allow.

Allison kept her right side forward—her good half. The side with a working arm, capable of blocking blows. Her left arm, having long since lost all movement, was kept to her back.

She had no way to compare, but according to research, the cheers should sound twice as loud funnelled through her ears. It was her animal trait, the sign of a Yatrice inheritance, marking her as neither a raw human nor mage. Some Yatrice had a tail or claws. She had the ears of a brown bear. Through those fluffy mounds on her head, she *felt* those shouts. The cheers and boos included both her name and her opponent's. Paying customers were ecstatic to watch a flesh-on-flesh cage fight, no mana allowed. Permitting a mage her spells was the equivalent of granting a human a battle tank, and it made equally as much sense for the martial arts contest. Not even being at the bottom of the lightest weight class could undo such bias.

Dodging the next strike, Allison delivered a kick of her own. It was all she managed before skidding backwards, her back pressing into the cage. It left her nowhere to go, and she had no way to block with only one arm. Allison bent her knees; ducking and weaving around the strike, she stepped in with her own jab, which landed in Rose's stomach.

The strike rocked her, sending Rose down onto her back. *A tactic, obviously.* She looked vulnerable, but

Allison knew fighting on the ground meant accepting a grappling contest, which she guessed was probably the fastest way to ensure she lost. She was a striker. It was only natural, given her training focused on knives. And with her crippled left arm, even having the skill would not be enough to utilise it. Taking the centre of the cage, she waited.

They weren't engaging, which was a sign to the ref. He used his hands to signal them away, giving Rose time to back up. Then he said 'fight', and they went back in. The moment she was back in range, Allison feinted with a punch, following with a kick to Rose's shin. It was the seventeenth of its kind over the two rounds, and she knew the payoff was coming.

Her opponent went for a wide rear hook, but neither its power nor speed mattered. She wobbled, missing her step and flailing just a touch. It was over right then and there, the ref just hadn't called it yet. Rose overreached, making it far too easy for Allison to get into range, sending an uppercut into her chin. Clean, hard, and powerful. Almost enough to flick the light switch.

Her legs collapsed beneath her. She wasn't even down, and Allison had already thrown two more hits. She only stopped when the ref used his full body to separate her from her opponent. Rose stayed down as cheering erupted throughout the room.

Without her glasses, Allison saw only a blur beyond the first rows. People rushed into the cage, pulling Rose off the ground and helping her to her feet. Only one person approached Allison, holding out her bottle. Even though he hadn't fought, his hair was an utter mess. It had been that way since yesterday, when Rebecca took scissors to it with untrained skill, trimming the long locks of dyed dark hair to just above the base of his neck. It was permanently messy, unless he spent the time to tame it, something she'd known him to do on only the rarest of occasions.

Like switching hats, the ref became the announcer, speaking into a microphone with a booming voice. "Your winner, in two minutes and seven seconds of the second round, by a technical knockout: Allison, bright eyes, Khione!" As the ref held her hand into the air, the cheering began anew.

Unlike the big-name competitions, there was just the single camera rotating around the ring during the fight and wheeled in for an interview afterwards. Truly a jack-of-all-trades, the announcer swapped hats again to ask her the common questions the winners always seemed to be asked. Half her answers came with a shrug. The place was amateur league, the audience was sized to match, and she knew she had no career within the sport. Not with one lifeless arm. Besides, fighting was her hobby, if not an addiction, and she had other dreams teetering on the horizon.

The moment it was over, she left with her brother at her side, backstage and through to her changing room. The room was empty save for her school bag. The far wall held a mirror that reflected her ash-white skin, making her figure appear almost ghostly. A smile spread across her broken lips; her golden eyes were alight with glee even as the skin around it continued to darken. Only just visible was the sigil she had tattooed onto her right shoulder blade, its curved branch enveloping a black and purple eye. Her scalp formed rows of white between the tight braids of hair. She stood looking into the mirror, her breath slowing down from the massive adrenaline surge as her brother undid the braid. When the last one came loose, she hurried for the shower.

Peeling off her clothes, she left a trail cutting across the room to the corner cubicle. The water rushed down around her. It was hot upon her skin, but she didn't waste a second trying to balance it right, instead focusing on using the soap to wipe away the blood and sweat clinging to her. Three minutes was all she needed. In the monastery, that was bordering on punishably slow. Back then, though, both her arms had been working.

There was a flash, some sort of blinking-into-the-sun moment, like the lights had been thrown on in a dark room. It made her falter under the shower, extending the time she spent under the water before turning the knobs and taking her towel. Her change of clothes was left on the shelf in the cubicle. Her bra was on the top, easy to shake out and slip through her right arm. The shelf made dressing somewhat easier, allowing her to hold up her left arm and thread the straps around. The lower half was even easier, far less affected by the dysfunctional limb. She left with her blouse in her hand. With Dakota waiting outside, she didn't feel it was worth the hassle.

Dakota sat by the far wall on a small stool before the mirror. His steel snake was coiled loosely around him. Even her animal ears couldn't hear its movement, telling her it was merely half summoned. It made sense. The familiar was only necessary when casting spells, an extra price for added power. Not quite there, not quite not. In that state, it wasn't even under his full control. It was an ethereal snake born as a conduit of his mana, and he used it as a pet.

That old voice spoke in her mind, directing her to use one herself. She almost stopped to look around, trying to find where her old sensei was hiding. But it was just an

5

echo, and hopefully one soon to fade. It had been four years of absence, and four years since she'd heard his cold voice, those unfeeling directions. Even now, she heard his list of every reason why she should use a familiar, how they lessen how much mana she would burn with every spell, and how they were an inalienable ally over a hundred of her siblings had chosen to accept. But it was not for her, not ever. To sign away the sovereignty to her mana was inexcusable, regardless of any convenience they might provide.

It wasn't just the snake; there was someone else in the room—someone she almost forgot in her absence. Their eyes locked as Allison stopped, half-dressed in the centre of the room, her brother talking to that annoying bitch queen.

'I am not!'

The voice resounded in her head, skipping her ears and implanting right into her mind. The girl was beautiful. Her perfect long hair was tied into a ponytail, and vivid blue eyes lit up the dark. Her delicate freckles drew in the eye, and her cheekbones were of the absolute perfect height. Her skin was silk smooth, like it was brand-new. To top it off was the amber heart pendant around her throat, the golden resin aglow, bordered by entwining silver spires. It was the perfect look for the perfect face. And her style didn't let her down. She wore plain white, like always—plain white blouse, plain white skirt, although plain black shoes. It was as if she was trying to make sure everyone that saw her immediately thought *angel*.

She embodied the type of girl every guy wanted, and every girl wanted to be . . . with only one drawback. And somehow, for some reason, she chose to date Allison's brother, someone who hadn't known what to do with love when it slapped him in the face.

6

Narrowing her eyes, Allison stared at the girl, focusing on her forehead so that she was not drawn into that beauty. "What are you doing here? It's not like you to watch me fight."

Approaching Dakota no longer felt worth the price, so instead she fumbled into her top where she stood. The only problem was her boots and sling were still at their side, and her ribbon in his pocket.

It wasn't just her looks that were near perfect. Even the girl's voice was a sing-song sort of velvet. "Can't I see how my friend is dealing with her mending heart?"

Allison rolled her eyes and relented, taking the steps forward and exposing the back of her neck to Dakota. He reached into his pocket, taking out the ribbon and tied it around her throat until it was almost so tight as to infringe upon her air, then folded the rest into a bow. Any looser and it wouldn't feel secure. Aside from the soft feel of the fabric, a second sensation rushed through her body as its power radiated through her. "We're not friends. And Josie left a week ago."

In the mirror she saw her appearance change before her eyes. The ribbon, her hallowed icon, now finally against her skin, allowed her spell to be cast at last. Her black eye faded into white, her nose realigned, and all the damage her body acquired reversed time by a whole hour, back to her peak shape. Even then, though, she would still be considered frail. For Dakota it was a scrap of wood, and for Nikita it was that amber heart. Just seeing it made Allison want to steal it, severing Nikita from her telepathic control.

In the end, Dakota stepped in. "She needs our help."

For a moment she froze, eyes locked on the other girl. "Why would *you* possibly need *our* help? Did you finally realise you need a personality transplant or something?"

7

Instead of taking on her flippant tone, Nikita's voice turned hard. "Someone's trying to kill me."

"What, just now? Took long enough." Allison said it with a smile on her lips, but it didn't reach her eyes. The problem with telepathic brats like her lay in the very nature of telepathy. If someone's thoughts ever displeased Nikita, she could simply replace them with an irresistible urge to lick her boots and serve her tea. Something contrary to that was nothing if not worrisome.

Broadcasting how she had read Allison's thoughts, Nikita said, "You think I don't know that? You think I didn't try? He got so bad I . . . I . . . ah . . . told him to kill himself."

"So what's the issue?"

"The issue is, it didn't stop him," she cried.

With one eye, Allison scanned the room for anything she'd left. "Nikita, if someone found a way around your telepathy, I'm not stopping them. I'm making them my tutor."

Her response came in like a subtle wind, chilling her from the spine out. "My telepathy worked. It just didn't stop him."

Eyes returning frontward, Allison explained, "Everyone knows that dead is dead. There must have been some trick."

"Allison, you are dark attuned, but I just watched you heal your injuries. *That* shouldn't be possible, so why is this so hard to believe?"

Clenching one finger around her thumb, she half turned to Nikita. "I use a time spell to undo the damage instead of healing it. That is not the same as coming back to life. It's. Not. Possible."

"But you've never tried."

Allison blinked. She didn't try to, but she had to stop and gawk. "God, I knew you were stupid, but that stupid? How would I use mana if I'm dead? It was probably just an illusion. Maybe if you could stop being such a stupid, cheerleading bimbo, you'd realise that."

It was only for a second, but there was something off when Nikita's lip pulled back, like that fury was not meant for her face. But all that ended with a swallow. "I'm not a cheerleader. Or a bimbo. God, why are you so mean to me? What did I ever do?"

Allison didn't answer, just started checking her school bag for anything absent. She could feel Nikita's eyes on her until Dakota spoke and diverted her attention. "I don't understand how he found you a second time. I thought you were in hiding."

Pausing a moment, Nikita shrugged. "I was. Until yesterday, I was in police protection."

And now you're back. Pursing his lips, Dakota gave a moment's thought. "You weren't using any telepathy, were you?"

"Sure I did. I got some pizza." In unison, the twins sighed. "What?"

Seizing the opportunity, Allison gave the answer she was sure Dakota would, just adding a few insults. "Because you left a trace for him to follow like a bloody idiot. *Yeah, just give me some pizza.* Then someone asks why they made a delivery when there was no order. Someone asks questions, reports it to the authorities, and bang, investigation into illegal telepathic activity. Even low-level telepaths know to give people a reason to help. I guess you're that powerful you forgot to ever actually learn any discipline."

9

"What do you mean? His reason was 'Serve me.'"

Dakota's voice had a clear exhaustion in it, similar to a teacher explaining something simple for the hundredth time. "It needs to be a reason someone would reasonable have. Make him think he's doing it for a friend who'll pay him back next time. Then make this fictional friend skip town."

Nikita sat stock-still, a furrowed frown on her face. "Huh," was all she said as time ticked away. "You might be right."

Allison was about to say something. She couldn't remember what. Couldn't remember anything at all. Nothing felt real, like everything after her match had been a dream. It lasted near a minute, her skull feeling like it was about to crack. A blinking light erupted before her eyes, a dizziness that rocked her body. It came from nowhere, and it came hard. Unable to get herself back upright, she slid down onto the floor, using the bench as a backrest to keep herself stable. Through half-closed eyes, she could see Dakota doing the same. When at last the moment passed, she shook away the sudden grogginess. "You alright?"

He nodded. "I'm fine. Nikita?"

She alone remained on her feet, standing still, her gaze absent as she frowned. Her arm moved mechanically towards her nose, her finger curled beneath it. "Huh. Blood nose."

Frowning, Allison pulled herself back up. "Do you get those a lot?"

She shook her head. "Not until recently."

"You must be pretty damn weak if hay fever is hitting you before spring even begins."

Nikita shrugged. "You two just suddenly fell to the floor. Don't go calling me weak."

With a shake of her head, Allison felt another wave of dizziness sweep at her balance. Hand to her forehead, she waited for it to clear. She rolled her eyes, pushing herself to her feet. "Okay, so you've learned from your mistakes, and when you hide this time, remember not use telepathy. Simple? Got it? Good."

She expected Nikita to give in, to hang her head a fraction and say '*fine.*' "I can't do that."

"What? Of course you can."

"I can't. I'm not going to live my life looking over my shoulder. I need him taken care of. Besides, if he can come back from my telepathy, then he can come back from whatever the police throw at him, and maybe even Temple. But you two, you could do something. Since, you know, you were . . ."

Leaving the past unsaid, she trailed off under Allison's warning gaze. Taking a deep breath, Allison let it out as two separate sentences. "Not. Happening."

Face tightening, Nikita leaned closer. "I'll pay you. You know I'm good for it."

"You're good to steal. Besides, this isn't about money."

"Then what? You hate me so much you'll let me die?"

Frozen for a moment, Allison's voice burned low. "Because what am I supposed to do? *Me?* Not Sydney, not Zero. Not the top ten, or the top hundred. Did you forget that he ranked us, or that I placed dead last? Four hundred and sixty-second of as many children, the weakest orphan from Koros. So tell me, what on earth do you expect me to do when you couldn't even stop him?"

In a slow, even movement, Nikita reached forward, her fingers curled onto Allison's shoulder. Her voice was almost soothing without its edge. "You know that's not true. You're not four-six-two, you're Cell, and nothing is impossible for her."

It hit like a truck. That name, those memories. The first time she'd been called it. It was already waiting at the edge of her mind, so familiar during her fight. And Nikita's words had just brought it back, the feeling of blood rushing from her sibling's neck all over her hands and face. It was visceral, feeling as if it was happening again. In a sudden movement she threw her off; Nikita's arms almost jolted. "Stay away from my memories."

Holding up her hands, Nikita made some sort of peaceful gesture that only served to make her more annoying. "Sorry, I didn't mean to do that. I'm sorry," she repeated with added emphasis. "It was an accident, I swear." Saying nothing, Allison stared hard at her. "God, you really do hate me that much you'll let me die."

That anger wasn't going away. Nikita was annoying, but not *that* annoying. It was something else. It was the memory itself, the feeling of fighting and training and *existing* as nothing but one of Sensei's assassins for fourteen years of her life that had her burning inside. She had to swallow back the memories, turn around, and look away.

"I don't want you to die. But I do hate you." In the mirror their eyes locked, Nikita's a blue deep as the ocean. "I hate how manipulative you are. I hate how you invade my mind with less hesitation than thieves breaking into a house." Her eyes glanced at the hair strands that fell before her face, clean and silky with the delicious scent of fresh shampoo. "I hate how you avoid responsibility like a plague. And I hate the way you act like you're above everyone else."

Once again, Nikita reached her arm for Allison shoulder, and it was just as soft and smooth as the rest of her. A part of her wanted to shake it off, but she couldn't. Something stopped her, not allowing her to even think about removing that bridge which connected them together. Nikita walked around her, bringing them face to face. Her breath was warm against Allison's skin. Then there were those fingers, reaching up to gently brush her hair. And finally, Nikita's almost breathless whisper, spoken right into her ear. "I don't think that about you. If you want, and you help me, I'll even let you have me."

Her heart beat like a freight train. She was unable to think, rolling automatically onto her toes and closing her eyes, as their lips came so close together. What happened next felt so much longer than just a single instant.

Allison's eyes snapped open as she forced an elbow into Nikita, just as she had to Rose, eliciting a breathless cry as her lungs collapsed. Dakota shouted, probably even more surprised than Nikita, dashing forward to catch her. "You sick freak!" Allison shrieked.

When she stepped again, Allison went all the way back to the wall. Her breath was heavy. She watched with tight eyes as Nikita huddled over, desperate for breath, in her brother's arms. She was trying to scream or cry or shout, but no words came out. Dakota's eyes locked on hers with confusion and anger and pain.

"Get it out! Get out of my head!" Allison screamed so loudly she almost wondered if someone would open the door to see what was going on. "How dare you make me feel like that, like I wanted you?" She closed her eyes, but all she could see was Nikita. All she could feel was her skin. It was all she could do to stop herself from shrinking into a ball. Her fist curled so tight it drew blood. The images didn't stop; the feelings didn't end. Her hair this time, her shampoo in her nostrils. Finally, she fell to her knees. Squeezing her temples, blood dripped from her palm down her cheek as she screamed, "Get it out get, get it out, get it out!"

Cradled in Dakota's arms, Nikita shouted just to be heard. "I'm not doing anything."

Tears started falling from Allison's eyes, and she honestly didn't even know why anymore. "Liar! You're always doing it. You never turn your telepathy off. Always reading, always looking, always after something to exploit. Take off your damned pendant for once. You thought I wanted that? With you? As if. I'd never want to be with someone like you. But you assumed I would, didn't you? And because you can't control your own power, you then put that idea in my head. Your telepathy made me feel that. Then, because you're so busy reading my mind, you read those thoughts *you* implanted. And you're so pathetic you let it affect your mind too, making us both do something neither of us wanted, as if that would please me. You're a freaking powder keg and you don't even care."

Forcing herself to her feet, she took her bag in her hand and stormed past the door, slamming it behind her. She needed some open air. And a place with no telepaths.

Just as Rebecca finished cooking dinner, the twins arrived home. They had only enough time to wash their hands, yet she already knew. She hadn't yet sat down, but she could see the glances swapped between her half-siblings. And when Allison refused to so much as peep at Dakota, any suspicion she felt became confirmed. And yet, there was no encouragement she could make to entice a word from either as they slowly consumed their dinner, the silence extending until Allison wordlessly disappeared into her room, leaving Dakota to help clean up.

Even the next day's breakfast was eaten in silence. A part of it hurt Allison, seeing Rebecca sad, confused, and wanting to know what was wrong. But she didn't tell her, refusing to bring Nikita's issues into their guardian's life. *She has enough stress as it is.*

As the day wore on, Allison opened the case to her violin. It was an old wooden instrument, polished and kept shiny. She opened a wooden box beside her. Also old, it was scratched and dull, and a little longer than her arm. The size was natural, given its contents: a leather gauntlet designed to cover from elbow to wrist. A black knife was clipped into the underside, and the thin wire that wrapped around its handle disappeared inside the gauntlet. Five metal plates covered the top side, each one filled with battle nicks. Imprints around the cuff were left empty, the small gems they housed still sitting in the box; each was one about the size of her thumb tip, a little red and translucent, containing a store of mana she could access only if one was crushed. It looked so out of place in their modern home, like it were some relic from a few hundred years ago.

Since she was dressed in dark jeans and a loose-fitting T-shirt, she didn't need a mirror to know the gauntlet looked strange as she fit it onto her left arm. Black threads escaped the ancient armour and wrapped around her arm, controlling it like a marionette. It pulled and relaxed, shifting her fingers around the violin's bow and pulling it into position as she began to play.

It was like her ribbon in so many ways—a hallowed icon, parts of her mana siphoned off to reside within it as payment for the spells she acquired. But it of was a completely different type. Of the six schools of magic, her ribbon was attuned to heat, which granted spells of time and water. Her gauntlet was instead attuned to an adjacent school of which she had a natural affinity: darkness, derived from the abyss. And while she wore the ribbon wherever she went, the gauntlet was reserved for practice only, left hidden in its box under the bed, a relic from an all-too-remembered past.

Her song came to its end. She had played it endlessly already, the music repeating in her mind, even as her door swung open to reveal the smiling face awaiting her.

"Wow, that was awesome."

Feeling the heat rising within her cheeks, Allison turned away to hide her creeping smile. "Thanks."

As her friend pushed into the doorway, Allison saw her twin a few steps behind. They seemed an almost unnatural pair. If his apathy was ever mixed with her bubbly behaviour, she guessed it might just create someone normal. "Well, don't stop on my account."

Even though she shook her head only slightly, her hair still managed to fly everywhere, leaving locks overflowing her shoulder. "I was just finishing."

With a visible pout, Katife slouched against the doorframe. She wasn't tall, but even slouching she stood above Allison. "But it's been so long since I last heard you play."

"Then what were you just eavesdropping on? Besides, my performance is in a few months. I thought you were coming." In her mind she'd kept it light, but even she could hear how her tone raised, as if genuinely unsure.

With a pout so large it was obviously an act, Katife whined, "But that's over a month away!"

It was small, but Allison let go of a breath she hadn't realised she was holding. "Well . . . look on the bright side." Raising an eyebrow, Katife waited for Allison to continue. "There's plenty of exam prep to occupy that time."

Katife's whole face, along with the eyebrow, dropped as she let out a sigh.

"Great, thanks for reminding me."

Returning her violin to its case, Allison shrugged into a jacket baggy enough to hide her gauntlet. Taking the lead, she left Dakota to lock the house behind them. She walked on the curb's edge, arms stretched out on either side for balance, while Dakota and Katife walked together down the centre of the empty road. He was taller than her, not that it showed. Hands dug into his pockets, back slouched, he looked a few inches shorter.

From behind, Katife called, "Hey, Alley? Where's your flower?"

Hand reaching automatically, she felt the empty space in the front of her hair often taken up by a small gemstone ornament. "Huh? Oh, right. I don't want Rebecca to see what we're doing."

"Wait, what? How does wearing that flower let her see you? I thought her power was to freeze time?"

In a calm voice, speaking matter-of-factly with no room for emotion, Dakota explained, "Rebecca's power creates a pocket dimension where time is frozen. That dimension includes a dome around all her flowers in the world. So if we take one with us, she could see where we are and what we're doing."

Thinking it through, Katife hunched forward just a little bit, enough to make Dakota the taller one again. "So you don't care that she sees everything at school?"

"I mean, she *can* see," Allison corrected. "But it also helps her transport us home. And if something ever happens, she's just an activation of a spell away."

Nodding, Katife added, "So do you normally only take it off for doing illegal stuff?"

Giving a one-shoulder shrug, Allison said, "I mean, I didn't have it last night. Just depends, I guess."

"Last night? Oh! How'd you do?"

She tried to hide it, but the slither of a smile escaped across her lips. "I'm now eight wins, four losses."

As if the smile was infectious, she saw it spread across Katife's face as well. "Hey, congrats. You've finally reached a two-point ratio."

She nodded. "Yeah. I think I'm finally getting my head around fighting with one arm. Not that I'll ever really need to."

The line of houses ended, replaced with empty land reaching to the road on the other side. It had grass and a small plastic playground, but for something called a park, Allison figured it really needed more plants. Jumping the metal rung that served as a fence, they made a beeline for the equipment. It was little more than a slide and monkey bars, another thing unworthy of the name. It came as no surprise that the place was once again utterly abandoned.

Summoning his snake from under his sleeve, Dakota stepped under the slide and let it coil on the bark, connecting to it and activating his power. It took a single spell, a simple one really, but one that was not easy to use. From where the snake touched, the bark and dirt gave way, the atoms shifting to turn it all into something else entirely. A case of reconstruction, an alchemy of sorts, turning bark into dirt and revealing a hidden room with a ladder beckoning them. "This is where you hid it?" Katife asked, disbelief evident all over her voice.

"I needed to hide a whole room somewhere close by. Where did you expect me to put it?" he asked in response.

Coming up behind Katife, Allison looked down into the darkness. "Don't worry, it's completely safe. Probably." With that she jumped, sliding down the ladder as if it were fire pole.

From down below, she saw Katife look to Dakota, and saw him give a reassuring squeeze of her hand before she finally nodded and descended. When Dakota followed, the snake closed the hole, sealing them inside.

Reaching into her pocket, Allison removed her scroll. Having not paid for one of the more expensive brands that offered a choice of colour, hers had a plain black rim. The sheet of clear, glass-like substance lit up in her hands, all her home screen apps facing her. She knew calling it a scroll was disingenuous, that she hadn't paid for the brand. But being first in the market, everyone just called the communications devices by that name, even those made cheaply for a shopper on a budget.

When she chose the torch, bright light illuminated the darkness. Four walls, a small doorway, and an inverted chandelier held up on a thin pole. It occupied the centre of the room, covered in tiny crystals dangling on rings. It was teardrop-shaped. Katife's eyes widened as she looked over the whole contraption. "How on earth did you get one of these? I thought they were government only."

Dakota stepped up beside her, admiring her approval more than anything else. "When I was doing my work experience at the bureau for mages and spells, I sent my snake down through the ground to examine it. It took the whole week, but I finally learnt how it was made."

"Wait, you made it? So why's this illegal?"

Answering for him, Allison spoke from behind the torch, which made her impossible to see. "Government, you know? As long as they have the monopoly on infusing icons, they get to know everyone's power and charge whatever price they want."

Half giggling, half cringing, Katife replied, "When you put it like that, it sounds corrupt."

"Katife, it's the government. Everything they do is corrupt."

Staring into the darkness looking for Allison, Katife

shook her head. "Okay then. So, what now?"

"*Now,*" Dakota stressed, taking back the conversation, "you show us what you picked to be your icon."

With a small nod, Katife dug into her handbag, coming out with a Game Stadium Lite. It was thin, made half of plastic, and about twice the width of a scroll. Searching her mind, Allison couldn't think of a single person who'd used a portable gaming console for an icon before. She sucked at her lip, deep in thought. "Well, it's certainly something personal. I'm just not too sure it's a good idea."

With a raised eyebrow, Katife asked, "Care to explain?"

"It's just . . . what happens when the battery dies, or if it gets wet? Or you need to go through a metal detector? You want your icon to be something you can keep on you all the time, and not something with a limited life."

Deflating, Katife fell back against the wall. "Well, then what should I use? I didn't bring a backup or anything."

With both her eyes and torch, Allison scanned her friend from head to toe. She wore an earring. *Easy to keep, but dangerous to store mana in.* She had hair ties keeping her hair back. *Too easy to lose.* Shoes, which would deteriorate, and clothes that would tear. Finding an answer of his own, Dakota asked, "Did you get an expansion card for it?"

Katife shrugged in the torchlight. "Sure. Adds thirty gigs."

Thinking it over, Allison couldn't help but smile. "Now that would be a unique icon."

Pushing herself off the wall, Katife turned her head

a whole hundred-and-eighty-degree arc to look between them both. "You want me to use my SD card? Won't that be crazy hard to draw on?"

Allison shrugged. "Nah, I practiced."

It was said so quietly she wasn't even sure Katife heard it, but under his breath Dakota muttered, "Which only matters if you're not too klutzy."

The way he looked, like a deer in the headlights of her torch beam, made it clear he hadn't intended to say it out loud. He froze, unsure what to say. She narrowed her eyes and held his gaze for a moment before snapping away and looking to Katife. "The choice is yours."

Katife looked between her and Dakota. Allison could see it on her face, that indecision, that slight confusion. But not about the icon. "Uh, sure?"

She removed the card from the portable console and handed it to Allison. Leaning her scroll against the wall, Allison used its light to guide her hand. She took the thin stylus from her pocket, another item Dakota had forged, and one by one copied the symbols onto the card. It was something normally done by professionals, sometimes aided by machines. She used her wires, wrapping them so tightly around her fingers that they removed even half a millimetre of sway. Her back was stiff by the time she pulled away and handed the card back.

Holding it to her eyes, Katife squinted to see it properly. "What's the next step?"

"We put everything into position and turn this bad boy on."

Guided by Dakota, Katife set the card down on the far side of the chandelier, about a meter from it. After that, Dakota guided Katife the opposite way. Somehow, she looked at home being steered by his hands. Allison turned away, heading for the door and letting them do the rest. She didn't need to see. She'd been through it herself twice already.

Even in the other room, a narrow hallway with nothing in it save darkness, she hard Dakota explain. "When we turn it on, mana will be taken from whatever is on this side, in this case you, and placed into whatever is on the other side. If anything else is in the room, it will be turned into a relay, wasting a bunch of mana. Considering you don't have an awful lot of that to begin with, you should probably take that seriously."

"So we need to get rid of the ladder?" she asked.

"That," he agreed. "And your clothes."

Allison imagined Katife blinking at Dakota as the silence extended. She smiled, glad she had removed herself before the awkwardness began. "Are you serious? Admit it. This whole thing was just an excuse for a teenage boy to see me naked, wasn't it?"

He didn't respond, which Katife seemed to take as affirming his candour. "If either of you so much as peep, the first thing I'm gonna do with this power is whip the living hell out of the both of you."

Hidden in the room by herself, Allison almost laughed, trying to imagine Katife even getting close to delivering on that promise. She only just hid her expression as Dakota came in. She didn't look to him as she spoke, offering only so much as a sidelong glance. "You think this will work?"

"Probably."

"You're such an ass. She trusts you."

"Hence why I made sure it will probably work." Breathing out, she shook her head as Katife yelled the word "ready" from down the hall. "I'm sorry. About calling you

23

a klutz."

Alison held her gaze fixated firmly forward, staring at the bleak wall. "Whatever."

She didn't see what he did, not with it being controlled by his snake, both to seal their room from Kaife's and to set the machine in motion. It started slow but got faster and faster until she needed to hold the wall to stop herself from falling.

Every second that the world continued to shake, she wondered what would be happening on the surface, if anyone would think an earthquake was emanating from the useless park. It lasted almost a minute, and finally she understood why it was normally done in floating rooms held aloft by chains.

For every second she waited with bated breath for a call from her friend, her mind played another image of what may have gone wrong. She saw twenty of them before hearing Katife call, "God, that was a lot of shaking."

Breathing out her worries, Allison released the tension in her back as they gave Katife the time to redress. With the scroll's light, they entered the room, focusing in on their friend looking down at her new icon. "Congrats, you're now bona fide mage. I think. How's it feel?"

Looking over herself as if she expected to see something different, Katife spoke hesitantly. "It's, ah . . . I feel exactly the same to be honest." She bent down, her fingers curling around the card. The moment they touched the card, she froze. It was a long moment, but this time Allison didn't worry. She knew what Katife would be experiencing now for the first time. "Is that normal?"

Allison shrugged. "Tell me what you felt and I'll give you an answer."

Frowning, Katife looked around the sealed room. "It

was like a breeze was rushing me."

"Well, that card is now attuned to the spirit school of magic, so obviously that's what you feel when you connect to your icon."

As Katife turned it over in her hand, Allison imagined her trying to see where the breeze was coming from. "So does the ribbon make you feel hot, then?" Katife asked.

For a second, Allison frowned. "No, why would it? Life spells are used for fire, remember? Heat is for water and time."

"Right," Katife said, giving an exaggerated nod.

Walking right up to her, Allison looked at the SD card. It looked exactly the same, but she could feel something from it. It was faint, but it was there. "Man, I can't believe how lucky you are for your affinity to match with the branch you wanted."

"Hey. Your affinity isn't that bad," Katife replied.

"Really?" Allison lamented. "Out of heat, cold, life, spirit, or light, are there any you would want less than dark? God, what I'd give for light mana. Then I'd be able to heal my own illness and live past thirty-five. But *no*, I get stupid-freaking dark, so not only can I not heal myself, others can't heal me either. And because I have this stupid muscular dystrophy, it makes things even worse. Face it, I have the worst possible affinity."

Arranged in a hexagon, the six mana schools each had two they were strongly compatible with, two they were weak with, and one they were outright immune to. *And of course I got the* one *I didn't want.*

As Allison ruminated over the horrible dice roll, Dakota rebuilt the ladder and opened the path outside. Katife returned the card into her console, and the moment she did, a new icon appeared on the screen. "So at a guess, how strong do you think I am now? Like, I've got to be at least C tier, right?"

From where he waited by the ladder, Dakota's mouth hung a little open, and Allison shook her head. "Do you even understand what those rankings mean?" Dakota asked.

With a shrug, Katife responded, "Sure, they rank you as a mage. And you two put me through a lot of training, so surely I must be somewhere good. Right?"

"Katife, that training was to get you able to use mana. You just got your power. There's no way you're anything but E."

"E!" she cried.

With a pat on the back, Allison cooed, "I mean, we're both only Bs, and think how long we've trained. It takes a long time."

Head sinking, Katife took hold of the ladder and began the climb. "So what's an A then? Or an A-2? I guess that's reserved for legends, huh?"

Dakota offered Allison the ladder, but she let him go next. As he climbed, Dakota said, "A-2 was created when mages broke what were once considered the upward limits. For a combat mage, A-2 roughly means you're the equivalent of an army unit. At a guess, I'd say that Nikita's probably one of the As."

"Huh." Katife's voice was distant, a little unclear. For a second, Allison even thought Katife had said "who."

Climbing up last, the moment she blinked away the sudden light she understood Katife's response. "Speak of the devil."

She was just an illusion, an astral projection of sorts.

She could tell from how Nikita's hair wasn't moving at all in the breeze, and because her skin looked too smooth, totally unlike yesterday. Without speaking, her telepathy put the words directly into their minds. *Got a minute?*

Dakota nodded, stepping forward. Following their gaze, Katife looked to where the image was. It seemed like she wasn't even seeing her, like Nikita hadn't added her to the telepathic chain. She looked ready to say something, but then quickly screwed up her eyes and fell forward.

"Hey, Katife, are you all right?" Allison yelled, lunging to her side.

Rubbing her eyes, Katife eventually managed a nod. "Yeah, I'm fine. What was that?"

"Ask her." There was venom in Allison's voice.

Helping her up, Allison looked to Nikita, trying to work out what was with her and making all three of them collapse in two days. It had never happened before. And yet all Nikita did was stand still, or her projection did, and speak in an absent tone. "Huh. Blood nose." As if noticing their eyes on her, she made the projection smile and brighten its tone a little. "You might be right about the hay fever."

From the way she said it, Allison knew she was trying to tell a joke, but it came out so flat Allison wouldn't have been surprised if she claimed otherwise. Allison didn't say anything. Her brows furrowed, and she walked with hurried steps back across the grass to the street. Katife fleetingly looked between Dakota and Nikita before hurrying after her.

The others started walking, but there was almost half the park's length between them. Allison didn't look back, just kept rushing forward. She asked Katife, knowing it was more about distracting herself than anything else, "So why did you want these spells anyway? Seeing and controlling trajectories seems really weird."

"Oh, well, I thought about it. Not only can I now make the coolest trick shots you've ever seen, but I figure if I could control my own trajectory, I could get myself to, you know, fly."

Hearing a slight breathlessness in Katife's voice, Allison pressed her lips and slowed her step. "You are going to need a hell of a lot more mana before that's possible."

Her enthusiasm too strong, Katife waved her off. "So I train for a bit. Won't be too hard."

"I suppose. I mean, once I could only reverse time by seconds, and now I can go so far back to become a child."

"Exactly. Um, just out of interest, how long did that take?"

Looking squarely into her friend's eyes, Allison said, "Katife, I won't beat around the bush. For me, that took four years of constant training."

Like bubbles bursting, her face dropped. "Oh."

Placing an arm on her shoulder, Allison gave her the best reassuring smile she had. It wasn't particularly good. "You're looking at this wrong. You aren't even from a mage family and never went through formal training. You shouldn't even have mana in the first place. That you've come this far is amazing. And supposedly impossible. So who knows how long it'll take you to be C ranked."

"What? Why C?"

Allison shrugged. "Just a guess of when you'd be able to do that."

"Oh." Swallowing, Katife nodded and started walking again at a normal pace. "So what kind of things did you do to get stronger?"

"Honestly? I was placed in a lot of life-or-death situations. Probably the fastest way to make your mana stronger. That is, assuming you live."

With a smile Allison couldn't tell if it was forced or real, Katife replied, "Well, we're fresh out of those."

With a heavy sigh, Allison sunk her shoulders, sparing a half glance back to the illusion of a girl behind them.

There's one closer than you think.

Dark cobblestone piled into the sky. It formed a perfect cylinder, and was held together by black mortar. There were no windows or doors. The roof was made of flat wood polished so smooth it would never give off a splinter. White dunes and black trees sprawled in every direction. She could see all the way to the horizon, even without her glasses or contacts.

Legs kicking over the edge, school skirt fluttering, Allison looked down from the sky. The clouds were like a game; lots of patterns to make it look infinite and real, but if actually counted, their limited nature was discovered. In all her life those patterns had never changed, unlike the fire. A ring of blazing inferno that once surrounded her tower had slowly stretched towards, and now at last past, the horizon.

Time continued to slowly bury her in the falling grey flakes. Her mind ticked like a lazy clock with glacial gears as the ash spilled over her hands. It fell like snow for the last four years, yet every time she entered the world of her soul, her tower was swept clean. She couldn't remember what it was like before when the trees were alive and the ground was a sea of green. The once tropical forest was now a desolate field of ash.

The peace, the quiet, the blissful solitude—none of it compared to the wonder of being free from Nikita's telepathy. All she needed to do was wait them out—stay at the tower until the lunch bell rang. She wouldn't hear it, not with the world of her soul cut off from the physical. But she knew she could time it right herself. There were twenty minutes left.

Would Josie come back if I could just stay here and count the clouds? Would she see that she was wrong, that I can change?

The tower, ash, trees, and all seven hundred and fifty-eight patterns of clouds all disappeared, fading away until she blinked into the school music room. The room was a clutter of chairs and music stands, but it was open to her as a music student, which provide the perfect lunchtime escape. Sighing, she made her way through the mess, knowing that it was all irrelevant, that Josie had been right. She said it herself: that in the four years since Allison had been taken from the monastery, the monastery had never been taken out of her.

Stepping out, she was immediately hit by the bright sun. From where she was to where she was going was across the whole school, all the way from the north block of classrooms to the southern row of portables. To enter that final row, she'd have to either detour around or cut through the hallways dedicated to year twelve lockers. It was brief, but that heated hallway only made the cold hit that much harder when she stepped out on the other side. Nestled between two of the classrooms was a gap two meters wide, with a single gate blocking them from the houses beyond.

Her legs stretched out, Katife sat beside the gate. Dakota was across from her with his legs folded in, Nikita tucked by his side. Sitting slightly apart to the side of Katife was a guy lost in thought as he ate his banana. Even so, he was the first to notice her. *Typical Theta.* "Hey. Where've you been?" he asked.

Allison gave a half shrug and dropped against the wall beside him. "In the music room."

"Ah," he said, and nothing else.

Her presence seemed to stifle their conversation, leaving it to Katife, the most extroverted of them, to cut the newfound silence. "And I just told you we were all out of these, huh?"

"Huh? Oh, right. Yeah," she said, remembering Katife only yesterday remarking that there weren't any more life and death situations facing them. Turning her gaze to Dakota, she just shook her head and let her eyes close. He didn't say anything.

With her telepathy to read thoughts, Nikita answered her unasked question. "A problem shared is a problem halved. Why wouldn't we get their input?"

Allison rubbed her eyes and kept them shut. "Because it could get them killed. And while you, me, and Dakota might consider those stakes normal, most people do not. I still don't understand why you don't want to leave it to Temple? It's literally in their name: Tactical Mage's *Protection* and Law Enforcement."

Pausing before taking his next bite, Theta nodded. "That's what I said. She said no."

"So, you're going to drag *our* friends into *your*

problems but then ignore their advice? What is that? The worst of both worlds?"

"Because," Nikita said, her voice strained from the repeated explanation. "I already tried that. What did you think happened last time?"

Allison stopped moving all together and just blinked, as if that would wash away the insanity she had just heard. "Last time you said police protection. There's no way you had a Temple guard and this guy still found you if all you telepathed yourself was a pizza."

With an exaggerated roll of her eyes, Nikita hissed, "Well, I'm sorry I'm not some criminal mastermind, Miss 'Been-an-Assassin-from-the-Day-She-Was-Born.'"

Allison felt sure her palm was ready to split open again from the force of her nails. Finishing his banana, Theta looked straight at Nikita. "It doesn't take a criminal mastermind to know something that obvious. All you need are two brain cells that are vaguely connecting."

Nikita looked ready to bite something, maybe Theta's head, but she stopped short. Maybe if she was there in person she would have argued harder, but the closer Allison looked, the clearer it became she was seeing nothing more than a projection. It left her wondering what the actual girl was doing right then, and for that matter, where she was.

Nikita's response proved there was not a moment she was not reading her companions' minds. "I'm staying at Katife's. Her family doesn't see me, so I'm kinda safe here."

Although finding out Theta had been dragged in had brought Allison down, this fired a boiling anger inside her. "What the hell? You're putting your friend's family in danger? How screwed up are you?"

"Hey! How about you have a hunter killer come after you, then I'll accept your criticism. Oh, wait, normally you're that killer."

Nikita's words were like fuel, making that fire burn higher. She could feel her cheeks turning red as the blood rushed to her face. Even Dakota's interjecting voice didn't quell the flames. "Which is why we need to do something quickly. We were planning to bait him into the empty house."

Another pump of her fist, and she knew that bleeding would begin soon. "Dakota, we don't even know what his icon is. That's rule one of mage combat."

Nikita's voice was flippant, as if she was simultaneously filing her nails. "It's probably an axe. I saw him use it when he, well, you know . . ."

She said it with confidence, and perhaps a sense of smugness. In an instant, that was destroyed when Theta, someone who wasn't even a mage, replied, "And what if he has two?"

Lapsing into silence, the school cadence overtook the air. Finally, Nikita had nothing to say. The bell sounded, ending lunch twenty minutes too late. The sounds changed as people congregated from the entire school grounds towards the classrooms.

Shaking her head, Allison whined "So that's it? That's your big plan? Pretend to hide in an empty house?"

Dakota nodded, not seeming to realise her disdain. "All I need is to get my snake inside the walls. We can offer him a bargain to make him stop. If he won't take it, we kill him."

From the tightening in Theta's jaw and the widening of Katife's eyes, Allison saw that Dakota's suggestion did not pass without judgment. Pushing himself up, Theta shook his head and left. She looked at him, then quickly whipped her head back to Dakota. "We're not in Koros anymore. *You* made sure of that."

As Allison followed after Theta, Dakota called, "He's trying to kill her, Allison. I have to do this."

Pausing at the mouth of the alcove, she looked directly at her twin. "What will you do if someone else gets hurt in the process?"

It was like she'd called him the nastiest word in the book, enough for him to physically recoil at the suggestion. "I won't do that. You know me. Just the target. No one else dies."

She could see Katife shrinking away, clearly not comfortable with the topic of murder. "Conspiracy to homicide will be the first charge on your rap sheet. Don't expand it. *You* should know that things never go to plan."

Not looking back, she left the alcove, chasing the one rational person in the group.

"Why am I doing this?" she asked for the fifth time. The first was after his request, the second was when she strapped her boots on, the third when she took her gauntlet out of her room, the fourth on the bike ride, and the fifth now as she hunched on the roof opposite the abandoned house. But the answer was simple. He asked. In eighteen years, he'd only ever asked for one thing. *A bitch of a time, forcing me to choose.*

The cold air made her thankful for the decision to bring a beanie. Darkness kept rolling further, overtaking the cobweb-infested For Sale sign. She'd used her own scissors to cut her hair, making it short enough to bunch under her beanie. If the worst came to pass, purple hair was too easy to remember, especially when matched with Yatrice ears. For the cold, her choice of jackets was lacking. It was dark and double layered, sewed together by her, with a piece of soft metal shaped by Dakota in the middle. It was enough to stop a light blow or glancing blade, but little more than that.

The room inside was lit with movie like precision, so as to pretend that someone there was hiding within it. It was a room at the back, on the second floor, with its curtains closed. The only way to see that escaping sliver of light was to peer between the roofs of the neighbours behind. She watched police walk right up to the door, only to turn around a second later. It was more than breadcrumbs, but not quite neon fireworks. Whoever was after Nikita would be coming; she just had to wait.

It didn't matter that her left arm had no sense of touch; she still felt the gauntlet's weight on her shoulder. Just like on Katife's hallowed icon, her runes were somewhat hidden underneath the metal band. The difference was that she had only four sigils engraved into it. The first made wires, which she used to climb the roof and control her arm. The second was in use right then, embracing her in a cloak of shadows. It did little to protect her against the cold, but plenty against sight, and more against attacks.

The last two were left unused. One served as a second brain, a parallel processing spell to control the wires when there were too many for her own mind to handle. She shuddered to think what would happen without it. *My own wires would probably kill me.* The fourth was no spell at all. Instead, it bargained her limits, making her spells cost more the further they went from her body. In contrast, as long as they stayed within her skin, they cost near nothing. It was the same family of magic to a familiar, a rune designed to weaken some part of her magic while making another part stronger.

The police were the last visitors. Some people walked past, but no one stopped. Not for three hours and eighteen minutes. Then a silver car drove up for the fifth time, this time stopping at the curb. Its license plate was hidden, but she already had a photo from its second pass.

Sending a quick message to her brother, she opened her camera on her scroll, snapping as many pictures as she could of the man exiting the door and crossing the road. He looked both ways. *Not a local.* It was a giveaway. In that neighbourhood, nobody looked; they just ran out, car or not. Draped in a shapeless coat, he stepped onto the pavement and up towards the front door.

He looked back for a moment. For him, it was an opportunity to see if someone was following. For her, it was a moment to get a picture of his face. Seeing no one, he reached under his coat and revealed a black-bladed hatchet. Just like Nikita said. At the peak of her zoom, the image became blurred, but she was able to capture his movement, placing the blade inside the door like some sort of liquid, and a moment later, pulling it out. With his other hand he gently pushed, and the door swung open, only to be pulled back as he stepped inside.

Only watch. As she sat, perched across the road, her mind raced with its decision. To watch or to follow? Watch, as Dakota asked, or move, like her body desired? Josie's words sounded in her mind, those chiding remarks that the orphanage was still within her. *I hate how right she was.*

Using a pipe and shimmying down the roof, Allison hurried, doubled over, her silent steps carrying her to the door. There was a split in the door, but no splintering like an axe would create. Pushing it open, she crept inside. Even with ears better than any human's, she didn't hear any footsteps, only the creaking of the stairs.

She kept her feet spread to the ends of the steps where the wood was strongest, which allowed her to follow with no noise at all. Light spilled from upstairs over the staircase, making her breath stop entirely. She could see his silhouette. He was big, in both height and size. She just hoped the bulk was fat and not muscle.

Stepping past the threshold, she watched the door fuse shut behind him. She heard the footsteps. Familiar footsteps. Straightening up, she turned to her brother.

"I thought you didn't want to get involved," he hissed.

Sighing and shaking her head, she just muttered, "Shut up."

Stepping up to where the door had been, she saw nothing but a blank wall, like it had always been that way. Muffled by the plaster, a voice with an accent she'd never heard called out. It was a strange accent, clearly not originating from any major nation, nor a common result of second language adoption. It was something entirely new, and yet, at the same time, familiar. "I should have guessed she would hire more help. Whoever you are, I warn you, that girl is not worth the effort."

Dakota's snake retreated from the walls, wrapping itself around him instead. She could almost see the shift when it let go, making the changes permanent. As Dakota held his hand to the wall, the snake made the tiniest of holes, burrowing in with its eye pressed close. When Dakota's eyes closed, there was no question he was looking through his familiar's. "Put down the axe and step away."

There was the sound of a slight thud, followed by that accent again. "Now what? Will you kill me?"

She saw the tension in Dakota's jaw as he contemplated his options. She didn't know what he was seeing, but she seized the moment to avoid anything unnecessary. "We came to bargain."

He laughed softly. "That is . . . unexpected. Who

could possibly be protecting that girl and yet ask for a bargain? Who you are?"

"We're just here to stop unnecessary violence."

A slight pause. "I never expected the minx who uses others to settle for a bargain, but I must admit I am intrigued."

Ice broken, Allison pressed on. "Tell us what she did and I'm sure we can work something out. Did she steal something and now the telepathy has worn off? Make you do something stupid?"

Though she was hoping an apology would be enough, her heart began to sink when he started to laugh. "I think you have made some mistake. This is not about me. This is about the greater good."

In that moment, she stopped talking. Nothing else came to her mind. Something stolen could be returned, and anger could be patched over, but ideology was something near impossible to reason with. Whether he noticed her silence or wanted to know for himself, Dakota asked the question, "Nikita's just a girl. What greater good could killing her possibly achieve?"

"I would hardly call a cursed child who is one of the most powerful telepaths in our world 'just a girl.' And know that if there was a better way, I would have found it by now."

As Dakota rubbed his head, the snake momentarily moved, but it was only a second before it returned. "Greater good? Are you insane?"

Muted sounds of exhaling breath drifted to Allison's ears. "It would be easier to talk if I had a name," the man said.

It could have been automatic, a response born from how similar the feeling was to back then. It was a name she hadn't used in four years, something left back in the orphanage. Knowing their shared father, witnessing their birth certificates, Rebecca knew the given names for them to return to. Since that day, she'd never gone back, and neither had he.

"Zero," Dakota said.

"Zero? Interesting name. Mine is Soul. And the girl?"

Choking for a split second on nothing, Allison grunted as he addressed her. "Cell."

"Cell and Zero? Interesting."

Not giving him another moment, Dakota pressed in. "What do you want, Soul?"

"I already told you that."

Dakota paused, clenching a fist. "Pick something else. I won't let you have her. But if it's in my power, I will attempt to help."

There was a strange tone in his voice, desperate almost, and Soul heard it too; an emotional defence for Nikita's life. "You're more than just a contractor. What do you think she is to you?" Dakota didn't answer, which she guessed was the safer play. But the damage was done; Soul made that clear. "You think she cares about you. You think you care about her. You even think your choices are your own. But you know her power. You know what she is."

Limiting his answer, Dakota reflected only what Soul had already claimed. "Like you said, she's a telepath."

"Yes. An uncommonly powerful one."

"So she scares you? You fear what happens when you can no longer overcome her power? That's not a reason to kill anyone."

A human ear wouldn't hear it, but she was sure he clicked his tongue. He sounded annoyed, as if Dakota's words were offensive. "This isn't about me; it is about her. About *them*. Those cursed children will cause only calamity upon this world. And she already has."

She could hear Dakota's emotions rising with every exchange, and as much as she loved the idea of seeing Dakota expressive, she knew it wasn't helping. Keeping her voice level, she cut him off. "What curse? Just because she's a bitch doesn't mean she deserved to be killed."

Soul gave pause, and when he spoke again, he sounded calmer. "I like you. Please do not make me hurt you."

"I can take care of myself."

Another pause. "You are a mage, are you not? A most capable one, I imagine. Know that I hunt those who hunt the children, and Temple themselves will not stop me."

Shaking her head, she tried to arrange a priority to the questions erupting in her mind. "Nikita, a hunter? That girl barely hunts for her own shoes."

"No, no. My apologies. I hunt the monsters in the dark, those which deliver a fate worse than death. To that girl, *I* am her saviour."

"You're a special sort of freak, calling yourself the saviour of the girl you're trying to kill," Dakota said. He didn't shout, but there was an emotion in his voice Allison hadn't heard before, at least not in a long time: deep venom and raging anger.

Soul's tone became that of a preacher speaking from the stand. "You know nothing. You have no clue what is going on or who you are up against. I have stood where you stand now; I have seen the path it wrought. This is the only option, and if you truly want to save that girl, you would hand her over so this may end in peace before someone innocent is caught in the crossfire. Otherwise, you will learn what true regret tastes of."

There was the clenched fist, the stiffness of Dakota's stance, and even his words. "I never hurt anyone but my target. There will be no crossfire." The subtle movement of the snake and the curl of his lip told her everything, even before Soul gave a shout of pain, followed by the thump of him falling to the floor. She froze, listening for any sounds from the other room..

"What the hell was that?"

Even in the dark she could see him seething, a bubbling box of boiling rage. "He's still alive."

Manipulating the atoms making up the wall, Dakota pulled it back into an archway. Just like every other room around the house, this one was empty of furniture or signs of life, the owner having long since moved on. Yet now, the room was reformed, plaster turned to iron spikes piercing the man and pinning him in place.

He was older than them, maybe mid-twenties. His skin was fair, but tanned from work in the sun. His dark hair was kept short. And that size was muscle. His voice had changed to raspy breaths. Even bound, there was something gripped tight in his hand. "You are making a huge mistake. I pray that you come to your senses before we meet again."

He hadn't finished speaking when Soul used what little movement he had to throw the grenade in his hand. She didn't know how he'd gotten it out under Dakota's watch, but that didn't matter when it landed between them with a thud. Diving for cover, Allison went for the room to her side while Dakota dove back towards the stairs. The moment his attention shifted, his spell undid itself, the spikes disappearing and the room returning to normal a moment before the grenade went off. Sounds blasted in her ears until all that was left was an indistinct ringing. Even lying on the floor could not save her balance. She relied on the feeling of the roaring wind to know when the blast was over. She saw the blackened walls and the hole in the floor that had opened right where it had landed.

She couldn't hear them, but she could feel them—footsteps, heavy as they ran towards her. No longer pinned in place, Soul ran for her. *No, for the hole.* Diving forward, she grabbed his arm just as his body dipped below the floorboards. Her body slammed into the wood, his weight holding her down. Grunting, she summoned both her spells from the gauntlet. The dark reinforcement coated her arm while the strings sprung to wrap around her bones, helping her hold on. A glance to her side showed her brother had fallen back towards the stairs with half his body aflame, his instincts dulled from years of Rebecca's care. "I am so sorry about this."

Soul's words pulled her attention back towards him right as his face disappeared from her sight, replaced with the floorboards that had been blown apart. She couldn't feel her grip anymore. She couldn't feel her arm at all. Her right arm, her good arm, extended only a little beyond her shoulder before it was cut off by the floor. In that one moment, all the damage had undone. The ringing in her ears, the flames on her brother, the blackened walls, the hole in the floor—all at once reverted to their pre-explosion state. Her arm, which extended through the gap, was now severed by the floorboards' reappearance. And the pain was unlike anything she'd ever felt.

Her eyes watered as she screamed. Her arm felt like it was on fire, the arteries cut off but blood unable to escape. She couldn't move, her arm fused into the floor, allowing not a millimetre of movement.

Looking around, she saw her brother. Her voice was raspy, needing every drop of effort to cry out. "Get after him!" Looking to her, Dakota hesitated, wanting to help, wanting to do what she asked. "God dammit, Dakota, your snake is gone. Go."

Realising the truth of her words—that until his snake had recovered enough to be resummoned, he was powerless to help her—he ran, disappearing down the stairs, allowing her to focus on her own current nightmare.

Without a moment to so much as think, she released more wire, looping it around her arm and increasing the pressure. She knew from countless training and assignments exactly what it was capable of. She knew how thick to make it to scale a wall, support her arms, or become invisible to the eye. And she knew how to use the wire to cut into skin. For the first time in her life, her wires purposefully cut into her own flesh. There was little resistance all the way until meeting bone. She had no breath left to scream, just to grunt and bear the pain. Cutting became harder. It became blinding, her eyes unable to see. It became deafening, her ears hearing nothing over the pounding of her blood as she pulled away with all her might. The loop closed in, severing her arm in pieces. The force threw her onto her back, her stump now expelling all the trapped blood eager to escape her arteries. And for that moment, all she could do was scream and kick and wail as she fought to connect her mana from her body into her ribbon.

Her left arm dropped, dead. She couldn't afford the mana to move it, nor the delay between using the icons. Heat and dark were close, but they still needed some time to switch. The moment she could, she set to reverse the flow of time surrounding her arm by just a minute. Her sleeve didn't come with it, but her right arm was back. There was no sign of her arm in the floor, not even a hole. Not healing magic, but time, and right now it was as if she hadn't shed a teaspoon of blood. The physical feelings of pain died immediately, but that didn't stop her mind from reliving the echoes.

She dragged herself up by the wall, hobbling one step at a time to the front door. Outside, Dakota desperately tried to slow Soul down, the door to the silver car already open. Without his snake or poisons, and against a bigger man with an axe, delaying was all he could do. Maybe if Soul was unarmed, or when Dakota was fresh out of the orphanage, there might have been a chance.

Rushing forward, Allison coated her body in shadows. She sent those wires inward, as thin as they could go. They dug under her skin, wrapping around her muscles and weaving amidst them until they were one. It wasn't a full job, but it was enough. The wires formed powerful muscles in her legs and arms, and with them she was able to close the distance so much faster. Her third spell kicked in, taking control. Millions and millions of muscle fibres in a single muscle alone; she doubted the smartest person alive could micromanage all that effectively. Her mana stores were depleting. She didn't know how much she had left and lacked a gem to top herself up. Seeing her running, Soul made one last swipe at her brother, swinging his axe with one hand while using his other to reach under his coat. Pulling out another grenade, he popped the pin and continued his defensive assault as its seconds counted down.

Run at him and blow up, or stay away and let him get away. It didn't matter. He already dropped the explosive and in their scuffle, it was kicked towards her. She had enough time to cross her arms and brace herself, activating her ribbon before it even hit. She saw Dakota turn to see her, saw Soul use his hesitation to shove him towards her. And no matter how much mana she poured into her ribbon, it wasn't enough to withstand the blast that ripped her body until no life remained.

Snow kept falling, expanding the film around the mountain more every day. It was all he could see, the ever-increasing rise before him, along with the occasional trees. He couldn't count how long it had been since he'd last laid eyes upon the broken buildings he knew.

The peak, hidden since he'd left the village's plateau, had returned to view. Pressing on, he came closer and closer, so close to reaching the top, where he would finally be able to decide where to descend to.

As he scrambled on hands and knees, red liquid started seeping through his skin. It fell onto the snow and changed its colour. It came from his knees, then his hands and legs. And yet, when his feet finally reached the top, the wounds became nothing but red marks across his skin.

The clouds were all below him now. He saw nothing but sky in every direction, and the village was but a cluster of tiny dots before the matchstick of the bridge. Beyond, white-covered trees extended into the distance, constantly getting lower until suddenly they stopped before a vast carpet of blue. It stretched as far as he could see, eventually colliding with the sky. It was so much bigger than he ever could have guessed. He'd never seen beyond the bridge, or beyond the village, really.

Of all the mountains, only his soared that high. They dotted the land in every direction, except towards the blue. His lips curved into a smile. He didn't know why. His body felt stronger than ever, like he could walk another twenty cycles of light and dark. And if he did, he knew exactly where he would go. Around him he saw a land so much larger than he ever knew, but still so empty. Only the blue offered something new.

Sitting on the highest point, he watched the light arc across the sky. Its touch warmed him. The air fed him. And he stayed there. When the dark overtook the sky and the stars came out, he could see so many more than usual. And for all the distance he ascended, they didn't look any closer. They were so beautiful and bright as he waited throughout the dark.

The boy stopped counting the cycles of sun and stars passing him by. After seeing the performance over and over, he started looking elsewhere. They always rose, they always fell. He was getting sick of it—sick of the sameness all the villagers prayed for. They were content to sit and wait as life ticked by and their bodies thinned out, some of them becoming nothing but white sticks held together in a vaguely similar shape. He couldn't take it a moment more. Not the sameness, the emptiness, the complete apathy. Anhedonia on a mass scale. He couldn't take any more of those people who had lost everything and given up on caring. Those with enough effort to speak could chant all they wanted that it was a mountain of belonging, but the boy knew that for whatever reason, he did not belong. He had lost nothing, only the years wasted since his birth.

The boy felt pain in his legs as they moved for the first time in a long while. Going down was so much harder than going up. Afraid of the long fall that would await him, he was careful not to trip. The dark brought back the stars so many times, and each time he had to stop. Without light he didn't know where his feet were landing. Eight cycles of light and dark went around him as he returned to his village. Only then did it come back into view. And for the first time he lost his step. Slipping, he rolled down the rocks. It was so much faster, but he paid for it with that much more pain. When he finally stopped, he could no longer move. His body screamed all over, but no matter how hard he tried, it wouldn't respond to his efforts to move it.

The village was right before him, and through the broken wall he could see a woman sitting inside, her back stooped over. He called out, his voice the only thing working. And the woman turned, her eyes meeting his. She watched him, staying inside that dilapidated building as dark came back and went, saying not a word, moving not a muscle. She just watched with those half-glazed eyes as the snow slowly began to bury him.

The first thing she saw was the vibrant blond hair falling in a thick plait as the hand shook her awake. There were still flowers embedded in that hair. The face was round and rosy, containing two golden eyes just like her own. "If you don't wake up now, there's no way you're getting to school on time."

Forcing her eyes open, Allison blinked her clock into focus. With a sleepy smile, she tried pushing herself up. Instead, she found not a single muscle reacted. The second grenade had torn her flesh to pieces, yet for a second time, Soul had used his spell to undo the damage. All her mana was spent trying to defend herself from the blast, leaving her nothing to undo the damage her wires caused to her own body as they strangled out her organic muscles. "Alright, I'll be out in a sec."

"Okay. I, uh, like your hair. It's . . . different." The moment Rebecca left her room, keeping her door wide open, Allison focused on her ribbon. Had it not still been tied around her neck, she didn't know what she would do, which was why she had insisted Dakota leave it tied on when he carried her to bed. With a night passed, she had ten hours to reverse to get her body back to when she was sitting on the roof, leaving her already drained of mana as she rolled out of bed. It meant leaving her hair poorly cut and short for the time. *Worse, Rebecca saw it. She'll think it's weird if I change again so quickly. I'll have to wait a week or so.*

As she stepped into school at the first ringing bell, she still felt that hollow feeling, that utter emptiness from after she was blown apart. The pain of the explosion was one thing, but what came after was something else entirely. Like infinite nothingness and the most soul-sucking feeling, to the point she thought it was literal. It made it hard to focus recalling the feeling when she returned to life in the middle of the road, watching Soul drive away. It was something beyond the capacity of words, to have done the impossible and returned from death. *I owe Nikita an apology. Bloody hell.*

By recess, the feeling had her head over a toilet bowl as her breakfast came out faster than it went in. The question of how Soul did it rang in her mind. By lunch she was hungry, leaning against the wall in their usual alcove with her brother and friend. Even Theta couldn't reason any answer. For Katife, that was expected; she was new to mana. But to find not one suggestion between any of her friends left a harsh implication of its own. It was theoretically impossible, but evidently achievable. Even spirit mana was primarily focused on wind. Closing her eyes, she tilted her head back, counting out the near five hundred different powers she had known from the orphanage. There was only one that felt even remotely similar. Looking back to her friends, finally sure they had no better answer, she gave in to what she knew had to be true, announcing, "He's not healing. It doesn't make sense. He has to be using a time spell."

Dakota nodded his agreement. He'd seen what happened to the house yesterday, the damage undone. Wood was easy to change, but there was nothing natural about the way it happened—like it was beyond Soul's actual control. *The way he said sorry just before it came back.* Her words were quiet. "He's like me. He's reversing time."

Having sat in silence, eyeing Allison the entire conversation, Theta finally spoke up. His voice was disinterested, like he was reporting the weather. "Perhaps. But from what you described, it sounded like a global power compared to your surgical precision. It's also possible it wasn't a heat spell. He might set checkpoints, like in a game. Or they could be illusions." It was a detached way of speaking, but she could hear the care in his words.

With a voice more fitted for weekend gossip, Katife chimed in, "Sounds more like a 'set and forget' power to me."

Leaning forward, Theta raised his voice, with an almost defensive feel to it. "You're not thinking that through. That would mean he turns the spell on and leaves it. This was most likely global, which affect everything equally for a duration."

Katife responded by speaking louder and sitting forward. "Exactly. He turns it on, and then whatever happens, his spell kicks back automatically. Whereas if it was global, it would affect the whole world, not just a small range."

"Just because it's called global doesn't mean it works on the whole globe."

"That's why it's called global!"

She rolled her eyes and he rolled his, each turning in opposite directions and asking the same question. "Which do you think?"

Even Dakota's stoic face widened under Katife's glare, and Allison was sure Theta's was having a similar effect on her. Quietly, she stammered, "It, uh, sounds like you're using different words to describe the same thing."

It was enough to get Theta to stop glaring at her, but even when Dakota nodded his agreement, Katife was slow to look away, like she wanted his approval. Bringing back control, Theta cleared his throat. "I guess since it's not the main issue we can agree to disagree, even if I'm right."

"Sure, but you're not."

Shrugging with apathy, Theta continued. "Logically, a spell like that must be limited by either needing a recharge or having a short range. On top of that, it's probably costly. Now, how to slip that info to Temple without implicating yourselves is the real question."

Nodding as she leant back, Allison saw her brother do the opposite, glaring at Theta as if he shouldn't have dared suggest it. Seeing his expression, a part of her wondered what he would do if he was still Zero: a nameless child and proficient assassin, raised in a hidden monastery up in the mountains. *Would he use that flower, the one traced on his back as the tree is on mine? Would he make something more horrifying than anyone here could imagine, just to protect Nikita?*

Instead of proposing that nightmare, Dakota looked sidelong to Katife, speaking from the corner of his mouth. "Hey, Katife? Do you have any contacts from your work experience days to run a plate for us? Or get a sketch artist?"

"Oh, so you want the police help now?" It came out snarkier than Allison intended, but shrugging internally, she decided that it didn't bother her.

"Using all available resources is different from going to the police."

Cutting in, Katife called, "Um, guys? I don't think it matters. I might know a few cops, but that won't help for something like this."

With half a laugh and enough sarcasm to drench the school, Theta teased, "Yeah, you'd be better off planting the info at a fake crime scene and letting them run with it."

Raising an eyebrow, Dakota started talking, and the moment he did, Allison felt her heart shudder. "That actually isn't that bad . . ."

"Yes it is. It absolutely is. God, don't even think about that."

"Yeah, Alley's right. That's kinda messed up, Dakota," Katife added.

Eyes narrowing, Dakota sighed. "It can be on the back burner then."

Softly, under his breath, Theta muttered, "Why did I open my mouth?"

Allison's lips were becoming dry, and no one was saying a thing. After a long moment, Dakota seemed ready to declare that "back burner" ready to be lit up. Theta saw it, and Katife too, considering her sudden interjection. "I can check the car rego online, see what it finds. Let's at least do that first."

For a second, Dakota's mouth was open without sound, until he found the thoughts to stop and nod. Eager to add onto that hesitation, Allison declared, "And I can check out the Bureau of Mages and Spells. We know Soul's power, and his first name, I guess. Might get some information on him."

Shaking his head, Dakota said, "No way. That place is a bureaucratic hellhole with privacy clauses for decoration. You won't get anywhere near that info before they make you want to leave yourself."

Her dry mouth only became more arid as she soothed her racing heart before giving her suggestion. "Well, what if I just ask nicely?" she said, twirling her hair with her finger.

For a moment, they all looked at her in something between shock and bemusement. Regaining her composure, Katife leant in and placed a hand on her knee. "Alley, dear. Are you suggesting using sex appeal?"

She shrugged. "Sure. Why not?"

Briefly biting her lip, Katife nodded to herself. "Okay. And which of us exactly is supposed to do that?"

With another one-shouldered shrug, Allison smiled a little. A clear implication, and yet to Katife, it was a trigger to shake her head. "Sorry, girl. As Dakota said, no dice."

Throwing her arm out, Allison exclaimed, "Why not?"

Katife opened her mouth, but before any sound came out Dakota interjected, giving an answer to what she guessed Katife was yet to ask: why Allison thought it would work at all. "Back in Koros, Allison was often sent in to charm people. But back then, she was a child, and people found her so adorable they sometimes forgot to search her for knives."

"Exactly. So why can't I do that now?"

"Because you're not a kid anymore. And there's a world of difference between having people forget to check you and having them pay so much attention they override safety protocols. Best case, they'd call the police to investigate Rebecca for grooming."

"Then I just go as I am now."

Dakota closed his eyes and Katife bit her lip. It ended up being Theta who had to speak up. "Allison. Please don't make me explain why that won't work."

Turning to him, she tried narrowing her eyes but couldn't. Even as she asked, her heart already knew. "I'm making you explain."

He sighed, seeming to look for the best tone to say it, yet knowing full well none could go well. "Because you're not sexy. Not enough if your goal is seducing someone into breaking policy."

Shuffling where she sat, Katife moved right beside her to stroke her hair. "You know we all think you're adorable. But what you're suggesting, it's kind of insane."

"You don't think I'm good enough." It was a statement, leaving no room for Katife to respond. Not that it stopped her.

"Alley, come on. No one is enough for this, not even a photo-edited supermodel. It just doesn't happen."

"I've seen it happen."

"TV doesn't count."

"Not just TV! I had siblings from Koros who could do it. I know it happens."

"Just how much degeneracy did your sensei push onto you?" Theta whispered.

Exhaustion in her voice, Katife looked hard into Allison's eyes. "What is this really about, Alley?" Her gaze dropping to her knees, she said nothing. With a soft sigh, Katife used a finger to guide Allison's head back up. "Look at me. This is about Josie, isn't it?"

She swallowed; she didn't even try to. Her lips became even drier, and she tried looking away again. "I don't know."

Blinking slowly, Katife's voice was like a soft ocean wave, constant and gentle on the shore. "There will be others."

"You just said I'm not attractive. Why would anyone want to be with me?"

"No, we said you're cute and adorable. That's not the same thing." Pausing, Katife gave Allison a moment to return her look, which she didn't take." Look, Alley. You're like a puppy. They're cute and cuddly. Everyone loves puppies."

Allison's lips twisted into a pout. "I don't."

Lost for a moment, Katife was fast to find a new angle and re-attack. "Then maybe something more like a platypus. What do you say?"

Quietly, under his breath and nearly indiscernible over the schoolyard noise, she heard Dakota *actually* chuckle. The others heard it too, their gazes all swinging his way. It was nothing particularly noticeable, and if it was anyone else nobody would care. But from Dakota, it was like he had just fallen to the floor in laughter. With enough decency to look ashamed, he looked away. "Sorry, it's just . . . a platypus is so perfect. Cute, but with deadly claws and poison. It should be your spirit animal."

Unsure how to react, unsure how to even feel, Allison stopped and swallowed. "Poison's your thing, not mine."

Mouth left slightly opened, he finally shrugged it away. "We know a snake's my spirit animal. My familiar kind of gives that away."

With nothing to say, she fell back against the wall. "Fine, whatever. Is it so wrong for me to want people to see me as a girl and not a platypus?"

Katife's arm went around her and her face was so

close, Allison could almost feel her friend's soft smile. "I'm sure that's how Josie and Sydney saw you."

In a moment, her heart rocketed up into her mouth, enough that it felt like she couldn't breathe. She turned away from Katife, twisting out of her hold. "Josie left, and Sydney . . . isn't here anymore."

Just saying her name rekindled the old wound in her heart, the pain about the friend she'd never see again. It was all she could say, and she was surprised she even got that many words out. Even as the temperature was beginning to heat up with the mid-September day, she felt a sudden chill rip through her. Speaking in soft words, Katife whispered, "You never talk about it. Do you want to? Just you and me; we can send the boys away."

For a moment she was ready to say something mean. She wasn't sure what, only knowing that it would feel good. Then she stopped, slowly nodding instead. Katife smiled a soft, sad smile and turned to the others. She never got to speak. Instead, Dakota's voice rumbled in a lowered tone, "Why don't you want to talk to me?"

It seemed impossible that Dakota would sound so insulted from just a few short words, but it was there and it was real. "No offence, Dakota, but you have no clue how I feel. I'm right here, and there's no one else you've ever cared about. You don't know what it's like to lose someone important." She was wrong. It wasn't hurt. It was anger. It was soft and only just above the surface, but it was raging inside him; she could see it in his eyes. The best part of twelve years she'd known him, and there was nothing that could explain that glare. "It's just who you are," she added, partially apologetically.

He spoke slower than normal, actually taking the

time to think before he spoke. "You think I've never lost someone? Who do you think leaves those flowers?"

She knew what he meant instantly. She'd told him about them, the flowers she sometimes saw whenever she went to visit *her*. Always the same sort, always a little to the side, as if allowing space for someone else. But *she* had no family left, no one to leave them for her. In an instant, Allison felt something snap. She didn't quite know what, just that it was something that made her want to take her twin by the throat and slam him backwards. "Don't you dare. You two couldn't even stand being in the same room. Don't talk like you gave a damn when Sydney left."

It was sudden. Her mouth had moved faster than her mind, and now her words were lost. Across the alcove, behind Dakota's eyes and in his voice, she felt the anger bubble within him like she had never known before. "You think I couldn't stand *her*?"

"Well, I don't see any other possibility for how you used to act."

More than just words, his response was an explosive shout loud enough to turn a few heads. "I couldn't stand how she looked at you!" As fast as the anger came it went, and Dakota's voice dropped to a near whisper, as if overcorrecting. "She chose you. The only person in Koros I could talk to. The only person who knows my . . . who I told things to. You really thought I couldn't stand her?"

Not another word was spoken. He looked at her, and for a time, their gazes held. Then his dropped, and so did hers. Theta and Katife were silent. None of it felt possible, but she knew that look hadn't been faked. For better or for worse, he meant what he'd said. It made her feel even dizzier than before. Like she couldn't stand much longer.

There was just one thing, one rule, that made it feel possible. It had happened before, more than just once, when life took something she knew to be true and proclaimed it all a lie.

Is this what it means, to be an orphan of Koros?

She paused at the iron gate as if unsure for a moment if she should even enter. Rebecca stayed where she was, hovering by the road. She'd wait until Allison was out of sight, just in case she turned back. Swallowing, Allison disappeared inside.

Outside was a proper road; inside it was bevelled with a brickwork gutter on both edges. The overhead canopy of trees stretching inward created an almost peaceful image. *Almost.*

She turned at the bridge. She kept her arm still, her fingers tight around the bouquet. Rebecca helped pick them out. She had enough flower knowledge to open a florist, were she willing to take the pay cut.

There was neither haste nor dawdle in her steps. She passed people every so often, most paying no heed as they knelt by the grass and stones. Sometimes even a car overtook her. She wished they wouldn't, that the park would ban them. It wasn't speed or threat. It was the feeling—seeing and hearing those lumbering machines while in that place made it impossible not to think of that day.

They were little more than tablets protruding from the ground, stone rows swept away one after another. There was no need to count anymore; her feet knew the way. She swallowed, reaching Sydney's, and tried her best to smile. For *her* sake.

"Hi, Sydney. Sorry I haven't come to talk recently. It's just . . . Josie felt weird about it. But I'm here now, in time for your anniversary. And I've got the whole day to talk. No Josie this time to . . . well, I guess you remember. And as you probably noticed, it's just me now. She's too gone to drag me away." Choking on the words, Allison had to blink away the forming tears. "It was all the remnants of Koros, apparently. That's why she left." For a long moment she lapsed into silence, as if waiting for a response. Then with a sudden energy, she added, "Oh! I brought you flowers. Rebecca helped pick them."

Placing the bouquet before the stone, she took a small rock and laid it to rest over the end, pinning them in place. She saw the other flowers, left by someone else. *Left by Dakota,* she reminded herself. Legs bent, she sat down, using her knees to hold herself up. The stone was a dark grey, the only real colour being the photo near the top. Sydney's photo was taken only a few weeks before that stone was made. In it she was smiling, flashing her pearl-white teeth. Her hair fell in tight curls out of the frame, her milky eyes peering into the camera. Even her dark skin was vibrant in the image, and it wasn't because of the gloss. Once she had been the older one, but now time had frozen her in place while Allison moved forward two more years.

"I thought that after the train I'd be over all that

insanity, but then we had that accident, and now . . . now it looks like things are getting bad all over again. I mean, I'm about to do something so freaking stupid, and I don't even know how I survived the last one."

She laughed, not that she felt it. "If only you were still here. You'd know what to do. You might not even need us. I bet you could take him out all by yourself. But I don't think I can. He already beat me once. And Dakota, he was there too. And Katife's got involved as well. You remember Katife, don't you? Now there's also Theta. Sorry, I can't remember if you ever met. Well, he came up with this idea to find the guy. I mean, it was a joke; he didn't mean it. But Dakota liked the idea, and I can't believe I let him talk me into agreeing. Every other lead went nowhere. Even the car. It was rented, paid for in cash. God, it is such a dumb idea. Wish me luck. I'd need it even if mine wasn't naturally god-awful.

"Oh, speaking of Katife, you'll never guess what we did. Dakota made one of those chambers, and it worked! She's a mage now. Cool or what? I didn't think it would be possible since she was supposed to be human. Maybe there was some secret crossover in her family history, huh? Maybe they eloped, and the mage decided to pretend to be human after that. Otherwise . . . I just don't see how it's possible. I mean, humans don't have mana circuits. I guess it's a mystery, huh? That girl . . . you two really would have got along, I'm sure of it. It's a shame you didn't get more time together. Nikita on the other hand . . .

"Oh! You don't know. Dakota found a girlfriend. Crazy, right? My twin. The one who we joked was named after the amount of emotions he has. *Zero*. But hey, he got her, and she is just whack. Like, I mean it. She's actually insane. All self-indulgence and narcissism.

But what do you expect from a telepath, hey? Well, she's the reason for this mess. I almost want to just throw her under an actual bus and let all this be done with. Don't worry, I won't actually do that. I know how much you hate greater good arguments.

"Hey, ah, just thinking. Dakota said something crazy the other day. Not to mention he got super angry, at least by his standards. He said you two were friends. There's no way, right? I mean, he was Zero. And you two never talked, so . . . surely not, right? I mean, he couldn't have left those flowers, right?"

Clouds moved to cover the sun, while the dirt started moulding to her print. She couldn't leave, not then. She had too much to say, too much to think. Too much pressure. From Nikita's hunter, who chose to arrive just as exams were really turning on the pressure, and her violin competition was just around the corner. Too many things, each as prominent as the last, culminating in a simple fact: that in that moment, she needed Sydney. She needed to hear those words she used to say. That the past was just that. That she needed to live for the next day. Her promise to make her own destiny had once sounded like a fairy tale, yet she had done everything to make it true. Until one day, that destiny was gone.

A car, a trip, a field of flowers. How they rolled and danced and ran. It was long ago, and far away, and seemed so very far. Back in a time when Allison's arms both worked, and her heart was in one piece. A magnificent outing, with a horrible ending. The last time Allison ever heard her speak, after the car tumbled end over end. Those words reverberated in her mind as if Sydney were saying them right then and there instead of in the wreckage that took her arm, and Sydney's life.

Don't cry, dear Cell. Don't let yourself break. I know you've suffered; I know you're in pain. I know sensei gave you demons you hold to this day. But if you can learn to accept these shadows coiled around your heart, and live with both your light and dark, then one day you'll be a beautiful, imperfect creature, so strong and wise and full of grace.

To look up into the sky and see any form of colour with the clock still reading seven twenty-five was the clearest sign of winter's demise. Not that it mattered when every building flooded the streets of Isoval with synthetic light, casting a veil to hide the stars.

From the train station under the city's centre to their destination was only a short walk, ending with a shortcut through a z-shaped alleyway. Reaching the other side, Allison saw the entrance, so different to how it looked online. Lights spilled out the door and ignited the footpath.

There was a line wrapping outside filled with people all clustered around their age. Music leaked out the open doorway in a mindless rhythm, the type of beat you feel in your heart like a bass drum. It was something she would have been beaten for had she ever played it back in Koros.

Club Lunar was written in neon letters over the entrance. On the same wall, seemingly as far away as possible, was another door, this one going up, leading into the building proper where a day business of some sort was closed for the night.

Her sleeveless yellow dress left her shoulders defenceless against the cold, her thin jacket adding flimsy protection. Her neck had it worst, especially at the back where she was accustomed to the windbreaker of her hair. After the disastrous self-inflicted cut, she had to rewind her hair's time to make it work. It meant going back to when she was still growing it years earlier, when the length was just a touch longer and the cut cleaner. Any more, and Rebecca would question her constant changes. It gave Allison the length she needed to form a loose bun at her back, which she'd pieced through with the stem of Rebecca's flower to hold it in place.

The closer they got, the more the escaping air felt like warm breath surrounding her. The volume doubled as they stepped inside. After Katife's brutal reminder of her unsexy appearance, she didn't begrudge the extra time spent scrutinising her ID, the date of birth edited by a week. Whatever changes Dakota had made, they were enough to allow them in.

Reaching the metal staircase descending onto the floor, Allison reached into her pocket to remove a set of mufflers. They were small enough to fit within her ears, with a dial to change the amount of sound let in. Most Yatrice with ear traits had a set, allowing them to control a world designed for human ears, but it was the first time she had stooped to using them herself.

She'd been to parties all her life, often as a performing musician with a hidden agenda. And yet, there was not a single similarity she could spot. Instead of polite conversation there was rowdy chatter. Instead of waiters roaming around carrying trays of fine wine there were only a couple of bartenders all behind the bench. Instead of a small band of violins, flutes, or other similar instruments, techno music blared over speakers.

Katife fit right in as they stepped to the dance floor, swaying naturally to the beat. To Allison, it was an utter impossibility. Nothing she did felt right in the artificial environment. Shouting over the noise, she had to gesture to communicate her words. "How long do we need to stay for this to look legit?"

"Are you seriously already complaining? Alley, it's your birthday. Try to live a little."

"My birthday's not for two days."

Shaking her head, Katife called, "You really are too uptight, you know."

Allison rolled her eyes, though the effect was lost in the low light. The people moved in such unpredictable ways that a bump here and a push there soon had her hopelessly lost. It didn't help that her head was spinning. First Katife was right beside her. Then there was a person between. That person became many, and then an ocean. Within minutes, she was on her own in a sea of strangers.

It could have been one song later or fifty—they all sounded the same. No matter where she pushed through the throbbing crowd, neither her friend nor brother were anywhere to be found. Somehow, her efforts to get back overshot until she was by the bar. Even the people sitting there were tapping a foot or finger, nodding their head, or showing some movement. In contrast, her stillness was as alien as a toad in an electronics store. There was nothing for her to latch on to, nothing in the music that moved her. Music was drilled into her as an excuse, a reason for her to approach a target. Even now, it had shifted only so far to become a passion for the performance. "Hi."

Spinning on the spot, Allison jumped back and raised her good arm, fingers flexed up. It made her look startled, as opposed to preparing for an incoming strike. A little tired, fresh off the dance floor (judging from the sweat), and a little older than her (judging by intuition), the guy who tapped on her shoulder smiled from under a sheet of facial hair. "Want something?" she asked.

"I was just standing there, and I noticed a girl standing here, looking unhappy. So I figured I'd say hi and see if I can brighten your night a little."

"Hmm . . . Nah, I don't think so."

"You sure? You really look in need of some good vibes."

"And yet you look all out."

He didn't know what to say, but he clearly took the hint, nodding once and backing away to an inner crowd who laughed at his empty-handed return.

With her party lost in the crowd, Allison skirted the edge of the dance floor. There was a second story overlooking the floor, divided by tinted windows. She kept her eyes on it until it was above her head as she hugged the wall. Closing her eyes, she tried her hardest to let the world wash over her.

She didn't know if it was because she had become a wallflower or because she appeared to be alone, but something about her was sending off an open signal. *Maybe being in a club is all they need.* There was a dark-haired edgy guy, some university athlete, a clear geek, and others she couldn't sum up so quickly. By the seventh time, it had become so exhausting she chose to leave herself, bracing into the crowd and making a beeline for the bathroom.

She slammed the door open and stepped inside, feeling an almost heavenly release as the door closed shut. She extracted the mufflers, letting her ears feel air again. The music was still loud but dampened and distorted by the heavy door that looked capable of withstanding a fair amount of punishment.

For a public bathroom, it was far from bad. Clean walls and floors were more than she could ask for, and the metallic-grey wall tiles provided a nice atmosphere, if nothing else. Stepping up to the mirror, she turned on the tap and splashed her face with cold water. She checked her scroll, looking at the clock. Seven forty-three. Still a long time to go.

Allison stayed where she was, leaning against the far wall, nose buried in her scroll. Feeling the pull of the flower, she took it out of her hair and laid it by the mirror. Every time the door pushed open, her eyes darted up, and every time she identified the occupant as someone other than Katife, they drifted back to the different card games she'd pulled up.

There was a girl in a blue dress. It was short, revealing a lot and catching her eye. The girl stood behind the mirror, reapplying lipstick and refreshing her eyeliner. Between moves, Allison's eyes drifted up. She was pretty. Nothing spectacular, but as a distraction from her fifteenth game of solitaire, she made for a decent sight.

"Hey," the girl said. Immediately, Allison looked back down to her scroll, feeling her cheeks reddening a little. "Hey," the girl repeated.

It was only the second time that Allison realised the voice wasn't accusatory but curious, like she was asking, not demanding. Looking up, she saw the girl looking sidelong at her. "Hey," Allison replied, her voice soft.

For what had immediately felt like a threat, the girl barely looked at her. "You've been there for a while."

"So have you," she muttered back.

The girl shrugged, continuing with her task. "I'm here for the mirror. You're just on your scroll." Allison said nothing. Finishing up, the girl returned her things into her purse and turned fully towards Allison. "Someone out there you're trying to avoid?"

She had an accent. Down south, more like France. Lowering her scroll, Allison gave a soft answer. "No, not avoiding anyone in particular."

"So it's people in general then?" Allison just shrugged. "Whatever floats your boat. I would have thought a girl like you could near have her pick in there."

This time, she did look back down. "I'm not really interested in all that. And I don't feel like talking about this with a stranger."

If she took offence, the girl showed none. "Sure, whatever. Look, I don't mean to pry, it's just . . ."

"It's just what?" Allison snapped.

Her voice calm, the girl pressed on. "I don't know, you seem lonely. Like you could use someone to talk to."

Allison started to bite back a retort, but there was something so apathetic and distant in the way the girl talked that she just couldn't. The girl didn't care about Allison, not specifically. She was just being friendly while occupying herself. Probably a social butterfly-type. Talks to everyone, never invests. She softened her tone, realising there was no value at all expending energy to be angry with someone who couldn't care less. "Sorry, I'm

72

just not interested in this loud music or being hit on by annoying guys, and that's all that seems to be out there."

The girl's eyes narrowed just a touch as she looked Allison up and down. Then, with a twitch of a smile, the girl rushed away. "I'll be right back."

Allison's mind slowed to a snail's pace as she tried to decipher the girl's meaning. Left alone, Allison muttered, "Wasn't going anywhere anyway."

It only took a minute for the door to reopen. Like before, her eyes drifted up. The girl was back. Only this time she wasn't alone, having dragged in another. "Okay, Tara, I'm here. What did you want to show me?"

The girl—Tara she guessed—stopped by the door, basically whipping the other girl ahead of her. She stumbled a little in her high heels, recovering, and in the process looked up, right at Allison. She had milky eyes and long, curly hair. At five and a half feet tall, she had a perfect hourglass figure held inside a modest blue dress. Their eyes caught, and before she knew what was happening, Tara disappeared again.

The girl looked back, seeing her friend gone, trying to work out what was going on. Looking to Allison with a smile that was part mischievous, part awkward, she started, "Hi."

"Hi," Allison repeated, her sociability forcibly raised, at least temporarily, in response to Tara's.

"I, ah . . . I'm sorry to bother you. My friend insisted there was something here I should see. You wouldn't know what, would you?"

Eyes glancing around the empty room, Allison said, "Search me."

The awkwardness faded from the girl's smile, becoming ninety percent mischievous. "I'd like that."

Allison's hand twitched, putting pressure on her scroll. Any harder and it may have broken. She swallowed. The girl stepped closer, stopping at a tap and running her hands under the water as if to justify her approach. Even as she looked away, Allison couldn't. Good cheekbones, smooth skin. Asian, or some such descent. This girl was definitely *very* cute. *She might even be beautiful enough to get info from the bureau.*

"I'm guessing you don't come to places like this very often, do you?"

Allison tried to speak but found her mouth dry. Forcing her lips apart, she croaked, "Ah, yeah."

"Thoughts so far?"

Her mind blanking out, she said the first thing that entered her mind. "The music's too loud."

The girl laughed. "Yeah, that it is. Not too bad in here, though." Returning the look, her eyes shifted towards Allison's ears. She gave a tight-lipped smile, seeming to really understand how seriously Allison meant it.

Feeling too awkward to look away but with her mind failing at speech, Allison's body turned stiff as her eyes wandered. Cracking, she broke the silence. "Aren't you going to go back out?"

Smiling without looking back, the girl said, "Why would I? There's no one out there who interests me, and I'm kinda tired from dancing."

Swallowing, Allison struggled to maintain the conversation. Thinking of the friend who dragged her in, Allison asked, "No one?"

The girl looked to the door and shrugged. "Nah, not really. Although there may have been one. A cute little bird, all alone against the wall. If she asked, I think I would have danced with her."

She said it so casually, yet Allison felt her heart

launch. There were those sideways looks which made the girl's meaning clear. Wishing for the wall to open up and swallow her whole, Allison finally focused her eyes back on her scroll, using the power of awkwardness alone. The screen had timed out. Countless hard swallows made their way down her throat. The door opened again—someone who came to actually use the bathroom for its purpose. Feeling the girl's eyes on her, Allison returned the look. "I'm Yifei," she said, a faint smile on her lips.

Taking a final swallow, Allison tried pushing herself off the wall and straightening up without making it clear she was doing so. "Allison." She croaked, her mouth coarse beyond any reasonable expectation. With every word spoken, the part of her wanting to run and hide became both smaller and stronger.

"Allison? That's a nice name. It matches perfectly with your lovely eyes."

Immediately Allison blinked, keeping her eyes shut longer than normal. When they opened again, she looked to the ground, hiding the gold as much as possible. "Thanks. So do yours."

Yifei laughed. When Allison didn't say anything more, Yifei looked down her body. "Do you mind me asking what happened to your arm?"

Allison replied quickly, too quickly she guessed. "Car crash."

"Oh, sorry."

Allison shook her head. "It was two years ago."

Yifei must have been unsure how to respond, allowing the dance floor's cadence to once again overtake the air. Finally, she came to a decision. She stepped away from the mirror and towards Allison, holding out a hand.

"So? What will it be, little bird? Care to dance?" Her voice was soft and calm and completely lacking any sign of anxiety. Allison's eyes darted to the door.

"I'm not going back out there."

"Who said anything about going back out? There's plenty of space here for a small little waltz."

Her lips dry, Allison tried wetting them without Yifei noticing. Yifei stepped closer, and Allison could feel her body heat. "You're clearly bored. How about some innocent fun to pass the time?" Glancing back up, she met her eyes. *They really are beautiful.* Milky green, nestled under a soft brow. She became so captivated by the girl's eyes she didn't notice the arms coming down over her shoulders, interlocked fingers held behind Allison's hair. The moment their skin touched, Allison jumped. It brought her closer, right up to Yifei's face. The scent of rosemary filled her nose. She could feel her breath. They were so very close. "Sorry, I didn't mean . . ."

No words came to her mind. It was like both languages she knew just disappeared and she couldn't manage a word. In the end all she could do is shake her head, allowing Yifei's arms to return.

Yifei led her in and through a dance she didn't know. Her body was stiff and rigid and moved like a robot's, while Yifei's flowed and swayed. It was like she was in a haze. Her body moved as she told it, not a millimetre more. She felt like her right arm was a second left arm, and her boots were on wrong. Not that it seemed to bother Yifei. If anything, it made her enjoy it more.

A vibration started at her hip, working through her body. It made her freeze, which made Yifei pull away.

"Something wrong?"

Words coming faster than her mouth could say them, she stammered, "Yeah, it's just . . . I think I got a message."

Stepping back, Allison opened her scroll and looked at the screen. Under Katife's name was a message asking where she was, saying they were ready to leave. Typing back a response, she hit send and returned her scroll. "Sorry, I have to go. It was, ah, nice meeting you." Allison didn't wait to finish, her feet already dragging her away.

"Yeah, it was nice meeting you too. Is there, ah—" Yifei stopped, cutting herself off with Allison already halfway to the exit.

Allison turned back. "Is there what?"

Shaking her head, Yifei looked away. "Don't worry about it."

Another hard swallow, difficult against her throat. "What?"

Batting her lashes, Yifei gave a soft smile. "Is there any chance I'll see you again?"

Allison shook her head. "I don't really like these sorts of places."

Yifiei nodded slowly, like she was disappointed. "Right. I mean, you could always give me your number, then we could meet somewhere . . . quieter."

Allison utterly froze. A big part of her wanted to move, to chase after Dakota and Katife, but she just froze. It was so different to what she was used to; Theta had been her friend for weeks before they exchanged numbers. This girl barely knew her, but was already being so forward with her. Her mouth went even drier, if that was even possible.

She saw Yifie's shoulders sag just a little, a sign of

defeat. Allison looked away, unable to look as she recited the digits to her scroll. She didn't wait for a response, turning and practically running out the door. In the mirror, she saw her cheeks were bright red.

Rushing through the crowd, she took the stairs two at a time until she was in the outside air. Its freshness hit her like a fist, making her shiver as she stepped faster towards the alleyway. Rounding the corner, she almost knocked right into Katife. "Alley, hey! Since when do you not pay attention to where you're going?"

Blinking didn't help, but she did it anyway. Over and over, as well as shaking her head. "Katife, I am so sorry. I just got so . . . doesn't matter. Where are we up to?"

Katife frowned, alerted by something in Allison's voice. But before her questions had a chance to arise, Dakota spoke up. "Done. Just need to make the call."

Looking past them, Allison saw what looked like a small puddle of blood by one of the two dumpsters. Props made in the service of a plan Theta never meant to be used. And yet, she'd missed the whole display, didn't get to verify with her own eyes it was done right.

To use Dakota's power to create a lifeless body that would look like it once lived. To piece it with a knife carrying the fingerprints from the house, then dump them both in the street for the police to investigate. The size would need to be right, which meant a second body, one to hold the knife and do the deed. To create a struggle, show signs of bruising. An entry point right for Soul's height. So many details Dakota spent an hour setting up while she was down below.

So many pieces, so many parts. Please God, let none have gone wrong.

Trapped beneath the snow, his fingers were becoming numb, his lungs struggling to fill. But his strength was returning as the air fed his body. His skin healed over, his energy came back, and finally he was able to push himself up, the snow cascading around him. The dark had come three times, and yet the woman hadn't moved once.

Since he was too exhausted to tread over the surface of the snow, deep footprints tracked in his wake. He didn't spend much time there. The woman made it easy, her apathy as he lay in the snow. Stumbling through the lane of dilapidated buildings, he entered the one called Home. It was broken like all the rest, but held together the best, giving a slight protection from the cold and snow.

The floor creaked. The place was empty. There were no possessions, no changes of clothes, no toys, no heirlooms—just a couple of people comfortable in the spot they found amidst the decaying wood. They had been there so long it seemed that they were becoming a part of it. He knelt before one of those people, a thin woman who looked ready to cease movement all together. It had been a long time since she had talked to him, since she had acknowledged his existence. There was a part of him that hoped his long absence up the mountain would rouse her interest. She barely even looked his way.

"I leave," he said to her. She said nothing. "I not come back." Still, she was silent. Her hair pooled beneath her in a tangled mess. In his earliest memories, it had been far less long and tangled.

The woman's eyes were hollow, deeply sunken into her face. Her chest rose and fell slowly and steadily. She didn't care in the slightest. She just sat there, savouring the decay, her place to live beyond pain or suffering, her place to merely exist.

Outside, the world darkened, and the boy waited, sitting on the floor throughout the darkness. When the light returned, he pushed himself to his feet, leaving the decaying building behind him. "Goodbye, Mother," he said to the woman as he stepped towards the door. It was a word she told him to call her. That had been back when she still spoke, before she had resigned herself to the rotting hut.

With his strength returning, his steps didn't track so deep. They skimmed over the surface of the snow, through the village, and to the rope bridge that spanned the deep fissure into the earth. He couldn't see the bottom.

The bridge swayed with his slightest touch. He didn't look back; he only stepped onwards, off the land for the first time ever. "Don't cross the bridge," the woman had once warned, long ago. "The world out there is cruel and hard. There is so much that can hurt you, kill you. It is better to stay here. It's such a gentle place. A peaceful place. A safe place for us to exist away from all the pain. Don't cross that bridge; the world outside is not safe."

The boy didn't know what lay beyond the bridge, but he knew there was nothing in the mountain for him. Gentle, for what? Peaceful, for what? Safe, for what?

The bridge swayed with every step, but no fear could slow his pace. There was no pain or horror that could be worse than the rot of the mountain town, where people existed but never once lived.

It happened so fast, the police blocking off the alleyway and the small areas around it. Police cruisers parked by the entrance, one with its door open for Katife to sit in, a welcoming gesture for what they thought was a horrified witness.

They watched the police in plain clothes, cheap suits that looked good on a budget, leave the alley in their direction. "I'm Detective Lee, and this is Detective Casey. Would you mind telling us what you saw?"

Even now, Katife kept her eyes lowered. She didn't say anything until Dakota put his hand on her shoulder. It made her look up. She had tear stains running through her makeup. *Damn, she's good.*

She described everything as if it were real, leaving out only that Dakota had puppet-mastered the whole thing. With the subtlest of movements, Dakota guided her lies by squeezing her shoulder. She stammered and stuttered and kept her eyes wide. Ten minutes later they were walking away from the police line, Detective Casey's card in Katife's pocket. Still hearing them talk, she slowed her step a fraction to listen. "What do you think?" Lee asked.

"I don't know. She didn't seem to see much. Not sure how good of a witness she'll be," Casey replied.

"Shame there were no cameras."

"True, but we can't help that now. The real problem is that an alley like that exists in the first place."

"That's what you get when they build new buildings around the old and try to take every bit of space they can."

Releasing her breath, they finally left hearing range. Already Katife had begun a call with her mother, and immediately the shouting between them began. Allison's palm moved to her mouth, stifling her laughter. "I'm actually glad we don't have a mother right now."

Dakota didn't return her cheeky grin, instead casting a sidelong glance. "In that case, you're up for calling Rebecca?"

Her laughter turning into a sigh, she poked out her tongue.

He took the hint, using his own scroll to send out the call. Just two rings later, she answered. *Someone's been anxious.* Dakota explained what happened in his cold way of speech. It didn't stop Rebecca returning with a worried voice, desperate to come get them. At that point, Allison leant into the frame, a sly smile on her face. "Hey, Rebecca."

"Allison?" Rebecca said, her voice a welcome and a warning.

Allison closed her eyes, not looking at her half-sister. "Yeah, um . . I've got some bad news." Her eyes narrowing, Rebecca waited. "I must have dropped your flower. Sorry."

On the screen, it honest to God looked like Rebecca wanted to throttle her. But it only lasted a second, and her cooler head prevailed. "Alright. I can try to find it on my end and then meet you."

"It's probably in the club. So there'll be a bunch of police there."

Sighing, Rebecca relented. "Then there's one in my office. I'll be there in ten."

With nothing else to say, they agreed where to meet and ended the call. The closer they travelled to the central business district, the lighter the foot traffic became, allowing them to arrive far ahead of Rebecca. Allison sat on a designer stone wall between the metal divides supposedly stopping skateboarders from ruining the beauty, a task they managed to complete themselves. Her eyes sunken after the call with her mother, Katife sounded far closer to Dakota than normal. "So, where did you disappear to tonight?"

Shrugging, Allison leant back with her hand against the stone. "I hid in the bathroom. Only place where I could get away from all the people."

"You realise people is part of the point, right?"

"Yeah, but I expected you to be a part of those people."

Throwing an arm around her, Katife cooed, "I'm sorry. I didn't mean to leave you like that."

"It's alright. Some good may have come from it."

"Oh?" Katife had time to mouth, right as Rebecca rounded the corner. She was dressed comfortably in a sweater and slacks, the formal type of casual.

"Hey, Rebecca," Allison said. "Sorry about the flower."

Her attitude completely different from the call, Rebecca shrugged it off, stepping closer to where they sat. "Don't worry about it. It won't be hard to get back. So, what were you talking about?"

Allison answered quickly, leaving no room for anyone to toss in something embarrassing. "Just how crowded that place was."

Rebecca's expression was blank as she nodded. She was young enough to remember what it was like having a guardian she wanted to keep things from. "You might want to try looking for low-key places next time. I might remember a few you'd enjoy."

"Ah, thanks. Next time I go clubbing I know exactly who to talk to." Her attempt at enthusiasm did not bleed into her voice, instead making her sound hollow.

"With your upcoming exams, next time better not be until the three of you are safely partying in Salbador." She said it with a fierce tone, but a kind smile. No one gave any response. With a heavy breath that may have been either dejection or frustration, Rebecca turned to Katife. "You can come back with us if you want. Our places are close by, so it should be much faster than public transport."

Stalling with a long "uh," Katife looked to her friends for some confirmation. Dakota gave a slight nod, which Katife copied for Rebecca. "That would be great, thanks. Saves me catching a train."

Smiling and nodding, all while removing the flower from her hair, Rebecca held it by her chest. It was made of coloured glass or a semi-translucent stone. The core was already healed from its last use, ready to activate again. Taking each of their hands, Rebecca crushed the gem under her thumb. Around them the world flashed bright, the city disappearing and being replaced with a sand sculpture replica, down to every last person. The twins let go, half stepping away onto the now frozen street. The flower's gem was back together, glowing in its place. Katife's grip doubled, putting a strain on Rebecca. "You can let go. It's just getting in and out where we need to be touching."

"Oh, okay." Letting go, she looked around the world.

Allison could see the domes in the distance of all the places where a flower was left. One was close by—hers, she imagined—and another two were in the air. One would be Rebecca's office, and the other she guessed was their father, living somewhere on the outskirts of the city in some apartment. This close, she was seeing more of him than ever before, yet it was only an empty building wall.

Nothing else moved in Rebecca's world of sand. On the outside, time stood still. Compared to the real world, the space was compressed between Rebecca's orbs, making a walk that should have taken hours accomplished in a few minutes, although by the time they took her hand again and she crushed the gem for a second time, not even a second had passed.

Once they emerged inside their house, they were bathed in darkness. Hitting the light, Rebecca turned to Katife. "Welcome in. You can wait here if you want."

Giving a grateful smile, Katife called her mother again. It didn't take long for her car to pull up and her mother to beep her horn. Giving both of them a hug, Katife rushed down the lawn and into the car. The moment it was out of sight, Rebecca turned to the twins. "Both of you, couch. Now."

Each swallowing, looking to the other, they obeyed her direction, crossing inside and folding into the tan sofa. "What happened tonight?" she asked, remaining standing before them.

Dakota looked to Allison, and Allison looked to him. Allison looked harder. "We went out, Katife saw someone getting mugged, so we reported it."

"No. Not that."

"I . . . don't understand."

Rebecca sighed, rubbing her forehead. "Do you think I was born yesterday? Are you suggesting the first time you go into the city you just happened to stumble onto a crime scene? And after losing my flower first? Maybe if you were ordinary kids, but with your history, I don't buy it."

Realising the conversation had swung to her anyway, Allison protested, "It was an accident."

"Allison, please. You're careful and deliberate. It's one of the amazing things about you. But it means that if you lost it, you wanted to. So just . . . talk to me."

"Come on, Rebecca. It wasn't long ago you were going out and partying. I doubt you'd be happy with Connie strapping a camera to you everywhere you went."

Rebecca's tone dropped, her eyes slightly narrowing. "I never demanded you take it everywhere. Leave it here if you want. I'm just trying to look after you two."

"Us?" Dakota cut in. His voice was distant, but not quite apathetic. It was mild, but she could hear the tinge of judgment. "Or you?"

"God, Dakota, what's that supposed to mean? I just don't want anything bad happening to you."

"Hence why you're okay spying on us."

Rubbing her forehead Rebecca said, "What? I have never once spied on you."

"But you could, with your power."

Screwing her eyes shut, she pinched the bridge of

her nose. "Do you realise how hard you two make it for me to keep you out of trouble?"

Dakota opened his mouth, ready with some retort. But before whatever it was came out, Allison spoke in a quiet voice, looking at her knees. "So don't. You're not our mother."

A single strand of Rebecca's hair falling would have sounded like a gunshot. Rebecca was frozen, her eyes locked on to Allison's. "You should go to bed." It was an order dressed up as a suggestion.

Feeling the cushion shift beneath her as Dakota stood up, Allison followed after, avoiding looking at Rebecca. When her hand reached the door, her half-sister said, "Goodnight, Allison."

Allison slid through her door. Taking careful steps through the dark, she crossed to her bedside lamp. It provided light enough to read from, but not quite enough to reach the far corner of her room. Slipping out of her sling, she threw it down on her bed. She reached behind to undo the zipper of her dress, letting it fall to her feet. Digging into her handbag, she removed her scroll and tossed it lightly onto the bed, followed by her wallet. From under the pillow, she removed her folded pyjamas. She didn't see them, didn't feel them, or anything else really. She only knew that she was wobbling, unable to hold still as she tried getting dressed. In her mind, she kept replaying what she had just said to her sister.

Clearing her head, she dropped her top to shake out the pants. She had to sit on the bed to feed her left leg through. Her breathing was loud in her ears. Standing up, she stepped towards her desk, taking back her scroll. Chewing her lip, she turned it on. Immediately, she saw the small icon of a girl smiling broadly into the camera, her hair blowing in the wind. There was no doubt she was the girl from Lunar. Her eyes turned to the friend request icon, staring for a second. Instead of pressing confirm or reject, she shut off her scroll and dropped it back onto her bed.

She could feel her own need for a shower. But Rebecca was still outside, and she didn't want to walk past her to the bathroom. Even irritated teeth seemed a worthy trade to avoid that. Besides, her pyjamas would need washing the next day, a day before her birthday. Leaving it, she resigned herself for the night. Sitting down, the numbers of all her upcoming dates and countdowns ran through her mind.

It wasn't just her birthday, it was everything else: school holidays, exams, and her violin performance. All of it was so close together. In just five weeks, it would all be over. Then the next chapter of her life could begin. It would have a similar first page to all the other chapters: working for someone she didn't like, doing something she didn't want, and the chances were someone would end up dead.

Finally, Allison looked back at her scroll, returning right to Yifei's picture. She was a girl she didn't know; she didn't know what she wanted or who she was, or why she had asked for her contact number. It didn't seem unreasonable to assume it was some plot, some scheme Sensei was pulling to bring her back. Maybe he discovered what was happening with Nikita and wanted to pull some strings. It felt contrived, but that far from ruled out the chances.

Putting the scroll down, she left the screen on and returned to her pillow, pulling on her top. There was the sound of an opening door, of footsteps receding towards the bathroom. She could hear her brother, unfazed like she had been. Closing her eyes, she listened as Rebecca's voice invaded the silence. "I know I'm not your mother."

"I know."

Allison's throat was constricting just listening to her. "I just want you two to be happy."

"I know," Dakota said again.

This time Rebecca took longer to respond. "I'm sorry I don't know what I'm doing. I don't know if I should be acting as a sister or a parent, or how strict to be, or what to let you do. I'm just . . . not sure how to keep up."

"I know."

"Is that all? *I know*? No remarks, no advice? I need something if I'm supposed to get better at this."

His voice was dull, but there was a tinge of tenderness, ever so slight, in its softness. "We disagree. But you're my sister, and I know you're doing your best."

They said nothing else. She heard Dakota close his door, and that was the end. The tightness left her throat, and she almost collapsed across her bed. The movement made the screen's light play on the periphery of her vision. Sighing to herself, she crawled over to the foot of her bed, looking over it. Her finger hovered over the button, just a few centimetres away. Then the screen darkened, ready to turn off. In that second, her finger lurched forward, pressing down onto "accept." The second she did so, the screen lit back up. Eyes widening, she shook her head, as if that would undo anything. She pushed her scroll away; it slid across her desk. Crawling back along her bed, she switched off her light and covered herself with her sheets, head and all.

Cracking through the silence, her scroll's notification

sound blasted, throwing back the layers of sleep that had started rolling over her mind. The accompanying light came on, flashing into the darkness every two seconds. Groaning, she sat up, letting the sheets fall away. Scampering back over her bed, she pressed the button on its side, intending to turn off the volume before going to sleep. The screen lit, showing her Yifei's page once again. The request button had disappeared, and instead she saw an icon indicating a new message.

~And here I thought you gave a wrong number~

Picking the scroll up, she rolled back onto the bed, her head on the pillow. She didn't turn the screen off. She just rested the scroll on her abdomen, unsure what to say. Finally, deciding to say something, she gave the simplest response.

~Hi.~

The next message came quicker.

~Watcha doing?~

To say the truth—that she was trying to sleep—felt too rude for her to type, which left her with nothing better to say.

~Nothing~

Yifei's response came even faster this time.

~Fair enough~

~Hope U R well~

~Did you see the police tonight, or did you just miss them??~

Sighing into the darkness, she cursed the promise their actions compelled them all to—a lie she had to protect for the rest of her life.

~Yeah just saw it. ~

Yifei went back to her near instant responses.

~ U ok? ~

She typed *yes*. Her finger hovered over the send button. Erasing it, she retyped her message to sound less formal.

~ Yeah. ~

By now she was used to the other girl's pace.

~ Thank god ~

Putting down her scroll, Allison again closed her eyes, trying to imagine the girl wherever she would be, typing the messages as they went. What she was thinking—to be thankful someone she only just met was safe. When she lifted the scroll back up, she saw a new message.

~ I have to ask ~

~ Are u really 18? ~

Smiling a little, she closed her eyes for a brief second before responding.

~ Not until Sunday. ~

She saw the dots to indicate a reply was in the making, but it took its time before coming to life.

~ When's the party? ~

Breathing into the darkness, Allison whispered to herself, "I don't even know that."

~ That was it ~

As the dots reappeared, she wondered what essay Yifei was writing.

~ Please tell me you didn't just spend your birthday party locked in a bathroom alone ~

With a soft smile, she said aloud, "Well, when you say it like that . . ." Then, considering Nikita and their real purpose tonight, her eyes began drifting to sleep with the ominous feeling that the truth might somehow be worse. Her eyes closing, she barely had time to type *goodnight* before her mind switched over to a state of deep slumber.

After a Saturday filled with endless studying and intermediate texting, Allison woke to a morning of fat pancakes and presents. It was a family breakfast with her brother and half-sister. She had over four hundred siblings from Koros, and she was stripped down to a family of three. Only fifteen of those siblings had stayed in touch enough to send a birthday message. Buried within them was one from Katife, Theta, and finally, Yifei.

-Happy Bday. Can't wait to see you again-

Typing back a reply, she once again confirmed the location that Katife had suggested. Four years in the local area, four years of places she had visited, and not one suggestion had come to her mind, forcing her to rely on her friend's recommendations.

Heart racing, she looked down at herself, at her dark tracksuit and long, baggy top. Riffling through her wardrobe, she picked out a black pleated skirt with purple rims and a blouse coloured the same. The finger brushing of her hair for Rebecca's barrage of photos no longer felt any better than bed hair. Nothing she did made it look right; its light weight raised it up around the sides. Turning to her ribbon, she reversed time just for her hair. But when she reached the moment just before she'd cut it, she decided to keep going, reversing to before a previous cut, back when it was long enough to reach past the bottom of her shoulders. Suddenly it went from being frayed and bending upwards to held down and swaying with every move. She added a hair band, keeping it from her face.

With exams on the rise, her time was divided into study blocks by a poster on the wall, one of which she wasted purely on her preparation.

Marching on with a relentless pace, hours retreated to minutes. Slamming her books shut, she pressed her feet into her boots, squeezed her wallet into her purse, and ran for the door. Rebecca was sitting at the table behind her laptop. Either the sound or the rush of movement caught her attention, dragging it to Allison's fleeing form.

"Hey, I'mma . . . heading out for a bit. Gonna meet a friend."

Turning back to her screen, Rebecca shrugged. "Sure, why should I care? I mean, I'm not your mother."

Heart lurching, Allison fell against the door instead of opening it. Her mouth started drying out. "Rebecca, look, about what I said . . ."

"Don't worry about it. It's true."

Closing her eyes, she leant her head into the door. "I didn't mean it like that. It's just . . ."

The sound of typing keys slowed as Rebecca looked to her. "Please, Allison, will you just tell me what happened?"

If it were possible, she fell even further onto the door. "Katife witnessed a crime on the way home. I was a little behind, so I didn't even see anything." She hated how easy it was to lie to her.

Rebecca spoke slowly, taking time on her words. "You really do expect me to believe on your first night out, you just happened to see a violent crime?"

Trying and failing to recite any sort of crime statistic, she said, "It's not like Isoval's the safest place."

"Nor is it the most dangerous."

Eyes half closing, she exhaled slowly. "Then I'm a bad luck charm. What else is new?"

With Rebecca's face the type that was built to smile, even a subtle change towards sadness hurt so much to see. It made Allison's heart drop. "You know you can talk to me, right?"

"There's nothing to talk about. Like I said, I'm a bad luck charm. It's how I was born."

Rebecca kept her ground, still trying to force her way in. "There's a difference between bad luck and putting yourself in bad situations. And even still, you're closing yourself off more and more."

"That's so not true."

"You have! Allison, you don't talk to me like you used to . . . "

Allison protested, shouting, "I'm talking to you right now!"

"With vapid responses and metaphors! Your door is always closed, your violin is sounding violent, and that's when I hear you at all. When you come home from school you always look so angry. God, you're not even looking at me now."

Slamming down her foot, Allison snapped her gaze

hard to Rebecca. "There. Are you happy now?"

"Of course not! I don't want us to be like this. I want to be open, but you keep shutting me out. I don't want you to go back to being the kid you were when I found you."

"I was fourteen. That's not a kid."

"You acted like one. You both did." Rebecca's voice slowed, and she lowered her eyes. "Is this about Josie?"

Screwing her own eyes shut, Allison curled her hand into a fist. "God no. Rebecca, I swear to you, there is nothing for you to worry about, and this has nothing to do with her."

Opening her eyes, she saw Rebecca leaning closer to her over the table, her hair falling around her laptop. "I can't not worry. You're my sister and I love you. There is nothing that will let me sit back and watch you spiral down some dark path."

"Did you forget I was born with dark mana? Kinda late for that."

"I don't care about your mana's affinity! I don't care what happened at Koros either. I care about right now. I care about the girl standing before me. Not Cell. Allison Jane Khione. And right now, you're scaring me."

"Rebecca, I . . ." Allison had to stop, taking another breath. "It's just exam anxiety. I've got a lot on my plate."

It was like her words were a hand removing a weight from Rebecca's shoulders. "Why didn't you say so?"

"Because it's not important. It'll be over once we get uni offers."

Shaking her head, Rebecca folded her laptop's lid. "Then something else will come. Allison, there will always be something to make you anxious, and if it's hurting you, it's important to me."

She didn't know why, but she couldn't look at Rebecca. "Everyone goes through this. I know I'm just being irrational."

"Allison . . . Allison, look at me. Please." Turning her neck was like opening a rusty door, her joints protesting every degree. "There's nothing irrational about asking for help. I remember what that was like, you know. It wasn't that long ago. And Mum . . . Connie was there for me. I know you have your things, and it might hit you worse, but just . . . know that I'm here for you. That will never change."

It was a lie. The anxiety was a lie. That's what she told herself. Yet Rebecca's words had her crying, unable to keep herself up. Nikita was an extra stressor, but even if she disappeared and took all her problems with her, everything else would remain. Her violin, her designs, her future, all of it vying for time that she wasn't sure she had. Without even thinking, she whispered the words, "I just don't know what to do sometimes."

There was no force left at all in Rebecca's words, just the soothing feeling of a cold drink on a hot day. "You will. I know you will."

Eyes closed, she nodded slowly as her heart began to steady. "You're a good sister. I should know; I've had hundreds." Rebecca didn't laugh, and neither did she. "Sorry about what I said."

"It's okay."

With nothing else to say, she turned around and opened the door. With one foot outside, one still in, she said, "I'll probably never know my mother, but even if she was here, I'd trade her for you in a heartbeat." She closed the door behind her before she could so much as hear her sister's response, closing herself into the garage with her waiting bike.

The fresh air helped, clearing her mind as she clipped on her helmet. She jumped onto her seat and began to pedal down the centre of the street, feeling the wind pull at her hair. The breeze got stronger as she entered the back paddock. Her left arm in a sling, she used her other to steer. Once it surprised her how easy it was; now it was natural. There were some changes she had to make, like moving both brakes to her right handle and adding a dampener to make steering more stable.

A train horn blared as she got closer to the station. Veering onto the roads, she weaved through the streets and entered the shopping strip. Squeezing the brakes, she stopped the bike two stores down at the closest bike ring, looping her helmet straps through the lock. Satisfied it wasn't going anywhere, she walked back towards the cafe.

The place was far from empty, but even further from full. Once she found a table by the back, she took a seat facing the door. Around her were the sleek white walls, while behind the bench was crisp black machinery. Above it was a menu disguised as a chalkboard. The extensiveness of coffee offered looked like it must have included every possibility under the sun. She couldn't think of a better contrast to Koros' set menus.

The clock wasn't ticking. It was digital, with its display loudly telling her how early she was. Using the time to scan the board, she searched for anything drinkable, which meant discounting everything that had the word coffee in it.

Someone walked into the building through the front door, looking around as she did. Same black hair, same long curls. Yifei's eyes scanned right past her. Swallowing, Allison raised her arm and waved. The movement was enough to capture her attention. Smiling broadly, Yifei slipped into the chair opposite her. "Wow. What happened to your hair? Did you go to one of those mage hair salons or something? And I'm sure you weren't wearing glasses last time."

Without thinking, Allison ran her fingers through her hair, brushing the arm of her glasses. She turned away, realising how silly it had been to grow out her hair through her mana. "Don't you like it?"

For a second Yifei sounded taken aback. "What? No. It's great, just . . . unexpected. But it must have been expensive, right? Everyone says those places don't come cheap."

Allison shook her head, speaking into that regrown hair. "I uh, did it myself."

One country south and she would have expected that sentence to call a mob down upon her; one county north and no one would have cared. Here in Emnalor, Yifei seemed more stunned than anything. "You're a mage?" she asked.

Giving her best attempt at a smile, Allison stammered, "Surprise."

Instead of showing indifference or anger, Yifei's eyes went wide. "Wow. I don't meet many mages. So, what? You have hair manipulation or something? Can you turn it into different shapes and hold things with it?"

Allison laughed. "No, I can—"

Before she had a chance to finish, Yifei raised a finger. "Hang on a second. Let me guess. Let's see . . . Are you a shapeshifter?"

"Not even close."

"Hmm. Medusa aspect or something?"

"What even is that? Can't I just tell you?"

"Nope, this is way more fun."

"My power's really weird. No one has ever guessed it before."

Leaning back on her chair, Yifei sighed. "Fine, you can tell me."

Moving her hand towards her ribbon, Allison felt the bow. "I can reverse time. But only for my body."

After a moment of confusion, Yifei's jaw dropped. "Now that is cool. Is that why you look so young?"

A sudden pang ripping her chest, Allison looked down. "No, that's . . . other stuff."

"Oh. Is it a spell or a . . ."

She shook her head. "Genetics. My muscles break down at a stupidly fast rate. It's called dystrophy. It, ah, might be a perfect microcosm of what I am."

"I don't know what you mean by that," she replied.

Finding the words to explain, Allison said, "It's like, a disease, but it's also a divine symbol. I'm decaying on the inside, just like I'm doing to the world on the outside." Shifting her eyes up, she tried giving a smile, which only just came through. She saw enough to know Yifei didn't know what to say, and probably wasn't going to come to any response soon. "So . . . I can reverse any part of me. If I want, I can reverse an injury, or even bring an old one back."

Shaking her head, Yifei made a show of avoiding Allison's earlier statements to instead focus on the later ones. "Wow. You're right, I would not have guessed that." Her words were not enough to reverse the gloom of Allison's statements, so after a moment, she looked back up with a smile and pushed through. "So, what's your order? My treat, by the way."

Throat catching, Allison stuttered. "You really don't need to . . . "

"I think the birthday girl deserves to be shouted." Unsure what to say, she looked back to the board. "I don't know. If it was a bit warmer, I'd go for a milkshake, so maybe hot chocolate instead?"

Yifei laughed. "Are you asking me or telling me?"
"Telling?"

Shaking her head, Yifei mused, "God, you're adorable." Standing up, she stepped around the table. "Alright, wait right here."

"You really don't have to," Allison called, even as Yifei had already stepped away. She left only the hint of rosemary scent in her wake. A minute later she placed the cup before Allison. "Here you go. One hot chocolate, an innocent drink for the innocent girl."

Instead of taking the cup, Allison frowned. "I'm not. Innocent, I mean."

Hanging her jacket over the chair, Yifei slipped into her seat. "Sure you are. Even if it's just for some things. Like how you forgot this."

She reached into her bag and pulled out Rebecca's flower.

Allison's eyes widened, and she reached for it on instinct. "Oh god, thanks. Rebecca was not happy that I lost it."

"Well, now you don't need to worry. So, how's your day been? Get any cool presents?"
Sipping her own drink, its heat made her almost drop the cup. "Rebecca made pancakes. I didn't realise she even knew how."

"Cool. And Rebecca, she is . . .?

Swallowing, she smiled. "My legal guardian. And my half-sister."

"Mum's side or dad's?"

"Dad's, not that I've ever met him. Or know anything about him, really. She doesn't like to talk about him."

Yifei nodded. "What about your mum? What was she like?" Allison just shook her head and shrugged her shoulders. "Nothing?"

"Not a photo or a name or the colour of her hair. For all I know, she could be an alien."

Scoffing, Yifei leant a little closer. "Yeah, I'm sure she is," she said with a big smile. Silence started to battle its way in, and as if she saw it coming and wanted a preemptive strike, Yifie asked, "So what was it like in an orphanage?"

It was a detail she regretted telling Yifei, but as their long text conversations stretched in the previous days, it slipped out before she could stop herself. *At least I had the sense not to mention it was Koros.* Allison just shrugged, unsure what really to say. "Life, I guess."

"Yeah, that basically means nothing."

"Maybe once I know you better."

Throwing her hands up, Yifie held them out as a peace sign. "Alright, that's fair. What do you want to know?"

Testing the hot chocolate again, Allison was rewarded with a rich taste. It was no longer tainted by such extreme heat that left her tongue tingling. "Well, or starters, what are you doing?"

"What, like right now?"

"You know that's not what I meant. Like with your life. You look too old for school."

"Oh, thanks," she replied with mock offence. "No, I'm in uni, studying my second year of bioscience. And I'm also working. Needa pay the bills somehow."

"Oh, that's cool. So where do you work?"

"Well, it used to be a place like this until they went and shut down. Now I'm in a bookstore." Allison started laughing through her nose just trying to picture the leather-wearing girl in a bookstore. "Oh, ha ha. Laugh it up. Any chance I'll see you between classes next year? If we go to the same place, it's practically fate."

Shaking her head, Allison took another drink. It had cooled to the point of perfection. "I've applied to a bunch of schools, but I'm hoping for IIDT. I doubt they teach bioscience."

Frowning, Yifei repeated the letters. "I don't think I even know what that is."

Realising her mistake mentioning such a niche school and expecting it to be known, Allison rushed to explain. "It's a design uni. That's what the *D* stands for."

"Design? What, you want to be a designer or something?"

Shrugging, Allison said, "Or a patternmaker, not quite sure yet."

"I, ah, don't know what that is."

Lapsing into an almost automatic explanation, she said, "Well, the designer makes the design itself, the patternmaker cuts and sews it together."

"Get out. That is so cool."

Smiling inwardly, Allison looked down. "I love sewing, but I'd also love to have my own store. But, ah, bioscience, huh? Sounds tough."

Prompting the conversation into Yifei's area, Allison had to stop and listen just to understand what she was saying. She passionately described things that didn't even make sense to Allison. After a few minutes, Yifei saw the confusion Allison couldn't hide and stopped. "You don't have any scientific background, do you?"

"Textiles, music, language? I'm practically an honours student," she said with a laugh. "But uh, yeah, I've kinda stayed away from any of the hard sciences."

"Well, I guess bioscience isn't everyone's cup of tea."

"Sorry."

She shook her head. "No, don't be. We all have our own interests. I'm sure there's a lot of terminology you could go into that would lose me."

They kept talking while slowly draining their drinks. They talked about where they lived and what they saw there. About what university life was like, and how it was to still be in school. Yifei talked about her grandparents still overseas, to which Allison had no response, not knowing her own recent ancestry. Yifei talked about her sister, Allison about her messy family tree. Her drink came to the dregs, and from Yifei's reaction, so too had hers. "This was nice, wasn't it?"

"Absolutely. Top two birthdays, easy."

"Top two? Wow, harsh crowd."

"What can I say, Rebecca went all out once she adopted us."

Smiling, Yifei laughed into her hand. "You are one strange little creature."

Her words were playful and innocent, but they resurrected older ones into Allison's mind, ones that ignited a phantom pain in her left arm. She felt herself choke as her expression darkened.

Mirroring hers, Yifei's expression started to change as well, her smile turning into a frown. "What's wrong?"

Closing her eyes, Allison felt her lips quiver. "I'm sorry. It's just . . . you reminded me of a friend."

"Oh. Did something happen between you two?"

Shaking her head, Allison wiped her eyes with her wrist. "I told you I lost my arm in a car crash. I didn't say there was someone else. Someone who . . . didn't make it."

As tears began to fill Allison's eyes, Yifei reached out her arm to take hold of her. "Hey, it's okay."

Fighting the tears, she cried, "I just miss her so much. I still can't believe she's gone.

"I'm so sorry. Did you want to talk about it?"

Nodding, sucking in a sniffle, Allison nodded. "We were on the way home. Someone ran a light and hit us from the side."

Feeling Yifei's fingers on the back of her hand felt like the only thing holding her back from really bawling. "That must be so hard on you."

Nodding, Allison said, "I haven't been in a car since."

Yifei's mouth opened, but no words came out. She just sat there, a calming presence. After long last, she said, "I don't know what to say."

"What can you say?" Allison pleaded. "She died. She sacrificed herself to save me after celebrating my sixteenth birthday."

Yifei gawked, "She died on your birthday?"

Sniffling, Allison nodded. "A week before. My life was her final present."

All Yifei could do was shake her head, which had an almost hypnotic calming to it. After a long while, she stood up. "Come on."

"Huh?" Allison asked.

"I'm taking you to the nearest ice cream shop. You really need a good cry, and I'm not letting you go until you're feeling better."

As she pressed the button to open the garage door, Allison felt certain she would not be crying anytime soon. Her tears were now spent and dried. Equally, her stomach was so filled with ice cream that eating seemed impossible.

She kicked out the stand and stepped off her bike. The car was gone, which told her Rebecca was too. She had either gone shopping or somewhere new; otherwise she would use her flower. The garage door started to lumber down behind her as Dakota opened the door into the garage. "Hey."

"Hey," he responded. She could see he wanted to say something, but for whatever reason, he was silent. She raised an eyebrow and stepped towards him. "Dylan's coming."

She stopped, blinking, and for a split-second questioned who he was talking about. "That's some interesting timing," she murmured to herself. "What makes you think that?"

"Rebecca said so," he answered with a decimal less than perfect calm as he stepped aside to let her in. "Apparently he called to tell her he's on his way. She was out, so she then called me."

With a sigh, she undid her shoelaces and stepped into the house. "Any clue what that deadbeat wants?"

"Maybe to wish us a happy birthday?" he answered, following behind her as she made for her room.

With a sigh she dropped to her bed, toeing off her boots. "I somehow find that unlikely." Pausing as she struggled with her second boot, she grunted before going on. "Are you gonna meet him?"

Eyes scanning the room for a moment, he replied, "The world's not burning."

She gave a slight nod as she leant back to lie on her bed. "Yep. Although I'm kinda curious what he looks like."

"I'll go if you do."

This time she shrugged more visibly, pushing her doona cover with her shoulders. "I said I'm curious to see him. I have no intention of meeting." He nodded, his lips tight.

It wasn't long before a car pulled onto their driveway. It wasn't Rebecca's. Hers was an old secondhand thing that wouldn't even have had airbags if it were a year older. Time had stripped the car, leaving it with a sound distinct from any other, especially with their animal hearing. Creeping into their sister's front-facing room, they stood framing the window as they were taught in Koros. Allison closed the blinds, using the slit between each one to peek onto the driveway. The thud of the closing car door sounded, followed by a knock on the front door. They were as silent as the grave, waiting out an insistent second knock.

With Rebecca's mother a pure human, it was clear their shared traits had come from their father, which implied that their amplified hearing was something he would share. "Hello, kids?" His voice dipped; she was sure any human would miss his next sentence. "Ah, what were their names again? Think, think. Ah, right. Dakota, Allison? It's your father. Please come out. I'm here to see you."

Sitting beside her, she saw Dakota's finger running along the flower Rebecca gave him. It was a blue one, similar to a sunflower in almost every other way. He glanced at her for confirmation. Her mouth was dry as she waited in thought. With Rebecca absent, it really was *the* opportunity if she wanted to meet her father—no distractions, no guardianship debates. *But he struggled to even remember our names.* Nodding, Dakota pressed the gem, sending a message to Rebecca's.

Outside, Dylan continued calling out. Finding the doorbell, he rang it twice. It was quiet, perfect for the occupants. His footsteps changed as they went from walking over the concrete to over the bark of the garden, crunching towards their window. Three steps in, his silhouette blocked the lines between the blinds.

Then Rebecca arrived. No car; she hadn't bothered waiting to drive back from wherever she was, instead using her power and arriving in an instant. Lacking any semblance of welcoming softness, Rebecca called out in a raw voice, "I told you not to come. I spoke very clearly. What part of that did you not understand?"

The footsteps receded, his voice turning warm and inviting. "Becca, hi, how are you?"

"How do you think, you . . . boar?"

"I would never get away with talking to my father

110

that way."

"I somehow doubt granddad would approve of how you acted as a parent."

With a slow and level tone, Dylan spoke with a pace that would be normal for Rebecca. "They're my kids, Becca. What right do you have to stop me from seeing them?"

"I'm their guardian!" Her voice was loud, but she lowered it, speaking slower through gritted teeth. "Look, Dad. I want you to be a part of their life; you know I do. God knows they need a father. But *that* is what they need, not a man who swings by whenever he feels up to it. They—we—need someone who will be there. If you want to see them, then you need to promise me now. You can't do what you did four years ago. You have to commit to the kids *you* abandoned. Then we can have dinner as a family. But you need to commit."

"It's not that easy, Becca. I have my own problems. I can't just be there when you're feeling sad."

It felt like a partial explosion, like a dash of hope was shot and Rebecca went straight to angry. "You need to be there when it's tough or you don't have the right to call yourself their father. That's what I've had to do. God, do you realise how much responsibility I've had to take up because of you? The hell they went through? Because you wouldn't raise your kids."

"You missed the first fourteen years of their upbringing, coming in once the hard work was done. And you want to talk to me about responsibility?"

"Done? Done!" Rebecca's voice was becoming less human and more banshee. "What part of this is easy? What part of balancing the job I didn't want with taking care of them is easy? What part of cooking for three every day is easy? What part of my life is easy, taking care of others when I was struggling to take care of myself?"

His voice was starting to rise, but Dylan's voice was still relatively calm. "I tried helping you."

"You tried two years ago! A whole two years after I found them!"

"Well, I'm sorry. I'm sorry, Becca. Is that what you wanted to hear? I'm sorry you can't be a carefree hippy anymore, partying every other night and getting high on gems. I'm sorry your life isn't a breeze, but you know what? Neither is mine. So, I am sorry I wasn't there to hold your hand and help you out as an adult. And now you want to complain when you wouldn't let me come back? How is that fair?"

"How dare you! You saw me every other weekend. Don't act like you know me. I always assumed that was a custody thing, but now I know Mum wanted you to be a part of my life. So what, did you have to ask to *not* have custody when every other father is out there begging for more? And now you want to complain about me, that I won't just give to you what you abandoned? Do you even have any concept of what they went through because of you, because of your inability to front up and take responsibility for getting their mother pregnant? What on earth makes you think you deserve to be involved in their lives?"

Finally, his voice raised into a shout. "Because I am their father. Just like I am yours."

She scoffed loudly. "Some father you turned out to be."

The sounds of movement died away. When he spoke again, his voice was softer. "What happened to us? You used to love catching up on holidays and birthdays. Why can't I have that with my other kids, with you anymore?"

It was as if she was matching his vocal change but in the opposite direction, and Allison began counting the seconds until one of their neighbours came out. "What kind of conceited jackass are you, acting as if you deserve it? Mum has been there for them more than you have, and they're not even related. Hell, you're still calling me Becca! No one's called me that in years, but you're too bloody absent to even know that."

"Calm down, Becca. You're causing a scene."

The raging curiosity battled inside her, pushing Allison to lean forward and peer through the blinds. It was just enough for her to see through, not enough even for her eyes to be seen. She saw only his back, facing Rebeca as she stood on the driveway in front of a police cruiser. A part of Allison never believed it when she was told her father was an officer. Even with her permanently rosy cheeks, Rebecca's face lit up in a whole different way. "Don't you dare tell *me* to calm down! You sent my siblings off to live as child soldiers! You have no right to tell me anything."

Dylan wasn't responding, but she could hear his heavy breathing. He stepped closer to her sister. "I didn't know."

Rebecca's anger hadn't died down enough for her to laugh; it just twisted it into something hateful. "That's bull and you know it."

This time he got louder. "I swear Rebecca. I didn't know. I went to a church because I thought that would give them a better chance than being with a single parent on a government salary. I thought it would keep them safe. I had no clue what was going to happen."

"You just didn't care. Thousands of people get stuck with a child alone, be it through an unwanted pregnancy or their partner dying or whatever. And they don't trade those kids in for an easy ride. They stick with it and raise their kids."

"I was doing what was best for them!" Dylan roared. "You know what happens to those kids with single parents? I end up arresting half of them. For killing the other half."

Allison almost didn't want to look, convinced her sister had become a banshee.

"Screw you!" Rebecca's chest heaved with shallow breaths at a rapid pace. If her head wasn't going light yet, it would be soon. She seemed to realise that too, forcing herself to quiet down but maintaining every drop of venom. "I know having a single parent is bad. I went through that until Mum remarried. But it sure as hell is better than none."

Dylan was frozen, struck motionless with no response. Without thinking, Allison leaned in closer, pushing the blinds apart with her forehead. The movement catching her eye, Rebecca turned towards her. It was only for a moment, but it was enough that Dylan noticed. Seeing where she was looking, he spun around and rushed over the garden. Dropping the blinds, Allison retreated into the room, the outside once again nothing but thin slits of light that morphed around his shape. "Kids! Kids, come out and let me see you. I want to see how much you've grown."

In four years, through thick and thin—rain, hail, or shine—Rebecca always maintained a certain calmness. Even when she was fired up and angry with them after realising they were sneaking off to do mixed martial arts, her tone was always at a normal level. Now that was all being blown apart in a single conversation. "They're not your kids anymore. You gave that right away, and you do not get to decide when you see them. It's when they say, or never."

The figure through the blinds didn't even look away to respond. "I don't care what you say. All of you are still my children, and you always will be."

"You gave them up! You gave them up, and the second you did, they were no longer yours. They became mine—my kids, my problem. I sacrificed for them, worked for them. I was in no better a place than you. No, screw that, I was in a worse one. You had a job, I was a temp. And despite that I made the time to bond with them, to care for them. While you left your responsibility." From the loudest cry to the softest speech, her voice became little more than a whisper. Not from desire, but from her voice dying on her. "We needed you, and you abandoned us. No one made you do that. Just you. You don't belong here. You need to go."

"I'm not leaving until I at least talk to them."

Rebecca was going to say something, Allison could hear it coming. But it was never realised. A new voice broke in, heavy and slow. "Excuse me, sir, but if you don't stop giving my dear neighbour a hard time, I'm going to call the police."

His presence made a change, calming Dylan and making him move away from the blinds. "I'm already here."

"Sir, your vehicle says city police. You're a long way from home, and outside your jurisdiction. I very much doubt the local department will appreciate their citizens being harassed by a renegade officer."

Dylan spoke calmly, like he was on the job. "This is

a family matter; nothing for you to be concerned with."

Allison knew that voice. It was of their neighbour. He was an older man, and he had that look, like he had once been a trucker or a biker, with a long, old moustache and developed fat. "Rebecca, is this true, or should I be calling the police?"

Rebecca was out of sight, but Allison could imagine her reaction, swallowing and nodding to him. "Well, there you have it. Now I suggest you go, or when the police come, I'll make damn sure you lose that badge of yours, if nothing else."

In a final protest, Dylan insisted, "I have a right to be here."

"A right?" The neighbour asked, sighing before adding, "Won't you take some more boy? It's more than you deserve."

For a long time, there was nothing but silence. Then the shuffling of boots on mulch as Dylan walked back to his car and opened his door. "I'm not giving up, Rebecca. I will see my kids again." Slamming his door shut, he reversed out so fast his bumper bounced as it hit the road. Dylan paused, blasting the siren for a moment before leaving them behind.

The moment Dylan was gone, the force keeping Rebecca standing dissipated and she fell to her knees. At the same time, Allison no longer felt frozen, rushing out the door to the front yard. She smiled briefly, giving a nod to her neighbour as her sister turned towards her. Just as Rebecca had done for her, Allison wrapped her in her arms and let her cry into her shoulder.

Closing the book, Allison started to understand why her teachers called it a "study break" instead of a school holiday. Finishing a practice essay, she permitted herself a moment to look through the handful of notifications on her scroll. Most were from Katife, including a few missed calls. Hitting "call back," Katife's face appeared on-screen near immediately. "Hey. What's up?"

"What's up? I'm with the police is what's up." The screen panned, showing the inside of what looked like an interrogation room of some sort.

"Oh my god, what happened?"

"What do you think? They had some more questions to ask. But they want all three of us, so I've been sitting here for the last hour waiting for you to answer your scroll. I seriously need you to get here ASAP."

A lie to last not just the night, but the rest of our lives. "Okay. I'll be right there. I just need to eat something real quick."

"Allison!"

"I'm sorry. I'm seriously hungry."

"And I'm not?"

"I promise I will be really fast. One toast, maybe two. With honey."

Katife sighed again. "Ugh. Can you at least get Rebecca to take you?"

"I'd love to say yes . . ."

"Then say yes."

". . . but she's at work right now."

"Oh, you are freaking kidding."

"Don't worry, we'll be as fast as we can."

"I hate you. And remember to drag Dakota here too." With that Katife hung up.

Placing her scroll into her pocket, Allison left her room. "Dakota, we're going into Isoval. Call Nicky too. Time for her to track the police." Without waiting for a response, she fixed herself a toast.

Repeating her last bike ride, they veered off at the end towards the station. There was a place to chain their bikes, and from there they had to run to catch the train. For nearly half an hour it rushed closer to the city until diving underground as it got close. She typed a message just as the sun was cut from view.

~Gonna be in city for a bit. Wanna hang out?~

At the third subway station, they exited the train, flowing with the foot traffic headed for the surface. When the sun came into view, her signal returned and a message came through.

~Sure, but got class. What time u thinking?~

~No clue. Maybe an hour.~

~KK. Msg me when you're done~

~Okay, see you then.~

Putting her scroll away, Allison stepped outside with her brother, practically onto the tram stop. It was standing room only, which wasn't bad for ten minutes. They got off on a platform where eight people waited, one of which was a familiar blond. "Hey, missed you."

"Missed you too," Dakota said. They didn't kiss or embrace or even shake hands. There was wind in the city. It played with Allison's hair. It didn't play on Nikita's. She was just a projection.

A few steps behind, Allison listened in as Nikita talked about the building she was staying in, pointing to the high-rise just a few buildings down from the police station. Detective Casey was waiting for them once they walked in. "Sorry to call you in like this," she said. "It's just how things are."

As they arrived at the room Allison had seen on-screen, Katife groaned in either relief or to show her disapproval of the delay. "And here I thought you'd left me to dry."

"You know we'd never do that."

Lowering her eyes, Katife muttered, "Yeah, well, it felt like it."

There was a two-way mirror in the room; they weren't even trying to hide that. Being only an image in their minds, Nikita showed no reflection. There were a few chairs set up for the twins to sit in, and another two on the other side. "Can we get this over with? I don't have all day."

The lines on Detective Casey's face made her look permanently stressed, unless that was just her work face. "Thanks for coming. The investigators will be here soon."

"What?" Katife near-screamed, but cut herself off when two people walked in.

They both wore suits from off the rack. *A good rack,*

but a rack nonetheless. The man was tall with dark hair cropped on the sides, the woman with a ponytail so strict it made Nikita's look relaxed. "Hello. I am Special Agent Paul and this is Special Agent Carter. We're from Temple's investigative unit." As he sat down, Allison saw Paul's arm had been replaced with a prosthetic.

Without missing a beat, the woman, Carter, continued. "We need to ask you a few things about what you saw."

"Sure, fire away." As she spoke, Katife made a loose shooting gesture with her hand.

They started with all the usual questions about the things Katife had told the police. Her answers were the same, or near enough to make no difference. Then the questions started to change. "And you were sure that knife was his, correct?" Carter asked, laying a photo of the knife before them.

"Uh, yeah."

"And have you ever seen him before? TV, newspaper, anywhere at all?"

Katife's widening eyes and frown showed her confusion plain as day. "What?"

Both agents maintained blank faces, even as they added a second photo to the mix. This one was not taken from the alleyway. The light was synthetic, suggesting it wasn't even taken from outside, but the tight cropping made it hard to tell. Leaning in, Allison peered at the image. It showed a face with a grey wall behind him. The man faced the camera, looking down a little. It was almost an exact replica of her own photo of Soul, only here he was years younger, built smaller, with a look of fury on his face. "Is this the man you saw?"

The image was enlarged and just a little on the blurry side. Taking a close look, Katife nodded. "Yeah, that's him." Satisfied, Carter removed the image from the table. "Mind telling me why Temple's up in my grill now?"

Inclining her head, Carter said, "We believe this man is a combat mage."

His voice even enough to match the agents' faces, Dakota asked, "Are we in danger? How powerful is this guy if he's getting you involved?"

Clever, to disguise information fishing as concern.

The agents shared a glance. "That's classified."

Banging her fist on the table, Allison spoke up, laying the impression of a teenage brat on thick. "Classified my ass! Katife's a witness. What happens if he comes after her? We deserve to know what's going on."

"I'm sorry, we can't—"

"I'm not asking for his home address. I'm asking for the type of mage you think he is. His ranking, even. How much danger are we in?"

Sharing a glance that seemed to communicate a whole conversation, Paul answered her, sort of. "He's very powerful, and very dangerous."

"That means nothing!" she said, slurring the words and drawing them out. "Are you saying he can win a fight with a boxer or break into an armoured car?"

There was a long moment of silence, and it was Paul who eventually gave an answer. "That photo came from inside a Temple base. I can't say any more."

Against a mage, a single human was easy to beat. So were noncombatant mages. But Temple was the armed faction of mage police. Even Sensei warned against engaging them. She could remember the times her siblings did engage, after which they often never returned. "We need protection. If he comes after us, we're dead. You have to help us."

Now if we can just include protection for Nikita, this can all be over.

"I'm surprised to have a child from Koros asking for help."

Carter's words shouldn't have surprised her, but they did. Obviously they would do a background check first, and it wasn't like Koros was a secret anymore. "I have one arm. You just said he soloed a Temple base. Do the math."

Agent Paul cut in, breaking his poker face a little. "He has no reason to go after you. It's not like he knew what you saw."

Making a show of calming down, Allison took a deep breath and let the interview continue. Agent Carter took the reins. "We have a few more questions we'd like to ask."

Rolling her eyes, Katife said, "I told the police everything I saw. Nothing's gonna change for you."

"What about what you heard?"

She blinked. "Excuse me?"

Carter continued. "Did you hear anything? Something they may have said, perhaps?"

"Look, I'm sorry to burst your bubble, lady, but I had blood pumping in my ears, and that's what I got to hear."

"Please, just think. Anything at all." If Paul was the good cop, he wasn't doing a great job.

Thinking over everything Soul had said, Allison wrote the script in her mind, hoping Nikita would transpose it to Katife, and that something good could come from her ever-present eavesdropping. Rubbing her temples, Katife closed her eyes. "Ah, he said something about calamity, and, and . . . I think he mentioned a curse or something."

The first word got no reaction, but even the poker-faced duo couldn't hide their interest at the second. "What curse?"

"I don't know. Like I said, blood pumping, not much hearing."

For just a moment, Allison felt a lapse of Nikita's presence. It was as if Nikita's focus became solely pinned on the agents' minds; she couldn't spare any of her power on them. "Nothing from the victim?"

"I don't know. He said something like 'What curse?' Something along those vague lines. That's the best I got. Now can I go? I have exams to prepare for."

"Just a moment."

The two agents left, closing the door behind them. There was too much soundproofing for Allison to be sure, but she was guessing they were behind that mirror. Five minutes of nothingness passed. They said nothing, did nothing, and thought everything. Then the door reopened. "Alright, have a nice day."

Rolling her eyes, Katife kicked off her chair and left, rushing out onto the street and leaving the building behind. Allison had to dash to keep up with her, and Dakota was a step further behind. Nikita's projection faded in at half opacity. "Guys, I want to follow these two for a bit. Just head to the apartment and we can talk there. Room 403. I told Dakota which building." He nodded, and she faded completely.

The twins caught up to Katife on the street. Katife turned to them and said, "You know, I've lost a lot of daylight. I might just head home. We can always talk online." Katife was shifting her weight, almost anxiously, as if she felt blocked from leaving by some imaginary force.

Chipping in, Allison added, "I promised to meet someone, so I'll be heading off soon as well. Dakota?"

Before he could answer with his own plans, Katife cut in with renewed energy, her anxious shifting gone. "Whoa. Hold up. What's this now?"

"It's really nothing . . ."

"Yeah, yeah, yeah, spare us the obligatory lies. When are you meeting this person?"

She opened her mouth, but no words came out. "I don't know." With a swallow she turned around, sending a text to Yifei. She got no response. "Not yet, I guess."

"Alright. Lead on, then."

The apartment Nikita was squatting in was nice enough inside, with carpeted floors and paintings on the walls. It was nothing super flashy, but it was far from humble. *Especially since she's not paying.* The elevator moved fast, taking them up to Nikita's floor. Her door was unlocked. It was a small dogbox apartment featuring a combined kitchen and a single couch. There were two doors: one connecting to a bathroom, the other to a bedroom. Nikita was sitting on the couch with her head back and eyes glazed over, blood leaking from her nose.

Waiting around her couch for her to return to her body from her telepathic scouting, they each glanced around the apartment. There was little to see. It was empty aside from the bare basics and unfurnished with anything personal, just the things Nikita had on her back. Plain white like always, cotton—a blouse and skirt. Only it was a little duller and dirtier in person.

Hearing her scroll message, Allison clicked it open.

~Ugh, I hate pharmacology. I think I need a dose of

you to cheer me up~

She bit her lip to stop it rising, replying with a smiley face.

~So, where are u? ~

Giving the street, she waited for a response.

~Wow, that's really close. I'll be there soon. ~

Light returned to Nikita's glazed eyes as her mind returned to her body. "Well, that was interesting," she said.

"Find something?" Dakota asked.

Interlocking her fingers and pushing her arms out, Nikita made out as if she was preparing to do some intense typing. Only then did she notice the blood. She didn't even frown as she ripped out a tissue and whipped it away. "Well, first off, those people have a history with our guy."

"I mean, they mentioned the base," Allison replied.

"Yeah, but there's more. I know you noticed Paul's arm. Three guesses what happened."

Allison felt ready to curse, yet Dakota spoke slowly and calmly. "I still don't see what any of this has got to do with you."

Nikita shook her head. "Me neither. Temple may be the enemy of our enemy, but that doesn't mean they know why we were involved."

"Any chance that prison break they mentioned is somehow related?"

"Dakota, I think I'd remember being a Temple prisoner."

"I meant if there was any connection at all. A relative or something."

She shrugged. "I'm an orphan too, remember? I got no family."

"You were adopted as a baby. Don't pretend you don't have a family." Allison interjected.

Nikita shook her head, while Dakota scratched his chin. "So we've got dirt-all?" he asked.

"Well, not nothing. Their minds went crazy at the word 'curse.' Hell, they even gave me a list. That's what I was looking into just now. They seemed obsessed with it."

"And this list is related?"

Nikita shrugged. "I can read their minds, which means I can only piece together what they know. Paul had this memory from years ago. He was at the Spanish Fringe doing some trade. The guy who cut his arm used that exact same phrase. Whatever Soul's after, it's not new."

Nodding, Dakota muttered, "Knowing what he wants is the first step. It'll make it easier to predict what he does next."

"Ah, we don't know what he wants. Just that this curse might mean something to him. Do we even know what it's a list of?" Allison asked, looking to Nikita.

She nodded. "Names. It's a list of people who might be 'cursed.'"

Closing her eyes, Allison leant against the window. "Okay. That's something. So, we look into these people and see what we can find. Best case, we find a bargaining chip. Worst case, we know where he might show up."

"Whoa," Katife called, near jumping off the couch. "What happens if these people can't help you? What if Soul doesn't want them? Or they're worth nothing to him?"

"Then"—Allison bobbed her head, looking for an answer—"we move to plan B."

"Ah, yes, plan B. What exactly is plan B?"

"Plan B is . . . it's, ah, it's the plan where we . . . do something."

Katife narrowed her eyes. They bored into Allison for a moment. "You're hiding something from me."

"What? No. It's just . . . you know . . ." She couldn't say it: that they would take Nikita and hide without her. They'd even picked a place, some house in the woods. She almost thanked her scroll out loud when it went off.

~I'm here, where r u? ~

Smiling with a breath of relief, she typed her answer.

~I'll be right down. Give me a sec. ~

Lowering her scroll, Allison said, "My friend just arrived. Katife, we can talk tonight, okay?"

As fast as she moved, she wasn't fast enough to escape Katife's words. "Sure. But I want to hear what this plan B is. Then we can talk about this date you're dying to get to."

"I am not!" she shouted, spinning around on the spot. "And it's not a date."

Her defence only made Katife look brighter. "Alley, please. You can lie to me, but you can't hide your tells."

"I don't have tells."

"Please. I found Dakota's tells; I can find yours. And right now, the tells are telling me you're excited."

Allison's mouth opened but no words came out. Her cheeks flushing, she spun and left with a muttered goodbye. She pressed the elevator call button five times. It took thirty-seven seconds to arrive. Stepping in, she heard Dakota's footsteps as he rushed up, making it just in time to join her. "There's something I want to talk to you about."

"Sure, what's up?"

He was hesitating. Of all people, Dakota was

hesitating. "Allison . . ." He paused to take in a breath. "You've been different since Lunar. Especially since our birthday."

"Please, Dakota, don't start being the clingy father type."

"That's not it. I just . . . I want you to leave Nikita to me."

The doors slid open, but neither stepped out. "God, you're not serious, are you? You can't just plan B me. It was my suggestion."

He shook his head. "It's been something I've been thinking about for a while. Ever since I . . ."

"Ever since you . . . ?" she prompted.

He hesitated. "Since I saw you get killed by Soul's grenade."

She was shaking her head without even trying to. "You can't cut me out. Besides, I came back to life, didn't I? You can't—"

"Do what you planned to do to Katife?" he finished.

Her jaw opened, but there was nothing for her to say. Closing her fist, she pressed the button to open the door and stepped out.

"Allison. Allison, wait . . ."

As she stepped out into the ground floor, natural light overtook the dimness. "What?"

"I'm serious about this."

"I'm sure you are."

"You didn't even want to help. You're the one who said to leave this to the cops. You should be happy to stop now."

"And leave my baby brother in danger? No way."

He stayed back but called firmly, "You have to stop walking the path Sensei carved for you."

That made her stop, turn around, and stomp her boot. "Say that again," she challenged.

He paused but was not deterred. "You're thinking like Cell again. You called yourself that again. The longer this goes on, the more I worry you're becoming more *her* and less you."

"It's just a name, Dakota. No different than Zero."

"No. Cell was a girl who did whatever she was told with a smile on her face, even when it killed her inside. Cell only knew how to follow Sensei's orders. Allison is my twin. Allison loves the violin, and sewing, and scrambled eggs on pancakes." It seemed so foreign, the softness in his voice. "And Allison is my beloved sister."

She closed her eyes, shaking her head. "And what about you? Aren't you the same, continuing Sensei's teachings?"

His lips were tight as he held her gaze. "No. I'm worse. I'm empty inside—I always have been. But I care about Nikita, and as long as we're together, it's my responsibility to take care of her. I won't abandon her like Dylan did to us. And you too. You're my beloved sister. It's my duty as a man to take care of you, not the other way around." They stood glaring at each other and didn't move for a long while. There was a real tenderness to his words that she couldn't bring herself to believe.

Shaking her head, she gave a final protest. "It's my choice."

"I know. I know I can't stop you. That's why I want you to promise me this. Please, promise you will let go of this remnant of Koros and actually begin to live *your* life. Promise you will leave this dirty business for me."

It seemed so strange, so wrong, and so unlike him. Even so, even if she didn't know what tells Katife referred to, somehow, she knew he was being honest. "Okay. I promise."

Her violin gleamed in the dim evening light of her teacher's home, the sound of its strings enveloped the room. Her teacher stood opposite her with hands folded across her chest. "Stop." Complying mid-note, the sounds immediately died.

Ms Jozkier's voice was crisp and sharp, unlike Allison's playing. "How is it that in two days you have lost all sense of tempo and forgotten how hard to press the bow? And here I thought you were ready."

"I'm tired," Allison replied.

"Something I'm sure the judges will consider." Her eyes were narrowed, disbelief written in them. Letting out a sigh, she asked, "What's wrong, Allison?"

Part of her was angry about her teacher's frustrations and demands. It was for Koros she first took up the violin, and it had never been intended for her to perform seriously. And yet, there was another part of her that was angry at herself for letting her teacher down and not being good enough. "I'm nervous."

"Oh? Are you starting to take this seriously?"

She shook her head. "No. I mean, yes. It's just, Dakota and I got into a fight."

She looked away to where the room's piano stood, its lid closed. Catching her gaze, her teacher remarked, "You're siblings. Sibling's fight. And if we have to change the accompanist, I need to know now."

Shaking her head, Allison said, "No, he'll be there. Of course he will, that's his whole point. And I know that. It's just . . . something was different about this argument. Like he *really* meant it."

"He really meant what?" Leaving the question hanging, Allison failed to reply, realising the absurdity of complaining to her teacher that Dakota wanted her to start spending more time practicing the violin instead of combat. "He wants you to stop playing?"

"No!" Allison shouted, mostly on instinct. Quietening, she explained, "It's actually the opposite. He wants me to stop doing something else."

"I see." Her voice was sharp and simple and crisp.

"It's not just him. It's Rebecca too. They both think Koros was so horrible that I need to leave it all in the past, but it's not like I can just undo fourteen years of my life. And if I did, then what? Shouldn't I drop the violin too? I mean, Koros is the reason I started it."

Ms Jozkier shook her head, looking away from Allison. "Oh, I have been cursed with such a painful student."

Smiling shyly, Allison said, "You know me, Miss. I'm a pinnacle of modern decadence. What else is new?"

Taking a large breath, Ms Jozkier sighed. "Oh deary me." Pausing, she added, "You are indeed unfortunately filled with your own indulgence and degeneracy. But you

132

also make a poor habit of confusing your virtues with your vices, especially in all matters issuing from Koros. Perhaps it would be best if you stopped worrying about what they thought and asked yourself instead why it is you keep practicing. And ask the same of your past, for that matter. How does your former exploitation make *you* feel—both about it, and about what you've become as a result?"

Startled, Allison had no response. "I don't know how I feel about it. I mean, a part of me knows what happened was wrong, but another part wants to hang on to what it made me into," she replied in a small voice. After a long silence, Allison added, "I applied for IIDT for a reason. I want to go to that school. And I like playing. That's why I'm here. The sounds move me like nothing else. But that's the same for combat. I can't pretend my body doesn't crave it."

Her features softening, Ms Jozkier gave a sad smile. "You really are a painful student." Her comment made Allison frown with a deep, sad expression. "Perhaps we should stop for tonight. Spend the next few days screwing your head on straight. For your own sake. I don't want to see you waste this opportunity."

Returning her violin to its case, Allison slipped her band off her wrist, losing all movement in her arm.

"If you don't mind, I would have a word with your sister before you go," Ms Jozkier said.

"Oh. Ah, okay, I guess."

Rebecca was right on time, appearing nearly the instant Allison pressed the flower. Ms Jozkier told her she wanted to chat, relegating Allison to the living room to wait.

"I'm concerned about your sister," Allison heard Ms

Jozkier say.

"Did something happen?" Rebecca asked, parental concern consuming her voice.

"With that girl, something's always happening. Perhaps now there is something new, but I believe whatever this is, it has been years in the making." Rebecca gave no response, or more likely a nonverbal one Allison couldn't see. "I won't beat around the bush. I believe she has been stifled by your love."

At that moment, Allison froze, diverting every fraction of focus she had to her hearing as Rebecca gave a delayed, somewhat shocked, answer. "I am trying to give her the best life possible."

From the faint sounds of swaying hair, it sounded like her teacher was shaking her head. "You are trying to give her the best life *you* can imagine. No one could claim you acted from anything but kindness, but if she comes to feel ashamed of her life, she will not grow the way you intend."

"What is that supposed to mean?"

She imagined Ms Jozkier standing, slumped, her voice so tired Allison was thankful she wouldn't be driving anywhere. "It means you have never stopped to put yourself in her shoes, to consider how a reality fit for anyone else has been shunted into an awful misfit for her soul. Scars left across the hearts are not something to take lightly, nor can they be ignored."

"I'm doing everything I can to heal that pain."

Her teacher answered with harsh, powerful words. "Rebecca, you must know that some scars cannot be healed, and some abuse cannot be ignored."

In contrast, Rebecca was getting louder. *It's Dylan all over again.* "What do you know? I'm the one who sees what was done to them every day. I saw her unable to move after her own spell destroyed her body. Why do you think I gave her my flower? So that day or night, I can drop everything to protect her."

"And as such you've spared her having to realise there are consequences to her actions. That some things cannot be undone. Trying to undo Koros, a central pillar of her upbringing, lends itself to the idea that her own actions can be reversed, no matter how much damage she inflicts. Especially to herself. She has the power to reverse time, and want to or not, it made her complacent with her footprint on this world. These intervals where we meet have made it clear she is being torn apart now that the bill comes due. The more you stifle her with love, the more impossible it will be for her to learn that there is always a cost."

Ms Jozkier quietened. "You can't destroy the darkness that monastery instilled within her. Back when I performed, I learned that you accept the shadows of your heart, integrating them into your whole, or shun them until you are consumed whole."

Her voice soft, Rebecca's words were hushed, like she didn't want Allison to hear. "I don't know what you saw, but there's no way it's the same."

"You are right. She is far worse."

"Then you know I can't accept that darkness. It's unnatural, immoral."

"True, what happened to her was most unnatural and indeed immoral. And it is true that you can try to fight the tendrils clinging to her heart until the day she dies. Although . . . isn't that what you've already been doing? How has that worked out so far?" She clicked her tongue, which ought to infuriate Rebecca. "Do you really think any person can thrive while being at war with herself?"

As she shook her head, Rebecca's hair sounded far louder than her teacher's had. "Koros deserves much more than a war for what they did to her."

With a force usually reserved for when Allison messed up her practice badly, Ms Jozkier called, "You must help your sister understand her trauma and how it affects her, not teach her to run from it like a scared pup."

Ms Jozkier hadn't finished speaking when Rebecca's footsteps came quickly, returning the way they came and entering the room Allison waited in. Over her shoulder, Rebecca shouted, "You're just a music teacher. Don't tell me how to do my job." She didn't wait to take Allison's hand, instead reaching for her and immediately shattering the gem in her rose, transporting them into her world before another word could be said. She said nothing, which was convenient, as Allison was left frozen by what she had overheard and wasn't sure what she could possibly say to her sister.

When they appeared back in their home, Rebecca muttered something about dinner and let go of Allison's hand. Left alone, Allison tottered towards her room. She crossed Dakota in the hallway right before she opened her door. He stopped whatever he was doing, looking to her with concern and stepping closer. "Are you alright?"

His words hit her mind, parting the fog that was gaining control. She blinked as if awaking and looked at him squarely. "I'm fine."

"You're shaking." There was actual concern in his voice, his volume lowering.

She looked down, raising her hands to her eyes. She hadn't even noticed. Careful not to drop her violin, she lowered the case. "I don't know why that's happening."

She spoke as if the shaking were from some separate entity removed from her and not her own body. But from the corner of her eye, she spotted that velvet-lined box containing her gauntlet, soaked in darkness. The band that was a piece of it, the only piece she needed to play. Really, the only piece that mattered anymore.

If alternate worlds existed, she wondered in how many of them he would have believed her. Not many, and certainly not this one. But he kept up that thin smile, turning away just as a new voice cheered into their minds. No footsteps, no warning. One second he was leaving, another Nikita had faded into existence between them with circus-like energy. "I've done it! I found them!"

Under her breath, Allison muttered, "Great, now you're here."

"I'm sorry. Am I interrupting something?" Watching Nikita's mouth move was like watching a film with dubbed voices, only less sincere.

"Why do you even ask when we know you'll just read our minds anyway? Whatever. What is it?"

Nikita turned, looking to Dakota. Allison wondered if he saw the same image, or if to him Nikita was always facing his way. "I just came to tell you that I found them."

"Found who?" both asked.

"Who do you think? The people on that list!" Allison had to look past Nikita, but she could see the tightening expression on Dakota's face. "Now, I will admit that most of them ended up being dead or had disappeared sometime over the last few years, no doubt thanks to my stalker, but there were eight just on the Southern Continent, and three here in Emnalor. None from Isoval, but there's one near the fringe, one at the southern border, and get this: one in Salbador!"

"Salbador?" Both echoed Nikita. Allison's voice held confusion, Dakota's concern.

"Yeah. Or you know, in that general area. Isn't this perfect? You were already going there, so this won't even be out of the way. And we have a hotel booked and everything! It's just perfect!"

"This is very far from perfect," Dakota muttered, but she couldn't tell if he was talking to them or himself.

Ignoring Nikita, Allison practically looked through her to her brother. "What's the big deal? It's a big city with lots of people. And there's no way I'm cancelling my schoolies. The deposit's already down."

"You promised me. No more."

"And? I never said I wouldn't be in the same geographic region as someone who may or may not be a target of Soul's. That would be absurd."

"But . . ."

"Come on, Dakota, think about it logically. What is the worst thing that will happen if I'm just in the same city? We probably are right now."

His lips were tight, his expression dark. Looking between them, Nikita asked with that same dubbed look, "What the hell is going on between you two?"

Dakota answered, the defeat in his voice. "I'm taking care of you from now on. Allison will be doing her own thing."

She wondered what expression Nikita showed just then—the real her, not the projection. She hoped it was shock. She was savouring the idea of it being shock.

"Wait, what? Why?" Nikita said.

"Because he's a hopeless romantic who wanted to save his love on his own, right?" Flashing him an over-the-top smile, Allison's voice rose with a blatantly fake sing-song tune.

Instead of responding to her taunt, he turned to Nikita. "It doesn't matter why. We decided she's staying out of harm's way. I'm still going to do whatever it takes to protect you. That hasn't changed." Nikita didn't respond.

The poor girl probably has no idea what to say. This might be one of the first times she's ever been caught unprepared. After long enough of saying nothing, Dakota asked, "So, who is it?"

Her projection faltering in Allison's mind, Nikita stammered, "Uh, just this girl named Arya. Family name's Daharak. Seems like she's rich, although she might also be some kind of recluse."

Dakota nodded, taking in the information. As he did, Allison frowned. "Hey, you know I have to tell Theta about this, right? Any chance he might pull out? We can't afford the hotel without all four of us."

Her voice chipper, Nikita replied, "Does it matter? If he does I can just . . . you know . . ."

She did know, and she hated that she knew, and hated that Nikita would suggest tampering with their friend's thoughts so easily. It was almost like Nikita wasn't a part of the group.

Then again, if it wasn't for Dakota, we might not even know her.

The light had only fallen once, and already his stomach was growling. The bridge was long gone, and even the peak of the mountain became hidden. He had to focus on his steps, making sure to track over the top of the snow and not sink in.

There was no path, just an endless downhill. Darkness fell much quicker here than up high as shadows were cast by the mountain. Using sticks, the boy made fire, which delivered just enough warmth to his body.

The second day was no easier with the pain in his stomach dragging him down. Another day went by, and he wasn't sure how he would keep walking. Settling against a tree trunk, he closed his eyes and waited for sleep.

Waking, it was harder than ever to get back on his feet. Never before had he felt so weak. He didn't know how to end the pain, how to regain his strength. It was like getting further from the top somehow made him weaker. Yet, the boy continued, step after step. Onwards and downwards.

The day was halfway done; he could tell from the position of the light in the sky. Then, he saw it in the distance.

Just like above, back in the village, there was a hut—small, broken, and covered in snow. It was still a long way below him and off to the side. He knew the chances of finding something there was slim, but the possibility of something was more than he could resist. Veering towards it, it took so long to get there he almost couldn't stand anymore, half dragging himself through the broken wall and into the mostly empty room.

No people were inside, only one of those bundles of white sticks resembling one. It was sitting against the back wall, just like so many people in the village. It wore a metal helmet, and in its hand was a tightly gripped stick. This one was an actual stick, brown and thick and about as long as his arm, with a dark wedge at the top. He didn't know what it was, but there was something about it that made him want to take it. His fingers closed around the handle.

The world disappeared and was replaced with a scene familiar, yet different. He was atop the mountain, with nothing but those carpets of blue in every direction. And he wasn't alone.

Before him stood a man made of a silvery liquid. He was taller than any person the boy had known. The man's voice was soft and echoing. "Hello." Pushing away, the boy retreated to the pinnacle. "No need to be afraid. I cannot hurt you here. This is your internal world we are in."

Voice shaking, the boy demanded, "Who you?"

"Me? I am but the soul of the deicide arm contained in the axe you held."

"Axe?" the boy asked. "Deicide arm?"

"Yes, an axe. Don't you know what that is?" The boy shook his head. The shoulders of the silver figure dropped. "That is . . . interesting. And deicide arms? Have you never heard of the weapons, like myself, who were forged to fight against gods and their servants, such as those horrible monsters across the border?" Again the boy shook his head, and again the silver man sunk a little. "Well then, do you want to tell me who you are? Or when it is? It has been so very long since I last talked to another. As you saw, my last owner died long ago."

The boy looked all around for some sort of escape or way to make it all make sense. There was nothing. "Are you alright? Did you hear me?"

Instead of responding, the boy continued to look around. "Where am I?"

"Hmm. I'm sure we're still on the mountain Urkinhorn. Although if you mean this place, it's your internal world."

"Internal world?" the boy repeated.

The silver man seemed to sink a little. Even though he was made of liquid silver, there was something lively about him. "I guess you know nothing about mana then. Well, that wasn't that uncommon amongst the villages we used to raid. I'll tell you what, kid. If you take me with you, I'll tell you whatever you want to know."

Holding his stomach, the boy asked. "Why pain here?"

The silver man frowned. "Don't you know what eating is?" The boy shook his head. "It seems I have much to tell you. Take me with you, and I can help take away that pain."

Hair held in a tight braid that kept her locks from sweeping the floor, Rebecca looked somehow off, as if she were an imposter. Allison took the opposite approach, spilling her hair over the shoulders of her handmade dress. A shade lighter than her hair, it had thin sleeves that just covered her shoulders, while the skirt dropped to her knees. Her violin case cast a shadow over the silver trim, which equally adorned her neckline.

In sharp contrast to his usual appearance, Dakota wore a plain suit, slick and dark and minimally tailored. Allison had already smoothed out the wrinkles once. His hair was held back by a pool of gel, leaving it firm with a slight shine.

She had only just entered the building and already she could feel that it would be nothing like those times for Koros.

The building was a long, arching ring with windows on one side and slightly orange walls on the other.

Everyone was dressed in the same league as them, and amongst every set someone carried a violin case. Guests, visitors, and judges would be arriving later. Right then, it was staff, contestants, and immediate family.

When others arrived, the familiar lined face of Rebecca's mother was not far behind. She wrapped Allison in an embrace the moment she was close enough. "Oh, you look magnificent. Truly gorgeous. You are going to shine once you get to IIDT."

Voice muffled by the woman's shoulder, Allison said, "I have to get in first."

With a gentle tug, Rebecca pulled them apart. "Okay, Mum. I think Allison needs some space."

Pulling away, Connie swapped to embrace her daughter, and then finally Dakota. "Oh, and you are so handsome."

Before any more of Rebecca's family could arrive, Allison saw her teacher walk in. She could still remember the fight between the two and dashed away to talk to her in private.

"Nervous?" Ms Jozkier asked.

She shook her head. "I'm trying not to think."

Ms Jozkier nodded. "Just don't forget to enjoy yourself. This is for you, after all."

Allison nodded, smiling in appreciation. Then Ms Jozkier began her list of all the questions she needed to ask. Had she tuned her instrument? Did she practice in the morning? Was she hydrated? And on and on.

From her position by her teacher, she saw Rebecca's old household gather, her half-brother and stepfather greeting Dakota. Once, Allison had drawn their family tree, but with so many half relatives involved, it just became a mess. It made things simpler to confine it to their household and view Rebecca's family as cousin and uncle. *Although Connie probably deserves the description of grandmother.*

The auditorium doors opened, and Allison returned to her family for final words of encouragement. Katife and Theta had gathered, both overdressed for the occasion. Then they split, her and Dakota heading backstage, the rest towards their seats.

Seventeen pairs waited with them. Some were sitting in the halls, some chose walking restlessly, while others were already heading for the stage entrance itself. With time before she went on, Allison found a seat further from the stage, warming up her wrists and fingers and running through the exercises she had done a thousand times before. She became aware of the calluses her fingertips had developed over a lifetime of playing that became not only natural, but a necessary part of her performance. Her arms were bare save for the gauntlet's band at her wrist, as well as its black threads that wrapped around her arm. There would be a camera upon her, ensuring none of those threads came in contact with the instrument. It would look unsightly, but the only alternative was wearing gloves, and as a violinist, that wasn't an option.

The last thing she did was tune the instrument. She had tuned it in the morning and the night before, and even again just before they left. Her heart started racing, and it was only the slow cycle of breathing that kept it under control.

The band was cold on her wrist. It was far from practical, slipping with the movement, made for something larger. It was not a good icon by any means, even if technically it was just a piece of one. *Of an icon that's lost its purpose. Too unwieldy for the violin, not practical enough for design. Something utterly outdated.*

"Hey, Dakota?" If it were a hinge, the slow movement of his neck would have suggested the need for some grease. "That room you made for Katife. Would it be possible to use it again?"

Eyebrow raising high, he asked, "You want another icon?"

"Not another one, no." Biting her lip, she waited, unsure what to say. If she said it, it became real, while as long as she didn't it was just a silly idea in her head. "I've been thinking. Maybe if I do well here, I might break the gauntlet and reconfigure my spells. I mean, I only need the wires now, right? I just need to move my arm. Everything else is useless. So maybe I swap shadow wires for water ones. Then I can add them to my ribbon. What do you think?"

He nodded, not even waiting for her to finish. "If I do it, no one will know you made the change, so you get that surprise element. I ah, don't know how well it will work though."

"Oh," she said, looking away.

"But . . ." She could hear him taking a deep breath in through his nose. "I think it's a good idea. Let's give it a go. Worst case, I'll take you to do it officially."

Nodding, she could almost feel the seat let her sink into it. "Thanks, Dakota. But it's only if I get through tonight."

Her time approaching, she rose, leading the way to the wings. She needed to be close, to be ready. From the wings she watched the sixth performer. He stood upon a large, wooden stage with thick, black curtains raised above. Rows of seats disappeared into darkness. She searched that darkness, seeking the familiar golden orbs of Rebecca's eyes. Beside her she found her family and friends, everyone she invited with one exception. Yifei wasn't there. She knew she wouldn't be. Her family had bought their tickets months in advance, whereas Yifei bought hers last minute. She was nowhere to be seen amidst the crowd. Her heart raced faster, destabilising her breathing. In her extremities, she felt herself shaking.

No human would hear the counting, soft and low and quiet even for a Yatrice. Little more than breath itself, Dakota counted the seconds in lots of four. Latching onto it, she forced her breathing back to match, slowing her heart and stopping the shaking.

The music stopped, and the boy bowed before leaving the stage. "Next is eighteen-year-old Allison Jane Khione, with the accompaniment played by Dakota Khione."

He gave her the slightest of nudges. It was all it took for her to take the first step. After that, it was one foot ahead of the next. She walked out through the first layer of curtains onto the stage amidst a wave of applause. Dakota stayed a few steps behind. She bowed from her position as Dakota took his place on the piano bench. She turned back for but a second, enough for them to lock eyes and know he was ready. She moved into her first position.

Dakota hit the first notes, keying her in. Two bars in, she started. It was slow, her bow sliding to create the distanced notes. It continued four more bars before Dakota had more keys to press. The pace quickened, the tempo rising. Her fingers followed, making the notes more powerful as she swung her arm further and faster. Her fingers became like a spider's legs as they ran over the neck of the violin. Her bow glided over the top like the wings of a bee, flying so rapidly it could barely be seen.

Dakota's notes became hidden behind her wall of sound. He was the wooden frame of a house. She was everything else. Some bars he stopped playing all together, sometimes he needed a slow, single lingering key. She couldn't see what he was doing; she didn't have the luxury of looking back. He was behind her, and her eyes were closed.

Her back bowed and arched at the music's demand. It took control of her in a way the thudding beats of Lunar never could. She could feel the tension in her cheeks as her tongue pushed against the wall of her teeth. Sweat gathered around her neck and forehead. She got louder; she got faster. Dakota followed right behind. She played until the music demanded she pause, where Dakota keyed in. Then he stopped, and she took over, igniting a relay of sound.

The tune slowed to become sombre, and that sadness took control of her heart. It stayed slow for two whole lines before it began to change. Then, it became joyful, almost jovial. She could imagine herself playing at a ball, playing for the nobles of old, the ones her family had been a part of hundreds of years ago. She could even imagine herself as one of the dancers. She saw all the parties she had played at as a child, the highlights of Koros.

Then she felt something wrong. Like the wire was wrapped around her fingers, like they were tight from tension. Like it used to be when the party was over and she did what she was there for. Violin wire made for great sound, but she'd felt enough people go limp in her arms to know it had other uses. On stage, watched by hundreds of people, she felt that phantom sensation wash through her body.

Again, her breathing got away. Trying to smother the feeling, she focused on her playing, which made everything unstable. Like thinking about how to move your arm, like reciting the steps to riding a bike. It didn't seem possible how her limbs were moving. Her head was becoming light, and she kept breathing faster, desperate not to feel her past happening again.

It was an illusion; she knew there was no other option. It was not Nikita's style of bending her mind, but something more natural, something more horrible. Her own mind not letting go— of the past, of her actions, of what *she* had done.

Dakota's notes shifted, slowing before their time. For a moment, she wanted to scream at him. But she didn't. It wasn't sabotage, it was aid. She was the one who had lost her time.

Instead of herself, she focused on him, on the keys. He filled her silences, matching her rhythm and making it sound right to someone who didn't know better, like it was what she was supposed to do.

The pace picked up, her tune feeding into what was written on paper. Five long strokes, requiring her to roll her bow. Each one was underscored by a low key by Dakota. The beginning of the final act. Her arm increased its speed, her fingers crying from dancing over the strings. They felt just about ready to bleed. Sweat formed under her hair.

Her back arched with the music. It felt like she must have moved, must be close to the edge. Even walking a literal tightrope had not felt so unbalanced. The final section barrelled in—fast notes paced with low sounds, happy but tinged with bittersweet sadness. For three beats she paused, and Dakota filled that gap with his keys. Then the final bar began; another two notes until she came to the end with one last, long, lingering note, perfectly in time with her brother.

Every sound died, not a muscle daring to so much as twitch as her breaths grew heavy, and the violin became the hardest thing to hold, the bow awkward in her grip, and she felt certain that in a moment she would drop them both. She dared not breathe.

Everyone was shoulder to shoulder. The seventeen violinists were now all back on the stage, waiting as the announcements were read. It was a long process lacking the flair of the ring announcers from her fights, and she wasn't sure how well her knees were holding up. Thanks were read out to each and every person involved in bringing the competition to life, finally ending with the judges who were welcomed onto the stage. They stood behind a table draped in a red velvet, holding up three large trophies.

At long last, the final envelope was opened, with the winners written inside. "In third place, we have Stephan Brojek." Applause sounded as Allison's heart dropped.

As supportive as Dakota's accompaniment had been, her midsong falter meant first was not even a dream anymore. Now she knew third was gone too, and her heart began to sink. Like everyone else, Stephan was around her age. She watched as he stepped from the pack and bowed to the crowd. He approached the judges table to shake each one's hand and was presented with the first award.

There was that noticeable, yet brief moment of confusion where he was unsure if he was supposed to return to the group or exit the stage, ending when a judge indicated for him to stand just to the side of the table.

She knew her face had dropped, that she was playing the sore loser unable to smile as someone else won. Some took the announcement with hope that first was still a possibility. Others reacted just as she had, with dread. They all gave polite applause.

The announcer's eyes returning to the page, he read the next name. "Our second-place winner is Allison Jane Khione." That same polite applause played the soundtrack to her dropping heart. She reacted according to her fears and predictions alone. Nothing else mattered in that moment but her prior calculations, creating an even more awkward instant where her own hands rose in applause, clapping three times before she noticed.

First her eyes went wide, then her heart fluttered. Mouth slightly agape, she almost wished she had Dakota with her to give that push like before. She stepped forward, cheeks blushing as she dropped into a curtsy and raced to the table. There were so many hands to shake as she went down the line, finally being presented the second plaque. Even when she was standing next to the third placer, her heart still refused to settle.

She needed to get off the stage. She wasn't sure how much longer she could stand, or how long until her cheeks would burn through. But she had to wait as a long procession was made leading up to the final announcement—yet more thanks and a congratulations to the first-place winner. She didn't even hear who it was until she was standing beside her.

There was a final round of applause, and finally the contestants were allowed to leave. But not her, nor the two beside her. They had to stay as someone new took the podium to continue their announcements. "I want to give a special congratulations to these three whose performances highlighted the proficiency and possibilities of this instrument. I am sure I am not alone in my hopes for their future, and for what we will hear next. And, come January, I look forward to hearing them again as they move forward to the Emnalor National Violin Competition."

She didn't hear anything else; none of it mattered. All her brain and heart cared about was staying still until she was finally able to move. Time crawled. Then, like a switch flipped, time jumped into hyperdrive as she was ushered out to the wings and met with her brother, who took her violin and escorted her to a private room, where she spent ten minutes pacing as fast as her legs would allow.

Dakota didn't rush her, letting her burn off energy or excitement or something else entirely as he sat waiting on the couch. It took time, and by the time she felt sufficiently calm to gather her things and make an exit to the lobby, most people had already departed. Her family rushed forward to meet her, and Rebecca embraced her. "You won! I knew you could. I didn't doubt you for a moment." She had no doubt every other parent figure had planned those same words.

Stepping around the group, Katife punched Dakota's shoulder. "Hey. You were pretty good yourself. You should play for me some more." For a second, her eyes widened. "Us, I mean. Play for us."

"Not gonna happen." His lips raised into a smile. A ghost of a smile really, but then, it was Dakota after all. "But thanks."

"Come on. I've never heard you play solo before."

154

"Katife, I don't play solo."

"Never? Not once?"

He shook his head, and Allison saw the memory reflected in his eye. "I used to try, but all I'd hear is Koros."

She was sure Sensei had Dakota sitting behind a piano as long as he'd forced a violin into her hands. She remembered him performing once, for all the same reasons as she did. But in the years since, she'd never once heard why he stopped. *We never really talk about music. I tell him what piece I need, and he says okay.* He never sweated from playing and always practiced with drawn-on keys. "I'm not like Allison. I don't love music."

Too close to pretend she didn't hear, Allison stammered, "I wouldn't say I love it."

He shook his head. "Katife's right; you do have tells."

Mouth agape and lost for words, she almost shouted to break through her embarrassment. "Whatever tells you think you see are wrong. It's just . . . kinda nice, I guess."

Bathing in the warmth of her friends and family, the endless minutes passed in bliss. Then a curious glance caught another, someone holding back and hanging by the wall. She made an excuse and pulled away, chasing after her until they were both around the corner and out of sight. "Hey. Sorry I was late."

Allison shook her head. Even dressed up for once, she was confident nothing could stop her recognising Yifei on sight. "I swear my heart almost burst when I saw you at the end."

Allison's comment elicited a soft smile from Yifei. "Then perhaps I should hide more often."

"I'd hardly call giving a standing ovation 'hiding.'"

She just shrugged. "It's not my fault everyone else has bad taste."

With a slight giggle, Allison lowered her gaze to Yifei's chin. "Is it alright if we hang out today? I felt lonely when I thought you hadn't come."

Leaning in just as close, Yifei said something back. Allison didn't hear what. Her focus became consumed by seeing her sister's hair in the window's reflections, her whole family coming around the corner. "Family?"

Allison nodded with thin lips. "That's my brother. The two my age are friends. The blonde is my half-sister, and the other two are her family."

Yifei looked away from Allison to the ensemble. "Is today when I meet the family?"

She swallowed. "Doesn't it feel kinda early?" Moving her head, Yifei looked to the group. "Seems a little late to be worried about it."

"I know but . . . we could go somewhere."

"Like?"

Allison answered in an unintelligible mumble, so Yifei asked her to repeat herself. "What about your place? Just for a bit."

Looking between Allison and the approaching group, Yifei hesitated a moment before smiling. "My place works great. And for right now?"

Rebecca saw them but maintained enough courtesy not to go right up to them. *The advantage of having a guardian young enough to remember this side.*

Stepping back, Allison spun out of Yifei's arm and ran over to her family. Skidding to a stop, she looked only as high as Rebecca's neck, taking a hard swallow. "Ihaveafriendcametoseeandinvitedmetoapartytocelebra te soooooo . . ." Sucking in a large breath, she finished her sentence. "I'm gonna head out now."

No shock or confusion crossed Rebecca's face, while Connie's was covered in it. "I think I gathered." She nodded and made a move to stop her mum's input. "Okay, well, stay safe."

Leaning in, Allison wrapped her arm around her sister, quickly repeating the hug for Connie. As she turned to her brother, he stepped forward. "You mind taking my things back?" He nodded, already carrying her violin, and now added her plaque.

As she started retreating to the crowd, Rebecca called to her. "When will you be back?"

She shook her head, more to stir herself than to signify anything. "I don't know. I'll call you."

Rebecca swallowed. "Um, message me when you get there, okay?"

"Okay, I promise." Without another word, she rushed away, catching Katife's smile as she turned. She couldn't tell if it was supportive or mischievous.

Weaving her way back to Yifei, they rushed out the building, threading through the crowd until they burst into the afternoon light. "So, what now? Call a taxi?" Seeing Allison's face drop, Yifei stalled in momentary confusion. "Oh my God, sorry. I forgot."

Not wanting her to feel any guilt, Allison shook her head. "It's not your fault."

"Still. How do you normally travel?"

"I walk a lot. Or ride. But I can also deal with trams. Will that work?"

Thinking a moment, Yifei replied, "Yeah, but we'll need to change lines. It won't be quick."

Allison bit her lip, but if the alternative was a car, she'd prefer the delay. The tram they found plodded along for near an hour. Yifei took the window while Allison snuggled beside her. The city grew taller from sticks on the horizon to smothering buildings on all sides. They changed trams, heading out in the opposite direction towards Yifei's suburbs.

Fourteen years in Koros had taught her patience. She'd often been made to wait in ambush or hiding, sometimes for hours, sometimes days, sometimes even longer. Now, waiting in that tram car, she wasn't sure she could wait another second to arrive. It felt like an eternity of endless stops until finally, Yifei took her arm and pulled her up. The walk from there was no quick trip either. She couldn't imagine doing that commute daily.

The street was the busy sort of quiet. There would be no cars for a long stretch, then a short burst would come through. Very few pedestrians were out—a jogger here, a family with a dog there. The houses lining the street were all separated by the minimum possible space to not be conjoined. They were new enough to not be old, old enough to not be new. Two stories by and large, all built by similar architects.

Yifei let go of Allison's hands to reach for her keys. Unlocking the door, she led Allison inside, using her heel to kick off both her shoes. She never ended up messaging Rebecca.

***

"Can I ask you something?" Allison asked as they sat down for dinner. It was just the two of them around Yifei's small table, eating cheap takeout food delivered to her door.

Putting down the chopsticks that came with their food, Yifei shrugged. "Shoot."

Allison swallowed, gathering her courage. "Why . . .

back at Lunar, did you . . . you know"

"Aside from Tara telling me to?"

"You could have left."

Yifei just shook her head, picking up another bite. "Like I said back then, you seemed bored, and I was sick of the dance floor. Besides, you looked cool and interesting, and just a touch cute. I liked that."

"You think I'm cute?"

"What did I just say?"

Take that Katife, someone does *think I'm cute.* Allison smiled softly to herself. Then an idea came, and she tried her best to hide her smile as Yifei picked another bite from her takeout box. Reaching for her ribbon, she set it to reverse time, not just by seconds or minutes, but years. The table rose up to meet her and her dress began to swim around her. One year, then two and three, continuing until she was back in her ten-year-old body. "How about now?"

Yifei came to a dead stop, blinking and trying to piece what she was seeing together. "I didn't know you could do that." Her voice was purely factual, an admission on an emotionless level.

Smiling deviously, Allison said, "I reverse time for my body. I never said how far."

"Okay, well this is, uh, weird. This is very weird. Wait, then why is your arm still broken?"

Shrugging, Allison said, "No one knows for sure. My guess is the mana circuits there are screwed, but there's got to be more to it since my arm is young too." As she said it, she thrust her left arm forward, still lifeless but in line with the age of the rest of her body.

"I'll be the first to admit I know nothing about

159

mana, but that seems pretty weird. Oh, and please turn back already."

"What, you don't like me like this?"

"Allison, I'll put it this way. You're now a child, alone, in my apartment, and those clothes don't fit you anymore. Yes, I would really love for you to change back."

Mouth falling open, Allison blushed and undid the spell, eating through most of her mana already. "I didn't think that through."

"Clearly," Yifei muttered, placing the chopsticks down. "Since I really didn't need to see that, how about you repay me with a few answers?"

"Like what?" Allison asked, swirling the chopsticks like the knives she used to train with into a folded position. "Well, for starters, you never told me you came from the assassin orphanage. Is that true or just an internet lie?"

Allison lowered her eyes, her voice quieting to match. "Does that scare you?"

Lips parting slightly, Yifei's whole face seemed to drop. "You really were a child soldier?"

With a fake laugh, Allison responded, "It'd be more accurate to say 'child assassin.'"

Yifei didn't laugh. "That's not something to joke about, Alley-Cat."

Her smile disappeared off her face. "I know."

Leaning back on her chair, Yifei asked, "So what was it like, you know, joining the outer world?"

Allison shrugged, not really wanting to remember those days, but wanting to tell her at the same time. "It was weird, being split from all my friends and everything I knew. The reports weren't nice either."

"Reports?"

She nodded. "Yeah. All the news people writing how we were little traumatised dolls. All they really cared about was ad revenue. That was the worst part."

"What, the media?"

"Aren't they always? But no. Not *them* per se; it was more the way they made us feel."

"You're going to have to explain that one."

Her voice lowering a notch, she said, "They made us into victims."

Slipping into silence, she felt her heart rate increase, felt how it had only gotten faster as she spoke, how her words only got angrier as she remembered those days.

"Weren't you?" Yifei asked.

Allison shook her head, not strongly, but a little. "No. I mean yes, we were victims of some bad stuff, but they made us into *Victims* with a capital v. Like that was our whole identity. I know what happened wasn't good but . . . they made me feel like I was helpless. Like my choices, my life, was irrelevant. They made their articles about how much they cared, then treated us like spoiled goods who needed their pity. I didn't want pity or sympathy. I just wanted them to acknowledge our humanity. Instead, it's like they thought we were doomed to fail because of things we couldn't help. If that's the case, how's life even worth living?"

Yifei nodded, her eyes revealing hidden thoughts playing behind those gorgeous eyes. But they were thoughts she left unsaid. Were the situation reversed, Allison wasn't sure what she would have said either. As the silence dragged on, she felt something deep within her mind begging her to let it out, a secret she thought best kept. It would have been so easy to keep quiet, but there was something inside her desperate to let it out, even if she couldn't explain why. "There were two dozen of them."

"Two dozen of what?"

"Two dozen people. That I, you know." She made a clicking sound with her tongue.

"Wha...oh." Yifei paused, lowering her eyelids and thinking. "That's a lot. You weren't kidding when you said you weren't innocent." She paused, and then she frowned. "Why did you tell me that?" It wasn't accusatory, but inquisitive. "Alley-Cat, why . . .? Oh. Dammit, girl. You're not gonna make me ditch you."

"Huh?"

Not responding, Yifei just shook her head. "'Huh'? You're trying to push me away." Allison stopped, swallowed, and closed her eyes. That feeling, that one she hadn't quite pinned down, had just been nailed. "Look at me." Allison couldn't do it, instead keeping her eyes lowered. Yifei did not accept that response, taking her by the chin and forcing her to look up. "Look at me. Stop trying to scare me off. I'm not going anywhere. Okay?"

She held her there, not moving until Allison finally relented. "Okay," she echoed. Yifei nodded, but neither felt like taking back their chopsticks. After a long time, Allison muttered, "I'm sorry for that. I know I'm not a good person."

"For trying to scare me off?" Yifei asked incredulously. Shaking her head, Allison took a deep breath. "Yifei, people like me highlight the decadence of modern society." "Decadence?" Yifei asked. Allison said nothing, so with a sigh Yifei opened her scroll, finding a definition online. Reading it, she shouted, "In what way are you a moral decay?"

Her voice quiet, Allison replied, "In more ways than

you can imagine."

"Wow," Yifei breathed. "I've never been so insulted in my life."

Shaking her head, Allison protested, "I don't mean you. I mean . . . when I was in Koros, I did what I was told. Whatever I was told. I was only ever what they instructed me to be." Slowing right down, she added, "I killed my best friend."

"What?" Yifei shouted.

Swallowing, Allison said nothing. After their silence stretched over a minute, she added, "I told you, I really am decadence."

Taking in the longest breath, Yifei closed her eyes, muttering quietly, "You are one messed up girl."

Yifei's words brought to mind ones from years past: those uttered with Sydney's dying breaths. Unable to stop herself, Allison muttered "An imperfect creature. That's what I am."

"A what?" Yifei asked.

Caught in the spotlight of Yifei's gaze, Allison swallowed and lowered her head. "Someone used to call me that. An imperfect creature."

Rolling the word on her tongue, Yifei tried it twice. "An imperfect creature? Now there's a nice image."

"What? How?" Allison whispered. "It's a horrible image."

"Alley, there's nothing wrong with imperfection. Nobody is perfect, and no one should try to be. It's being broken that's the problem. There's a whole lot of shattered people out there who I don't envy one bit." Rubbing her hair, Yifei let out a long sigh. "Call your sister. You should go home."

Eyes turning downcast, Allison whispered, "You

don't like me anymore?"

But Yifei reached out her hand, gently taking Allison's in hers. "I told you; you're not scaring me away." She paused, waiting for Allison to look up. "But it's getting late, and I need some time to think. You've put a lot of images in my head, girl. And I only have so much space up there."

She didn't use Rebecca's flower. She didn't want her sister to arrive too quickly and bring this moment to an end. Nodding, Allison pulled out her scroll, and sent her sister a message. In both her head and her heart, Allison hadn't the faintest clue how to feel as she waited to be taken away.

From near the western extremes of Emnalor, over by the fringe, the train began rushing towards them. With Rebecca's aid, they arrived at the station early, bags packed for their two-week trip by the ocean, a celebration of the end of high school just as summer was warming up.

They clung to the shadows of the limited shade. Contacts left in her bag, she relished the sliver of shadow the frames of her glasses provided. It was a choice she found herself making more often since her performance. They were alone on the platform, while the one across the tracks had enough passengers for them both. Most departed on the city bound train, although a duo remained behind. They stayed for a moment, then disappeared from the platform, appearing again walking up from the underpass. "Heads up."

She guessed they were probably trying to seem less threatening by taking their time. Coming into view, they were clearer now. A pair of Yatrice approached with chipper smiles like they'd just won a jackpot. "Hi. I'm Laura. This is Aaron. How are you doing today?"

She was a bunny girl—the worst sort of Yatrice, in Allison's mind after the last one had left her lonely. Aaron had a tail of some sort. She didn't look at them, instead looking to where their train would come from. "Want something?" she asked.

The girl seemed deterred enough to look to her partner, but not enough to stop. "Me? Not particularly. I just noticed two fellow Yatrice hanging lonely and was wondering if you needed a place to stay."

Facing the girl for the first time, Allison stared her up and down, never looking above her hairline. "Do you just assume we're strays?"

"Aren't you?" Aaron asked, a sort of confidence in his voice.

"Did you forget it's schoolies time right now? We're going for some sun, surf, and shopping, not . . . whatever weird crap you two are into."

Finally taken aback, the pair put their hands up in protest. "Oh no, we're not . . ."

Seeing the longing way he looked to his partner, Allison guessed there was nothing there, and that he probably wished there were. *Or I'm choosing to see something because I'm bored and it's better than paying attention.* "So, you just go around inviting strangers to live with you all the time then?"

Using one of those fake smiles a jaded customer service agent would show, Laura stammered, "I think there's been some sort of miscommunication. We're with Occupy Yatrice. I'm sorry if we came across wrong. We're just trying to offer support to young Yatrice, especially if you're ever feeling lost or in need of a community."

A part of Allison wanted to groan and throw the girl

onto the tracks. Another part wished she had a bingo card to check off all the things she knew were coming. Deadpan as always, Dakota stated, "We're not interested in joining a domestic terrorist gateway club."

Their protest was predictable, given Dakota's taunting was refined to a tee. But seeing a second pair behind them, Allison threw predictability to the wind. "Besides, the community we need is right behind you."

When they twisted instinctively, the pair was directly met with Katife's stretched grin. "Howdy."

Laura bit her lip. The two looked at each other, to the twins, and finally, the human pair of Katife and Theta. The latter seemed to be their convincing argument, making Laura nod. "We, ah, should go. But please give it a thought." Laura tried handing the flyer over, but neither of them would take it. In the end, she left it on the bench and walked away.

Reaching down, Theta took the pamphlet. "This again?"

Leaning onto the steel back of the shelter, Allison sighed. "That's the sixth time this spring. I swear they come out with the sun."

Sliding down beside her, Katife spoke with a chipper voice more sincere than the bunny's. "Well, look on the bright side. Our train's almost here."

From city to city, the trip lasted almost two hours of constant movement. The coastal towers curved around the horizon just as Katife showed off how she'd learned to bend the trajectory of her scroll's camera. "You're improving fast," Dakota said. Katife smiled back and was about to say something, but stopped herself.

Eyes were on her, but for once she didn't seem

comfortable. "Speaking of mana . . ." Allison chipped in, steering the eyes towards her instead. "I'm finally going to do it."

"Are you really?" Theta asked.

She nodded. "I promised. I came in second, so I guess I'm getting rid of it."

"So why the wait?"

"I dunno. Nostalgia, I guess."

"What's so nostalgic about that place?"

Shrugging, she replied, "I don't know, Theta. It's just . . . It's gonna be so weird not having it under my bed anymore."

He nodded slightly, enough to show he understood. It was Katife who asked, "So how are you going to do it?"

Taking in a deep breath, Allison said, "Maybe drop it off the balcony. I mean, it's literally armour, so not the easiest thing to break, but . . . I'll figure something out. Then I can toss it into the ocean for good measure."

They all nodded with faint smiles. Even Dakota. *Especially Dakota.* The train screeched to a stop just outside the city.

Taking all their bags, Katife and Theta split off from the twins, boarding a city bound bus. "You're sure there's nothing on rails?"

In the queue for the hospital line bus, Dakota took Allison's hand. "I'm sorry, there's nothing."

Clenching her fist so hard her knuckles went white, she allowed him to pull her onto the bus. They sat on seats closest to the doors. With every curve, every bounce in the road, every pebble, the images flooded back—of the drive, of the impact, of her world flipping end over end. It left her on her knees ready to vomit by the time they got off.

He was left waiting behind her, gently stroking her hair as her world slowly stopped spinning. When she finally recovered, there was another ten minutes left to walk and clear her head. Looking at their destination, Dakota said, "You're just here to talk, remember?"

Stepping past the low brick fence, she moaned, "I just told you I was breaking my gauntlet."

The house they arrived at was two stories, twenty meters long, and deep from the looks of. It would have swallowed Rebecca's home five times over and still had space for more. The front door was thick and heavy and hidden behind a screen door. "Take a look at that side street. Someone's doing a stakeout."

He looked carefully, not making it obvious. "Cop?" he asked as they crossed the front yard.

"Looks likely," she said, pressing the doorbell and standing back to wait. Hearing the door being unlocked, she muttered, "Damn, it's getting hot."

Face half hidden behind the mesh, a girl with blue hair tied into twin ponytails opened it. Her eyes were hidden behind thin frames resemblant of Allison's own. Her skin was a dark tan. She wore a silver ring. She was similar, but not quite what Nikita described—way too young. "Who are you?" Her eyes focused mostly on Dakota. With a smile, Allison answered, "Hi there. I'm Allison, and this is my brother Dakota. We need to speak with Arya Daharak."

Just hearing the name had an effect, making the girl stand straighter, one foot forward. A defensive position. "What do you want?"

Feeling her own exasperation at the Occupy Yatrice duo reflected back at her, she risked trading friendliness for sincerity. "We have a friend who's in danger. We were told Arya might be able to tell us something."

Chewing on gum, the girl gave it thought. "She'll probably say no. But I'll ask." After she closed the door, they heard the girl running. It took a minute, but then it was opened again. Someone else stood there now. Her hair was longer and tangled in a clear bed head. It was bubblegum pink, which looked dyed, unlike the first girl's. Headphones were trapped around her neck. Her glasses had a pink lining, and her eyes were amber with rings underneath. Otherwise, the two almost looked the same, only about five years apart. "Are you Arya?"

The girl's voice matched her tired look, yet she fired in rapid sequence. "Yep. No, I won't give a comment; yes, the rumours were true; no, not anymore; no, I don't know who the others were; no, I don't want to go on record. Are we done?"

Blinking as she tried taking it in, Allison stammered, "I have no idea what you're talking about."

Her confusion was reflected on Arya's face. "You're not reporters or something?"

Almost unsure of what to say, with a slight incline of her head, Allison urged Dakota to answer. "A friend said you might be able to help us."

"What friend?"

"You won't know her."

"Right," she said, drawing out the word. Chewing on nothing, she glanced sidelong to her sister, who was standing at the edge of view. "You don't actually have any interest in me, do you?"

"Sorry, no."

Giving a final moment's thought, she nodded to herself and swung the door further open. "Alright, let's talk."

Swallowing, Allison asked, "You're not going to let us in?"

"Ah, no. Sorry not sorry. The last person who

showed up unannounced broke in, so no chances. For that matter, I should warn you security is watching, and if you try anything, they'll stop you. So, what does a pair of mages want with me?"

It took everything Allison had not to go wide-eyed. "How did you . . .?"

"Please, I have an affinity for dark mana affinity. I can feel how much that ribbon is practically drowning in it."

Mouth agape, Allison reached up and rubbed the fabric. Forcing her mouth to close, she nodded. "Not like we need to come inside anyway."

"Great, so let's get to it. But turn off your scroll. I don't want to find myself on a recording or something."

Allowing a frown to cross his face, Dakota commented, "You're not very trusting, are you?"

"After what I've been through? Why would I be?" Relenting, both made a show of taking out their scroll and switching it off. Seeing the screens go dead, Arya turned to her sister. "You mind giving us a moment, Riley?"

The younger girl—whom Allison assumed was Riley—protested. "Why?"

"Because I want to have a private conversation. Don't worry, I'll be fine." With a reassuring hand on Riley's shoulder, she sent her away. "Sorry I'm a mess. If I knew someone was coming, I'd have done exactly nothing differently."

Forcing a smile herself, Allison said, "No problem. Sorry we're interrupting."

"Nah, I was just about to crush a few gems, enjoy the trip. Ain't as good alone, but no way I'm doing it with strangers and . . . well, whatever. No offence."

Unsure what to really say, Allison just gave an open-toothed smile and said, "Uh, sure. None taken." Then, searching for something to reduce the awkwardness, she said, "Riley was cute."

"Yeah, she's my adorable bottle of sunshine."

Trying to keep it up, Dakota added, "She looks just like you."

"Yep, well . . . yeah. So, what's the deal with this friend of yours, and what's it got to do with me?"

Using her most flippant voice, Allison said, "No clue. That's kinda what we want to know."

"So, you want me to help you help a friend I've never met for a problem I don't know about?"

Allison half turned to Dakota and, confirming he was letting her talk, she started. "We had a photo and a recording, but it's on our scroll."

"Yeah, well, convince me to trust you. So again, how does this come to me?"

Allison bit her lip, hesitating a second. "Our friend is being hunted. Her pursuer mentioned something about cursed children, and following that lead led to you."

She didn't even have to finish for Arya to close her eyes and groan. "Of course. It's always about *that*."

"That?" Allison prompted.

"Ugh, that *curse*." She clicked her tongue, but then stopped to frown. "Wait, she's being chased by someone after the curse but she doesn't know what the curse is?"

Allison shrugged. "I guess so."

"That makes no sense. And you found me through her?"

"Evidently," Dakota muttered.

Exhaling, Arya seemed to deflate a little, like her defence was going down just a touch. "Okay, I am now at max confusion. This friend a mage?"

"Yep," they answered together.

"With an icon?"

With a slight pause, Dakota answered, "Is there any other sort?"

Chewing her lip, Arya breathed, "I don't see what this has to do with me, or how I could be of use. I mean, if she has an icon, she didn't commit the taboo, and if she didn't do the taboo, then I don't know who's after her. Probably not the taboo hunters, but that's the best I got."

Raising her arm with her palm open, Allison stammered, "Wa-wa-wait, what taboo? I've never heard of one. And taboo hunters? Our problem is hunters. Hunter. Could be."

Speaking slowly, Arya explained. "The taboo, you know, using yourself as an icon."

"But . . . you can't use yourself as an icon." Turning to Dakota, she added, "Right?"

Biting his lip for a moment, he looked to Arya. She looked back, waiting. "I've heard about people writing the sigils on themselves before. But that would break the membrane that insulates you from mana, so I never understood how it works."

"It *doesn't* work. That's the point," Arya replied, her voice laced with laziness and annoyance. *But not at us.* "It destabilises all your mana circuits, makes spells impossible to control. Gives a lot of power and minimises how much mana you have to spend, but makes your power go haywire. But, if this friend has an icon, it has to be something else. And if it's something else, it's got nothing to do with me."

The twins looked to each other. Tight-lipped, they each swallowed hard. Finally, Allison nodded. "Well then, nice talking to you. Sorry for wasting your time."

"Eh, whatever. Fun to talk to people not hounding me for a scoop for once."

Dakota grunted a sort of acknowledgement as Arya reached to close her door. The twins were both taking a half step back when Allison stopped. "Hey. Out of interest, and I guess just in case, who were these hunters anyway?"

Her whole expression darkening, Arya stared hard for a moment. "I don't know the particulars. Hell, we don't even know their names. It's just what we call the group of psychos that hunt down people like me."

"But why would they do that?"

Arya tightened her fist. "A few years back, some people escaped from them. They said these guys were running experiments using people with the taboo. The types that don't pass ethics."

Dakota froze, speaking in slow, deliberate words. "Creating a fate worse than death?"

"I'd imagine so."

Soul's words rang out in her mind. *Saving them from a fate worse than death, the one who hunts the hunters.* Then there was what the Temple agents had claimed about Soul leading a prison break. Urgency erupted into her voice. "How did you hear about the hunters?"

Arya looked away, her unease growing. "I didn't. They came for me."

Allison's mouth was growing dry as Dakota kept up the questions. "Did you ever hear of someone going after them?"

Arya nodded. "Like I said, a few got away. Some say a boogieman let that happen."

Thinking the pieces through, Allison asked, "What about Temple? Have they got anything to do with this?"

That made Arya frown. "The mage police? Don't see why they would."

Nodding as she thought through the information, Allison closed her eyes. *They could have smudged some facts to not give us too much info. But then, wouldn't Nikita have picked up on that? Could* she *be the one lying to us?* Opening her eyes, she spoke clearly. "I need to show you something," Allison said, staring directly at Arya and taking her scroll from her pocket.

Either from the force of her voice or some mixture of curiosity and pity, Arya nodded. She waited as Allison powered it up, then quickly navigated to Nikita's list from the agents' minds.

"Recognise anyone?" Allison asked, holding the screen to the wire mesh.

It didn't take long. The first few names seemed to be enough to make her face drop. "These are all students of Fredo Pedro." Seeing the questioning looks on their faces, she explained, "I'm not talking about him. You can look him up. But if this is the list of people . . ." She left the rest unsaid.

Almost immediately, Allison changed to her photos. "And him? Do you recognise him at all?"

She had to zoom in since Soul's photo was taken from across the road. It made him a little pixelated, but it didn't change his appearance. "What the . . .? Where'd you get that photo?"

"I took it," Allison responded. "When he was trying to kill our . . . friend."

Arya swallowed, fear creeping into her face, an

answer itself. "Riley! I know you're listening. Come here a sec." The twins shared a glance, but it ultimately ended in a shrug as they waited for the younger girl to return. "Hey, I need you to take a look at something." Cranking her neck, she indicated the twins should show the photo.

Allison did so, holding it again to the screen door. The recognition was clear on Riley's face. "That's the guy from the other day."

"Wait, he's here?" As he said it, Dakota's whole face dropped.

"He was here on Tuesday," Riley said.

Arya seemed to sink, seeing the panic in the twins' faces and realising there was more. "I told you someone broke in. He came in at night, stole a bunch of things. We thought he was some robber."

"He is not just some robber," Allison said, remembering their brief interaction and how it had ended. "I don't get it. If he was here, did he give up on Nikita? But then why did he just steal some things? Why didn't he . . ." She couldn't finish the sentence, not to Arya's face.

"Arya wasn't home," Riley said.

"Shush, Riley."

Arya's expression was different now, panicked as she looked behind her back into the house. Then she spoke with a softer voice. "I was out with a friend when he attacked. Lucky timing, I guess."

"But then why wouldn't he wait for you to return? There's no way he was after jewellery or whatever."

"He didn't steal jewellery. As for why he left, that's obvious. Our alarm was going off."

Shaking her head, Allison stepped back and paced across the pavement. "I don't get it. He went through effort to get Nikita alone, then attacks you at home? Why is he even here? Shouldn't he still be after Nicky?"

His voice maintaining a sense of calm, Dakota answered, "We don't fully understand his reasons. Three months is a long time; he could have considered Nikita a lost cause. That would match what we did at Koros. Then, if he wanted to stay in Emnalor, that only left two options apparently. It's not exactly a coincidence. And as for Nikita, he did assault a Temple blockade."

"Right, but that was a final resort if he was going to get to her. But attacking a home like this as step one?"

Her voice soft, Arya asked, "What if I don't go out?"

Brows furrowing, Dakota asked, "Didn't you just say you weren't in when he came?"

She shrugged. "No one knew I left. I don't take the front door. And when I'm out, I'm not in public. Anyone watching would think I'm a full-on recluse."

"Then . . ." Allison began, turning her head.

Dakota did the same, looking out to the yard. ". . .we just confirmed that you're in."

"God dammit," Arya breathed, taking a step away from the door.

There was nothing in the street even remotely suspicious, only the one cop. No obvious sightings of Soul. "He's going to come back. Probably sooner rather than later. Unless . . ."

With a single nod, Allison continued, "Unless he can hit you while you're out again."

Shaking her head, Arya cried, "No way I'm going out like this. Margaret can come here next time. We can hang out in my room."

Nodding, Allison stopped looking for any signs of him. "Sorry to be the bearer of bad news."

Arya looked ready to complain, but instead nodded.

"It's better that I know."

Keeping his even tone, Dakota asked, "How good is your protection here? If he already got in—"

She cut him off. "More people, more cameras. My parents make a few calls and we'll become locked up tighter than Pandora's box."

"Then . . . good luck, I guess," Allison said, trying to lighten the mood with a failed smile. Arya rolled her eyes but nodded as well.

Allison was ready to leave, to step away. They delivered the news, downed the mood; she didn't know what more they could do. But Dakota stepped back towards the door. "If he comes, give me a call. I'll stop him before he can hurt you."

"What's some teen gonna do?"

"We fought him once already. We have some idea of his powers. It could be helpful."

She shrugged, relenting, and took down his number.

"Stay away from the windows," Allison said. "And don't answer the door yourself. If he's watching, he knows you're home, but if he's not, you do not want him to know for sure. I doubt he'll want to risk two duds."

She nodded. "Sounds fair. Why do you guys care so much about me? It's not like we've ever met."

"I don't," Dakota said in one of the most tone-deaf responses Allison could imagine. "I just want him gone."

Allison wondered if it was better—that brutal and stark truth—or to give some sort of lie. Arya closed the door, and they heard it bolted and triple locked. It was a sunny day so close to the beach, and yet she felt her heart fill with dread.

The *Promenade Eclipse* stood proudly less than a block from the ocean, its name spelled atop the rounded building, ready to alight once the sun went down. Inside the lobby, two receptionists waited behind a desk while a shelf held a brochure of every conceivable attraction in the city. Allison, Dakota, Katife, and Theta took the elevator, rising slowly but comfortably to their floor. Everything was dressed to make the budget hotel look lush.

Room 704 was as far from the elevator as possible, rounding the bend on the left side. The room itself was small but contained a lot: a kitchenette, a glass table with straw chairs, a couch and TV, and a beautiful view of the ocean. Just off the combined area was a master bedroom, a second bedroom, and a bathroom.

Their bags were dumped beside the beds in the second bedroom. It was plain and mostly unfurnished, aside from the two identical beds with identical side tables and identical lamps. Perfect for twins. Allison's bags were by the bed closer to the window. Theta was in the main bedroom, while Katife was using the pullout bed in the couch. It was the only option with three votes in favour.

As the sun rose on their first full day, Katife's outfit was the perfect explanation of why they were in Salbador: a summer dress with a red over white floral print, a wide straw hat, and sandals. Beach and sunshine.

Starting with an all-you-can-eat breakfast, they spent the day lazing by the beach and walking the streets, collecting as many brochures as felt relevant. The second day they started with a jet boat ride through the river system splitting the land. Between the open waterways and lack of traffic or wheels, Allison found the speedboat a mode of transport she could enjoy.

The day ended with a night club so unlike Lunar. It was built on the ground floor with open windows, and the music was dialled low, leaving no blaring tone ringing her ears. She couldn't tell if it was made with Yatrice in mind or if the owners decided they preferred that atmosphere. Allison danced this time. She was rigid and stiff, but the upside was not being hit on. Something about their group of four was keeping them at bay.

Three theme parks dotted the city, most on the northern side. With an hour-long vote, they chose which to visit. From roller coaster rides that left her hair blown to log rides that left it saturated, nothing Allison did could keep it tame. Katife's was the same, and even Dakota's was worse than usual. It was only Theta, with a hairstyle cut in such a way that a quick brush with his fingers set it back to normal, who was not left a mess in all the photos. There was a haunted house no scarier than a rom-com, and tiny cars that left her wanting to puke. If it weren't for the queues, there wasn't a moment they weren't on some sort of adrenaline-pumping action. From the ones her friends took on their scrolls to the one she bought from the park itself, Allison amassed a bank of photos she couldn't wait to send.

Then came the fourth day, which—despite her brain advising her not to—they spent a long time at the beach. They waded out into the surf, diving into the waves and enjoying the sensation as the water cooled while the sun cooked. Every day the mercury seemed to be inching a little higher. At some point, Dakota failed his attempt at body surfing which Theta talked him into, instead being dragged head over heels through the undercurrent back towards shore. Bursting from the water far behind them all, he stood hunched over, gasping for air. "What was that?"

"What?" Theta asked, riding a wave back to him.

"Why . . . why couldn't I breathe?" Looking at him, Allison judged that he was breathing fine. "When I came out of the water, my mouth was open, but I couldn't get any air in."

Theta shrugged. "Don't know. Might be a G-forces sort of thing, like with jet pilots."

"How are G-forces related to water?"

"Dakota, sometimes you have to accept what just happened, even if you can't explain it."

His look darkening, Dakota said, "I couldn't breathe, Theta. I thought I was going to suffocate."

"Stop being a baby. You went out into the surf, then let yourself get swirled around. There's a price to pay for every action. So even if I don't know the physics behind why you couldn't breathe, I'm not wrong about it being your fault."

From that point until they were all back in their

apartment, Dakota glared every time his eyes fell on Theta. By then Allison's stomach was growling and her mouth was dry from the salt water. She waited, unmoving, as Katife took a shower, having felt the sunburn with every step on the return journey. Through gritted teeth, she muttered, "God, that was a bad idea."

When Katife finished, Theta took a small bundle of clothes to take his shower next. "Were you hoping to tan or something?"

Grumbling to herself as she shifted her weight, only to be rewarded with more pain in her thigh and foot, she winced. "Clearly I'm too pale to tan. Look at this," she said as she held up her hand. "This isn't a tan; it's just red. I look like a tomato."

Laughing into her hand, Katife conceded. For a moment, Allison contemplated giving her friend a nice, solid slap to the face. The only problem was how much that would kill her own hand. "Can one of you get my icon? I don't care if a tan might come from this, this pain is crazy." Doing as she asked, Katife went to Allison's room, but still took every opportunity she could to tease her until her skin returned to snow white.

As night rolled in, the four of them returned to the streets. Ending at the beach, a pedestrian only road stretched into the distance, packed with restaurants occupying nearly the entire ground floor of every building. Those which weren't fully occupied had a staircase leading to an eatery on another floor. Choosing a burger shop after another prolonged vote, they stepped into the air-cooled room. Like in the cafe, the menu listed more variations of a single item—this time burgers—than Allison knew existed. While Dakota opted for the simplest one, a hamburger that still held far more toppings than any she'd ever seen, she decided that the one listed as "tropical" sounded even better, with an added pineapple slice in the mix. Theta's had everything the shop had on offer, except for the lettuce he had an argument with the cashier to get rid of.

From the slice of tomato threatening to slip out to the sauce dripping over their arms, their meal left them all a mess. Battling off the offending stickiness with the napkin, it wasn't until they were back in the hotel using soap and water that they felt clean again.

As the night deepened, Allison stayed up as long as she could, until one by one they went to bed. Katife went first, the least used to the physical exhaustion and the most tired from the day, but was soon followed by the rest. No matter how Allison used her ribbon, it would never fight back the oncoming sleep, unlike her scroll's blue light screen.

The last one up, Dakota switched off the lights in the main room and began pulling back the sheets on his bed. "Hey, Dakota. Look at this."

One foot raised to slide in, he paused to look to Allison and her scroll. "What is it?"

She shifted her weight, inviting him to sit on her bed and see. He did just that, his body turned away but twisted to look at her screen. "I was just looking into some of the things Arya said. This was that Pedro guy she mentioned."

Passing him the scroll, she waited as he read the page, his jaw tightening with every paragraph. "This is real?"

"Verified by bipartisan news sites."

He handed it back, the article still up describing a mage tutor who visited wealthy homes, only to defy their trust and make them perform the taboo Arya mentioned. "This is . . ."

"Messed up? Seems like it was big news while we were in Koros. Katife and Theta both knew already."

"So he just . . . ruined a bunch of lives for no reason?"

"The families were all wealthy. Maybe he was an 'eat the rich' loon. I dunno. But look at this." Running her finger down the screen, she scrolled until the paragraphs were replaced with a list of names. "These are all his victims." The list was chronological instead of alphabetical. Third from the bottom was Arya's full name spelled out.

"Arya. This was Nikita's list?"

"Seems like it. But look at the bottom name."

His eyes scanned lower, reaching the name at the end. She saw a nauseous look develop in his eye. "Nikita Quinn? You do know *our* Nikita's surname is Castell, right?"

"Maybe Soul made a mistake, or maybe she changed her last name. I don't know."

Not even letting the thought settle, Dakota's expression turned harsh. "That would mean she knows what he wants and is lying."

As best she could with only one arm, Allison held up her hand as if to show she was unarmed. "Look, I don't know. I'm not saying it's her, but it could be the reason she's being targeted. Because everyone on this list is turning up dead, especially the old ones. Except for one," she said, scrolling back up and pointing to the fifth name. "Lucina Aries. The only one of the first thirteen still alive. I found her name listed as one responsible for the destruction of a whole city in northern France. Make you think of anything?"

She could see by the look on his face that it did. Soul's rant about innocents caught in the crossfire, connected to Arya's warning of destabilised mana circuits. "What happened to the town?"

"From what I looked up? Everyone was burned to a crisp."

"Goddamn . . ."

"Yeah. Thing is, the buildings were left untouched. People, dogs, cats—all burned. But bricks and mortar? Absolutely fine. How does that even happen?"

He shook his head. "That would take serious anti-personal weaponry."

Tilting her head, she asked, "Such as? That's your field, not mine."

For a moment, she saw him cast his mind back to the types of things he looked at in Koros. "Probably some sort of burning smoke screen or chemical fire. Something like napalm or white phosphorus."

Breathing out, she relaxed into her pillow. "I do not want to get involved in that."

Handing back her scroll, he nodded his agreement. "No wonder Soul left that one alive. Besides, you won't be. How long until you break the gauntlet?"

She could hear it, the edge in his tone, hoping for an answer closer to "right now" than even "tomorrow." "Hmm," she hummed, finally closing her scroll. "Halfway sounds good." He didn't like her answer; she could see it in his eyes. But he didn't say so, leaving for his own bed and turning off the light.

Sleep took its time as her mind refused to wind down. Eventually it found her, and when it left again she found her sheets in such disarray, she had to admit it would have been a disaster had anyone shared the queen bed with her.

With the dawn came the next day. The city was becoming packed as more graduates flew in to celebrate their temporary freedom. The city was already alive but was rapidly becoming akin to a man on every stimulant, a description apt for many of the arrivals. Parts of the beach were cornered off just for them. The streets became a dance party, the night sands lit up with green and red lights—ruckus and rowdy and chaotic. It was enough to enjoy for a little while, but come nine, Allison felt her head splitting and retired back to the hotel. Katife joined her, leaving the boys in the town.

They turned on the TV, keeping the volume on low. There was a movie on, something Katife had seen and claimed was alright. A romantic chase, a will-they-won't-they type of plot. The heroine was a dud, some girl who was wrapped up all in herself and never paid attention to the guy's efforts. Allison was almost ready to yell at the male lead to move on to the best friend when the door to their room flung open and Dakota ran inside, heading straight for his bag.

"What's going on?" The words came instantly, Katife speaking before Allison even had a chance to open her mouth.

Dakota never answered. Riding in his wake, it was instead Theta who gave the explanation as he crossed the doorway. "That girl called. And now someone's thinking about being a hero."

Rifling through to the bottom of his bag, Dakota shouted, "I'm not being a hero. I'm doing what I have to protect Nikita."

"Dakota, what happened?" Allison asked, but he wasn't answering, and Theta hadn't finished talking.

Raising his voice louder than usual, Theta called, "What you need to? This is what you want to do."

Reaching the bottom of his bag, Dakota began laying out all the vials he'd brought. After that he found a pair of shorts, a singlet, and worst of all, his jacket. It was the same as the one Allison had worn on the roof the day she first encountered Soul, the one she still had tucked away at the bottom of her own bag. "Dakota?" she asked, standing up and blocking the doorway.

Looking up at her, his voice was like steel. "He made his move."

"He attacked Arya?" she asked instantly, but Dakota shook his head.

"He has her friend. He's using her to bring Arya to him."

"Goddamn," Katife breathed.

Stepping forward, Allison came up right behind him. She could see all the things he had laid out, his final remnants of Koros. "What's she going to do?"

Done with his bag, he let it fall to the floor. "Arya's staying where she is. You saw her house; he's not getting in. But if Temple even gets close to the South Salbador Boat Club, he's going to kill her."

Not waiting to be invited back in, Theta proclaimed, "And so *Mr Hero* over here decided he would sweep in and save the day."

Spinning around with a glint of anger in his eyes, Dakota spoke with such force it left her stunned. "I have to do this. Arya stays safe, the friend doesn't die, and Nikita's protected forever."

"No one is protected forever. This is an excuse, and you know it. If you really wanted to keep them safe you would do as I said and CALL TEMPLE." She'd seen Theta mad, but the force in those last words left her completely stunned.

Slowly, methodically, Dakota stated, "If Temple shows up, the girl dies. I'm not Temple. I'm not a cop. I'm an assassin. This is the best shot at keeping everyone safe."

Although Katife had never entered the room, she

had still listened, and her quiet words now broke through like a cold knife. "If you fight, what's to stop her being killed in the crossfire?"

Dakota stopped, and Allison saw that old look pass between them. He softened, taking her by the shoulders. "Katife, I won't let that happen. Say what you will, Koros trained us well. I never leave collateral victims. Only my target. Nobody else."

"And yet somehow, you don't see how wrong it is to have a target in the first place." Dakota said nothing back, simply returning his things and getting ready.

He didn't even wait for them to leave, he just kicked off his pants right there and replaced them with the shorts. Theta closed his eyes, turning away and leaving the room. But not out of embarrassment or sadness or shyness. Disappointment. It was written over his face. When Dakota was done, the vials stuffed into his pockets and his attire replaced, he turned around and looked at his sister. "Don't follow me."

Her voice small, she said, "You can't do this alone."

"I can. And you're breaking your gauntlet. Tomorrow."

Her eyes drifted to her bag as if she could see through the layers to where her gauntlet lay. In the end, she could only nod. He paused a moment, indecisive and hesitant, ending it by enclosing her in an embrace. It shocked her for a brief instant. Then she leant in, wrapping her arm around him too. "Theta's right, I think. You're making an excuse."

She felt rather than saw him shake his head. "No. I need to protect Nikita."

"Nikita isn't here. Soul's moved on."

"He could come back."

"Or he might not."

"I'm not going to waste this opportunity. I might not get another."

He pulled away, looking hard at his sister until he turned to leave. Only Katife managed to watch, her eyes pleading right until he disappeared out the door. Then came the elevator ping, and Allison knew what she had to say, running out and shouting loudly, "I hate Nikita. I owe Arya nothing. You know Theta's right; you know it's an excuse. I know because . . . I want to go too."

She knew he must have heard her, but when she heard the elevator doors close, she lost all sounds of him. Slinking back in, Allison closed the door behind her. She collapsed onto the couch, unable to focus on the movie again. He would be stepping out now into the night air. She didn't know where the boat club was, but probably not far enough to use a bus or taxi. She closed her eyes, the feeling of misery overtaking the air. Theta's words were like a poison, seeping into her heart. It wasn't his intention, not Theta, not ever, but she knew the consequences were sometimes hard to foresee. "He's going to get himself killed."

She had seen it back at the old house. Dakota was no match for him. Soul had won back then, and it wasn't like Dakota had done any real training since. If everything else stayed the same, she knew Theta was right. She considered them all, from weapons to setting to time. None of it was enough, and after a minute she breathed, "God, you're right." She felt like a zombie as she hobbled towards her room.

"Where are you going?" It wasn't just a question; Theta's voice was a demand.

She didn't look to him—couldn't let herself do that. If she did, she knew she would stop. "I'm going after him."

They both spoke at once, both her friends with different forms of concern etched into their voice. "You can't!"

Swallowing, she shook her head. "You're right, Theta. He will die. At least if he goes alone. Our best bet is together. I mean, we're twins." She said it with a smile, shining it back at them. But her eyes were closed tight, refusing to look.

She mirrored him, pouring out her bag and dumping everything on her bed. She didn't prepare, just took what she needed and stuffed it back in. Her gauntlet came first, along with all the gems attached. Then her holster and all the knives no one knew she had brought. She intended to throw them all into the ocean along with the icon as part of some set. And now she was using them together. Finally came the jacket and a change of clothes. Without waiting, she followed him out.

"Allison. Allison. Allison!" Theta called, loud enough to drag her to a stop. "You don't have to do this."

Shaking her head, she said, "He can't do this alone. We need to work together."

"No. All you're doing is ensuring that you both throw yourselves away."

"Theta, I . . ." slowing down, she took a breath. "I'm chaos, I'm destruction. I'm a terrified girl who's seen both sides of far too many atrocities. I'm broken and confused and lost. But he's my baby brother, and I'm a decaying girl." She didn't look back. She didn't let him approach. She only froze for a moment in the doorway. "Wait twenty minutes, then call Temple. If we're not

191

done by then, we never will be."

It was the best she could do, the greatest concession she had in her. Closing the door, she took the elevator. An echo, through and through. Only she didn't know where to go. The reception was open, so she asked there. The answer was quick, coming after a little tapping of keys. A decent walk, a very short drive. "Get me a taxi. As fast as possible. I'll pay extra, I don't care. I have to be there now."

She hadn't meant to raise her voice, hadn't meant to let the fear creep in. But it had, she saw it in the receptionist's reaction. But the taxi was called, finding the closest one who picked her up. She sat in the back, getting changed and sorting herself out. She didn't have all her gear, but she had more than enough.

She lodged the gems into the slots around the wrist of her icon. Arya said she would crush some herself, but the way she said it implied a pseudo-stimulant, a mage's replacement for traditional drugs. Hers were the mana supplements she'd stored for years. Next was her shoulder strap, suspenders of sorts with pockets for her knives. Three to a pouch, it came to a total of twenty-four blades. Then there was the final piece, a pouch that clipped onto her straps around her lower back. It carried a knife of its own, longer and more deadly than the rest. She covered the thing with her jacket, the twin to Dakota's. She left it open, granting access to her knives.

The further they drove, the darker it became. She had no clue where she was, or if she came before or after her twin. She paid the driver double the fare and jumped out the door. She took her bag with her, leaving it between the footpath and the water's edge. Somewhere she would find it again, but far enough away that it wouldn't get in the way.

The building was before her on the edge of the river. The taxi drove on, leaving her alone. There were no sounds of combat. Creeping forward towards the riverbed, she stepped over the sand and closer to the building. A spillway crossed from the fenced walls into the water. There were tarps covering what she could only imagine was a row of boats, and a two-story building with light spilling out. She slowed down, making sure no one would hear as she got close enough to hear inside.

There were ragged breaths coming from within, mixed with slow and even ones to counter match. The doors to the spillway were open, leaking light outside. She didn't dare breathe, holding still as he walked halfway down the length of the spillway. Then she set to work.

Spools of wire spilled into her body, tightening around her muscles and forming thick bands of artificial tissue. Her natural body was practically crushed within. The threads of mana were stronger than her real ones, and no less flexible. No amount of stimulants or weight training could compete with her augmented self.

Her second spell came next, the dark shadows reinforcing her skin like a suit of armour. It even served a second function, providing concealment within the dark night. The third spell then flicked on, seizing the automatic control which allowed her to function with the billions of wires within her. Finally, she unlatched her first knife, the one hooked under her gauntlet, and stepped forward, crushing a gem at the same time.

She felt that distinctive sensation of someone else's mana filling her. With millions upon millions of fibres to control, demanding an expensive spell to keep them all in check, those gems would soon be the only thing keeping her walking.

Lower down the spillway, Soul stopped, as if to really feel the air. He did a one-eighty, his eyes passing right over her. He had his axe gripped loosely in his hand. Every step was careful. She ducked low, keeping the moonlit sky behind him. His silhouette gave him away, while she blended into the ground.

Soul standing on the spillway caused a problem. She would either have to clamber up or strike from below. Her feet didn't leave the sand, refusing to risk a movie moment and step on a twig. She was getting closer, but he was also walking further out towards the water's edge. Then he stepped off the wood and onto the sand. "I know you're out there. You're good, but I've been hunted by wolves."

Her heart came to a crashing halt. He turned to look at her. *No*, around her. It was the hairs on the back of his neck, that sixth sense. He knew she was there, but he didn't see her. To respond was to abandon the benefits of stealth. She had to act fast or else stall and wait for Dakota. It would be safer to wait if he actually managed to get there first instead of some possible accomplice. There was no indication of one, but she couldn't discount the possibility. She swallowed, calming her heart. Ducking as low as she could go, she leapt forward, her blade a homing missile locked on to his throat.

He had a split second, which was apparently enough for him to jump back while sweeping a long and wild swing, his arm outstretched, creating a protective arc enforced by the sharp edge of his axe. It was like a guillotine, forcing her to dig in her heels and kill any forward movement in order to keep her neck intact. "You again?" His voice dripped with utter surprise.

Without a word, she pulled her knife back in, twisting out of his way. "We can still trade if you'll listen."

He shook his head, only just visible in the dark. "We had this conversation last time."

"You could have reconsidered." Pausing a moment, she tried something else. "I know about the taboo now. Help us find a solution where nobody dies. Isn't that better for you too?"

She could see him pause, but even so, he was keeping his distance. "Were it so easy. Lucina Aries proved that was impossible."

Allison frowned, recalling the article she'd read about the burned town. "A few bad people doesn't mean you should murder the bunch."

He shook his head. "Lucina was a good girl. But this curse cannot be controlled. She lives with the memory of what she did every day. That is why I must do this. For their greater good, not just the world's."

She shook her head, thinking of Sensei, of the choices he made, the things he had them do, and his favourite phrase he would say each time. Those three words echoed in her mind. *For the cause.* "That's not your choice to make." She slipped her middle finger inside the ring of her first throwing knife, flicking her wrist outward. In one movement, the blade was sent flying towards him. Even as it curved end over end, she knew it would land on its pointed side. Even if she didn't have her training, her third spell ran the calculation for her, controlling her arm for the perfect swing. Fast as lightning, he blocked her knife with his axe.

She was nimble over the sand, decimating the distance between them. But so was he. Even with her lighter frame she couldn't run like him, his feet gliding over the top. For her, the sand was like a death trap. Her only options were rushing for the spillway or the wave-hardened sand. But neither were possible, not if she had to turn her back to do it. Instead, she dug down as firmly as she could. His swing was telegraphed enough for her to dodge with ease, ducking and sending her own knife up. It slid across his shirt as he twisted and grabbed her arm. It was a strong grip, enough that without her protective coating it would have crushed her wrist.

She spun the knife in her fingers as she faced him. He tried twisting away. Then she raised her leg, tearing it from the sand and sending a rounded kick targeting his ribs. She used what movement her wrist maintained to drop her knife to the other. Before he was able to adjust, she'd sent it straight in, piercing his eye.

It made him loosen his grip. He stepped back with a kick, crashing into her stomach. It seemed impossible just how fast Soul was. Yet despite his speed, she couldn't help but feel his arcing slashes relied on power alone, so that even with her limited movement she could weave away from danger. Once they separated, he pulled the knife out of his eye, blood oozing from the socket. She pressed forward, targeting his now blind side. She focused on her left knife, the one from the gauntlet, sneaking it in under his ribs. He returned with a knee, but she gripped the wire connecting the knife to her gauntlet and tugged. The knife pulled out, tearing skin as it sailed back to her waiting hand. Then the bleeding disappeared.

The blood and tissue vanished from the knife, his

eye returning to its socket. He took the split second to blink, his body returning to before she stabbed him.

She took out the next blade, calling one of the threads within her arm and twisting it out from underneath her fingernail so it could wrap around the handle. Between his size, weight, the axe, and his agility over the sand, she couldn't afford to let him in close. While her legs stepped back, her arms tossed both knives. They formed an *X* in the air, their intersection behind Soul. Then she pulled on the wires and focused on their mana. Doubling back, her knives created a guillotine. Using his axe, Soul deflected the left side blade, while the other cut in.

Pulling again, she arced her free knife before him, forcing him to retreat, step by step. Finally she was off the soft sand, and he was into the water. Her deadly arcs continued, chasing him further into the lake, until suddenly he disappeared.

Dropping onto his stomach, buried underwater, he escaped her sights. Left in a gamble, she chose to dash for the spillway before he returned, not risking him resurfacing off to the side. Keeping both knives windmilling in inverse swings, one up while the other was down, she was ready for his return.

Pinging uselessly on her dark armour handle side first, the knife he'd stolen fell by her feet. It was probably meant as a distraction, but the water was still over his ankles when her eyes found him at the end of the spillway.

He charged, and her angle changed while the wires extended, allowing her blades to dance towards him. Again, he brought up his arm. The knife sailed past, and only then did she pull, changing its direction and making it wrap around his arm. She pulled again, this time overbalancing him as she sent in her second knife. Taking a quick step forward, he created enough slack in the wire to move the axe, cutting right through one dark thread and using the other to pull back, creating a deadly game of tug of war. His arm bled from where the wire bit in, but he had enough power to force her a step forward and off balance. In that second, he ran.

Tossing her final knife of the first pouch, she regained her balance and braced for impact. It bit into the soft skin of his arm just as he resurrected their tight brawl. He didn't give her an inch, not even to refresh her blade. Her only recourse was to use a wire to pluck it from its holster and carry it into her hand. The sounds of their blades hitting were drowned by the waves. *He's good, but I'm better.* The slices opening up in him proved it, as bit by bit he was turning to ribbons. It was savage and brutal and fast. Her feet acted on their own, using the tiny space to circle as much as she could while maintaining the pace. And she couldn't stop smiling.

That feeling, the thrill. She didn't know exactly what it was, if it was some chemical in her brain or an acquired lust for combat, but the closer he got and the faster their blades collided, the more her face twisted into a smile. If she had the breath to spare, she would be laughing, enjoying the moment, the feeling, the ecstasy. Her blood was rushing through her veins. Her strings undid the laces of her boots, allowing her to kick them off towards Soul. He dodged. Using the split second reprieve, she dropped her two knives towards her feet. More wire leaked from her toenails, taking the falling blades and fastening them to her toes as if they were fingers.

Mixing kicks with her thrusts, every strike put Soul at risk of being sliced. And he couldn't defend against it.

Not with four armed limbs all chasing after him. She spun on the spot, constantly trading which limb she used to swipe at him. Like a ballerina, she kept her eyes on him, twisting her neck to spot her turn as she became the human embodiment of a spinning top. And she was pushing him back towards the water. She was already tearing him to shreds. His spell undid some damage, but the cuts that stayed were more than just injury; they were information. *Looks like someone has a cooldown.*

She kept spinning, using every limb and every rotation to gain power, locked on and shredding his skin like paper. With every casting, his spell was becoming more obvious, a green light appearing from his chest whenever it was active.

Her smile couldn't be stopped; she relished the nostalgic feeling. It was something the mixed martial arts could never achieve. They were too safe, lacking the thrill of her mind reading every move her opponent made and working to stop it inches from taking her life. It was something she never realised she'd missed.

Even when he got strikes in, cutting into her arm, managing one into her chest, it didn't matter. She still had mana, which meant she could keep healing, creating a war of attrition she had no doubt she could win. Her spell didn't have a cooldown, and she still had those gems.

Soul's feet splashed against the water. There was only a little of the spillway left, and once he was off and onto unstable ground, he was as good as hers. Her spinning, dancing, twisted twirls gave no inch nor indication of which direction the next strike was coming from. The only shame was the knife at her back was not a part of it. Then Soul jumped back, off the spillway and onto the water. Preparing the wires to make up the distance, she readied her final combination. Then he tossed the axe, sailing easily past her without even touching a strand of her flowing hair. Then came the click and the thud as once again he dropped a grenade to her feet. Her smile died just before the blast eroded her lips.

In that moment, she was sure of two things as her skin melted from her body. The first was that Soul was caught in the blast. The second was that his spell had to be active.

If he heals before me, this would have been for nothing. Pouring everything into her ribbon, she burned and healed, both at the same time, causing a constant, agonising pain. She fell to her knees before it was over. Dashing around and over the sand, Soul was already on her other side before she could get to her feet. Drained, she was forced to crush her fourth gem.

He had burned away her combat high, leaving her in plain fury. And now the fatigue of endless swirling was getting to her, zapping at her energy. Then came the sound of footsteps. It took both of their attention, turning it towards the boathouse.

"She's here," Soul said. In his hand he held that same grenade, his spell making it as though it had never exploded. He pulled the pin again, counting the seconds. She couldn't see his chest, couldn't tell if his spell was on or not.

Bursting from her gauntlet in every direction, her wires wrapped her into a cocoon, tightening and forming until she was locked inside. The coating went around the outside, hardening into a shell and protecting her from the explosive, even as it rocked her. It stopped the blast from killing her, but she felt her skin begin to peel and burn as some fire got through. Using another gem so soon after the last, she undid the spells.

Soul was rushing towards the doorway, eager to greet the newcomer. Meeting Arya once was not enough for Allison to memorise the sounds of her footsteps, but she knew the ones they were hearing, and smiled, knowing Soul was in for a massive disappointment.

Every day, the voice of the silver man whispered in his mind, telling him, teaching him. As long as he held onto the axe, the silver man who called himself its soul— whatever that was— spoke to him.

The first thing he taught him was food. He said he couldn't understand how the boy had survived so long without any. Next, he taught him how to find it. He knew a little about hunting, which he passed on to the boy.

He'd point out a creature, and the boy would creep as quietly as possible, using the axe to slice it dead. The warm juices of his first deer filled the boy up, heating his body from the inside. From the very first bite, he wanted more. There were no words to describe it. The silver man also pointed out plants, but cautioned many were dangerous, and that he didn't know which.

Eating made everything easier. It took time and made the journey down the mountain very slow, but bit by bit he was getting closer.

The top of the mountain was becoming a blur in his memory. His clothes were tearing and wearing out. It was cold and getting colder with every rip, and the only thing he could do was to light a fire at night.

The worst were the wolves. They attacked sometimes. The silver man told him to run, to get away and drop any food he had, to climb a tree and escape. One time the boy found one sleeping alone. He crept close, using the blade to end its life. Afterwards, the silver man taught him how to use its fur to replace his torn clothes. It was very warm.

Something the silver man called a year had passed before the ground got less steep. By then, hunting and surviving has been infused into his very being. It became easier to walk, easier to run and hunt and find food. Although the further he got from the top, the more the animals fought and ran. A sweeping stream blocked the path before him. Dropping to his knees, the boy scooped handfuls to his mouth to quench his raging thirst. He was able to get water from the snow, but it was not so simple and plentiful as the river. "I remember this river. It spans far; we will have to cross it. The ocean is still a long way to go."

One foot first, the boy immediately jumped back, the cold nipping at him and zapping any energy in his foot. "Cold."

"My body is an axe, boy. Cut yourself a bridge."

He told the boy which tree to choose, where to cut it, and how high to swing. Soon the boy had gone from frozen to sweating. He got about halfway through when the tree started to creak, titling and then falling across the river. It made it to the far side, the dead leaves resting upon the shore.

The tree bridge rocked with his movement, similar to the rope bridge, but different. Arms to his sides, he put one foot after the other, slow and careful. He got halfway, but unlike the rope bridge, it didn't get easier after that. This tree bridge rotated and spun. He tried to keep the tree stable, but overcorrected and went a little too far, and his yelp pierced the soundless day as he tumbled into the water. It was deep enough to engulf him. He kicked his legs, grabbing at the tree. It scratched his hands, but he found a branch to hold to pull himself halfway up. He was close to the end now. He tried to rise on his own strength, but his arms were sore and the wolf skin was so heavy. Instead, he drifted along, using the next branch to drag himself closer to the riverbank. Finally, his feet hit the riverbank and he was able to walk. It was slow, and hard, and so very cold.

When the boy stepped out of the river, the water left a trail behind him. Falling to his hands and knees, he crawled forward. Its dampness clung to his skin, freezing him even more. He couldn't stop shivering. He tried moving faster, hoping he might heat his blood. But without food, and with his body already cold, he lacked the strength to do so. He couldn't even gather any branches to start a fire. The river was still just on the edge of sight when he could move no more, falling onto his face, shivering uncontrollably.

"Sorry, boy, but thanks for getting me closer to water," the silver man said. "Hopefully someone will find me again."

Freezing, lodged into the snow, he was utterly unable to go on.

Soul ran inside, blade still in hand. Just in time, he narrowly avoided the lashing jaws of Dakota's snake. Taking slow steps, Allison began to catch her breath and refill her mana. Dakota would need help, but she decided he could hold his own while she recovered, especially with gas already seeping from his pockets. *His impenetrable, undefeatable, armour.*

The boats inside were all open top, their cabins exposed to the expanding fumes. There were three of them, identical to the one they rode, only with different branding. There were benches and worktables by the wall, which she could only assume was where Dakota found the oversized wrench he swung from his right arm. Around his left, the snake coiled.

Soul ducked easily, retaliating with his axe. Flinging the wrench toward the ceiling, Dakota sidestepped to attack again. The way he moved with his balance off centre created an opening so obvious, she knew it was intentional. *Clearly being hunted by wolves didn't prepare him for feints.* Aiming for Dakota's neck, Soul put himself right in line for the wrench to plummet into his shoulder, knocking him off course and bypassing the defence of his spell.

Soul's human instincts kicked in, demanding he turn to the source of pain, offering Dakota a free pass to send a powerful hook into his chin. Recoiling, Soul reached for his waist, and that same old trick. Before he tossed it, Allison called, "Grenade!"

The warning was enough; Dakota batted it away into the middle boat. There was a moment just before it went off that she heard muffled screams. The blast launched the boat forward, forcing Dakota to scramble.

Calling to her brother, she said, "His spell lasts about fifteen seconds and needs five to recover."

Reaching the doorway, Allison slid the next set of knives from their sheath. Using her augmented muscles, she launched them at Soul; all three sunk into his soft flesh. They were not deep enough to be stuck, but were painful enough to buy a second for Dakota to choose his next canister. As the can thudded toward Soul, the grey clouds spewed out, bathing him in its toxin.

Five seconds was a long time to stand unprotected in the gas. It left him no option but to charge recklessly ahead, offering her the perfect opportunity to lunge into combat, jumping for the space just outside the cloud's reach. His attacks lacked composure, and Dakota deflected Soul's escape, keeping him in the gas with Allison now covering the other end.

Without space to unleash her wires, Allison kept her blades gripped in her hands. She pushed in from behind while Dakota mimicked from the front, ripping Soul apart like a meat grinder. She saw him reaching for the grenade again, and this time she determined it would not leave his hand. The moment it was in the open, she shot a knife toward it, pinning his finger to the casing. Unable to get let go, he wasted a flailing second trying to understand, but then came to a quick and horrifying decision. When he thumbed out the pin, the fuse began. Seconds later the grenade went off, taking them all with it.

It could have been a second or an eternity. That hollow feeling made her sick. Soul was more prepared for the revive than they were. As he ran for her and cut into her belly, she felt her life slipping away seconds after it returned. She had no choice but to activate her ribbon, allowing Soul to slip past and tighten his arm around her chin, holding his axe to her throat.

"Stop!" he called. "Zero, right? I'm sure she can't survive losing her head. Whose life is more important: hers, or that of a cursed child?"

His hands were tight, and her energy was fading. She wished she'd been faced the other way; it would have made things easier. Craning her neck forward and cutting herself on the axe head, she slammed back as fast as the tendons in her neck allowed, smashing full into his nose.

Skulls are stronger at the front, giving her the more painful side of the blow. She didn't care, instead taking a different prize: shock. It allowed her to dive, desperate to escape to the left. He reached for her, his fingers clawing around her right arm. The one she was forced to dismember because of him. She returned her body to that day when her arm was no longer attached to her body, leaving him holding a severed limb.

More shock, another surprise. The snake came in,

diving for the floor at Soul's feet, reforming the concrete into rising walls, imprisoning him in an instant. Dakota's snake did not let go, allowing it to change the walls at a moment's notice.

It took mana to rip off her arm, and more to bring it back. Rubbing where the stump had just been, she looked at Dakota and asked, "Is it over?"

He didn't answer, instead fixing her with a glare of burning wire. "You promised to leave this alone."

"Ugh. We won, right?"

"You were almost killed." Seeing her brother with that much emotion almost had her smiling, even if his was pure fury.

"Key word being almost. A lot of bad things *almost* happened; what matters are those that actually did." Stepping toward the pillar, she knocked twice. "Can he hear us?"

The voice was muffled, but she could make it out. "Yes, I can hear you."

"Well, I guess that answers that," she muttered back.

Hopping onto the tire guard for the middle boat, she craned her neck to look inside. Immediately, the source of the earlier muffled screams became obvious as she saw the gagged girl around Arya's age inside. Her eyes were filled with tears, and Allison almost felt pity as she cut the ropes binding her. "You might want to GTFO." The girl nodded, scrambling out of the boat, and tumbling out onto the floor.

With her Yatrice ears, Allison heard Soul mutter, "What on earth are these two?" His disbelief elicited a smile from her.

Dropping onto the tire guard, Allison turned to her brother. "Apparently that Aries girl who was involved in the whole scorched town thing is part of his motive."

Frowning, Dakota asked, "How so?"

"According to him, she was a 'good girl' who just lost control."

"A good girl burned a town?"

Through the wall, Soul called, "Yes. And the same will happen to all these children. That is why I must do this: to save them from themselves." She rolled her eyes.

"Nikita's a telepath; she's not burning down any towns."

"I did not think such a capable fighter would be so naive. The moment she loses control, the outcome will dwarf what happened to Lucina."

"That's bull," Dakota shouted. *Finally, something to stop him looking at me like that.*

Soul didn't stop, instead becoming louder, his voice clearer. "Telepathy has the power to warp a person's mind, influencing even basic survival functions. How to walk, how to breathe. That is what is at risk when she erupts. And her power has unprecedented range. I fear the aftermath of Nikita's eruption will be hell on earth."

She could see Dakota was trying to bite back a response, but she cut in first, speaking in a calm, level voice. "One problem. Nikita didn't commit the taboo. And what about Arya? What does your magic orb show her doing?"

"It is not prophetic to read the writing on the wall. Her shadows will clog the lungs of all those around her. Chaos and calamity are all that awaits these children. Why will you not understand this?" His voice had risen to anger, leaving them with nothing to say. As seconds ticked by, Soul calmed his voice back to his slow and precise way of speech. "I am not an unreasonable man. At our core, we seem to hold the same desire. I will grant you a promise if you grant me mine."

She eyed Dakota and knew he shared her caution. "What promise?"

"I was once like you. I tried protecting them from the hunters, thinking that would be enough. History taught me my approach was flawed. But I am but one man. Perhaps it was my approach that held the flaw. If you promise to protect all the children from both the hunters *and* themselves, then I will promise to do whatever you ask in service of that end."

Dakota snarled, "You're insane."

"I do not care, Zero, who or how those children are kept safe. Death before they taste despair is my answer. You demand another. I would be so very happy to pass on this burden, especially to those who still have hope. Is this not the bargain you sought?"

Biting her lip, Allison looked down to her gauntlet, feeling its weight on her arm. It had felt so good, like a drug she could use forever. The fight, the high, the thrill. But there was something else, something clear in those glimpses of death. "I can't fight anymore." She said it quietly. She didn't even know if Soul could hear it.

It was as if her words broke a spell cast upon Dakota, and finally his features softened completely. He looked almost relieved. "That wasn't a bargain; it was an ultimatum. I fought you to protect Nikita. I will die to protect my sister. The others are none of my concern."

Whatever he expected, Dakota's words left Soul's voice laced with a deep tone of sadness. "Then I have no choice. I am truly sorry."

She saw it all, every moment of what happened next. And she was powerless to react. As before, Soul's axe phased right through the wall, spinning end over end and slashing right through Dakota's face. It peeled the skin from his cheek, blood splattering as he screamed. The snake disappeared, and with it, all the modifications he made to the floor, including the imprisoning walls.

Soul sent the grenade chasing after them before she could even stand. Sailing just past her, it landed under the trailer. Its explosion sent a rocketing force, slamming the boat forward and pinning her to the concrete. Springing from the gauntlet in both directions, her wires did everything to stop her being crushed.

Her knife in his hands, Soul rushed her brother. It came down, slicing at him with attacks that never should have touched him. She had a perfect view as he tore her twin's face apart.

Sparing a single wire, she sent it after Soul's leg, wrapping around it and pulling hard. She tried winding it, getting it under his skin. All she needed was an opening in his skin for a wire to sneak inside his body. The plus side was he was already covered in countless such lacerations. If she could just sneak one into his heart, wrap around and squeeze, it would all end.

She couldn't tell if he knew what she was doing or just felt Dakota was already beyond being a threat, but he turned and charged at her. His axe was back in his hand, and while she lay pinned, he swung down upon her arm, severing it at the elbow. Her arm dropped, taking the gauntlet with it. Just like Dakota's snake, her wires all vanished, and without their support, the boat crushed through her hips. Her gauntlet in hand, Soul escaped into the night.

Crying through some of the most painful tears of her life, she called, "Dakota! The boat!"

Bloody beyond recognition, her brother had enough

mana and sense left to summon back his snake, sending it for the boat. It felt like a lifetime as it slithered slowly, reaching for the fibreglass and, upon connecting with it, severing it into billions of pieces, each the size of dust. It didn't matter that some got into Allison's mouth, she couldn't register anything over her pulverised hips.

Everything, from her focus to her mana, was driven into her ribbon, pulling for the spell to take her back just one minute. It was all she needed to undo the damage, but it felt so hard and exhausting. It left only a third of her mana remaining, not nearly enough to fight. Her left arm had no movement, and she was so very tired. She looked to her brother, then after Soul.

Poisoned, injured, exhausted. There won't be another chance like this.

Stumbling as she went, she began her chase.

Over the sand and back on the road, she saw him faltering ahead through an empty intersection. Hobbling forward, she sent more knives after him. Of the six she sent, only two even hit—one in his leg, and one to his back. It was the first indication of how exhausted she was. She stopped at the curb as he turned to face her, wearing the look of a wounded animal.

Her hand hovered over her last pouch, waiting for him to step first. She needed the moment; her lungs wouldn't hold up without it. He paused as well. *Just as tired, just as in need of a break.*

Soul moved first. He got two steps down before there was another knife in his thigh. He stopped, grunting. She could see he was close to collapsing. He stepped again, and this time she matched it. Her second knife found a home beside the first. Gritting his teeth, he refused to stop. There were sounds of cars and sirens in the distance as they closed in on one another. They were only a few meters away when she hurled her final throwing knife. This time he blocked it, and when his arm obscured his sight, she reached behind for her final blade, a completely different sort from the rest.

It was longer, sharper, heavier. It came to a fine, curved point, its inner edge serrated. The knife itself was made from a dull, black metal. Her red gem was lodged into a gap in the handle, five exhausts connecting it around the blade. The grip was moulded for fingers larger than her own, making it hard for her to reach the trigger built into the top imprint. The symbols written into the blade denoting an ancient history of an icon whose owner was long since gone.

She didn't block against Soul's attacks, not while he wielded that phasing axe. Instead, she focused on dodging his strikes, on reading his movements and staying out of the way. They circled around the centre of the intersection. All she needed was a moment, a few seconds of her blade facing towards him. She kept circling, staying just out of his reach.

Soul went for an overhead strike. She jumped in and to the side. In that same instant, she raised her own up blade, slicing into his fingers. With a cry he dropped the axe, and as it fell, she kicked it off into the night. She didn't wait, going in for the kill.

He reached for his thigh, taking the pain of extracting two knives in exchange for something to block with. They formed an *X*, catching her midswing. If she had two arms, it would have been over already. Using all her body weight, she forced the blade down, aimed right at his throat. With a final smile, she went for the trigger.

She missed. Her own hands were too small, and the pressure of his guard pushed them low on the handle. She had to stretch her finger, missing with the first attempt. Her force and focus diverted, his own defence pushed her away just as she reached the trigger. That red gem was crushed in an instant, and the spell inside was let loose. A fire gem, unleashed inside the handle. With nowhere else to go, the flames shot through the exhausts, sending a burning tongue around the blade. It missed his throat but still stuck him squarely. He screamed. Pressing the moment, she swept at his legs, tripping him against the gutter and bringing him down onto the pavement. In that moment, she realised just how exhausted she really was, the effort bringing her down as well.

He used the same block, but this time crossing his arms to stop her blade. She wished for another gem, but there was only room for one within the blade. The fire outlived his spell, flames sticking to his clothes despite those on his skin extinguishing.

With her knees at his ribs, she pressed down with her whole upper body. After everything, it was down to a battle of attrition—whoever's energy would outlast the other. Her hair fell around them like a waterfall. He moved his lower arm, losing resistance in favour of a grip on her neck. When he moved the other one to follow, her knife went straight into his collarbone. His grip was hard, cutting off her air. It left her too weak to push any further. He rolled, pinning her underneath. When he removed the knife, his blood splattered down, dropping onto her face.

She was losing her breath. She knew how long she could hold it, but that was when she started with a full inhalation. Her vision was fading, going black around the edges. Putting everything she had into her legs, she raised them up, wrapping one around his neck, the other under his shoulder. She pushed with her back. It tore his fingers from her throat, and in the process allowed her to put pressure on the joint in his arm. With two arms and energy left over, she could have broken his arm right there. Instead, it was all she could do to hold him in place. "Don't you ever . . . run out of mana?" she wheezed.

He saw it first, the lights that swept around them. They came on fast—the headlights of a car. "I think . . .I have enough . . . for one more." He stopped struggling, stopped trying to get away. Changing grip, he focused purely on keeping the two of them down, rolling over the road.

She had nowhere to go, and neither enough time or energy to escape. Trapped in her own attack, she heard the screeching tires as the car tried to stop. Unable to, it rammed into Soul, leaving her only a split second to escape.

"Hey, kid! Wake up!"

Muffled by the snow, the cold, and his exhaustion, the sound was but incoherent noise. His jaw was locked in place, his eyelids frozen shut. It didn't take long for the darkness of unconsciousness to return.

There was no telling how long it had been when the boy at last began to wake. It wasn't cold anymore. There was something heavy wrapped around him. His clothes were gone too. As was the silver man's voice. When he managed to open his eyes, he woke to a room he had never seen before.

The heat faded the moment he pushed back the blanket. Even then, the air was only cool on his bare skin, like a fire was burning close by. Wrapping himself in the blanket, he pushed open the door. It swung with just the touch of his hand, opening into another room. The floor was soft on his feet, embracing every step. The room was long and thin with doors on every side. The one at the end was half open, and there were sounds gushing out.

Another room waited beyond. There was a board on the wall, the image it showed constantly changing. Two people sat in the room, both of them big and tall, but he'd ever seen either of them. Their hair was smooth, with no strands standing out. They saw him and spoke. "Well, look who finally woke up."

Pushing through the door, he stepped into the room, looking around. The moving picture had been replaced with black. There were gaps in the walls, but they didn't look like the ones up high—they looked purposeful, and there was a slight gleam, like something invisible was there. "I never expected to find a kid out in the snow, let alone for him to still be alive. Are you all right? Do you know where your parents are?"

He didn't answer. He just kept looking down, croaking his own question. "Wolf hide?"

This time the other man answered. "Your clothes were soaked. We had to get them off you. They are in that room just there. They should probably be dry by now."

The boy turned to where the man pointed and immediately started in that direction. "Hey, kid, slow down, okay? My name is Harold, and this is my house. I called a doctor to take a look at you, but he will be a while. There will also be an officer soon. He will help you find your family. So, I guess I want to ask you where you came from."

Pausing, the boy gave a single word. "Up."

Harold shook his head. "Up? There are no more properties on this side of the Alps."

He just said it again. "Up." The man swore. And the boy recoiled. "Up mountain. Near top."

"I told you, kid, there is nothing up there."

Speaking up, the other man said, "I mean, there might be. We don't know that for sure."

"Oh, not you too."

"I'm just saying. No one who has gone that high has ever come back. Who's to know there isn't some old tribal village up there? He was certainly dressed the part."

Harold turned away from the boy, fully facing the other man. "Don't you think if there were people up there we would see something? Lights, travellers, anything?

The boy just looked up at the two men. "Town has no light. Only decay."

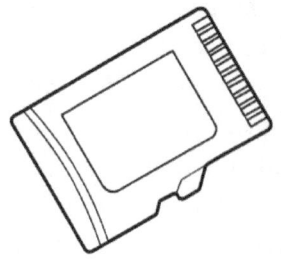

Leaning over the balcony rail, Katife counted every person that passed her by. Theta was inside, doing something similar by the door. Slipping past her watch, a banging at the door roused her from her trance-like state. "Katife, Theta, open up."

Dakota's voice. Her heart raced as she almost skipped to unlock the chain. "Sorry, I'm comin— Ohmygodwhathappenedtoyou?!"

As the door opened, she saw him holding a red-soaked pad to his face. The moment the gap was wide enough, he pushed inside. "Doesn't matter. Where's Allison?"

"Wasn't she with you?"

He shook his head. "She ran off."

Her throat constricting, she relocked the door. "Great. And what happened to you?"

There was nothing for her to see on half his face, just the blood-soaked pad. From his arms, he dropped a cloth onto the table, covered in the same red, spilling Allison's gauntlet and knives over the glass. "I need to borrow the bathroom. Tell me the second she gets here." As he disappeared behind the door, their conversation quickly died.

Stepping to the bathroom door, she called, "Need any help?" He didn't answer.

After a minute of silence, she collapsed beside Theta. Taking a deep breath, she saw him look tiredly at the door. His look of judgment was gone, resigned to the reality of what was. Watching him looking as though he wanted to see through the wood, she almost smiled as an idea struck. She reached for her Game Stadium Lite and rushed for the door. "What are you doing?" he asked, peering at her screen.

Taking her scroll into her other hand, she opened its camera. "I can alter trajectories, right?"

"Right."

"And that includes the camera's vision. So logically . . ." She didn't finish, her intention clear.

He didn't admonish her for spying, instead nodding and letting her give it a go. Activating her power, a red laser-like cone appeared from her scroll's camera, an indication of everything in its trajectory of vision. She focused on it, curving that light under the gap and up into the room. *It's working!* She saw Dakota unwrapping the pad and what was underneath. In as high a voice imaginable, she yelped at the sight.

"Katife!" Dakota roared, using the same tone as someone angry at their dog.

Without thinking, she was on her feet, storming for the door. "Dakota? I'm coming in."

"No!"

She knocked hard. "You need to see a doctor."

"I've had worse."

She felt eyes on her back as Theta stared, not knowing what she had seen. "I don't care if you've had worse; you can't fix that alone. You need a hospital."

His only response was a single word, shouted in a shrill, breaking voice. "No!"

There was enough force in that word to push her back a step. "This isn't about a doctor," she said, whether to him or herself she didn't know. Stepping closer, she put her ear to the door.

She heard only his slow, ragged breathing. His voice was quiet. "I need to be here when Allison returns."

"Dakota, we'll still be here . . ."

"She was low on mana. She lost her gauntlet, and she was tired. I need to be here when she comes back."

Shaking her head, Katife insisted further. "Look, we'll still be here when she does, regardless of whether you—"

He cut her off, his voice hard and firm. "It was my fault! It's my fault she's in danger."

Behind her, she could just hear Theta whisper, "'Bout time you realised."

Dakota paused, whether from needing a moment or recoiling from Theta's words, she couldn't tell. "We had him. All I needed to do was let go of the walls, make the change permanent. But I screwed up, and now she's in danger. I have to be here for her."

She searched for the right words, but none came to her. Swallowing, she turned her screen for Theta to see the image of Dakota's face, the left side a bloody hack job. Theta looked him over, making his decision. "I know how good he is and how good he thinks he is. Get him to the hospital. Do whatever it takes."

Taking a second to mull it over, Katife returned to

the door and knocked again. "Dakota? I know you heard that. Theta will stay here. He'll call you the second she gets back."

"I said no, Katife. I'm not leaving."

Closing her eyes, she took a calming breath. "Then I'm calling Rebecca."

It was as if the world froze. Even the sound of breathing stopped. After ten seconds of nothing, she heard his footsteps, then he opened the door just enough to show the right side of his face, free from damage but still smeared with blood. "You wouldn't."

"I know Allison brought her flower. One call and Rebecca will be here in an instant. Are you going to come with me or explain to her?"

He physically sagged, defeated by her words. He returned the pad to his face, stopping more blood from pouring out. Taking her wallet and a room key, she led him by the wrist. "Call me the instant she gets here," she said.

Theta nodded. She swallowed, towing Dakota away. They rode wordlessly away from the city with an air so sombre, even the taxi driver killed the music. Once they were dropped off at the emergency room, she once again took his arm, pulling him inside. He tried brushing her off, but unrelenting, she held on. Reaching the front desk, Katife let his face do the talking. There was a crisscross of scars along Dakota's left cheek that formed a sideways *A*. At its highest point, it almost intersected his eye. The worst was below, where a large patch of skin had been peeled back like a door on a hinge.

They were asked to take a seat in the crowded room and told that it wouldn't be long. She knew that was just ER talk for at least an hour. Fifteen minutes in, Dakota's scroll rang. He jumped, his hand diving for it. Then he put it back the moment he saw it was Rebecca calling. "Shouldn't you answer?"

"I need the line free for Allison."

Over the next hour, Rebecca made two more attempts, both left to voicemail. After fifty minutes, Katife ran for the bathroom, returning to find Dakota still sitting there, his scroll ringing once again. He only gave it a glance. "She's persistent," Katife remarked. Dakota grunted.

As she sunk into her seat, a slight glimmer caught her eye. For a split second she saw a large coin with a purple and gold face being twirled between his fingers: one side with Allison's tattoo drawn on it, the other depicting a flower. The moment her eyes connected, he closed his fist around it. "What's that?"

He dug his hand into his pocket. "Nothing."

"It's clearly not nothing." She paused, but his mouth was clamped. "Why does it make you feel so guilty?"

Even under the pad, she saw him frown. "How . . ."

With a soft smile, she said, "I told you, didn't I? I know your tells."

"Allison doesn't—"

She cut him off. "Allison is your sister. I am your friend. We don't see you the same way." Turning away, she added softly, "Just as you don't see us the same way."

Shaking his head, he leaned back into the chair. "I've known her for twelve years. She should be the one who understands me, not you."

Twelve? Not eighteen? Inhaling a long breath, she said, "She's your whole fricking world. But Allison's different. She has a life outside of you. That's why I'm the one who can read you best. You might be her twin, but you're my best friend."

He just shook his head. "You know nothing about me."

Suddenly her face dropped, and with it, her kind tone. "Why don't we test that? If I'm right, you call Rebecca. How about it?"

"Test . . . What? How would you even—"

Cutting him off, she stated as a matter of fact, "Right now you're wishing you never met Nikita." His dismissive attitude disappeared, replaced with abject shock. "You're thinking that if you hadn't met, Soul never would have mattered. Then you wouldn't have fought, and Allison wouldn't have run off. You think that if it weren't for him, you could have convinced her to break the gauntlet by now. But Soul posing a threat to Nikita meant there was some chance of a fight, which you both secretly wanted. And lastly, you're wondering what you can do to make me stop talking, but in a way that won't hurt me. How did I do?"

Dakota didn't respond. He sat frozen, his eyes glued on her. His breathing increased, and finally, he looked away. Then, with slow movements, he called his sister. "Hey, Rebecca. What's going on?"

She had hoped talking to his bright, vivid, smiling sister would somehow cheer him up, but it only took a second to know she was horribly wrong. *Stupid. Whoever calls predawn with good news?* Her heart started to gallop as she saw the screen, and tears staining Rebecca's cheeks. "What happened?" Dakota asked, a newfound urgency in his voice.

Wiping her eyes with the back of her arm, Rebecca breathed a sigh of relief. "Oh, thank god you're alright. When you didn't answer, I thought something might have happened to you too."

That one word, that pesky, final word. It spoke volumes, more than any one word ever should. Not *you*, but *you too*. Her heart felt ready to split.

The same building. After everything, and of all the places in the whole city, they ended up in the same building. Copying Katife, Rebecca demanded he see the doctor or else she wouldn't tell him where Allison was. Even over the scroll, her tears could only stop her seeing the bloody pad covering his face for so long.

Finally called in after an hour of waiting, forty-eight stitches attempted to hold his face together, taking twenty minutes to complete. Dakota didn't say a word, acting as if it were his tongue that had been slashed. The peeling skin from the massive gash on his cheek left him feeling like someone was holding his features in place. The doctor applied some sort of cream to cool him down, following up with bandages that wrapped around his whole head. By the time they were finally able to search for Rebecca, the sun was already rising.

The intensive care unit. That was what Katife said. While he was seeing the doctor, Rebecca had texted her with the ward she was in. The moment Katife uttered that name he ran, taking the stairs two at a time. Long lines marked the floor leading to each ward of the hospital. He followed the yellow one.

There were stark white walls, constant antiseptic bottles, and people in scrubs walking past in half a hurry. It felt like the right place. "Dakota, slow down." Lacking his same fitness, Katife struggled to call out while matching his pace. Even though he desperately wanted to stop, he couldn't bring himself to do so. He read the above sign telling him he'd found his destination. A desk was at the front across an alcove, where all his answers waited. He made it halfway there when he saw something out of the corner of his eye that stopped him short.

The alcove was filled with hard plastic seats of a pale green colour so close to grey it could have been either. Seated at the back wall he saw those distinctive golden locks. He turned on the spot, and she saw him as well. In an instant, Rebecca was off her seat and her arms were wrapped around him. "Thank God you're okay." Pulling away from the hug, she stared at the bandages and her eyes fell. "You're not. Oh God. I'm a terrible guardian. I let this happen."

An hour waiting gave him a long time to come up with a list of every possible mistake he had made, every reason leading up to the night's horrors. Not one was her. "It's not your fault, it's mine."

She didn't listen. "I'm your guardian. I made that choice, and this is my responsibility."

He couldn't look at her, couldn't take those big innocent eyes. "Where is she?"

Swallowing back tears, Rebecca said, "She's still in surgery." She hadn't even finished when she broke down, crying into his shoulder.

Eyes reddening, Dakota took her tears for ten more seconds before he had to look away. "I need to see her."

Rebecca blinked at him, those massive orbs obscuring his vision. "I know. But all we can do right now is wait."

He shook his head. "I have to get to her."

"She's with the surgeon, Dakota."

"She doesn't need a surgeon. I can save her."

For a short moment, she froze, unmoving until anger boiled over. He could see her face reddening in a different way, and before he knew what was happening, the world turned to sand. He didn't even see her pull out her rose, or crack its gem. Having activated her power and dragged him into her frozen world where time stood still, she didn't even give him a moment to process what she'd done before she started screaming. He had a feeling of whiplash. The last time she'd brought him here was with Katife and Allison, on the way home from that club. "Give it a break. For God's sake, she's in surgery, don't you understand?"

"I can fix her. My snake . . ."

"You're not the only mage here."

"No one has a power like mine."

She started laughing, like the whole thing was hysterical. "You mean a power that can't affect organic things?" She let the words linger a moment before going on. "Get over yourself. This is reality, this is life. And your sister is now in surgery, and God, your face . . ." Catching her breath, she slowed and softened. "You're only human, Dakota. You're not perfect, and you're not a god."

Freezing over, his voice became stilted. "I just . . ."

wanted to help."

"Who? Who were you possibly helping?"

Nikita, I needed to protect her. Arya too, in a way. Looking around, he couldn't even say those words.

Letting him be, Rebecca waited a long while until her cheeks weren't so red and his breath was under control. Only then did she hold out her hand to take him back to the real world, out of her world of sand, to wait as hours ticked by and no one came. As they sat together, he noticed the flower in her hands, purple petals spinning around—the flower she had given to Allison. It was now clear how she managed to arrive so fast. The sun was above the horizon and in the sky when finally, someone in uniform came to see them. But it wasn't scrubs. "Excuse me, miss. We need to have a word with your son."

For a moment, her gaze caught on the police officer before she mumbled, "Brother."

Touching his sister's hand, Dakota followed them. They were older than the previous pairs, far more tired and far more upset, like they had been personally attacked. "I'm sorry about your sister." Dakota didn't respond. "I know this isn't a good time, but we need to ask a few questions. When was the last time you saw her?"

For a long while, he didn't answer; he just stared back into the officer's eyes. They made no sign of leaving. "At a beach party. Around seven. We split up after that." It was hardly a lie since his eyes were focused on Soul during the fight.

"Will anyone be able to confirm that?" Frowning, Dakota asked, "Why? You think I did this?"

"Sorry, I just needed to ask. Are you aware of what happened?"

He was sure he knew more than the officers, but

whatever that final piece was, he didn't have it. Shaking his head, he told them so.

The officer nodded slowly, as if less speed made it sympathetic. "I'm sorry. According to the hospital records, she was admitted late last night. The way she was brought in was rather strange." The officer paused. "Do you know if your sister is involved with anything? Drugs or gems perhaps? Any information could help us understand what happened."

Lips tightening, Dakota tried and failed to relax his expression. "We just came here for a holiday." *If only that were true.* "What did you mean that the way she came in was strange?"

Looking at each other, the first officer spoke. "Last night we had a report that a patrol car was stolen and an officer assaulted. According to the report, the hijacker loaded an injured girl into the back. We believe that girl to be your sister. Can you think of anyone she was involved with who may have done this? A boyfriend, a dealer, anything?"

Soul. A name which seemed so much but was worth little more than spit. A mystery man obsessed with his crusade.

Even as the pieces of the night fell into place, they still didn't make any sense in his mind. He couldn't understand why after such a fight, after going after each other's lives, Soul would possibly traffic her to hospital. "I don't know anything."

The officer gave a reflexive smile. "Well, if you think of anything, let us know." Handing him a card, they let him go. Stepping back into the waiting area, an uncomfortable weight crushed his mind: that Soul's DNA would soon be linked to two separate crime scenes in two different cities, both of which they were involved in. *My clock is ticking.*

Sitting back in the hard seat, what felt like eternity ticked by until finally the correct uniform came to speak. Standing up to greet him, Rebecca shook the doctor's hand. "The operation was mostly successful, although she is yet to wake."

Rebecca spoke with forced calmness, depicting a strength that went against the buckling in her knees. "Do you know when she will?"

The doctor shook his head. "Cases like these are hard to predict. I am sorry." Speaking slowly and easily, the doctor gave her time to digest his words. "The injury caused damage to her spine, which only light mana can reverse. Because of her dark affinity, there is the possibility your sister may never walk again." A moment of silence passed, mixed with an empathetic look cast between them. "I imagine you are eager to see her. She's in room four twenty-three. Please limit yourselves to only two visitors at a time."

The strain in Rebecca's voice made it clear she was desperate for some positive news. "She uses time spells. She should be able to undo that." The doctor nodded, not wanting to add confirmation or take away hope.

As he guided them to the room, Katife waited outside. A pale glowing sun lit the inside. Aside from the one bed and two chairs, the room was mostly empty. Walking up to the blue sheeted bed, Rebecca rested her hand along the side. Her hair sprouting in all directions, Allison lay still against the pillow. The only movement was the rise and fall of her chest, assisted by a ventilator strapped around her face. Not that she would have been able to move with her body locked up in a brace. Tubes ran into her arm from an IV drip. Her eyes were closed, loose with no tension. Somehow, she looked peaceful.

Every step sapped at his oxygen. It was so similar to last time: the same position, the hospital tubes, and plaster around her. Only then she had been awake, crying over Sydney when the surgery had failed. This time, she was the one unconscious. Falling to his knees, Dakota's head fell onto the mattress, right beside his twin's hand. Slowly his tears darkened the sheet beneath him as he clung to her for dear life.

This is stupid. I already know his answer.

Coming from Salbador, the two domes looked so close together, yet as Rebecca approached, they felt worlds apart. There were chores to be done back home, all the things she let slip with the promise of two weeks to herself, which was disrupted by the knock on her door in the early hours of the morning.

Rubbing her eyes, Rebecca collapsed her spell, appearing in the dark room right before the frame mounted on the wall where her flower was pressed inside. It was the second stationed within the city, the first being in her office. Throwing on the light, she heard a feminine shout.

Her neck snapped on instinct as she turned to the couch supporting two people in different states of undress. The man matched her gaze, immediately recoiling in shock. "Rebecca? What are you doing here?"

Pushing away, the woman got off the couch. "What the hell, Dylan? Were you cheating on me with this blonde barbie?"

Rebecca was still flipping the woman off as Dylan set to calming her down. "No, Tan, this is my daughter, Rebecca. Do you, ah ... Sorry, why are you here? I mean, I'm happy to see you, but you should have called."

"Yeah, I can see that."

Sighing, he turned to the woman and spoke quietly. Nodding, she gathered her shoes and hurried out of the room, pausing only to whisper a shallow "Nice to meet you."

"So. You said you wanted time with your kids? Well, one of them is in a coma, so now's the time if you want to be there."

He had to shake his head as if he wasn't sure if he was hallucinating or not. "What?"

"Your daughter. She was hit by a car."

Rubbing his forehead, he seemed to finally understand this was no dream. "Okay. And why are you telling me? You said you didn't want me getting involved."

Squeezing her fist, Rebecca took a hard breath in and spoke through her teeth. "Because she's your daughter. I thought, you know, that you might be interested that she's fighting for her life. If you really want to be involved, now would be a great time."

Dylan's place was small, with little room for too many luxuries. It was a city apartment owned by a guy, and that reverberated in every pore of the room. "I seem to recall a hairy neighbour telling me to leave." Rubbing his head, Dylan sat down. "I can't help you with medical fees, you know."

Suddenly she was unable to stay still, stepping forward as her voice exploded in her throat. "Screw you. I already make more than you. I did the overtime, I took

234

the extra responsibility, I minimised sick days, so now, I'm not the one still stuck at the bottom of the totem pole. Unlike you. No, *Dad,* this isn't about money. It's about the daughter you pretend to care about who's fighting for her freaking life!"

With a groan, he leant backwards into the couch, rubbing his eyes and looking up. "Okay. Okay, I'll be there. So, which one was it?"

It had been hard hearing the news of her sister. And yet, those words hit almost as hard. "Which one? I said your daughter, and you know it ain't me. Which one do you bloody well think? Is there some other daughter I don't know about? It's Allison, Dad. Allison. *Which one?*"

He shook his head like he was trying to clear some grogginess. "What about the other one? Dakota?"

With every sentence she started to wonder if one of them belonged in the mental health wing of that hospital. "You can't be serious."

"What?"

"What? What do you bloody well think? Dakota's your son. God, how quickly did you dump them at the orphanage to not even know that?" Shaking her head, she retreated back towards the door, even though it was meaningless given her power. "This was a mistake. I don't know what I was thinking. Maybe that you might actually give a damn. I won't make that mistake again."

She stepped away, reaching for the flower in her hair. "Rebecca, wait. Look, I'm sorry. I'm tired right now."

"You didn't look tired when I got here."

"Look, Becca. I didn't know. I just remember their mother saying identical twins, so I assumed . . ."

Shaking her head, she dropped her hand. "You

235

assumed? Jeez, how much time did you spend with them?"

"Look, their mother . . . a lot of crazy stuff happened around her. It's kind of hard to remember some of it."

"I don't give a damn if you remember her; I'm talking about them!" A thudding on the roof reminded her that unlike at her or Connie's place, people lived nearby, and they could hear her yelling. Forcing her voice to be calm, she asked, "Who was she? I'm sick of nothing but vague nonsense." He shrugged. "Give me something here. A name, a race even."

Rolling his head back, he offered her a seat beside him. She didn't take it. "I don't know."

Her mind fought for the right words, and when none came, she settled on something that felt good. "You're sick."

"It's not like that," he protested. "She was a shapeshifter. It's why they have purple hair. I couldn't find her if I tried."

Her jaw dropped. "You haven't tried?"

"Why would I? She returned home and made it clear she didn't want me to follow her."

"Gee, I wonder why." She had to stop and sort through what he said to make sense of it. "So is there anything you do know?"

His voice becoming almost wistful, he said, "I remember meeting her. I remember our time together. When she told me she was pregnant, it was one of the best days of my life."

"You really show that."

"Don't you give me that. She gave birth prematurely, then immediately decided to disappear. I didn't know what to do. I didn't have anyone to help me. So, sue me for thinking they'd have a better life with someone else."

She was starting to reach the point of wondering if she were in a dream, unsure how else to justify the absurdity she was hearing. "So, you're saying she gave birth and then just decided to leave that same day?"

One shoulder shrugged as he said, "Basically. She was impulsive like that. I didn't know what to do, so I drove them out to a church."

"What, like, the same day?" she asked, completely unable to hide her disbelief. "And she was the impulsive one?"

"I was desperate, okay? We were saving for a place I couldn't afford alone. It's not like she gave me any time to prepare. One day she just went into premature labour, seemingly on her own command, then handed them to me and told me their names. The next minute she disappeared. So yes, I made the call. I always planned on seeing them again, and I never for a second thought that church would sell them off as child soldiers. I promise you I wouldn't have left them there otherwise."

"Yeah, okay. So if you could do it again, you would have kept them?"

He shook his head. "I would have found a better orphanage." She started laughing. She didn't know why, but she wasn't sure how else to respond. "I didn't have a choice."

In a fast moment, her laughter died. "Oh, screw you. We all have a choice. I chose to take them in when I didn't have to. I chose to look after them and make a home. You had a choice. Ask for help, go back to Gran, *something* to look after your own kids. But no, you just leave them for someone else. I can't believe my father is such a pathetic, spineless loser. Where's your masculinity? Where are your paternal instincts? Do you even have any?"

Dropping his eyes, he went silent. She stared for a long time, waiting, hoping he would say something in defence. Her breath caught when he finally opened his mouth. "I knew I couldn't raise them by myself."

In that moment, with his quiet words, all her anger died. She wasn't quite sure why, but all that was left in her voice was complete contempt. "You know what? I'm done. I'm just so freaking done. I'm taking my flower and leaving. I don't *ever* want to see you again. Come back before they want it and I'll file a restraining order." Turning, she reached for the frame that held her flower.

Standing up, he held out his hand. "Rebecca, wait . . ."

"No! I can't stand to look at you anymore. I don't want to see you, I don't want you on my scroll, I don't want to remember you exist. I am just so done with your crap." Pulling at the frame, she took it off the wall.

"Wait!" She did, freezing and waiting for him to speak. "That's my frame."

She didn't know what she had been expecting, maybe some sort of defence, a plea for her to stay. *Something to show he cares.* Instead, her heart sunk one last time, the message clear. Turning over the frame in her hand, she pulled off the backing and held the flower she had given him so long ago. It was the first she ever gave out, one of the ones she had taken such care with. And he had gone and stuck it behind glass. "Goodbye, Dylan." It was the last time she saw his room.

It took the both of them, plus Katife and Theta, but for four days Allison was never left alone as long as the hospital allowed visitors. Every day ended with Katife practically dragging Dakota away to the perfectly timed bus, along with all the other visitors who were kicked out.

There was one other visitor waiting on the second day. Wearing a headscarf and glasses, Arya was altogether dressed up to disguise her identity. "You saved my friend. I don't know what I would have done without you. It feels wrong to say thank you, but . . ." She didn't finish, but he nodded. "She's real pretty. She seemed nice that day we met. And she's here because of me. God, you must hate me so much."

He felt numb, and it was hard to move. "You didn't do this."

She didn't say any more but whispered a prayer for Allison. He was thankful for it. She left a flower on the windowsill, a sunflower, probably one from her garden. It was nice. Giving thanks once more, she left.

Then came the third day, and he was forced to leave again. Sitting back on the couch, he eyed the gauntlet resting on the table, waiting. For what he didn't know. Its owner, he guessed. Her knives had been returned to her bag, the blood bleached clean. A few were missing, those she still had when she ran after Soul. *Police evidence now, I guess.*

"Hey Dakota?" Her voice was low and soft, an invitation for him to get out of his head. Taking it, he turned his eyes to Katife. "Is your icon really just a scrap of wood?"

Giving her a half-shrug, he replied, "Yeah. Why?"

"It's just I was always told mages choose items of great importance for their icon."

With a nod, he unwrapped the bandage from his arm, which was coloured to blend with his skin. When the wood fell into his waiting hand, he held it for her to take. "They usually do. But it's a tendency, not a rule. Easier to keep something on you that you care about. Or, you keep it on you so much it becomes important. I'd imagine you didn't think about your memory card as much as you do now."

Holding it to her eye, she inspected the jagged edges, the frayed wood fibres, and the tiny writing. "I don't even think of mine to be honest."

He nodded, unsure what to say. Tearing his gaze from her fingers, he looked her directly in the eye and spoke slowly. "You should stay with Theta tomorrow. There's no point in us both being miserable while we're here."

With a swallow, she reached out and took his hand. Instinctively, he pulled away, and by the time the reflex passed, she had already retreated her reach. "I don't want to leave her any more than you do."

Briefly his jaw opened, ready to say something.

240

Then it closed, and he couldn't look her in the eyes; he could only look as high as her shoulder. "I don't know how I could do it without you."

She smiled. "Good thing you don't need to find out."

He didn't know why, but he didn't return to the hospital so early the next day, instead trailing behind his friend as they spent that morning like tourists for the first time since Arya made her call. She took him along an orange cobbled lane running through the centre of the city block. It was pedestrian only, surrounded by stores and cafes and buskers on every side, two stories high. There was a hotel at the end. Most of the places were small shops, but one on the second floor was the back entrance to a department store they'd walked past on the main street.

It didn't really make sense, but somehow Katife used her smile and her words and convinced him to buy her a dress. It was a blue floral thing made with an elastic tube to fit around her chest, with the rest hanging down beneath. It looked like it belonged on her, at least as long as they stayed near the beach. In the brief time they spent back in the room, she changed into it so that she may wear it sitting in the hospital waiting room. Rebecca was there by then.

As Dakota rubbed his thumb over the back of Allison's hand, the fifth day began to steadily drift by. Then there came a sound. It came under the cadence of rustling clothes, the beeps of the monitor, the wind from the window, and every other hospital sound. The sound of exhaling breath.

Grasping onto her hand tighter, Dakota all but flew out of his chair to press his ear to her lips. He heard it again, clearer this time. It was incoherent, but present.

Sound escaped Allison's lips. Rebecca moved almost identically. Everything else melted away, even as Rebecca took his hand. The sounds, the sights, the feelings—none of them mattered when faced with his sister looking ready to open her eyes. They flickered slightly against her skin. He found himself holding his breath.

He felt her hand become rigid in his. Then it moved, a slight, small movement. It made his heart leap. But her eyes didn't open, and a second later, that leap tumbled into a dive. Her hand started to vibrate, and her eyes started flashing beneath the lids. Next, her whole body started to shiver. That shiver turned into a shake, and that shake became a violent seizure as the monitor's beeping became galloping hooves.

A nurse burst through the door. In a flash, she took in the trio, focusing in on her patient. Then she took in Dakota, frozen as a deer in headlights. She forced apart his interlocked fingers, giving Allison space. A doctor came in next. He took the time to read the chart at the end of her bed and quickly made his decision. Taking medicine stored in the room, the nurse filled a syringe and flicked the tip before injecting it into the IV. Whatever it was subdued the shaking. Before he knew it, they were undoing the latches on the bed and pushing it out of the room, leaving him and Rebecca with the empty space.

Time became like a funnel, slowed to a crawl as they waited for the moment the doctor would return. Dakota felt stiff, his limbs begging to be stretched. There was practice in the doctor's words, the perfect tone of sadness and compassion, someone experienced in giving bad news. He wondered how hard it was to stand there and tell them they found a blood clot on Allison's brain and they wouldn't see her again that day. He wasn't sure he could breathe, let alone speak. Rebecca looked the same but somehow managed words. "Will she be okay?"

"Her condition is worse than we imagined. It's not clear exactly how she'll respond."

"So are we talking a few more days, or a week, or . . ."

Waiting for her to swallow, the doctor gave his levelled response. "Right now, we don't know how she will respond, if at all."

It didn't make sense to him how Rebecca was still standing. Her legs were shaking so much it should have been impossible. "But she was just about to wake up."

"Most likely those were the early signs of the seizure. I am terribly sorry."

It was irrational, but it didn't feel right for the doctor to leave. A part of him wished he would stay to talk to them after they had nothing left to say, just for a semblance of support.

They drifted to the cafe. Not wanting to go, not able to stay, it was the closest anchor they had allowing them to stay. They said nothing until Rebecca used her rose and disappeared, leaving him to drift away, Katife his buoy. The hotel was empty. She'd guided him back, short steps at a time. "I don't know what to do," he said to no one.

"Right now?" Katife asked. He didn't need to answer. "In general. I can't imagine . . . Do you, ah, need some sort of distraction?"

"What distraction could be enough?"

She shrugged. "I don't know. I guess the pool could do something."

"I doubt it."

"Yeah, I know. But sitting here won't do you any

good."

Moving only his eyes to look to her, he asked, "Will it be any better there?"

"I don't know. I, ah, I just think you need some fresh air. At least sit on the balcony."

Tired and unsure, he nodded, letting her guide him through the sliding door and onto the maroon-tiled balcony. There were two chairs and a small table tucked into the corner. Pulling the chairs to face out to sea, she dragged the table behind and between them. She didn't sit down with him, instead returning inside. Craning his neck to follow her, he saw the dress flow around her legs as she took seemingly delicate steps to the fridge. Before she turned back, he turned forward, not letting her realise that he had been watching her. She came back, placing two beers on the table. With the wind ruffling her hair as she sat down, he couldn't help noticing, despite how bad he felt, just how great she looked.

Opening one bottle, she handed it to him before taking the other herself. She *really* looked good, enough that it was almost off-putting having her so close. Their fingers touched, and he saw that smile on her lips. His favourite one. Cynical, a little upset, but not dim or dark and depressed. There was something about her face that just seemed to be built for that smile. Her cheeks and mouth were made for laughing, but it was her eyes that made it feel so right—tired, kind, and content.

It was part of what made her look so good. She didn't have some fantasy model-type figure, but still maintained a healthy and slim profile. Her face was a beauty, but she was showing lines of stress. Her imperfections made her more real than anything else in the world. Certainly she was more real than Nikita's projections. He was about to say something, not that he was even quite sure what, when someone else's voice made them both jump. "Enjoying yourselves?"

Calming his heart, he focused on the newcomer already sitting between them on a chair that didn't exist. Nikita, sporting a straw hat so large he was sure that were it real it would be giving him a slight feeling of claustrophobia. *Think of the devil.* "Hey, Nicky. Did you get here alright?"

The projection moved its lips, but the dubbing was worse than ever, like a robot body with a human's voice. "Yeah. I'm in a taxi from the station. So, what's the plan now?"

Through the image, he could see Katife watching him, not the projection. "She's not allowed any visitors today, so we'll have to wait."

The projection nodded. "Fair enough. Guess that means I'll find a place to take me in. Don't worry, I know to not leave any traces now. I'll make someone take me up to check out a room, then just forget me there."

Tight-lipped, he nodded. "Hopefully we can try tomorrow."

"Yeah, hopefully. I, ah . . . sorry." He nodded, knowing from her tone she had read his thoughts of the day's events.

She had nothing else to say, but she didn't retract the image. It made it so the three of them sat on the balcony together in awkward silence. Dakota looked right through the projection and saw that Katife felt the same. Finally, not able to take it, she asked, "Hey, Nicky. How do your parents feel about all of this?"

She shrugged. "They're dead, I think."

Katife frowned, rubbing her brow. "What? I didn't know that."

Shrugging again, Nikita replied, "Yeah, well, I don't know for sure. I haven't seen them in years, just heard it on the news. I mean, my father was a jerk, and my mother a bigot, so you know, I left ages ago, before anything happened." He didn't know what it was, but there was something wrong with her response. "Besides, it's not like they were my real parents. They just adopted me to make themselves look good."

Somehow, he didn't really care. Whatever it was, it was Nikita's problem. If it didn't affect Soul, it wasn't important. The only thing that bothered him was losing the chance to enjoy Katife's raw presence. It was something so warm and positive, he never wanted it to fade. Even when Nikita forced it to.

A sleepless night, a morning bus, and Rebecca was forced back to work. Alone, his head against the bus's window, Dakota felt the exhaustion more than ever. For once, he was going in for himself, to follow up his scars.

Removing the bandages, his doctor checked the damage. The new binding was with adhesive bandages, covering just his scars instead of wrapping up his whole face. Warning of a possible infection, his doctor wrote a prescription that Dakota took and scrunched into his pocket, freeing his hands for the sunflowers bought from the shop. They sat between his knees as he waited to be allowed in and for Nikita to arrive.

His eyes caught on the sleeping woman two seats down. Many of the visitors' and nurses' faces were etched into his memory, but hers was not among them. Her face was timeless; she could have been anywhere between seventeen and thirty-five. She was dressed way too hot for summer, and even had a thin scarf wrapped around her neck. Jet-black hair fell in spiked tips coloured a toxic-coloured green. Feeling his gaze, her eyes drifted open and she turned halfway towards him. "Visiting someone?" It seemed like a pointless question, but he gave her a nod nonetheless. "Me too. Who are they?"

There was a part of him that wanted to ignore her, but at the same time, there was something comforting in talking to someone else. "Sister."

"Ah. Mine's work. I'd imagine yours is worse. Not a good wing to have someone in. This and the burns ward are easily the worst to have to visit." He didn't respond, and after a moment of looking expectantly for him to, she added, "Sorry, am I bothering you?"

Her question made him look properly at her, making him realise she had a face which resembled a bird of prey. He shook his head. "Sorry. Just a little distracted."

"I get that. Those flowers for her?"

Glancing down at them, he smiled. "Yeah."

"I'm sure she'll like them." Just like Soul, she had some weird accent. She was clearly from France or somewhere close by, but from which former kingdom or minor nation he had no clue.

Hospital sounds rolled back in as he glanced at the clock. "You're not from around here."

He hadn't made it a question, but she answered with a faint, soft smile. "Yeah. First time I've left my homeland, actually."

"Hmm? Where are you from?"

She shrugged, looking away from him. "Metanna."

He couldn't help it; he gawked at her. "No way."

"Something strange about that?"

"No, it's just . . . my ancestors are from there. Apparently."

"No kidding? Half a world away and yet my home

248

is coming back to find me." She said it with a flippant tone, but she did not smile.

"I might be wrong. I mean, I'm an orphan, so who knows for sure. But I've always wondered what it's like there."

He didn't know why, but there was something about her, or perhaps it was just the situation, that made him want to talk. "Well, it's cold." He didn't know how to respond to that, and before he did, she added, "So, your sister . . . What happened to her?"

His jaw locked up and he had to look away. "Car crash," he said simply.

"Ah. Same. Cruel world."

He nodded. "How close were you? To this colleague."

She spoke with a sigh, her gaze dropping to her knees. "That's complicated. Honestly, I don't even know how to answer it."

Frowning, he added, "But you care a lot to come halfway around the world."

Shrugging, she said, "I'm partially here for work. It's a mess, but you do what the boss tells you."

Unsure what to say, he just nodded and looked away. But even then, there was something there, a sort of makeshift connection, that made silence feel somehow wrong. "So, what do you do? If it's partially work, it must be important to come so far."

Her response was a single word answered flatly. "Military."

He didn't know what he expected, but somehow it wasn't that. "I see."

Interlocking her fingers, she stretched her arms. When she brought her hands in, she looked to him fully and tilted her head. It only served to exacerbate that bird-like appearance. "Mind telling me what happened to your face?"

Arm rising instinctively, he felt the new bandages. They felt smooth against his finger, painful on his cheek. "I got into a fight."

"Ah, yeah. Been there. Does it hurt?"

"It's worse than it looks."

She smiled, and he wasn't sure if she was trying to make him comfortable or the direct opposite. "Been there too. Well personally, I think you look handsome. A rugged adventurous type, you know?"

He didn't believe her, but even still he smiled. "Thanks." Looking past her, he saw Nikita walk in. She was late. He didn't mind. Pushing out of his chair, he nodded to the woman. "It was nice talking to you."

"Likewise," she said, holding out her hand.

Dakota took it, her fingers locking around his and keeping him in place with a force that seemed impossible from her thin frame. "What's your name?" she asked in a way that left no room to refuse.

"Dakota."

Short, sharp, and harsh, she nodded. "So you are. What are the chances? The girl in the coma . . . she's your twin?"

Throat constricting, eyes widening, he asked, "You know me?"

She smiled, but it didn't reach her eyes. "By reputation. You made it pretty obvious. Although those eyes . . . they made headlines four years ago. I'm sure you can imagine that when the rare eyes of our nation's founder showed up, of all places, in a mountain monastery training children as assassins, it caused quite the stir back home." When she finally let go, he felt relief flood his hand. "Wish

250

your sister the best for me. And don't beat yourself over what happens next. It's beyond your control."

He couldn't talk, couldn't breathe. Her smile was friendly, but behind it was something predatory. *What on earth does she know?* Everything she said left more unsaid. Her words left either a threat or a promise or something totally strange nagging at his heart. For that moment, he wanted to stay there, ignoring his plans, and demand to know what she did. But even if he did, there was that shiver she sent through his spine, telling him to flee as fast as humanly possible.

He felt Nikita standing behind him, her hand on his shoulder. Her touch guided him away from the woman. He wanted to know what she meant, what *was happening next.* But for a reason he couldn't understand, Nikita was intent on getting away, like whatever she saw in that woman's mind was enough for even her to flee.

It wasn't until the door was closed and they were alone with his sleeping sister that his heart started to settle. Stepping to the windowsill, he laid down the flowers. It wasn't much, but they added some colour in the drab room. "Who was that?" Nikita asked.

Lips tight, he stepped towards the bed. "I don't know. But she knew me. Mind telling me what she was thinking?"

He couldn't tell what, but whatever she'd seen had jammed her mouth shut. The best she managed was to shake her head. He sunk a little, whether from disappointment or fear, he couldn't tell. Reaching into his pocket, he removed Allison's ribbon, handing it to Nikita. "Do you think you can do this?"

Taking the ribbon, she looked down to his sister. "I hope so."

"But you've never tried?"

"I don't exactly encounter a lot of comatose people."

Stepping up to Allison's head, Nikita spread her fingers around his sister's ears. The ribbon was pressed into Allison's hand by Nikita, keeping them in close contact.

Nothing happened. He knew telepathy wasn't a very visual power, but there was nothing at all to see. And from Nikita's expression, it wasn't hard to tell why. Dropping her hands, she turned to him with a downturned expression. "Sorry, there's nothing for me to latch onto."

In an instant, he let out his breath, and he deflated from more than just the expelling of air. He sunk into the chair, taking the ribbon back into his hand. Nikita sat with him, resting her head on his shoulder. Time passed slowly, letting him linger in Nikita's failed attempt to use Allison's mind to activate her own power. They sat there for so long he lost track of time, until a familiar-faced nurse asked them to step out for the midday rounds.

It wasn't until he was outside that he turned on his scroll. For once, there was a message waiting, and not from his friends or Rebecca. There was a voicemail and a bunch of texts from a number added recently enough for him to remember. Nikita heard the message, and understood what it meant. "Get to the hotel, don't let anyone see you." The moment she began nodding, he took off, leaving her by the bus. *It's happening. He actually stormed Arya's home.*

And I didn't notice.

The voice became more distant day by day, making way for the two men. Just as the silver man taught him about living in the snow, Harrold and Karl taught him about the house. And he didn't need to hold the axe to hear them. They fed him, teaching him to eat with these silver tools they called a knife and fork, and how to clean up afterwards. Within two weeks, he was almost used to it. A part of him wondered how long he would stay. He still hadn't reached the blue.

"Hey, kid, can you come here?

He was midswing, cutting wood into smaller pieces for the fire. He looked to the man, the younger one with slightly ginger hair. *Karl.* Lowering the axe, he walked up to him. "So, you may have heard us talking about how my wife is going to be arriving today, and I was hoping to get you a little cleaned up before then."

There were gaps, parts of the speech he still didn't understand, but he could see the idea of cleaning and dressing. He nodded. After all, a hot shower was one of the most relaxing things amidst the cold. Leaving the wood cutting behind, he did as he was asked. After the first time the men had put him under the water and washed off the dirt, he was amazed how bright his skin became. After running with the dogs, cutting wood, and helping to clean outside, he was filthy yet again, but it hadn't ingrained into his skin as much, making it far easier to wash off. The problem was his hair. Unlike the two men's, which was cut short, his reached down to his hip and was all tangled together.

Drying with a borrowed towel, he dressed in the clothes the men had given him. The shirt was completely unlike the wolf hide. It was soft and soothing against his skin, what the men had called a flannel. Buttoning it up, he met them in the front room just as a roar came from behind the trees. It was soft and constant, getting louder every second. A blue box on four wheels rode into the front and stopped moving, the roar dying. The thing opened up, and people stepped out. There were three of them, two tall like the men, the other similar to him. "Karl!" one of the tall people shouted as she ran forward and wrapped Karl in her arms.

"You finally made it," Karl replied.

"That we did."

The next person to speak was the small one, who ran up to him as fast as her legs could carry her. "Uncle Karl!" Scooping her into his arms, Karl swung her around. "Did you miss me?"

Shifting in Harold's grip as the trio came together, the boy saw Karl smile. "No."

The final person only waved.

Stepping back from Karl, the woman bent down

before the boy. "I take it this is the kid you spoke about?"

Karl's lips tightened. "Yeah. We found him a few weeks ago buried in the snow."

"Did you call the police?"

"That we did. The best they could do was stick him in an orphanage, so for now he's here."

The small one walked up to him, standing really close and peering closer. She spoke with a high-pitched voice that made him jump. "Who are you?"

He saw under her hood vibrant yellow hair that became even more apparent once it was pulled back. He looked up to Harold, who seemed to be trying to work out how to handle the situation. "Go on, kid. Talk." With that, he nudged him forward a little and let go. The boy swallowed, frozen before the girl.

Holding out her hand, she loudly exclaimed, "I'm Fraya. What's your name?" The way she spoke was just as vibrant as her hair, exploding with energy. It made the two men sound just like those on the mountain in comparison. "Well? Don't you have a name?" The boy shook his head, and her jaw dropped. "You don't have a name?"

He stood still facing her. "What is a name?"

It didn't seem possible, but her jaw dropped even more. "Are you stupid? A name is . . . your name."

He stood stunned, with his eyes locked on her. "Who are you?"

She rolled her eyes. "I told you. I'm Fraya, and I'm here to stay with Uncle Karl because of my curse."

"Curse?" It was a word he'd never heard, had no clue what it meant.

"You know, the taboo?" He shook his head. "Wow, you're stupid. It's something that if you do it, bad people will chase you. That's why I need to hide here now."

There were too many words she was using that meant nothing to him, making her speech as useful as a growling animal. "I don't understand."

Rolling her eyes, she pulled off her glove and held her bare skin against the house. The dark bricks turned yellow, then green, then red. They kept changing, an endless rainbow before his eyes. His jaw went slack. "How did you do that?"

She laughed. "It's my taboo. Whatever I touch will turn into whatever colour it wants."

In a calming voice, Harold seemed to finally feel the kid had spent enough time unable to respond. "Fraya, this boy lived up the mountain. I don't think he knows anything about mana. Or anything, really."

Tilting her head, she asked, "Weren't there any names or icons up there?"

"I guess not," he replied.

Looking back to him, she tilted her head in thought. "He needs a name!" Her eyes narrowed as her stare intensified. "Mamma, is this what you meant when you called that lady a wandering soul?"

"A what?" the boy asked, while one of the women nodded.

"You know, a wandering soul. Someone who doesn't belong anywhere. Like you." Her smile intensifying, she proclaimed to everyone, "From now on, that can be your name."

It felt like his run had only just started and already he could see a pillar of black smoke rising into the sky. The closer he got, the more the cars slowed. There was a slight burning in his legs when he finally arrived before Arya's gate. *Manageable, but annoying.* He slowed, watching the flames dancing over her garden. But it was something else backing up the traffic. A police car dead on the road, punctured with neat holes, its owner drenched in blood leaning against the door.

The concrete driveway was the only entrance free from fire. *If only I knew what was inside.* Spotting a shattered window, he commanded his snake to coil on the pavement opposite, making it rise. Hollowing out the new column, he transferred the concrete into a bridge to the window and sprinted through. The moment the snake let go, it all disappeared to nothing.

The room was a mess, yet showed clear signs of having been thoroughly searched. With the shattered window, his best guess suggested she'd used it as an escape, pausing to close the curtains behind her.

Rushing through the room, he saw another open, and heard muffled sounds coming from within. Checking both ways, he dashed for it. Inside was a study, or something similar. Arya wasn't there. But her sister was, huddled onto her knees. Beside her, a man was bleeding out from a dismembered arm. Dakota gauged the blood left, deciding only an ambulance in the next few minutes would save him. *And Riley's clearly in shock.*

Using the snake to soften part of the table into cloth, he tied it around the stump and tightened it as hard as he could. Enough to slow circulation, buying just a little bit of time. Gritting through pain, the armless man looked to him. "You're the boy she mentioned? He came for her. He's tracked her scroll." Looking where he indicated with his chin, Dakota saw a monitor with the city map and a blinking dot. "She said you promised you would help. She's running for the city. Please."

Standing back up, Dakota paced back and forth. There was no closing that distance, and there was no point wasting energy trying. He knelt back down before the girl. "Riley? I need your help to save Arya. Do you have a way for me to catch up to them?"

Eyes wide, she nodded, pushing herself to her feet. He had to help, pulling her by the wrist. Wordlessly, she took the lead, down the stairs and into the garage. The heat was rising as fire started invading inside.

There was a car parked there, something decades old, something an enthusiast would like. Not something he wanted to use for his crash course in driving. Spying a pushbike by the wall, he went for it instead. It was almost pathetic looking in comparison. He found a button by the door to open the garage; it was still rising when he jumped into the seat and began peddling, staying in the middle of the driveway to avoid the licking flames.

Desperate to regain lost time, he swerved through a red light, weaving between cars as he rushed for the water. It was a godsend that the whole thing was ever-so-slightly downhill.

A pillar of smoke erupted across the street, different to the last. Brake lights switched on and tires squealed. Another plus for the bike. The rolling mass of black cloud sweeping the street came from no fire. It was pure, unrefined mana, let loose into the world. He peddled harder.

People rushed in the opposite direction. The smoke was already becoming fog, allowing him to see the bobbing blur of pink hair. He weaved through people and cars, narrowly avoiding deadly crashes. There was a sidelong police car, stopped perpendicular along the road, a partner to the one outside Arya's. Its door was open, and dashing in a beeline between it and the pink, Soul was closing in.

The combination of wheels and the downhill let him close in fast. This time he didn't swerve, aiming right at Soul's back. He even snapped the handlebars sidelong to drift the bike and make the whole thing crash sideways into Soul. They both tumbled right in the middle of the street.

He had about two seconds at best. Two seconds to choose: to stay and fight or to take Arya and run. Running left Soul alive; fighting could end everything there. There was only one thing making the choice easy: that after his mad dash to her house and cycle to the city, he was left in no condition to fight. His snake wasn't even summoned. The crash would have hurt Soul, but he was fresh from the drive. Worse, the fight would be public, in the middle of the street.

Rolling over the asphalt, Dakota was back on his feet and running. Arya had frozen. It felt like her arm was going to rip from its socket as he dragged her after him, kickstarting her legs into gear.

She had run barefoot, and he could see the exhaustion taking its toll. Dragging her around the corner, they rushed onwards. Keeping chase, Soul never even let them break line of sight. *If we can't put two corners between us, I'll use a building.*

"My feet are killing me," she complained.

"If you stop, he *will* kill you." The harshness wasn't his intention, yet even still, she managed a meek nod and kept going. Raising his voice to the max, Dakota screamed, tossing a pointed finger back towards the chasing Soul. "Help! He's after us!"

He knew it wouldn't do much. It might give them fifteen seconds at best if someone actually decided to help. He couldn't afford to look back and see.

Finding what he was looking for, he dragged Arya into that same department store he'd seen with Katife, only this time through the front entrance. Straight ahead was an escalator to the next floor. The sign at the front said it was a three-story building, first for appliances, second for women's apparel. Twisting into the aisles, he spiralled closer to the elevator, refusing a direct line. "What are we doing in here?" Arya asked through her ragged breaths.

"Escaping out the back and hiding your hair." A glance down showed a third objective: needing to stop the trail of bloody footprints even a novice could track.

He called the elevator, pressing the button twice and wasting no time to enter the moment it arrived, praying Soul wouldn't cut off their escape.

They stepped out almost into a rack of hats. Most were caps that would do little to hide her pink hair, but there was a single winter beanie hidden between them. Pulling it off the rack, he ripped off the tag and handed it to her. "What's—?"

"Put it on. You need to disguise yourself." She hesitated a moment but did as he said. "Do you still have your scroll?"

"Yeah, why?"

"He tracked it."

She groaned but didn't hesitate to fit it onto a shelf and lose it forever. They stayed away from the centre and pressed closer to sunlight. Detouring through a shoe aisle, he took the closest sandal off the shelf that looked vaguely right. She knew this time not to ask, ripping the tag herself and slipping them on.

Dressed in a tank top, there was nothing Arya could strip to change her appearance. Betting on the beachside atmosphere, Dakota pulled off his shirt, tossing it over her. "Put it on," he demanded. "And take off your glasses. They'll give you away."

"Wait, what? I can't see without them."

"Glasses are binary. You either have them or you don't. If he's scanning the crowd for pink hair and glasses, he might not even see you. Hold onto me and pretend we're a couple."

Pulling off the lenses, she closed their arms and held them in her hand. "And your face? He'd have to be blind not to see those bandages."

"I'm open to suggestions, although I doubt he's seen them yet." She said nothing, and he decided to all but bury the bandages against her new beanie.

They walked out the back completely different to how they came in. He held his breath as they passed the scanners, praying he'd removed the tags properly to stop them beeping. He kept that breath until they reached the walkway and were outside the store. They went as far as they could along the second story until they had to descend down the stairs to the cobbled street.

Slowing their steps, moving glacially, his heart began to race. Instinct told him to run, but logic said to be discreet. He could see, and even feel, that Arya felt the same. Glancing back at the street entry, his heart skipped. Soul was there, up on the second floor, having followed them through. Scanning the crowd, his gaze passed over them, and Dakota pressed his face harder into Arya. Then Soul's gaze kept moving, and they passed from view.

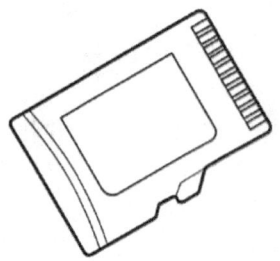

The waves were coming in, rolling over the sand. Tanning, lying on her back, she enjoyed the summer sun. From within her bag, her scroll buzzed with a text.

~I'm leaving Salbador. Just need to say goodbye to A~

Mind racing, she wondered when he'd left the hospital in the first place, or why he was going now.

~I'm on my way~

Jumping to her feet, she called to Theta. She threw a summer jacket over her bikini, and within minutes they were chasing down a bus. Wherever Dakota was coming from, they got to the hospital first. He never replied to her message.

Splitting up at the waiting room, Theta took a polystyrene cup and poured himself some water while she entered Allison's room. Hovering behind the chair, she bit her lip as she looked at her friend. "God, Alley. You're not going to recognise your brother when you wake up." Hearing the door, she stopped and turned. "Nikita?" she asked, seeing the flesh and blood girl step in.

"Dakota's on his way," she said in response.

"Holy hell, you're actually here."

Before the door could open again, the air shifted as Rebecca entered through her world of sand. *How long does he take to get water?* "Hi, Katife and . . . Nikita, right?"

Swallowing, Katife stepped away from the chair. "Hey, do you, uh, want a seat?"

It was only from the corner of her eye that she saw Nikita glaring at Rebecca. *I can't stand that smile. Those massive eyes, that cliché beauty . . .*

Twisting her face into a grimace, Katife pressed her palms into her temples.

"Katife, what's wrong?" Rebecca's words were enough, making Nikita realise and reel in her thoughts.

"Nothing. I just need some air, you know? Nikita." The girl rolled her eyes but nodded and followed Katife out. The door had hardly closed when she turned to her. "Why can't you keep your thoughts in your own head?"

Biting her lip, Nikita made a show of being troubled. "It was an accident."

"Ugh. This isn't the first time."

"Well, I'm sorry my power is controlled by my mind and not some darn a video game."

She was about to bite back when Dakota rounded the corner. Walking beside him, Theta's delay in getting water finally made sense. Whatever they were talking about was leaving a dark expression on Theta's face. "Is Rebecca in?" Dakota asked, his tone grim.

"Like clockwork," Nikita replied, not looking to Katife.

He nodded. "Alright. Do you mind giving me a moment first? Hopefully we can sort this out without you."

Nikita nodded. "Hopefully. Like I said, I can't make

any promises."

For a long moment, Dakota held a breath, considering something in his mind. Then, with a nod, he stepped inside. Turning to Theta, Katife raised an eyebrow, wanting to know what was twisting his face. Instead of answering, he inclined his head, pointing directly to Nikita. "Ask her."

Looking under her fingernails, Nikita said, "It's not my place."

"Yeah? Neither is erasing Rebecca's memories."

Unable to stop herself, Katife shouted, drawing the eyes of those around. "What?"

With a face built for poker, Nikita stated, "He doesn't want her to worry."

Head shaking, she stammered, "That's insane."

"No," Theta intercut. "The insane part is not knowing if she can put the memories back"

It didn't seem possible, but Theta's addition made her eyes widen even further. "What the hell?"

The voices behind the door got louder, overtaking even their words. "Nothing's been happening."

"Your face looks like a jigsaw puzzle and Allison is in a coma, so don't tell me nothing is happening," Rebecca near-shouted. "Why won't you just tell me the truth?"

"Because you'd never understand."

"Then help me understand. Please, talk to me."

"What's the point in talking when you never listen?"

By just her voice, Katife could tell Rebecca's shock was real. "When have I ever not listened?"

She was sure there was a volcano erupting inside that room, one that had laid dormant a long time. "Only every single time I say a word. After every single MMA match, or whenever we talked about our childhood. I mean, I'm sure you could just abandon the first fourteen years of your life and forget everything you were taught. And of course we're the ones who need to change, not you or the rest of this hellhole of a world."

"I thought you hated the orphanage."

"Yeah, well . . ." He quietened down. "The rest of the world ain't much better."

With the end of his sentence came a silence so deep she could hear them breathing. It took a long while for Rebecca to say anything. "So, what do you want?"

"I want . . ." He didn't finish. Katife peeked between the blinds. "I just want you to accept what we are."

"When have I ever not accepted you? I love you, both of you. But Dakota, what they did to you was so wrong."

His face changed, forming an expression unknown from all the tells she had collected, although the disappointment was so clear it didn't matter. "Yet you never stopped to wonder how thinking like that would affect us. Did you ever consider how much stress your ideals were putting on her?"

"She would have told me if they were."

"She didn't want to hurt you! She kept making me promise not to say anything so that you could feel good about yourself and what you've done."

"I gave you a home. I took you away from that hellhole."

"Your words, not ours. We had friends there. Memories. There were some good moments. All of that was taken away so that empty people could parade our images, write their articles, and pat themselves on the back for what a good job *they* did, all the while skyrocketing the number of my siblings winding up in a noose. Because every goddamn step of the way, it was never about us; it was about people with a saviour complex."

"That is so unfair, and you know it. I sacrificed so much for you. I took out a loan so we'd have a house. I spent my afterhours at work so you'd have food. I haven't gone on a date in four years to make time for you two. I've lost a lot of my life since you two came into it, but you know what? I wouldn't trade it for anything."

"Then why didn't you let Allison fight when you knew she liked it?"

Through the slit in the blinds, Katife saw Rebecca look down at her sleeping sister. "I don't know what I'm doing. I'm new at this whole guardian thing. If I'm doing something wrong, you have to tell me. I can't read your mind."

He paused, almost as if surprised by such a concession. His face started to go slack, and he gazed down just like her. "Just . . . watch over her for me."

Looking back up, she stared at him with a glare so piercing Katife felt it. "That sounds like you're going somewhere."

Nodding, he added, "I've got something to take care of."

There was a moment of hesitation, ending with her shock returning with twice the force. "You want to kill someone?"

She saw him shrug. "After what he did? What he's still trying to do?"

"This is wrong! You're too blinded by rage. You're not thinking clearly."

He took a moment, and Katife could hear every sound inside that room. "Is this your line in the sand?"

"Killing someone? Yes. It is."

She saw him nod. "Okay. Then I'm sorry."

Nikita was quick, stepping into the room behind Rebecca. Rolling onto her toes, she placed her hands on each side of Rebecca's head. Theta refused to even look. It wasn't quick. Nikita was standing there for so long she was sure her arms must be tiring. A minute ticked by, then another. Rebecca didn't move, and when Nikita finally lowered her arms, Rebecca fell limp. Dakota rushed forward, guiding her down into a chair, his sister now asleep.

He looked to his sister, then to his half-sister. "Get well soon, Allison. And be safe, Rebecca." After a second more, he stepped away, pausing beside Katife. "Don't follow us."

She felt her heart slowing, her body not wanting to move. Even knowing it was their plan, even seeing it happen, she couldn't believe what they had done. She felt like a robot as she twisted her neck to see him. "You're not going anywhere without me." He said nothing.

Even Theta's voice felt like it was in the distance. "You also told Allison to stop. Why was it only a problem when Rebecca said it?"

Dakota had no real answer, he stood there and hissed, "That was different."

Shaking his head, Theta added, "And another thing. I thought you only hurt your targets. What are you becoming?"

Dakota paused, looking his friend in the eye for only a moment before looking away again. "Whatever I need to be. And . . . this doesn't count. She's only forgotten something useless."

Katife could see Theta shake his head, speaking

slowly. It didn't take detective work to see the disappointment radiating from within him. "I'm going to stay here and look after *your* twin. And if anything happens to Katife, I will never forgive you. You have no clue how lucky you are."

Dakota made no response.

Everything moved fast from there. Back to the hotel, into the room where a pink-haired girl was waiting. Both froze seeing the other. No one explained anything. Dakota packed quickly. It took half an hour. He'd cleaned Allison's things but stopped to remove the remaining gems from her gauntlet. Katife packed as well, making it just in time to leave. They left their keys in the kitchen and took the elevator down, heading back to the train station they arrived on. The departed the city to the northwest, on a line which would cross the national border.

No one spoke in the mostly empty carriage. With a spare tennis ball, Katife passed the time by tossing it forward, and altering the ball's trajectory so it would always come back straight for her hand. She made it do all sorts of funny little tricks, like a loop-the-loop that made no physical sense. Wherever her power told it, the ball went. Focusing on her mana kept her mind occupied.

When the city was left far beyond the horizon, Katife raised from her seat and closed herself in the bathroom, finally having the privacy to cry. She didn't want Nikita to read her mind, to see what she had said to Theta in those last moments. How she had stood there, how he had stepped beside her. "What you're doing is a thankless task."

She had only shaken her head. "Something has to keep him in check. Now more than ever."

He had agreed, but not completely, "You have

feelings for him." It wasn't a question.

With a sad, sweet smile, she said, "I guess it's no surprise you'd know."

"If only you said something pre-Nikita."

She shook her head. "It doesn't work that way."

"I know. But I wish it did."

"I wish she'd wake up. I don't know what will happen to him if she doesn't."

"You do. We all do. He'll fall apart. He relied on her, like she was the only thing keeping him alive. Now all that's left inside is anger. I can't think of anything more stupid." Pausing, he took a breath. "Good luck, Katife. You'll need it."

Wiping her eyes, she turned away from the sleeping girl. "Tell me, Theta. Is it just me? Am I being some jealous bitch or do you also have this feeling? Like she just doesn't make sense sometimes? I don't understand it, but for some bloody reason, I feel like Nikita's happy about this."

Abnormally tender for a stoic like Theta, he laid a hand upon her shoulder. "You can't afford to think like that. Not now. Leave all that thinking to me. Because the answer is yes, I know exactly what you mean."

It was a long ride up the mountain. Leaning his head against the window, he drifted into his internal world.

It was different. Again. It was a forest, where tangled trees blocked the sky as only a forward path was left. The very earth had become twisted, ignoring any idea of gravity. Over time, he'd witnessed the land disappear, leaving only a few meters of earth before an infinite drop. It allowed him to see the sky. It was filled with a sea of stars drenched in a purple and green hue. And now it changed again.

He could always guess what caused the changes. But this time, there was too much too quick, leaving too many possibilities. Nikita and her danger, Arya and her flight, Allison and her coma. It could have even been Rebecca and what he had done. His internal world, a representation of his soul, had split into a flotilla of floating islands drifting in a sea of stars.

There was endless nothingness in every direction. Stepping onto the edge of an island so far from the next, he dared not jump. He wondered, for just a moment, what would happen if he ever fell. Looking down into that abyss, his mind returned to the bus.

Head against the window, he vibrated with the bus's movement as it dived deeper into Inngey Forrest. Leaving the train right before it entered a tunnel boring out of the country, the bus drove them higher and higher. The trees here were nothing like the ones in his world. These were rich and green and full.

It was just the four of them and three others on the bus. His stirring rocked Nikita just enough to wake from where she was sleeping against his shoulder. Katife sat across the aisle, speaking in hushed tones with Arya.

Almost an hour later, they stepped off. The sky was darkening, and by any metric they were in the middle of nowhere, save for the small sign at the crossroads. They'd had to ask the driver to pull over, and it took Nikita's telepathy to convince him. Dakota leading the way, they dragged what bags they had up the gravel path that twisted higher still, further from any signs of human life. Then finally, off in the distance, a wooden building came into view. A cabin in the woods. A very nice cabin with a pointed roof that failed to reach above the canopy. Its floor was elevated from the ground, built on stilts, requiring a small stairway leading to the front door. The garage was the only thing attached to the dirt. There was a path leading off into the trees. "How do you know about this place?" Katife asked between breaths.

"Allison and I looked it up ages ago, back when it all started." Turning to Nikita, he asked, "How many people do you sense?"

She didn't even falter as she reached her telepathy ahead. "Just the one. He's all alone."

Letting out a breath he didn't realise he was holding,

Dakota nodded, walking again. "This'll be easy then."

"Wait, what will?" Katife asked, kicking back into gear behind him.

"Clearing this place out. We can't have the owner here while we're hiding."

"Wait, this is someone's home? I thought it was a rented cabin or something." Katife gawked.

Nikita shrugged, spinning to offer a grin as she headed onto the steps. "Don't worry about it. I'll give him a holiday. He'll thank us in the end."

Following her up, Dakota knocked twice, while Nikita hovered over his shoulder. The echoes of the knock vibrated throughout the forest. Through the spotless windows, he saw the slow movements of someone approaching the door. There was no haste, as if whoever it was didn't care who had come to see him. The door swung open to reveal an aging man dressed in denim. His hair was freshly cut, which left Dakota a touch stunned. "There better be a damned good reason for a Yatrice to be knocking on my door."

"Yep," Dakota said, pulling the door all the way open and stepping inside.

"Hey!" the man yelled, completely unable to do anything as Nikita followed behind.

The man yelled louder, as if the problem was a lack of volume. "Hey! What the hell is this? You can't just walk in here like you own the place. If you don't leave this instant, I'll—"

He never got to make his threat. Nikita turned, and in an instant, her telepathy set in. "Kerry Davids, I think it's time you took a holiday. Is there anywhere you'd like to go?"

She said it with a plastic smile, the type that

reminded him of an air steward or travel agent, but a bad one, the type who hated their job but kept up appearances. He spoke robotically, like her telepathy was robbing him of emotion, which it probably was. "This is my home. It's where I want to be."

He saw her roll her eyes. He gave her a questioning eyebrow, to which she shrugged. "I was gonna send him to see some family, but turns out this guy's a loner."

Giving it a moment of thought, Dakota shrugged. "Then sent him to Salbador. We need Soul to find us somehow."

Giving in to what was probably more apathy than anything else, she went back to work, adding ideas into his mind. That he'd booked a holiday, that he had to leave. He packed with zeal, pulling his bags into the garage within fifteen minutes. There were two cars there. The one he took was an old four-wheel drive, perfect for the mountains. The other was some sort of sports car— low, sleek, and covered in dust. They watched him drive away, dirt kicking up in his wake. Only then did the other two finally surrender and step inside as the sky turned black. He heard Arya mutter as she stepped through the door, loud enough she wanted him to hear, "That was messed up."

Closing the door, he used the lock, rusted open from years of disuse. Hanging nearby, Nikita asked, "Hey, you got a minute?"

He shrugged. "We're in the middle of nowhere. I've got nothing but minutes."

Pausing, waiting, mulling it over and nodding, she finally said what she was thinking. "When we opened the door, I heard him think some things about you."

"Because I'm a Yatrice?" he asked. She nodded.

"Is that normal?"

Shrugging, he stepped further into the cabin, looking around. Dark, sleek, timber walls made it look like it was a holiday lodge retreat. "Someone's trying to kill you. I find it hard to care to be honest."

"But it's not just him. It's humans. We do this stuff, and it's horrible. And you shouldn't just not care."

Turning where stood, he sighed, then stepped forward and held her by the arms. "Nikita, I get to choose what bothers me. And when something happens five times in a hundred, it's really not a big deal. Besides, haven't you heard the things groups like Tooth and Claw have done to humans?"

"Dakota, you didn't hear what he was thinking."

He dropped her arms, rolling his eyes in the process. "I've seen people killed before my eyes and was trained to do so myself. Something like Soul that's trying to hurt me, that's what I worry about. Not some mean words. Its sticks and stones, Nicky. Words will never hurt me, okay?"

He couldn't tell what she was thinking, just that she wasn't happy. Finally, she nodded, and he led her upstairs to where they guessed the bedrooms were.

A study, a small library, one bedroom—that was the upstairs. And like children going on holiday, Katife and Arya had already laid claim to the bed. Nikita stopped and stared at them from the doorway. "You two want to sleep together?"

Katife smiled from where she sat at the foot of the bed, her bag dumped by her shoes. "After a train trip of bonding, a sleepover sounds like the perfect way to deepen this friendship." He could tell she didn't really mean anything by it. She had that high-pitched inflection indicating she was just making fun. But her smile quickly faded. "Maybe this was a dumb idea. We should swap . . ."

Shaking her head, Arya was already lying down on one side. "Nah, it's a great idea. 'Sides, those couches looked real luxurious. You might even be more comfortable than us."

Her comment made Nikita frown, wrinkling her features as she focused on something. Without her telepathy, Dakota could only wonder about what was in Arya's mind that was getting to her. Whatever it was, he wanted to bring her out of it. "Any clue if the couch was a pullout?"

It worked, making her stop frowning and look to him. Rolling her eyes this time, she pushed past him to the other room. He followed behind, returning to the couch to discover that Kerry did have a place for a guest to sleep. "Dakota, why didn't you help there?"

"Did it matter?" he asked, his tone completely flat.

"Did it matter? Dakota, we still haven't . . . Can't you see what I'm getting at?"

Loosening his shoulders, he leant back against the wall. "We just ran for our lives. I'm not thinking about that stuff now."

Groaning, Nikita dumped her stuff by the couch. "You better not complain if you miss your chance to be with this," she said, running her hands down her sides.

Placing his own bag beside the couch, he walked over to the window, looking back over the driveway as night rolled in. In an exhausted voice, he said, "Nikita, look."

Coming beside him, she did as he asked. "Trees?"

He shook his head, closing his eyes for a moment. "Not that. An open pathway with a lot of cover. We need defences. We don't know what help Soul has. We can't be wasting time and energy before we have this place fortified. I don't want to take any more chances. I won't risk him taking you. I can't lose anyone else."

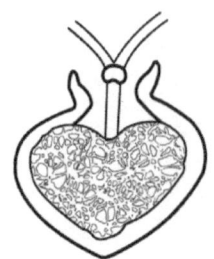

There was no fence, nor any sign of a border. She wondered if there was one closer to the road. Using the dusty car in the garage, Katife drove to town for supplies. Having a driver's license and lacking any immediately distinct features, Katife was the easy choice. Needing his own supplies, Dakota accompanied her, leaving Nikita with Arya to draw up their defensive lines.

The fence would be three stories of stone, ideally topped with barbed wire. They agreed to making it ten meters out from the house, enough to be defendable, but not too big that Dakota wouldn't be able to make it. Dakota insisted the trees would not be a problem, but she couldn't see how now.

On the other end, Arya was also inspecting where to draw the line. Stepped towards Arya, she asked, "Would making a roof work? Even more protection that way."

Nikita looked over the land, visualising the suggestion. "If Soul was coming in ten years, sure."

Arya didn't seem offended by the rejection, instead shrugging. "You know Dakota's limits. I don't."

Visualising the wall, Nikita considered the supplies Dakota was going to grab. "Once we put the landmines around the edge, a roof will be redundant."

"Wouldn't they break the walls?"

"That's why they'll be thick."

"So, a roof will drain him, but thick walls are fine?"

Nikita looked around her into the endless forest. "Just draw some lines so he knows where to build. I know his limits, and I can confirm we're clear."

Without a word, Arya took a stick from the ground, pointing it into the dirt. Nikita did the same. Starting back-to-back, they began drawing the outlines for four walls, leaving space for an inside trench just in case. Everything would be two meters thick, enough to stop Soul's grenade from becoming a pain. They left an entryway gap, a possible way in and out. Otherwise, there was the risk that if the defences were too strong, Soul might retreat and remain at large. Nikita couldn't wait for when the secret mines would be planted to make it an unassuming death trap. Turning away from the house, they drew lines for a four metre funnel at the front alongside the dirt driveway.

Nikita's hands were getting aggravated as the wood vibrated in her palm. Across from her, Arya walked with a thin fog surrounding her feet. Somehow her markings were left intact in her wake. "What are you doing?"

Twisting back, Arya blinked at her. "Huh?"

Pointing with her free hand to the smoke, Nikita continued. "That smoke trail. I thought you couldn't control your power."

Arya looked to her feet, raising her eyebrows as if she only just noticed the fog. "It's feeling the ground around me."

Voice rising, Nikita yelled, "Feeling? What could you possibly be feeling for? The only thing here is grass and dirt."

Arya just shrugged, completely indifferent. "I nearly never leave my house. Grass may be normal to you, but all I know is carpet and pavement. I just wanna feel as much as I can with whatever time I have left."

Rolling her eyes, Nikita scoffed. "Spare me the existential crisis. We're doing all this to keep us alive."

As calm as ever, Arya replied, "Things often find a way to go wrong. Especially when you can't afford it."

Nikita sighed in frustration, finishing the markings. Even only five meters away, Arya's thoughts were a tangled blur. It was like looking through the very fog at her feet. Using her telepathy, she spoke directly into the other girl's mind. *Stop for a sec.* Arya ignored her, making no indication she had even heard.

Pausing to bite her inner lip, Nikita rushed forward. She left Arya no time to react before she was dragged off her feet and into some makeshift grapple. "What the hell? Let go of me."

Nikita's eyes narrowed, putting all her effort into her telepathy. The fog didn't get any clearer. The minds of the townspeople fifteen kilometres away were more readable. With her arms wrapped around her as much as they were, it should have been the easiest read of her life. The only thing between them was their clothing, and their hands were physically touching. "I don't get it," she breathed.

"Yeah, I don't know what the hell you're doing either."

Looking up, right into the other girl's eyes, Nikita asked, "Why the hell can't I read your mind?"

"You were trying to read my mind?!" Arya demanded.

Again, she didn't answer, instead demanding more. "Quack," she said. "Become a duck for me." She said it aloud and as a telepathic command.

"What is wrong with you?" When she let go, Arya fell hard towards the dirt, stopped only by her summoned clouds. "God, you're one psycho bitch. You could have just asked."

Eyes wide, Nikita found her head shaking beyond even her own commands. "How is that possible?"

Pushing herself up, Arya made sure she had distance before speaking again, thickening the smoke in preemptive defence "Why? Cuz A: dark mana is two connections away from spirit. Makes it—"

"So freaking what? My telepathy works on people attuned to life mana, which is my exact opposite!"

Stepping further away, Arya changed her tone, speaking more carefully. "And B: I committed the taboo, remember?"

Nikita shook her head, unable to understand. "So?" Her voice rose as her face got redder.

"So? Have you ever met another taboo user? My mana circuits are mangled like crazy, and you think you can slip yours through them?" Shaking her head, Arya kept increasing the distance between them. "I get it now. You made Katife change her mind about the beds. You're a controlling, narcissistic, self-centred brat. Now I see why you earned the name 'bitch queen.'"

Nikita matched Arya's gaze, not sure what to say. She hated it—on these rare occasions it happened—when she had to talk to someone and not know what they were already thinking. She tightened her fist, taking a step back. *I can't trust her. I don't know what she wants.*

It was faint, and in the distance, but she could hear them—two voices getting louder—Dakota and Katife on their way back. Still ten or so minutes away. Ten minutes to stay as far from Arya as possible.

Dropping the stick, Nikita ran, slamming the door and deadbolting the locks. In all the time they were alone, Arya only tried the door once, then returned outside to sunbathe. Nikita counted the seconds as she waited by the front for the sleek car to crunch over the gravel, stopping right before the garage.

The dust had been mostly driven off by the wind. Shutting down the engine, Katife opened the door and the boot. "Hey, mind giving me a hand unloading?"

It was only then, with witnesses she could trust, that Nikita unlocked the front door. The boot carried three plastic bags, mixed with Katife's backpack and Dakota's duffle, all now full. Each scooped up their own as well as a plastic bag. Arya stepped up, taking the last two and closing the boot. Nikita stayed well away from the door as she glued herself to Dakota.

Dropping the bags onto the kitchen table, Katife looked back to Arya. "I got you some stuff."

"Cheers," she said, following Katife up the stairs.

Nikita kept a constant tab on Katife's mind, hoping for some hint of Arya's true motives. She saw her get changed, but that was it. When she came back down, Arya was wearing thin joggers with no real design. It was the furthest thing from fashionable, the two white stripes on the side notwithstanding. She said she loved them, which Nikita was convinced had to be a lie. Her shirt was replaced with some souvenir tank top depicting a waterfall.

They'd come down in time to see Dakota laying the purchases from his bag onto the table, the grocery bags all emptied into the fridge. "What's all this?" Nikita asked.

Spying the display of chemicals and leaves, Nikita watched as Dakota explained. "Katife came up with the idea to strip Soul's mana."

"Well, technically it was Theta's idea." Katife blushed.

"Wait," Arya called. "You know how to make Milton's Twilight?"

Dakota saw her shock, matching it with his own. "How do you know about that?"

"I used to take it."

Shaking his head, Dakota protested, "It's illegal."

"Not in Egypt."

In his mind, she could see Dakota searching for an answer, looking for a single reason someone would intentionally take the drug. "Milton's Twilight doesn't help with any known illnesses."

"Not an illness," she said, sighing and sliding into the seat. "You really don't understand the taboo, do you?"

"I understand there's a mana membrane around the skin that you ignored."

Pinching her nose, Arya looked hard at him. "Do you actually know the reason mages have icons?"

"Obviously. To control our mana flow."

This time she rolled her eyes. "Please. That's like saying we need driving to make cars. It's completely inverted. Icons bridge your mana circuits with the world, allowing it to leave your body to cast spells. The taboo gives natural mana open borders into your circuits. So there's always mana in my body; it just isn't mine. I can influence it, but I can't do whatever I want. Milton's Twilight is like building a checkpoint on the freeway. It tempered the damage until we found a better way."

Nikita frowned deeply, ready to ask a question. But then she didn't have to, instead getting Dakota to do it for her. "You say that like you managed to stop it."

Arya sucked in a long breath and curled her fingers around the hem of her new top, raising it to just under her chest, showing what had once been the flesh of her belly. Katife looked away, seeming ready to puke. The sight was enough to make Nikita feel the same. She wondered if it was Dakota's history in Koros that made him capable of looking without disgust at the deep, hideous incisions crossing over her stomach. The skin itself had been removed all the way from her lower belly button to just under her bra. It was too much for grafted skin to cover, and worse, it cut much deeper than just her skin. It was like a piece of her abdomen had been taken out. There was some sort of string tying it all together inside, creating a web within the actual pit in her stomach. And over the top was some sort of cover. Something transparent, almost like a cling wrap.

"That was where the symbols were drawn. They had to cut deep to get it all out. An arm you can amputate and replace with a prosthetic, but my stomach? This was the best choice I had."

Nikita couldn't look, and while Katife wasn't either, it didn't stop her from asking. "Does it hurt?"

Arya scoffed, letting go of her top. "I was wheelchair bound for years. Now? I barely even notice. The surgery gets easier every time, and it's much safer than it looks.

The only downside is I need a lot of medical work to maintain the webbing. They're trying to find some way to regrow anew what was lost, but even so, I'm almost normal now."

Finally looking up, Dakota's eyes reached hers. "How bad is the taboo to make this worth it?"

With a sigh, she leant back. "At first, it seems great. You become so freaking powerful. But then you reach the tipping point, and everything spins out of control. One day I woke up with no say at all anymore. You either stop it at all costs or become the next Lucina Aries. And I didn't want to have to live with burning down a town."

His throat was dry; she could feel it through his mind. All the things Soul had said to him were replaying for her like a theatre. They were now backed up for him by someone on the complete other side. But in there somewhere, he started to find an answer, causing his words to slow as they picked it apart. "Why isn't this public yet?"

With a heavy breath, Arya explained. "No one knows the long-term effects. I'm one of their guinea pigs. Two more years, and if I'm still good, they'll let the world know. Then the taboo will be as good as cured."

He nodded, taking it all in. "We might not need to fight after all."

Oh, you are freaking kidding. My own guards are going to get me killed.

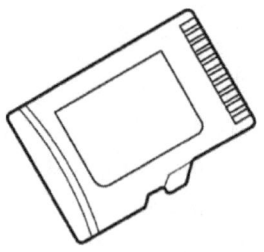

The sun was down, and the walls were halfway up. Placing her hands upon the dark stone, she heaved like moving it just a single inch would cure cancer.

The face of it was rough, but it would still be difficult to scale over. It was another thing that would need to be fixed before they could declare completion. There were still too many trees allowing someone to scale over, but they were thinned now, and would be gone tomorrow. Two days in, there was still no sight of Soul.

As Dakota lay on the floor, his mana depleted, Katife wondered what the burn felt like. Her spells were too weak to ever come close. School sometimes made them do long distance running, and she guessed the burning feeling in her legs may have some equivalence. Remembering those times made it hard for her to get annoyed as she dragged the chairs outside for their campfire dinner. Two chairs were from around the table, and the other two were camping chairs Arya found in the garage.

Arya did the cooking. She said it was one of her favourite pastimes back home. She carried out two plates, and Nikita took the other two. *Probably to minimise as much contact as possible.* With the sun gone, the stars were shining brighter than any she had ever seen. The fire was their only light.

Arya's dinner was as simple as could be: schnitzel, with an added can of peas. Dakota finally dragged himself up and onto a chair between Nikita and Arya. Dinner was silent, all of them enjoying the food before it could cool down. The way Arya ate gave her face a chipmunk-like impression. Halfway through her schnitzel, she swallowed it down and looked over to Dakota. "You said Soul used an unnatural amount of mana?"

Giving a half nod, his head bowed towards his dinner. His bandages were almost brown with dirt, in dire need of changing. "It must have been a high level spell that he used more times than I can count."

"And you said using multiple mana gems couldn't keep up?"

He suddenly looked away, and in that flash, she saw the clear look of guilt overtake his face. "Right. But she's a B tier mage with a double-A spell. It's not like she can't maintain it long."

"Right. But two icons with a strong spell and marathon usage is not an easy cocktail to maintain for anyone."

With an expectant lift of her eyebrow, Nikita asked, "You have some idea?"

Placing her plate on her knees, Arya looked up to the stars and exhaled slowly. "There's a possibility he isn't a mage."

Nikita immediately swore, not giving her a second more to explain. "He came back to life. What do you mean not a mage?"

Despite Nikita's voice rising, Arya's remained flat, with an ever so slight smirk on the side of her lips. Katife wondered if she was being calm just to annoy Nikita. "Right, and all mages know that dead is dead."

"Are you saying he's doing some sort of sleight of hand? You're insane."

Taking a deep breath in, Arya closed her eyes. "Do you know what the highest ever recorded mana store is? Not near enough to do what you said."

After one grew accustomed to the projection and its limited emotions, watching Nikita in real life was like seeing a whole different person. "And you're some sort of expert?"

Speaking like a teacher who feels superior and bored, Arya responded, "No, not an expert. But I'm in my third year of mana studies." In that moment, Nikita completely stopped talking, shutting her eyes and turning away. "Double A mana reserves require both crazy amounts of training *and* bathing in a high mana region."

Dakota blinked. "A what?"

The way she answered only further increased that exasperating expression. "Regions where the land is deeply infected with mana. Getting to one gives an insane boost to your mana stores, but God they are hard to find. And if you do, they'll still run out eventually."

Clearly resigned to being behind Arya's thoughts, Nikita sounded exasperated as she asked, "So what is your 'expert' analysis on how he's managed this?"

Stressing both words, she said, "Deicide arms."

The words froze the girls, leaving Dakota swinging his gaze between them. "Anyone care to explain this to me?"

Arya scoffed at his confusion. "You don't know what deicide arms are? That's like, grade five stuff." He shrugged. "They're a type of weapon that was developed during the mage/human wars. Their name derives from the Latin words for 'god killing'. Although really, they were used for killing the servants of gods. Like the monsters."

She remembered learning about them in school, back when Dakota would have been in the orphanage. "Why do you think he was one of those? It's not like they're common."

Pausing a moment, she considered the best explanation. "A deicide arm is basically a hallowed icon without an owner. You don't need to spend mana to buy spells. And since they were made for humans, they don't even take that much mana to begin with. If you had a big pool, you could fight until you dropped. But one thing. I never said he had *one*. The axe you described sounds just like one of the original arms, and the other power you explained? You can bet that matches up too."

Her own smirk sneaking in, Nikita spoke up. "One person can't have multiple arms. Boom goes your theory."

Scoffed, Arya retorted, "Sure they can."

Face reddening, Nikita nearly slammed her plate on her knees. "Are you passing that degree or just attending? Everyone knows you can only have one arm."

"No, everyone thinks that. It's actually just rare, since most arms hate each other's guts and are unwilling to share their host's internal world."

Dakota frowned. "You talk as if these weapons are

alive."

"I don't know about alive, but they've developed a soul of their own. They're basically a homunculus."

Rubbing her eyes, Katife muttered, "Having Nikita's voice in my head is annoying. I can't imagine an extra two."

Nodding in agreement, Dakota asked, "Wouldn't that have driven him insane ages ago?"

The best he got was a shrug. "You think he's not? Look, if I'm right, the axe is pretty basic. It phases though, and that's about it. The other one? I don't know what it's cased in, but there was talk of an arm that could halt causality."

All three looked to her in confusion. "What?"

Taking another bite of her cooling dinner, Arya explained, "It means that for a period of time, nothing in the world can affect you. Of course, it works in reverse too. So if you kill someone, once the spell wears off, you never actually had an effect on that person, so they're alive again. I always thought it was a useless power since any damage you cause will be undone, but I guess I was wrong."

Sighing, Dakota looked to the sky. "Thanks for the info. I wish I knew that last time." She said nothing in response, which Katife guessed was for the best.

Each of them focused back on eating, not letting their food get cold. It was a brief respite of peaceful silence, the insects and fire the only sounds. Finishing his plate, Dakota muttered, "I doubt any arm would want to share my world."

Tilting her head, Arya asked, "Why not?"

He looked to her with sad eyes. "It's just not a very nice place anymore."

"You know, they say an internal world is a reflection of your life."

"Thanks," he muttered in response.

Shrugging, Arya said, "If I could, I'd love to share mine. It's a greenhouse filled with plants, trees, and birds of the most amazing colours."

Katife's jaw dropped. "Oh my God. I knew there was something I liked about you. We're internal world twins."

With a raised eyebrow, Arya questioned, "Really?"

"Well, maybe siblings," Katife conceded. "It's an ocean floor, not a greenhouse. And they're fish, not birds. But the idea's the same." Even just describing it brought the wistful feeling over her.

"Hmm. Sucks we can't share them. Without marrying, I mean." Giggling in response, Katife nodded. Smiling back, Arya turned to Nikita. "What's about yours?"

Instead of answering, Nikita stared into her plate. "I don't want to talk about it."

Scoffing, Arya muttered under her breath, "Surprise, surprise."

Looking back with pure frustration, Nikita jumped from her seat and looked hard at the girl for a long while. Then turning, she stepped away from the fire. "Where are you going?" Dakota called.

"I'm going to bed. Today's been exhausting, and this didn't help."

Looking awkwardly between them, Dakota rushed behind to follow her inside. Suddenly everything felt quieter. But not the awkward kind of silence, the floating on water kind. "They didn't take their chairs."

"Yeah. Should we start packing up?"

Katife looked to the fire before answering. "Honestly, I kinda wanna wait the fire out."

Arya replied with a half laugh. "Sounds like a plan."

Sliding off the bottom of her chair, Katife lay on the grass. It was soft and comfortable on her back, although she could have done without the ticking behind her ear. Snorting, Arya shook her head and watched, only to quickly relent and do the same. Her top rode up a little, and Katife could see the edge of the pit in Arya's stomach. The fire's crackling sounded loud and natural, a serenity of its own. Even the idea of getting up and cleaning seemed too cruel. If it wasn't for the wind, she may have tried staying out all night. "Hey, Katife?"

"Yeah?"

"I want to ask something."

Katife shrugged, even though it would go unseen. "Shoot."

"Are you in love with Dakota?"

She almost choked, stifling it into a laugh. She pushed off the dirt and looked down at Arya. "What gave you that idea?"

Arya laughed a little in response. It was stifled, just like Katife's own, their brains demanding they stay quiet in the night. "Please, you're basically throwing out neon signs."

Scoffing, she said, "He's with Nikita."

"That's not an answer." Arya stopped, waiting to see what Katife would say—what defence she would concoct. Time dragged on, and Katife had none to give. "It's why you wanted us to take the bed. It had nothing to do with being friendly with me."

With a groan, Katife fell back onto the grass. "Nikita's my best friend."

"Coulda fooled me."

Frowning and chuckling at the same time, Katife asked, "What's that mean?"

She shrugged. "Honestly? You talk as if Allison is your best friend. I mean, maybe I only met her once, but hell, I get it. She wasn't actively unlikeable."

Katife took her time, thinking back to those days in school. They were so far away now they'd blurred together. "I don't know. It's like a dream."

"What, this whole Soul thing?"

"I mean yeah, that too. But Nikita, she's like a dream."

Almost head to head in the grass, Arya half looked away from the sky. "She seems closer to a nightmare to me, to be honest."

Sighing, Katife closed her eyes and thought of how to phrase it. "I don't mean like a fantasy. I mean like, you've had a dream, right? Suddenly you're somewhere and it all just makes sense. Like, why was I fighting a robot jaguar? It just made sense, and you don't even think about it."

Chucking, Arya said, "You have some weird freaking dreams."

"No, it's like . . . Well sure, but that's not the point."

Whistling, she sunk further onto the grass. "I get it. You're friends but you don't remember why?" Nodding, Katife looked back to the sky. The fire was dying down between them. She guessed in ten minutes, there would be only embers. "You know, I have another theory."

"About Soul?"

"About Nikita." Katife raised her eyebrow. Arya seemed unsure of whether she should say it or not, but finally taking a deep breath, she did. "I wasn't sure, but that dream thing makes me think I'm right."

"About what?"

With bated breath and a long pause, her mind tried guessing at what Arya was about to say.

"I don't think she's what she says she is," Arya finally said.

"Wha . . ." The words were barely out when suddenly it clicked and Katife's eye went wide. "Stop. Don't say any more."

The way Arya pushed herself off the grass seemed hesitant, like they were clinging to her. "I like you, so I can't let you go on like this. She was trying to manipulate me yesterday. She said she wanted me to think I'm a duck or something."

Holding her hands to her ears, Katife shook her head. "Stop! I can't hear this."

"Please, Katife, listen. You know she's a telepath, and that's borderline illegal for a reason. Isn't it at least possible she messed with your memories just a bit?"

"No! Please, Arya, stop talking."

"Katife, she's not your friend. Nikita's using you."

"I know!" Even with her brain telling her to be quiet, she all but screeched it. Then she repeated it again in a small voice, her words soft.

Suddenly the expression on Arya's face changed, dropping into confusion. "If you know, then . . ."

Shaking her head, Katife pleaded, "Then what? I'd stop her? She can rewrite my whole brain on a dime. If it's a deicide arm that's keeping Soul alive, then what are we supposed to do?"

Pushing up, Arya looked into her pleading eyes. "Her power doesn't work on me, so I can . . ." She stopped, never finishing the thought.

"If I know, she'll know. And if she knows, I won't.

You're too early."

"*Too early*? For what?"

Katife shook her head so hard her hair whipped her shoulders. "I can't. He said we need more time. He's doing all the thinking for a reason."

"I don't understand. What's going on? Who said you need more time?" When Katife didn't answer, Arya added in a softer voice, "How long have you known?"

Pushing herself onto her knees, Katife wrapped herself in a hug. "Since Allison. There's no way she'd act that way to a friend."

"And Dakota?"

She shook her head. "She's had too much time with him. And he was the one who told her how to do it."

"Do what? Katife, I don't understand."

Katife shut her eyes, as if not seeing would make it not real. "They told her she needed a reason, not a command. Make someone want to help her. And Dakota loves her. Which means *he* will stop us. You're too early. Theta said we need another day."

"Who?" she asked.

"Theta. He's a friend. He's been texting me slowly about what to do. They're too far apart for Nikita to get to his mind. At least, I think he is."

Understanding dawning on her face, Arya nodded. "You don't know your own plan. And she can't read what you don't know."

Nodding, Katife recited, "So far, he wanted me to tell Dakota to use Milton's Twilight on Soul and text him when it's done. Which Dakota said will take another day or two. I need to forget right now, or this whole thing will go up in smoke."

Katife swallowed, desperately looking for something

295

she could use on her memories. She reached for her psychology classes, recalling all the lessons about memory. It was far from her best subject, and there was so much she'd already forgotten. It seemed ironic to forget how to forget. There were models describing how things moved in the brain and became a part of long-term memory. Models that said memories needed time to consolidate. *And if that was disrupted . . .*

"You can't use electricity, can you?" Shocked and taken aback, Arya shook her head profusely. "I need something . . ." Katife said, looking around the yard. The fire, the chairs, the walls. And Arya. "I have it," She declared.

"What?" Arya begged, leaning forward in anticipation.

"I need you to choke me. If I pass out, I might forget."

"Wait, wha . . ."

Katife was on her knees before her, tears in her eyes. "If I black out, that memory might be disturbed. But I can't do it alone. My survival instincts will kick in."

Arya pulled her hands away, her voice turning shrill for the first time. "Are you insane?"

Katife shook her head, shuffling forward and taking back her hand. "Do you have a better idea?"

Pulling away, Arya scrambled back. "I'll think of something. Just give me a sec." Raising to her feet, she paced a few metres away. "You just need to black out?"

Nodding, Katife confirmed, "I think so."

"Then just . . . wait here."

Pushing herself up and to her feet, Arya skirted around Katife and sprinted inside. She looked around, trying to see or hear anything that may help. A minute later, she scrambled down the stairs, two bottles gripped between her fingers with glasses in her other hand. "Are you a lightweight or a heavyweight?"

Closer now, Katife could see the label on the bottles. One liquid was clear, and the other a little brown. "I can hold my liquor."

Folding onto her knees, Arya held the two bottles on her thighs, the glasses on the grass. "Then pick your poison. You've got a lot of drinking to do."

Raided from the cabinet, Arya held tequila in her left hand, vodka in her right. Sighing, Katife rolled her head back. "I am so stupid."

"Yes, absolutely. But you were panicked, I get it."

Sighing a second time, Katife whispered, "I've never been blackout drunk before."

"They say there's a first time for everything. So, what's it going to be?"

Looking between the two, she reached out with her left hand. "Tequila. I might as well enjoy this."

Taking the bottle, Arya filled the glasses, passing one to Katife. "See you in the morning."

His eyes opened as a violent shaking forced him to wake, looking into the face of Fraya. Her lips were sporting a mischievous grin. Pushing off his pillow, he rubbed his eyes. "And here I was having a lovely dream."

"Oh? I bet it was of Darcy."

Tossing back the sheets, Soul shook his head. "Actually, it was of the day we met."

Punching him in the shoulder, she smiled. "Aren't you too young to be reminiscing already?"

It seemed impossible that the young girl who had given him his name had grown so tall, almost as tall as him. Her hair had darkened over time, her voice wasn't as shrill, and she was much, much more beautiful.

Nothing could have prepared him for how life changing it would be to cross that river eleven years ago. Waking every morning for school, meeting friends. Being adopted into Harold's family. And even if Fraya always claimed it was a small town on the edge of the world, it was bigger than anything he'd ever known.

Now even that was in the past, as they woke in a bustling town. Instead of a mountain, it was a plain. Instead of white snow, it was orange sand and dirt. Instead of buildings so far apart you couldn't see your neighbour, the buildings were physically adjoined. And stranger still, according to the world map, he'd barely moved.

It was called the Spanish Wall, named after the empire it had carved across, built to stop the flowing tide of monsters. Its population looked a little different. Darker from the sun, and with different animal traits. Yatrice. He'd only ever heard about them in class.

And then there was the wall. Its shadow engulfed the hut they stood under. Mounted armaments and defences lined its top. It was slowly being torn down and replaced. Once a wooden barrier, it was replaced by stone. But now it too was in the process of being traded for something taller, wider, and stronger. It even looked better, with a sheer white face made of steel, cement, and a whole lot more. Bridging the gap where the old was down but the new was not yet up, a rotating roster of soldiers kept watch, a bubble defending against the monsters. The sounds of rifle fire rocked every few hours.

The crowd of volunteers could not compete with those they aimed to help. He still wasn't sure where she had come to the idea, but once the notion of volunteering at the starving fringe got in Fraya's head, there was no stopping it. Before long he was standing in the slight shade of their little stand, faced with a long line of Yatrice. The closest one was a woman he was sure was young, but her tangled hair and frayed clothing that reminded him of up the mountain made her look much older. Soul passed her a bowl and she shuffled down the line, just one person in a long queue for the pittance of food they could supply. Behind the tables, sweating over the steaming pots, Fraya helped prepare the soup.

It was not until the line was gone, and even then, not until the pots and bowls were all cleaned that he, Fraya, and the forty-four other volunteers were given a moment of respite. Between the sun, the steam, and radiated body heat, sweat engulfed his skin. It was uncomfortable just to move, and he couldn't wait to strip his clothes off and enjoy a shower.

When the sun faded and he returned to his bunk, he lay on his stomach to write a letter detailing everything to Darcy. They'd met during their final years of school, and there was nothing more alluring about going back than seeing her again.

When the next day rose, he followed Fraya onto an elevator up the new wall. Hand in hand, they looked over to the scorched earth beyond. "Isn't it breathtaking?" she asked.

He couldn't help but nod. "It's like being on the edge of the world."

All he would need to do was turn around to see people gathered in swarms, low buildings stretching far out, and the roads that transported cars along. There was the main road, the only one that extended beyond the streets and into the empty space behind. And yet before him, on the other side of the wall, was empty land as far as he could see. Rolling sand dunes, no trees, no water, no buildings, no people. Nothing but the throngs of darkened creatures milling around. Sometimes, when they had been adventurous, he'd seen them through the gap in the wall. He'd never realised how many they were, and the only thing that kept them out was a wall and the soldiers guarding it. It wasn't hard to see from there, to be given perspective of what he was doing, and to know that there was merit to it, to providing even a little to the starving fringe.

He glanced to the girl beside him, the one he'd come to call his cousin. He couldn't help but understand, seeing all those creatures, the fear her mother had had. How on the morning of their flight she had pulled him aside, showing to him a small wooden box of darkened oak. "We bought this from the black markets when we fled here," she explained. "It cost more than our house."

"Well, it is certainly a very nice box," he said with a smile. She did not reciprocate it. "Look, Helena. Fraya is like a sister to me. You know I will never let anything happen to her."

"Not intentionally. But to go to the fringe . . . Oh, if only I raised a daughter with more notion of her own situation." Pausing, she looked back to him. "Soul, you don't know what the world is like, and the fringes are unlike anything else even if you had."

"Hey, I've been to Harverdale."

"That's one town over. Those places are something else entirely. Dangerous, poor, tension in the air. I need you to promise me something should the worst happen." Unlatching the case, she opened the box for him. All that was inside was a small leaf-shaped brooch with golden trim.

"You want me to wear this?"

"God no. It's a deicide arm, just like your axe. Wearing them both would kill you. But it is highly valuable. Now, if something should happen and the hunters get to her, I need you to trade this for my daughter's safety."

"Helena, nothing's going to happen. I swear."

She shook her head. "You're a good boy, but the rest of the world isn't like here. At the fringe, you'll understand that faster than you realise. And the hunters won't have forgotten her. I need you to promise me."

He rolled his eyes but took Helena's hand. "I would trade my own arm to protect her. My leg too. Trust me. I will not let anything happen to her."

With a faint smile, he banished the memory from his mind, returning down the elevator for another day of sweat.

What a view, what a world. How fantastic it is to be alive.

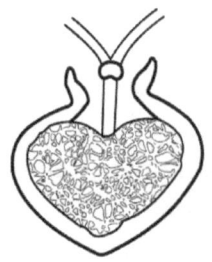

Arya has to go.

She was a wildcard, the unknown; needing her gone was obvious. With Katife out cold, her thoughts were near nonexistent; Nikita couldn't even see what had happened last night. Worse, there was something in the way Arya's eyes darted anywhere but at her, hinting that something had happened. And she didn't know what.

Theta and Rebecca were the first obstacles. Smart people always were. She could erase Theta's memories, but sooner or later he would reason out that something was wrong. And Rebecca was a danger in and of herself, with a power that would let her know too much if only she looked at the right times. But Theta had gotten himself out of the way, and Dakota actually gave her *permission* to erase all of Rebecca's memories. Photos of him would have been left in her house, but by the time she pieced everything together, Nikita knew she would be long gone. But Arya was different.

She was still with them. She was immune. And she had that look in her eye.

Sitting on a desk beside her, the Milton's Twilight brewed. All it needed now was time to set. It was in a large jar of some technical description, waiting on the study desk on the second floor. It would work on mages. But Soul wasn't a mage, or at least, Arya didn't think so, and her logic was sound. In her life, she had never heard of a deicide arm's user taking Milton's Twilight.

Finger pressing into the jar, she clamped on her lip as she watched the liquid move. *If this doesn't work, Dakota will have to fight. Which means no deals. Not a bad option.*

As she removed her finger, the jar settled back flat. She knew she couldn't spill it. It was too useful against Soul, and against Dakota if it came to it. Which narrowed her down to one option. It seemed impossible to get rid of a girl immune to her power. But there was a way; Dakota told her how to do it. She just needed a reason. And there was a reason so obvious it was almost a joke. She saw it every day in Dakota's mind. It just needed a little adjustment.

Through the window, she watched the snake extend from Dakota's sleeve and set into the methodical rhythm of sinking its teeth into the closest tree, heating up the chemical bonds to rearrange its form, and adding it as stone to the top of the wall. Molecular alchemy—the power to utilise equivalent exchange of atoms to turn one thing into another. Most people with that sort of power stopped at the elements, needing steel to create steel. Or, if they were smart enough, iron and carbon and whatever else steel was made of in the right amounts. But Dakota went down to the atoms, adding a whole new dimension of freedom, if he knew his chemistry enough to get it right.

It took hours, using enough of his mana to make sweat pour from his forehead. What had only two days earlier been a house in the woods had now started to look like a full-blown castle. The moment he was done, back at the front of the house, he was leaning against his new wall, unable to stand.

The others were downstairs, unaware where she was. Which made it the perfect time to give it a go. Exiting outside and stepping into the sun, she traced the wall to where he sat, collapsed against it. "You alright?"

He turned to her with only his neck moving. "Yeah. Just drained."

Nodding, she sat beside him. "So, all that's left to prepare are the mines?"

He nodded, barely. "There's also the Milton's Twilight. That should be ready tonight."

She smiled, running her hand along his face. Those bandages needed changing, that was for sure. "Which means there's nothing more for you to do right now."

Shrugging, he breathed, "I guess." Smiling to herself, Nikita pushed up on her left side, turning over so she was kneeling over him. "What . . ."

Before he got a chance to finish, she raised a finger to his mouth. She spoke without words. *I think you've earned a rest.* Leaning forward, she pressed her lips to his. She closed her eyes, feeling his mouth. He wasn't kissing her back. Not yet. He was shocked; that was ringing loud in her mind. But it was more than that. She felt him rejecting her, yearning for someone else. With a telepathic nudge, all those thoughts washed away.

It felt good once he was willing to go all the way. It

had been a long time since she'd last been kissed, let alone all the rest. But with him, it didn't feel as good. Implanting the thoughts she'd kept of others into his minds, she suddenly felt her pleasure increase.

It was basic, and obvious, and easy. The more contact she had, the better her telepathy worked. And there was no way to have more contact than she had right there, providing her access to the deepest recesses of his mind. It made it so easy to reach in and pluck out those feelings he had for the others, keeping his attention solely on her. She had to keep Allison, but she didn't matter anymore anyway. Next, she removed his idea about bargaining. And then, she added something for herself, something for a bit of fun. *Don't trust Katife.* With that much contact, her tendrils so deep, she guessed those changes might even be permanent.

Soul will be easy. She finished and stood up. Too tired to move, Dakota was left behind to watch as she smoothed her shirt and pulled up her skirt. She made for the garage. She knew Soul was in Inngey; she'd been monitoring the minds of the train station staff. It wouldn't take long to find him, but there was another mind she needed to reach, one that was much further away. And she needed to make the changes without a shred of contact; she wrote off more than an hour to get it all done.

Settling into the passenger seat of the car and lying it back, she closed her eyes and got to work. Her mind escaped her body, reaching the different consciousnesses around, connecting from mind to mind until finally she was so far away, she couldn't even feel her housemates. By the time she was done, her shirt was stained with her own blood, leaking from her nose.

There was a tissue box in the car. A small one. Half empty. By the time the bleeding had stopped, the box was done. Stripping off her blouse, she left it there in the corner of the garage.

Dakota walked past, making her realise how long she'd spent under. He carried wooden boxes under his arm, his duffle bag swinging from his hand. Katife scurried behind carrying a watering can they'd found. Sparing a quick moment, she saw not a peek from last night, the girl's memories fading sometime over dinner.

Neither saw her. They should have, but she made their minds go right past her, the opposite of her projections. She found her own bag by the foot of the couch. She had another T-shirt ready near the top. They all looked the same, plain white with a deep V-neck. Plain cotton. A style easy enough to find anywhere, blank enough to project whatever she needed. It showed off her pendant nicely, framed on her neck.

As she slipped it on, she saw Arya outside helping Dakota set up. She heard him explain what they were doing as he dug the hole and Arya nestled the wooden box into its place. "This is caesium?"

From his bag he took a glass cube containing a dark sloshing liquid, placed it inside the box, and nodded to Katife. With her watering can, she poured it in. "Yeah. It's the most reactive alkali I know how to create."

"Don't those things explode with air?"

"Hydrogen. Which, for the real reactive ones, means yes. This one though? It will just take some water." With the box filled, Dakota poured in a cup of Milton's Twilight and fitted on a lid, leaving just a small, square hole cut into the centre.

They moved to the next one, leaving a wooden

spoke beside the pit of the same width as hole. She knew the tactic. That short wooden stick would operate as a pressure plate or detonator, buried by the thinnest layer of dirt so that when it was stepped on, it would crack the caesium's glass underneath and expose it to the water. For now, they left it all open, not bothering to cover it back with dirt. That would come later when the last mine was buried.

"And this will be enough to stop him?" Through the two open minds, she could hear Arya's concern.

He shrugged, placing in the second box. "Either it stops him or it slows him down. The Milton's Twilight will also spray into the air and get into him. But, at absolute worst, it's an alarm."

She left the window, retreating deeper inside. She'd already seen the mines work in the history of Dakota's mind. When everything went perfectly, they could kill. But more than anything they maimed, which, with all thoughts of bargaining plucked from his mind, would mean Soul's imminent death. They would cover the entrance funnel, leaving no room for escape. And best of all, they were hidden, bypassing the frustration of his power. One by one, everything was falling into place, and she could taste the oncoming end of her yearlong nightmare.

The sun had passed noon, now falling back towards the horizon. The trio were still outside. She supposed there were a lot of holes to dig, and it would only get harder as Arya continued to tire. She looked to see how many were left. She counted sixteen open pits of the planned twenty-five. But something was wrong. Katife was taking a call, and the others had stopped to listen. The detonator spokes weren't fitted into place, nor were the mines buried.

From the window, she watched. It didn't last long. The call ended, and Katife lowered her scroll. She knew what had been said, knew who was on the other line.

"That was Rebecca."

She didn't even need to say it. Dakota was a Yatrice, his hearing better than any of theirs. He'd heard the call himself. He fell to his knees even without Katife's words. His eyes were wide as Katife whispered, "I'm so sorry, Dakota."

"What?" Arya asked, clueless.

Eyes dropping, Katife explained in four slow, simple words. "Allison . . . she didn't make it."

"I can fix her. If I go back now, I might be able to…"

Katife tried getting closer to kneel down before him. "It's too late, Dakota. She's gone."

The words choked in his throat, making it difficult to speak. "You don't know that. I can save her. I just need to . . ."

She shook her head, the tips of her hair whipping his neck. "You think you can get to Salbador in time? It's a two-hour trip, even if there was time."

His chest heaving, his voice grew louder. "I have to try."

"It's too late, Dakota." Her voice became as small as a mouse as she added, "She's already dead."

"She can't be! I need her."

In a voice like aluminium—strong but with a hint of give—Arya said, "If it were in your power, you already would have done so. There is nothing more you can do."

He saw Nikita looking at him through the window. She had an expression on her face he couldn't quite work out. He heard her voice, those soft, sweet words telling him it would be all right. A part of his brain recognised how unnatural it was, like an injection spreading something cool into his blood. Dulling his mind, slowing his breathing. "I need to be alone." Pushing himself up, he stumbled away. Away from the mines they were planting, away from the people he was supposed to be protecting, away from Nikita's lull, away from everything.

Finding the path they spied on their first day, he was carried along to he knew not where. All he knew was that it was well-worn by countless footsteps stamping the grass right out. It was taking him away, and that was enough.

Breathing was becoming harder. It was partially the exhaustion, but he knew the real reason was something else. He kept going until his legs threatened to give out. It was a long path, and all signs of the house had vanished. The sky was the only thing telling him how long he had been walking when he mounted a small hill, right before arriving at a cliff. There was a marking there, some sort of memorial stone. He went beyond it, right to the rocky outcrop. It rose at a slight angle, extending over the edge of the cliff. He took it to the end, a natural balcony over thin air.

The snake slithered from his sleeve, making three full loops around him. The moment its tail left his touch, it became something less physical, something pure ethereal. With his control severed, it became like a pet. The snake lowered its head, coming as close to sleep as a snake can. Comfort was impossible, not with how the rock protruded into him as he sat right before the drop.

He watched the clouds slowly drifting across the sky for a long while. His eyes traced one that he was sure looked like a knife as its form distorted and pierced the horizon. He turned away, tearing his wrist and removing the wooden piece from its hiding place. Dropping its wrapping over the edge, he flicked the wood into his palm and shot it forward as fast as he could, sending it spinning and flicking as it fell, gliding into the canopy below. He felt nothing as it left his grip forever. Below, maybe someone someday would find it, question why treated wood was so far in a forest. And if they did, they'd likely shrug their shoulders and move on.

He had to pull his pant leg all the way up, exposing his upper thigh. The tape there was different to the one on his arm, coloured to blend in with his very skin. In all his life no one had ever questioned it, never even considered something he went through so much effort to hide was just a fake. He started unwrapping the tape. The first layer was easy; it only stuck to itself. But the next three made him wonder what was wrong with people who voluntarily chose to habitually wax. He had to grit his teeth until finally the coin was exposed, stuck to the inside. It came off easy enough at his touch. The snake's eyes became fixed.

The years in hiding hadn't changed it one bit. All the scratches and nicks were still there. The side with the flower, its pedals fragmented and flying for the edge. An embossed outline of white. The raised edge had been scratched so much at points it was almost flush. Otherwise, it was still mint fresh, at least on that side. Then he flipped it over to the purple side, which housed the icon tattooed onto Allison's back. It was coloured in black, with the purple pieces that surrounded it filled in. It was the image described often as a twisted tree, perfectly symmetrical as it split apart and came back together into an incomplete circle. In the centre, the eye looked out at him. This side was scarred to high heaven, at some points the colouring almost gone. She had crafted the image for herself, unlike him. Sydney commissioned his from one of her friends, back in a time when he hadn't known Allison.

He flicked the coin, and as it spun, the eye looked as if it were enclosed by the flower. The broken petals seemed to fly, a desperate escape, but when it stopped, they had made it no further.

Scribbled onto the border were the symbols, similar to the wood, but different in all the important ways. They were undamaged. They were drawn after. "That's the thing from the hospital."

He'd heard her footsteps for a long time, listening to them slowly getting closer. He could tell she was trying to be quiet. He just kept looking at his coin and the sky beyond. "What are you doing here?"

"You've been gone a while. I was getting worried." Katife stepped closer, almost up to the snake "I know that tree. Allison had it on her shoulder, but . . . I don't think I've ever seen that flower before. Was it Sydney's?"

His eyes falling closed, he let out a breath and placed it down right in front of the snake. Its eyes were glued on her as she raised the coin between her fingers, holding it closer to her eye. Dakota was at the ready, so that in a single moment he could snatch it from her hand. He half-turned to watch her, to see her expression. It was so different from the way he looked at that coin. She was curious, not regretful. She knelt down beside and behind him, divided only by his familiar. Her features were soft. No smile, no laugh, her features not twisted in tears or sadness. *It was just . . . calm.*

She didn't return his stare. People always told him

313

how beautiful his eyes were. Such was a hollow sentiment, the greed drawn from the tainted hearts of men. Hers were a milky brown that he could just keep looking into, like they went on forever. They were so soft and inviting. He had to drag his gaze away, and clenching his fist, he focused on that pain. There was something about her, something he couldn't quite work out, but his mind was screaming at him not to let his attention fade, not to let her do something.

"So what is it? I take it you can't buy anything with it."

As he held out a hand, she gave it back without question. "That's none of your business. Just know it belongs to me."

She swallowed, clearly wanting to say something. But whatever it was, she pushed it down, nodding instead with incredible consideration. "Okay. I won't ask then."

Closing the coin back into his palm, he looked towards the horizon. Her voice was so very soft, calm, and gentle. "What happened was not your fault."

Frowning, he recalled another's words, so similar, but days older. "What's about to happen," he murmured. "That bird-like woman said the same thing. But how could she know . . ."

Trying to pin her warning down, his thoughts were disrupted when Katife repeated, "Dakota, it wasn't your fault. You told her not to go, remember?"

Her arms reached for him, making him jolt away, but the cliff's edge gave him nowhere to turn as her arms embraced him. Somehow, it felt like she was the only thing holding him together. So much so he stopped ruminating on the mystery woman.

"It is. I should have stopped her. I should have been better. Or at the very least, it should have been me."

Even feeling it coming, he couldn't bring himself to stop her hand as it flew to his face in an open palm slap. His cheek stung. When he turned back to her, she slapped him again. "Don't you dare talk like that. Don't you bloody dare." Her eyes watered again and her voice lost its clarity. "Why can't you realise that there are people who still love you?"

Those words hit him harder than her hand had, going right for his heart in a way that made it skip and drop and beat faster all at the same time. "Someone like you?"

At that she turned away. "Rebecca. You know she will do anything for you."

"She doesn't even know I exist."

"She'll remember. I know she will. However long it takes. Her love is stronger than some spell."

The words caught, holding in his chest, and making him stop. Rebecca said it all the time, but he always just dismissed it as words. Things she said because she was supposed to, not because she meant them. *And yet* . . .

"I came here to be alone."

Wiping her eyes with her wrist, she said, "I'm not leaving you."

"Please, Katife. Just . . . let me be."

But she didn't leave, or stand, or shuffle back. She looked to the coin and took a long breath. "Tell me about the flower. Then I'll go. If Allison's tattoo is on one side, it must be important."

Frozen in place, his mind took its time considering her words. His sense of time was gone, and he had no clue how long it had been. Finally, he nodded, undoing his top buttons enough to loosen his collar and lower his shirt behind his back. The air pressed in on the newly

315

exposed skin. Just as Allison's shoulder housed an image of her twisted tree, his held the fragmenting flower.

He felt her cool fingers, so gentle and tender, running along the ink. "We were only numbers in Koros. We didn't have names. But then someone came to an idea. Those who were still alive all chose an image, something to represent us. We all have one in that same place."

Her fingers traced every line of every petal. It took a long time, and she wasn't moving fast. "Why the flower?" she asked.

"It's a long story. One I don't want to talk about."

Eventually, she pulled away. The moment her skin left his, it felt like something was missing. She got back on her feet, the vibrations echoing in the rocks. "Don't take too long, okay?" He didn't say a word.

He knew he wasn't as good as she was, that she would be looking at him and seeing so much more. All he could tell was that she was sad, suffering, in pain. With every step, she faded a little more. He didn't look after her. The moment she was back on the track and out of view, he lay on the ground and looked to the sky. She had been right, and she had been wrong. It felt appropriate, almost, that two twins raised to be killers would die protecting someone else, like his life would get just a little bit of redemption in the end. Like it all would have been for something, that it would have done something. But it meant losing more than he even had. It would mean losing her. The worst part was, with his heart such a mess, he didn't even know who *her* meant anymore. Allison, Nikita, Arya. There was a part of him convinced it meant Katife, but something deep in his mind was insisting she couldn't be, because she couldn't be trusted. But even if he couldn't decipher who it was, it didn't change that losing her would be something so horrible that in no version of an afterlife would he be capable of holding himself together. He could only hope for an absolute end, and that was a risk he couldn't take, not when dealing with eternity.

Finally, the sun kissed the horizon. He'd seen it the last night, that things would get dark quickly. He stood up. Holding the coin, he commanded the snake, making it reach into the ground and pull forth the stone. Bit by bit, it grew until a replica of Allison's symbol was built onto the outcrop. He couldn't count how many he had made in a field outside those monastery walls. One for each of his fallen siblings. Their name, and their grave. He couldn't make the eye, but at that time, right there, the sun was in the perfect spot to make it for him. "I'm sorry, Allison. I wish I could have done more. I wish . . ." His eyes closed. He watched for a moment before finally turning back.

He stopped at the top of the mound, focusing on the thing he had seen on his arrival: a gravestone, pure and simple. Someone who had died a long while ago and had only lived a short time. The owner's daughter, he guessed. *A companion for whatever comes next.*

With slow and easy steps, he left the mound, returning to the trail. He could see why the owner had chosen that spot. It was a nice place, and an easy path. But not too short. A path he had walked many times. With the sun lowered, there was less light in the forest. Enough to see, but not enough to last much longer. He took it slowly.

There was a sound like a roar, like a dinosaur had come back to life just to scream in his ears. Not just one but a horde. The sound of his makeshift bombs, the caesium exposed to water, over and over again.

The final summer sun set forever. Their final week at the Spanish fringe began. The wall repairs moved fast. Moving like a Mexican wave, the old was torn away and a new was built in its place. In that time, his hair had grown long again, and Fraya's skin had become tanned, except for her hands, which stayed inside two layers of the world's thinnest gloves, all to ensure her curse never got revealed. It seemed impossible that her ability to change the colour of the things she touched would put anyone in any danger, and yet he never forgot the fear in her mother's eyes.

They were back in the hall, eating the little they spared for themselves. "Hey, did any of you hear about that orphanage down in Emnalor?"

Considering the map and how little he had moved, Emnalor was so far he could barely fathom it. It was the middle of three countries on the southern continent, with a fringe all of its own. According to maps, the entire western half had become a scorched earth infested with monsters. No one answered, and so the person who asked continued. "Apparently there was some orphanage using the kids as child soldiers."

"Oh, God. I thought they were civilised. And in peace."

The original speaker shrugged. "I have family there. They said this was just an isolated thing. But from what I've heard, it sounds like the kids got pretty messed up. Apparently, they were starved and made to kill each other."

"Sounds horrible."

Nods of agreement swept the table, while Fraya mused, "I wonder if there's anything I can do to help them."

"You want to help killers in Emnalor?"

"You said they were kids, didn't you? I bet they were the ones being abused."

The first interjector protested, "But if they killed people . . ."

Frayer shook her head. "Child soldiers are not monsters. They're people suffering. After everything I've been given, I want to help those in need. Besides, I bet they could use some friends."

The girl was about to protest again when a sudden loud screech rippled in from outside, shouts rocking the air. They pushed back their chairs, rushing for the door. People were in a stampede, putting as much distance between themselves and the wall as possible. And chasing them down, having breached the wall's gap, was a creature from the scorched earth. It looked like a wolf, only much larger, and with an almost humanoid body. He didn't know what he was doing, but Soul ran forward, unlatching his axe for the first time since leaving home.

He wasn't even thinking, his mind only noting that the monster presented a danger to Fraya. His charge caught the beast's attention. Shots were ringing throughout the town, but none directed at the monster before him. The creature swiped, forcing him to dodge back. It tried to block his swing. As he activated the axe's power, it slipped right through the beast's arm and became solid just before cracking into its skull. Its life draining, the beast became unbalanced, toppling on top of him.

Pinned underneath, his lungs were prevented from their full expansion. Seeing the threat gone, the closest volunteers stepped out to help him, lifting it off. Fraya came up behind them, hanging a step back right until she wasn't. A hand slid around her mouth, another her waist, and in a moment, she was pulled from view.

With all his might, Soul struggled against the heavy weight but could only watch as she was dragged to a waiting car. Slipping free, he gave chase, but against the mechanical gears, he could only watch them driving further away. "Fraya!" he called after her, and the others stopped to look, never realising what had happened.

Soul didn't stop. With only one road out of the fringe, he cut through the backstreets, twisting through the dilapidated buildings until he burst from the city. He sprinted for the road. The car was faster, but traffic and twisted lanes were enough for him to get there first. Skidding to a stop in the centre of the road, he faced the oncoming car.

After months spent in the fringe, months he had kept his promise to Helena, he wouldn't let that go now.

The car kept coming, and he adjusted the axe in his grip. Just before it would hit, he jumped feet first through the windscreen. The glass shattered as he half-entered the car. He fought for the wheel but that left him open to the passenger, who yanked his long hair. Soul thrashed wildly until he was stopped not by force but with words. "Stop struggling or we'll shoot the girl."

Turning as much as he could, he saw the man holding him was indeed using his other hand to hold a gun pointed into the back seat, where Fraya lay unconscious.

Swallowing hard, he did the only thing he could think of. He stopped struggling and instead reached with one hand behind him for the door, and with his other for the release to the man's seat belt. Kicking with all his might against the driver, he pushed the man out. But his grip held strong, tearing Soul along with him.

Rolling over the asphalt, the world kept spinning. The other man didn't get up, having taken the brunt of the fall. Lying on the road, he could only watch as Fraya was stolen away.

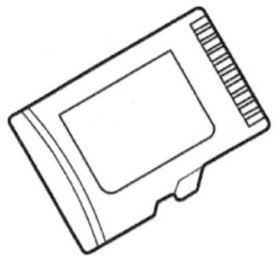

In the growing dark, it was like a whole different forest. Seeing the tall walls, Katife wondered if their foe would be able to climb them. But when she ran her palm along the surface, it was smooth, lacking any handhold. Veering through the entrance, she stepped around the exposed mines.

She could feel Nikita's thoughts leaking out even before she saw the girl leaning against the inner wall. "How was he?"

Letting out a breath, Katife said, "He'll survive. I need to talk with Arya real quick."

Her face dropping, Nikita looked away. "Arya . . . left."

From her muscles to her heart, Katife froze. "What do you mean she left?"

Nikita shrugged. "She said she wanted to see her family and that Temple would keep her safe."

"And you just let her go?"

"I'm not her warden. If she wants to leave it to Temple, who am I to demand otherwise?"

Shaking her head, Katife swore. "But Soul might already be here. She could be walking straight into him."

"Arya's a big girl. She knows the risks."

Shaking her head, Katife bit her lip. "How long ago did she leave? We might be able to catch up if we take the car."

Nikita shrugged. "Taxi picked her up about half an hour ago."

Katife cursed, stepping forward again and into the house. She took the stairs and entered the room they had shared until so recently. It was an absolute mess, worse than when she left. "What were you thinking?"

There was something painful in seeing the clothes she picked for Arya left out on the bed. Pushing the thought aside, she dragged her bag onto the bed and began packing. Then she frowned.

A pair of her own jeans were folded over her pillow, something she knew she had not done. Under her breath, she muttered, "Why are you folded when everything else is in disarray?" She shook the jeans, looking underneath. There was nothing. But she felt an extra weight somewhere. Turning the pants over, she saw a slight bulge in the back pocket, which concealed a small piece of wood. It was a jagged outcrop, like it had been torn from the walls and scratched. Its scars ran deep, made by more than just a fingernail. A part of her wanted to smile at the ingenuity of it, but more than anything she wanted to frown and shout in frustration. *he stole my sister.*

Inhaling her breath, ready to shout out, she stopped at the final moment. There was a reason. Why was it hidden and not just a message she'd given to Nikita. Sliding her thumb down, she saw a single letter it had hidden: *S*.

That one letter changed more than just a word, but the entire meaning. *She stole my sister.*

Swallowing involuntarily, she immediately opened up her scroll, sending a text all the way to Salbador. She was short and precise with her words. She didn't let her mind linger, instead focusing on the first thing to come to mind. The clothes made her think of packing. Setting to it, she waited with bated breath for his response.

When her notification sounded, its echoes hadn't even faded before it was in her hands so she could see his answer. Instead, she got a question.

~Is the milton's twilight rdy?~

With some already poured into Dakota's bombs, she didn't even need to think of the answer.

~Yes~

Theta wasted no time responding.

~Then here's what you're going to do~

Not knowing why, she descended into the garage and unlocked the car. He directed her next to drink a glass of water, keeping the glass in one hand and another glass in the other. No matter how she looked at it, she couldn't see the impact, puzzling it over in her mind as she did as he instructed. She could only assume keeping even her guessing was a part of the plan. Then he said to go to the study.

There was the mix of Milton's Twilight sitting ready, half its contents empty. Her hands curled around it, ready to move it. Theta's next text came, telling her to pour some into the empty glass. Leaving the used glass on the desk, she carried the drug outside, setting it down

324

outside the wall and entrenching it so it wouldn't fall.

~*Done*~ she sent for the seventh time.

His next request was for a photo of the yard. She obliged, stepping into the wall's opening. His response sent a chill down her spine as his plan became clear. It was a race now for whose power would work fastest.

Flying to the closest mine, she held the wooden detonator spoke Dakota created as a pressure pad but didn't have the time to rig up. In her other hand she held her Game Stadium Lite. Her power activated, showing her the thin red lines indicating the trajectory of all things she chose to see. It was her power; to see a trajectory—the path of a moving object through space—and alter it.

Right now she only focused on the detonator spoke. Its line showed it dropping straight to the floor. She'd curved the trajectory of camera lenses and tennis balls, but never anything as heavy as this. Using the app that appeared the day she became a mage, she used the joystick of her portable console. As it turned, so too did that red line. She didn't stop until the line curved up into the sky and eventually fell back towards earth.

It took her three minutes to set them all up, every last spoke—those pressure plate detonators— and then they all were gone.

After sending her final confirmation, Theta replied with his last instruction.

~*Get her into the field.*~

Fear suddenly erupted inside her, feeling the urgency contained in that final full stop. Katife stood right in the centre of the yard, calling loudly in both voice and mind. "Hey, Nikita!"

Eighteen seconds gone, spent waiting in the middle

of armed explosives, until Nikita stepped out onto the porch. "What?"

The positions were bad, and she was low on time. Swallowing, she took the easiest, most direct route, the one she could really get into her mind to hide the thoughts begging to rise to the surface. *In other words, to tell her.* "You stole Dakota."

In an instant, Nikita's tension disappeared, replaced with a half-closed eye, her contempt palpable as she stepped down the stairs. "Are you actually real right now?"

Swallowing again, she took an unwilling step back. "I was about to ask him. We were friends for years, and then you swooped in and stole him from me."

"I can't take you seriously right now. Katife, someone is trying to kill me, and you want to talk about boy troubles?"

For every step forward Nikita took, Katife matched it with a step back. She let the jealousy fill her mind, her petty reasonings boiling to the surface. Visions of the two of them against the wall replayed in her mind from when she had watched from the window "You didn't play fair."

Nikita gave a sly smile. "All's fair in love and war."

"Including telepathy?"

Nikita stopped, her breath catching. "You knew? That's impossible. I would have seen it."

Katife could see it on her face, proof Nikita was using telepathy as she spoke. "I bet you dismissed me this entire time as just some useless collateral friend. But after how you acted to Allison? I knew there was no way you were real."

For a long moment, Nikita did nothing. Then she started to change, giving a sweet yet far-from-innocent smile. It was self-satisfied. Nikita stepped onto the grass, and Katife backed into the entrance funnel of Dakota's walls. "His feelings for me are real. So what if I gave a little push."

"That is so effed. I can't believe you."

"You won't have to. Hell, you won't even remember wanting him in the first place."

She focused on the wall, on the distance between them. At every thought, her mind tugged at her to think back, and it was all she could do not to. "Is that all a friend is to you? Someone to manipulate to your own ends?"

Nikita's voice sounded almost like a condescending parent. "I'm doing this for you. You'll be so much happier. It'll make us..." She trailed off, and immediately Katife knew Nikita had noticed. She could only hide her thoughts for so long, and her words were practically begging Nikita to dig into her past ones. Her eyes widened, following Katife's as they both looked up and saw the wooden detonators raining back to earth. Katife dived, throwing her icon in the opposite direction.

STOP THEM NOW!

The command roared in her mind, telling her to change the trajectories. It was an unstoppable command, forcing her to reach for the console too far out of reach. She was on the ground reaching for it on Nikita's own order when all the spokes landed perfectly within their slots.

It was the wrong choice, but Theta must have known Nikita would make it. She could have run, or dived, or tried to knock a spoke off course. Instead, she relied on her mana, allowing the wood to crush the glass jars inside the boxes and expose the caesium to water.

The reaction was instant, detonating all across the yard. The entire field burst into heat and water and pressure. *Leave it to Dakota to invent a water-based grenade.*

She'd expected it to be a red and orange wave, but instead it was blue, as the water rocketed out of the pits they had dug together. Even still, the blast was strong, a frontal assault on all her senses. It made the hot day burn. Wooden rubble rained down as the porch was torn apart. She wanted to huddle into herself, making herself a small target, but Nikita's command wouldn't let her stop reaching. Her ears were ringing, and when she looked, there was only the smouldering wreck of the porch waiting for her.

The blast had treated Nikita like a ragdoll, throwing her off her feet and into the air. Finally taking her icon in hand, there was nothing left Katife could do to fulfil Nikita's telepathic command.

The girl was left lying close to the wall, with bits of wood stuck into her skin and droplets of water infused with Milton's Twilight drizzled over her. She didn't move; she just lay amongst the dirt and grass and debris, groaning incoherently. Katife had no doubt there would be broken bones and burns scattered throughout her body.

The Game Stadium was broken, the screen cracked and the system not waking up, no matter how hard she pressed the buttons. Flipping open the hatch, she pulled out her card, safe and intact. *Thank God for small mercies.*

Taking the glass she had prepared by the wall, she knelt beside Nikita. With one hand, she held her mouth open, and with the other, she poured the Milton's Twilight down Nikita's throat. Forcing her jaw shut, she didn't let go no matter how much the girl seemed desperate to choke, not until she saw the swallow.

Collapsing against the wall, Katife let out a long breath. "You can read all the minds in the world, but you really are one dumb bitch."

She'd planned to move her, to take her inside and tie her up. She thought she would have the energy. But her adrenaline had pumped as she waited for the explosion, and now it had worn off and left her exhausted. Collapsing, she prayed it would take effect before Nikita woke up. Arya claimed to know how the drug worked, and Dakota had made it, but she was not even sure the best way to administer it. For all she knew, the droplets in the mines were already doing the job.

As the sun began disappearing over the wall, she saw its last glimmer shine off Nikita's pendant. Biting her lip, she snapped it from the girl's neck, shoving it into her pocket.

"Katife! Arya! Nikita!" The voice cut through the silence that had fallen over her amidst the ringing in her ears. Dakota's voice was frantic, calling their names over and over, changing the order, growing louder.

Her voice was dry and in need of water, but it was enough to make him stop, to almost drop to his knees in what she was sure was relief. His snake was out, its head looking everywhere. It caught on the unconscious form of Nikita. "Katife? What happened? Where's Soul?"

She could only shake her head. "He's not here. Don't worry, I can explain. It's just . . . complicated."

Something in her words elicited a shadow of darkness to cloud his eyes. Before she could even process it as something she had never seen in him before, his hand was curled tight around her throat, slamming her back into the wall. "Dakota!" She screamed as her head hit the stone, leaving her in a daze.

329

His voice was low, snarling in her ears. "I knew it. I knew there was something wrong with you. You . . . you're working with him!"

Her eyes began to water as part of her still desperately tried to reason what he was saying. Her hands taking his wrist, she tried pulling it away but could do nothing against his strength. She felt faint. "Dakota, what are you doing? I'm doing this for you."

"Yeah, just like Soul wants to kill them for their own sake. I'm not falling for any more of your lies."

"When have I ever lied to you!? Dakota, please . . . I can't breathe."

Her legs kicked as her vision faded. Her shoe slammed into Dakota's gut, making him flinch and giving her a moment of respite, but not nearly enough. Eyes closing, she tried to get her leg under control long enough for one movement. *I'm so sorry.* With a sudden extension, she sent her leg out and up, right into Dakota's groin. This got a bigger reaction than the last time, enough that he took his hand off her throat. Kicking and crawling, she scrambled through the ruined yard.

It seemed impossible how quickly he recovered enough to turn around. Pushing herself to her feet, she ran, her feet catching in the piles of dirt. She got about four meters before she felt a sharp pain in her shin and fell forward. She saw his snake, its teeth pressed into her, dragging her back towards him. She couldn't fight it, couldn't stop the pain. She cried, the tears mixing with the soil, as she begged, "Dakota, please. Don't do this." He didn't listen, and when she was back at his feet, he knelt down onto her arms, pinning her in place. "Agh! I'm trying to help you, Dakota! Please."

"Shut up!" he growled, taking her throat once again

and pressing in even harder than before.

"You have to stop. Arya's in danger."

"There'll be one less danger soon."

Her own tears mixed with the dirt as it fell into her mouth. It made it hard to talk, but she didn't give up. "No! It's Nikita! She did something to Arya. You have to believe me!"

Her lungs started to burn, begging for air. He snarled into her ear, "Why on earth would I trust a word you say?"

She had time for only a few last words before her body gave out. "Because I love you."

Don't trust Katife. Three little words. They rebounded in his head, drowning everything else out. Even when she managed to spit out her last words, he could barely hear it. Lifeless as rocks, she fell to the dirt.

Nikita was still slumped by the wall. Pushing himself up, he took the first step towards her. Then, on the fourth, he stopped. Those three words disappeared from his mind so completely he couldn't even remember where they came from. Stopping midstep he turned around, seeing *his friend* lifeless in a ditch.

Five seconds wasted on shock, he stood and stared before finally, his legs kicked into action, rushing back and sliding into the dirt right up to Katife. She wasn't breathing; her heart wasn't beating. With shaking hands, he tilted back her head, putting her throat in an easy position to breathe. It didn't help. "No. No, no, please, no."

Three more seconds were wasted as tears welled in his eyes and dropped onto her. Placing his hands on her chest, he pushed down, firm and hard, enough to reach her heart. He did it again and again. She didn't respond. Moving his hands to pinch her nose, he placed his lips to hers to shove oxygen down her throat. Her chest raised, only to deflate when he moved away. He did it again, pushing against her heart and breathing through her. Every time he swapped between the two, he saw those eyes glazed open, not in judgement but sadness.

He repeated it three times, then five, then seven. On the ninth it became just movements, a possession upon him that would not let him stop.

He'd felt it himself at the beach that day when he hadn't been able to breathe. He saw what he must have looked like, only instead of water she was covered in dirt. Katife gasped at air, sucking as much in as possible. He almost didn't stop.

It took only a few moments once she had stopped chugging back oxygen before she was able to look around and know what had happened. He waited, ready for her to yell, or scream, or push him away. Instead, she cried, wrapping him in her arms. "I knew you couldn't do it. I wasn't your target."

As she cried into his shoulder, he could do nothing but hold her. It seemed like forever that they stayed there unmoving, and he did nothing to rush that time along. It came on its own, eventually, when she pulled back into the dirt. She had a doughy look on her face, the meaning of which he couldn't fathom. "I'm sorry. I'm so sorry, Katife. I can't believe I . . ."

Shaking her head, she stopped him with the sweetest smile. "Nikita. Anything else and I wouldn't forgive it, but I know that anything less wouldn't have made you do it."

"Katife, I—"

"Dakota, I know what she is. It's why I never wanted to tell you, because I knew she was too far in your head. And not through some pretty words, but through violating magic. I can forgive you. Just not her."

Pushing herself up, she rotated her gaze until it landed on Nikita. "I don't understand what happened. I had this feeling like I couldn't trust you, and then it was just . . . gone."

She was rubbing her neck. There were marks left on her skin. He couldn't look. "I gave her the Milton's Twilight. Her telepathy must have finally worn off."

Katife needed help moving, stumbling to just a step before Nikita. She looked a little different than the Nikita he remembered, enough to wonder if it was even Nikita he was looking at. Her freckles were gone, her cheekbones were lowered, and her body was a bit bigger. Her hair became more of a dirty blond, tangled and frayed, and her eyes a duller blue.

He'd rubbed his eyes, but it was clear there was no trick. All the little things that marked her projections from her "real" self were redoubled before his eyes. It was like every distinctive feature she owned just faded away. "What . . . why does she look different?" he asked.

Katife shrugged, instead giving a boot right into the girl's ribs. She was pushed heavier into the wall, finally starting to move. "Because she's a dumb bitch who wasted her mana on overkill makeup."

"But . . . why?"

"Why? Because she could. She had the mana to spare. After all, she committed the taboo. Didn't you, Nicky?"

Without thought, he rejected the possibility. He

knew she was a mage, knew she had an icon. Arya herself had said it, that Nikita couldn't have done the taboo. *Unless . . .*

Dangling between her fingers, Katife held all the proof there was. Nikita's pendant, her icon, removed from her touch. And yet he'd had to wait for the drug to strip her power. She handed it to him, and as he inspected it, something immediately became apparent. There were no sigils, no writing. It was just a pendant, not a hallowed icon. Nodding, he began to sink. He felt those memories fade, one by one. They started at the beginning, when they had first met. Then it reached Allison's last fight, but instead of fading, the memory was replaced. Allison was in the shower, and a girl with dull blue eyes walked through the door. She'd turned them into her brainwashed dolls, doing what she said and answering all her questions. And in doing that, they told her how to use her power, giving her the idea and changing the spell. That was when the headache erupted in both their minds, and when Nikita's nose first began to drip.

Beneath them, the girl was stirring. Slowly, she managed to raise herself just a little. When she finally cleared the grogginess from her eyes, she looked between the two of them. "What happened?" Katife looked to Dakota, and he to her, as if inviting the other to speak. "God, my head hurts."

Taking the invitation, Katife broke away and looked down at Nikita as she started pushing herself up. "Oh, really? How about now?" He saw it coming a second early as Katife wound back her leg to launch her boot back into the girl's ribs.

Shouting in pain, Nikita recoiled against the wall

and rubbed her ribs. "What the hell?!"

"Oh no. No, you are not 'what-the-hell'ing me.'"

"Huh?" she asked, trying to clear her head.

"That's it? That's all you have to say for yourself, you know, after lying for months?"

"Katife what . . . when did I lie to you?" Dakota saw Katife's knuckles go white as they tightened at her side. Nikita saw it too, and finally she paused. "Hey, where's my mana? What the hell did you do?"

Dropping into a squat before her, Dakota summoned his snake, letting it coil out from around his arm. "You drank some of the Milton's Twilight. You know what that means, right?"

For a few seconds, there was nothing but confusion on Nikita's face. Then that started to change, her face falling into a slate of fear. "No. You didn't."

Nikita swallowed, clamping her mouth shut. Now instead of pushing herself off the wall, she was basically trying to sink into it. "Guys, wait. Just talk to me. Tell me what you're thinking. Whatever it is I promise I can explain."

"Oh . . ." Katife said, making a show of examining under her nails. "We don't need you to explain anything. The moment that drug took effect everything became crystal clear with all your manipulations out of the way."

"What manipulations? Katife, you don't know what you're talking about." With every word there was a shrillness growing in Nikita voice, a dreading fear that had settled inside her.

"Oh, I think we do. But okay, help me out here. You used the police, like you said, and when that didn't work you went looking for someone new. Ended up setting yourself on two of Koros' children. Then you broke into their mind and made them want to help you, making us all believe we *wanted* to help you. And the reason Soul was after you? Well, it's obviously because you committed the taboo."

Fingers splayed, pushed out before her, Nikita called, "Katife, wait, you've got it all—"

He almost didn't see it. The form was bad, enough to almost split Katife's knuckles on impact. Not that it mattered. It was still enough to smash Nikita's jaw sideways, throwing her head back a little into the wall, her hand a useless defence. "I've been to a fringe. I stood on the wall and looked out over the scorched earth. I've seen firsthand the monsters that live there. But you . . . you are something else entirely. To copy my feelings for my best friend, to twist them to be all about you . . . You and Soul deserve each other."

Still reeling from the hit, Nikita struggled to clear her eyes. "Katife, no. Please, listen to me."

Shifting his weight, Dakota curved into her view, blocking it off. "Listen? Alright then. Tell me where you drew the sigils."

"Dakota, wait . . ."

"Where is it?" he roared, and she fell silent.

Nikita looked away, her eyes dropping, her shoulders slouching. He gave her a few seconds before snatching her wrist, constricting his fingers around it. "It's not your arms. Is it your stomach like Arya? Your legs? Your back, your neck, your head, your . . . Your head." He'd seen it the instant he said it, that twitch in her lip. Then when he repeated it, how she looked up to him.

"No, Dakota. Think about this. Think about what you're saying!"

With a fistful of her hair, he yanked her head until her nose was almost in the dirt between her legs. The snake slid onto the back of her head and severed the bonds of her hair, letting it drop onto the ground. She screamed and squirmed, but he only pulled her further, testing the flexibility of her torso. She finally stopped fighting, resorting instead to crying. The snake kept going, severing almost the entirety of her hair. It wasn't pretty, leaving tuffs and patches. When the strands he held were severed from her scalp, it left her head bare, the runes written dark and bold. "You really did it. Allison was right," he breathed.

"Wait, Allison knew?"

There was real surprise in Katife's voice as it rose from behind him. "She suspected it. There was a list of those who'd done the taboo. Nikita Quinn, I think it was. She guessed that may have been you. But I was too stupid to believe her."

Her features softening, Katife's hand fell onto his shoulder. His eyes closed, and as hard as it was, he gave her the slightest of smiles. "Is there anything else we want from her?"

Giving a single nod, Katife stepped in. "Yeah. Find out what she did to Arya."

"Arya? What do you mean? Where is she?"

Katife shook her head. "I don't know. She disappeared. Nikita did something to her sister, but I don't know what." Taking a long, final look at the snivelling girl, she looked away. "I'm going to get the car ready. Otherwise, I might just kill her myself."

Behind him, Katife stepped away, pulling herself onto the ruined porch and through the now missing door. Before him, Nikita was forcing back sobs, barely able to speak. "You were supposed to help me. He promised."

He frowned as he looked at the girl's tattooed scalp. Taking her chin tight in his fingers, he raised her head until she was looking right into his eyes. "He?" Like a blizzard had formed inside her, Nikita froze, barely even breathing. "Who promised?" She said nothing, trying to look away but unable to move. "Sensei. It was him, wasn't it?"

She must have heard the ice in his voice, something so harsh she snapped from clamping her mouth shut to blurting it all out. "Please, I promise I didn't know who he was. I didn't know what he was thinking. I couldn't read his mind. He just said to go down to the ring and I would see what he meant. Please, Dakota. I didn't know, I swear."

Keeping his gaze on her, he indicated to his snake. It started moving, wrapping its way further and further up her arm as it twisted in a tight circle right up to her shoulder. It stole her attention as she tried to pull away, but the snake just constricted harder to hold her in place. "I can't believe after all this, he was involved. But, you know, I think I can forgive him just this once. He didn't make you do it, now did he?" Her mouth gaped open, but no words came out. Forcing his mouth smooth, he stopped holding her so tightly to pat her head gently. "Nikita, be a good girl now and tell me where you hid Arya."

Lip twitching, she spat on his face, the saliva landing on the bandages over his nose and dripping slowly. For a moment, he held her gaze, staring back. Then he stopped, twisting his neck until he was focused on the snake wrapped tightly from her wrist to shoulder. "Crush."

Constricting fast and tight, the sounds of snapping

bone became machine-gun fire. Her scream was louder still. He didn't even wait for it to die to ask again— calmly, evenly, and not bothering to hide his hostility. "Where. Is. Arya?"

In the entire dictionary, he wasn't sure there was a word for what she did next. It was a part laugh, part scream, part cry. "I was going to tell you. That was the whole point. Trap Soul in a basement with Temple and you. Now you can go screw yourself."

Her lip twitched as she held the glare. He spoke with the same mock sincerity she always did, even if he'd never realised what it was. "Nikita, sweety, I've only broken one limb. You have four. And that's before I even start getting creative. Or, I can make the pain go away. It's your choice."

Sobbing, she said nothing at all. Taking her other hand, he didn't even need to move the snake before she screamed, "Lunar! I sent her to Lunar!"

Finally, he stopped, loosening the snake and looking down at her. "Lunar? As in Club Lunar?"

She nodded emphatically. "Yes, that Lunar."

"Why the hell would you send her there?"

"I don't know. It seemed appropriate. A nice death trap. Now fix my arm."

He didn't comply, instead asking another question. "How did you do it? I thought she was immune to you."

"Fix my arm first."

"How about I break your other?" The snake moved, showing it was no idle threat.

Shouting a curse, she held out just a second. "Agh, I sent her sister there."

He let go. "Are you serious?"

Finding the strength to resurrect her mock smile,

she asked, "Surprised? You gave me the idea. One look at your sick devotion to Allison was all I needed. Now fix my arm like you promised."

He stared hard at her. He said nothing, just thinking. She kept screaming at him to fix her, yet he didn't respond. She chose to spit again. It broke through his thoughts as he wiped his cheek. "When did I say I would fix you, even if I could?"

Standing up, Dakota began to walk away. The snake came with him, Nikita still wrapped in its body. She sounded like a banshee in the night as she was dragged over the lawn and towards the front steps. Led by her broken arm, her legs kicked as he took her right to the ruined porch. It was only then that he stopped dragging her, using the snake instead to form a chain, binding her from her broken arm to the posts underneath the house. It didn't give her the space to stand, forcing her to stay on her back.

Just as Katife had before, he pulled himself up onto the porch. He found her inside with his bags by the garage door. She stopped to look to him. "Well?"

Taking a breath, he stepped up to her to take his bag. She hesitated, their hands together on the strap. "Lunar. Looks like we're going home."

She nodded, letting go. They were left staring at each other for a moment before finally they broke apart. She took the stairs, and he followed, stashing the bag into the boot of the car. "I'm sorry. You've already done so much, and I hate to ask for more, but I don't know how to drive, so—"

Shaking her head, she gave a sad, soft smile and cut him off. "I wouldn't let you leave me even if you tried."

Stopping not just his body but his mind, he gave her

341

the truest smile of his life. "Thanks, Katife. Really."

"No problem."

For a moment, they hovered. Then she broke away, pushing a button to open the garage door. The moment it began to rise, Nikita's whimpering came back to their ears. "Just . . . give me a moment," he said, unzipping his bag and rifling through the contents. "What did you do with the rest of the Milton's Twilight?"

"Huh? Oh, it's still in the study. Why?"

"Nothing, it's just . . . Start the car. I'll be a second, and that field's a mess."

She swallowed but nodded as she keyed the ignition. Rushing back inside, he took the jar right from the study. There was some missing, and some spilt onto the table. He didn't know why, but it made him smile. He poured what was left into two separate flasks before rushing back outside. He put a stopper in one but left the other open.

Instead of making for the car, he went to the porch. "Arya's really at Lunar?"

Eyes drowned in pain, Nikita matched his gaze. "That's what I said."

Nodding, he snapped his hand forward to take her chin, forcing her mouth open. With his other hand he poured the open flask into her mouth and clamped her jaw shut. She coughed and wheezed but he didn't let go until it was all gone. Reaching into his pocket, he pulled out a jar filled with a clear red liquid. "Now, normally you'd read my mind and know what this is, but I guess this time you'll need an explanation." She said nothing, but her eyes bore into his. "I won't tell you its name. That would defeat its whole purpose. What I will say is it is going to cause you a lot of pain, and in two days, if untreated, you will die. Now, the good news is there's a

342

cure, and that you'll be in too much pain to feel your arm. Bad news? It's indistinguishable from another drug, and the wrong cure will be fatal. In other words, I'm the only person who will be able to save you. So if you want me to come back, you better hope I find Arya alive."

As he held it to her lips she pulled away at every turn, trying to avoid letting it close. She was no match for him, and within seconds he held her strong and forced it down the same as the last one. She was still spluttering as he stood up to leave.

In the growing dark, he was halfway to the car when she began shouting. "You sick son of a bitch. You think this makes you a hero? You think you're doing this for Allison? I know you're doing this for yourself, because you're a soulless, empty husk with nothing to live for. You were just using her to fill that void, and now that your beloved older sister can't do that anymore, you jumped on the first girl you found."

For a second, he froze in the middle of the yard blown apart by his own explosives. "You think I haven't known that from the start? You really are pathetic."

Without another word, he entered the car, leaving all their hard work behind, wasted, as Nikita screamed into the night.

Four hours. That was all he gave them to prepare for the trade. As the dark was invited over the land, he stepped up to the crossroads, the wall only a distant haze. His prisoner, tied to him by rope, was pushed forward into the intersection.

Helena had been right about the broach's allure. Tying the kidnapper's hands, he'd made an offer, which was met with practical begging to arrange the meeting. A simple trade: his prisoner and the broach, for Fraya.

Five people stood waiting before two cars just off the road. There was a lump in the man's pocket from where Soul had shoved the broach case in. "Hold it," a voice called from the cars. "Where's the arm?"

Soul inclined his head to the lump. "In his pocket." His hostage gave a nod of confirmation. "Where's Fraya?"

The people gathered shared a look, but the voice that spoke came from none of them, instead feeding directly into his mind. It sounded like a low rumble that teemed with bass. "Use me now."

The man smiled, turning around to the van. "Oh, she's right here."

That voice boomed so loudly that finally he relented just as the man turned back, but instead of presenting Fraya, he pulled a rifle. Soul's heart exploded, in an instant losing his grip on the rope and world alike.

There was no feeling, no sensation, no sight. He couldn't even tell if he had a body at all. It was like his soul itself was all that was left. And then, just as fast, it was gone, and he was back in his body, lying flat in the dirt, and that low voice rumbled. "Keep your eyes closed. Don't move. They think you're dead."

"What happened?" he asked, thinking the words.

"I erased your causality, as is my power. Now, you must wait and do what needs to be done."

There was no doubt the voice belonged to the arm he snuck from the box as he slipped it into the pocket. "What needs to be done?"

"You want to save your girl, don't you?"

He almost shook his head. "You cannot mean . . . killing them? That . . . is wrong."

"All I said was to do what you must to protect your girl. Whatever that means."

He swallowed, praying none of the men were watching. "They might have families."

"And Fraya doesn't?"

Right near his ears he could hear the rope being cut, and he ceased even the tiniest movement. "He had a second arm. That axe."

"Really?"

"Yeah. It's a first generation, but it's still worth

something."

With the prisoner free, there were six men around him. One walked right up to him and reached down. "Now, make your choice. Will you keep that promise, or will you let her die?"

Swallowing hard, he snapped his eyes open. *That's no choice.* The axe was only a little from his reach, and the man had not yet grabbed it. Stretching, Soul took it in hand and rolled with the motion, slicing it right into the reaching arm. A scream filled the air, but he hardly heard it. All he could sense was the next person as his axe kept going and embedded its blade into his hostage's neck. All four of the remaining men turned to him as he was already scrambling to his feet. Stealing the screaming man's pistol, he followed the guide of the voice and fired until it clicked empty. Most of the bullets hit only open air, but there were a few that struck through the men.

"Quick, use me again." A faint glow escaped his fist as he bent down for the axe again. He charged at the two men standing by the car. They shot, their bullets slamming him back. He spat blood but still managed to stumble forward, close enough to take the closest man's head as their clip ran dry. "My spell undoes in three, two, one . . ."

Just like with countless deer, he twisted, snapping the neck. While the final two fumbled with their knives, Soul sliced them both apart until he was standing alone with only the now armless man left alive. Breathing hard, he fell to his knees, his chest feeling hollow. "I just wanted to trade . . ."

That voice spoke again. "You did what you had to."

Swallowing back his bile, Soul pushed himself to his feet. Stumbling to the van, he held the handle and took a deep breath before sliding it open. There were computers and weapons inside, but no Fraya. He went for the car still missing its front window, but it too was empty. "Where is she?" he cried into the back seat.

"Look, by the dashboard. A navigator. It might be able to tell you where they went."

Swallowing, Soul wiped his tears and did as the booming voice commanded. Starting the car, he drove into the night, following the ping the navigator provided. Beginning the evening with hopes of ushering Fraya back to the safety of home, he instead disappeared into an endless quest, one that would consume his life, his heart, and his very soul.

Feeling every bump and sliding over the gravel, it was clear why the car was covered in dust. But the moment its tires met asphalt, they stuck to the road like a pig sticks to mud. Even in the rear view mirrors, those walls he'd made became lost from view. "I wanted to return the place to normal before we left."

Katife was different, her eyes glued to the road, her posture stiff. He wondered which was causing it: driving a stolen car or at speed, the calamity awaiting them, or what he had done. "He gets some nice walls; it's not too bad."

Something told him it was a joke, even if it didn't feel like it. He sat back as they entered onto the highway and the car shot ahead, faster than ever before. There was no one around to watch her speed. It felt natural, like the car was made to race that fast.

The engine purred, creating a cadence he almost managed to lose himself in, right until his scroll started buzzing. The caller ID made him frown. He almost didn't even answer, unsure how it was even possible. Then it clicked that all around the country, if not the world, Nikita's illusions would be fading away. Answering on its final ring, it opened to an image of his sister's teary face. "Dakota? What happened? Where are you?"

He swallowed, unsure how to have this conversation, how to tell her what he'd done to her. "Hey . . . Hi, Rebecca."

"Don't hey me! I just forgot I had a brother. You're going to tell me right now what the hell is going on and where you've been." Between her tone and her tears, he had no idea if she was crying or shouting.

Katife peeled her eyes from the road for a first split second, glancing at Rebecca. "I've been camping. With Katife. I needed some fresh air."

"Camping? What, Dakota? Your sister has . . ." Rebecca cut herself off as the tears came on so strong, she had no choice but to wipe them away.

Beyond any conscious control, he shook his head. "It's not like that. There was something . . . something important."

"It better have been damned well important."

Unable to meet her gaze, all he could do was close his eyes. "It was supposed to be."

He knew it wasn't his words. He could only guess it was his tone that stopped her, softening her own. "Dakota, what's been going on these past weeks?"

He shook his head. "I'm sorry, Rebecca. I didn't mean for this. I just . . . we were trying to help, but I think I may have just made everything worse." Forcing his eyes open, he saw her readying to say something. He quickly continued, knowing if she went on, he may not be able to. "I can't explain right now, but I promise I will."

Her lips were tight, her cheeks stretched. "When?"

"Tomorrow. Sunup if need be."

With gentle movements, she nodded her head, her cheeks redder than usual. "Okay. If you promise." After that she was silent for a long moment.

Lowering his gaze, he asked, "How did it happen?"

Her lip quivered. "Overnight. Without movement, and without her mana reversing it, her dystrophy accelerated, and her heart just . . .stopped."

Closing his eyes, he leant back into the seat "I'm sorry I wasn't there. I'm heading back to Isovale, and I'll . . . work it out from there."

With another slow nod, she gave the faintest of smiles. "Okay. Is there anything I can do?"

So ready to dismiss her offer, he cut himself off. "Actually, yes. Call the police, no Temple. Someone with a deicide arm is going to Club Lunar. If they can do something . . ."

She blinked. "A deicide arm? Dakota, what the hell is going on?"

"I told you, tomorrow. Right now, I just want to keep a friend safe."

In that moment, everything about Rebecca softened—her tone, her words, her eyes. And she nodded, like she really understood. "Stay safe."

Nodding, Dakota ended the call, wondering how it would even be possible to live up to her final words. For a long moment he just sat there, lingering on what he had said. The feeling it gave him, mixed with seeing Katife so determined behind the wheel, made him think of how they spoke by the cliff. "Hey, Katife?"

"Hmm?" she answered.

Swallowing, he spoke with delicate care. "That coin

you saw? It's my hallowed icon."

She nodded as if she expected it. "Why's it so damaged? Was it from a fight?"

Shaking his head, he slumped his shoulders, twisting to look into those milky eyes. "No. Or yes, in a way. I threw it out a window."

"Strange thing to do with an icon."

Behind his eyes, that old memory began to play. The memory that imbued the coin with his regret. "It made sense at the time. It was a present from Allison when we first met."

"You keep staying stuff like that. 'When you met.' You're twins. Didn't you always know each other?"

He shook his head. "Blood didn't matter in Koros. Back then we were grouped by our rankings. I didn't meet her until we were nine. By then, I realised Sensei was just using us. Because of that, I assumed she was another one of his ploys."

Katife didn't show any real emotion, no judgement on her face. Just something soft. "You thought it was a plot, so you threw it out a window?"

He looked away, his fingers curling around the coin in his pocket. "Yes. No. Because she made it. She cared, after I'd forgotten how to. I'm sure she had help, but it was still from her. And me, being an arrogant brat, told her I didn't want it. She was different back then. At first, she didn't believe me, said I was just being shy. So I . . . I threw it out a window. It's why they called me Zero. She thought that was a rank. Zero emotion, they said. Zero care for all her love and effort . . ." He spoke so slowly he wondered if she was getting whole thoughts in between his words. "And she . . . she smiled at me. She said that if

I didn't want a trinket, she'd kindle a bond through time."

"That sounds way more confident than the Alley I know."

He nodded so slightly that she didn't even notice. "She was back then. When she had nothing going for her, but went after it all anyway. I couldn't sleep after that. Even after curfew. So, I snuck down into the moat. It took me all night. I only found it at dawn really. No one knew I'd gone, but I was too tired to train properly, and so Sensei punished me."

Returning the coin to his pocket, he looked out to the horizon. "That's, ah . . . I don't know what to say," Katife said. "But I'm glad you told me. I must be one of the only people who know this is your real icon, huh?"

Closing his eyes, he lent forward onto his folded legs. "You're the first I've told."

Not taking her eyes off the road, she replied, "You mean the first outside of Koros?"

He shook his head. "No. I mean, Sydney knew since I needed her help. And Sensei probably found out. I assume Nikita knows, but otherwise, I've never told anyone."

"But you told Allison." He said nothing. "Right?"

He shifted his position. No matter how he sat, the seat was still comfortable, and he wasn't able to enjoy it. "She never knew."

She shook her head as much as she dared. "You don't keep secrets from her."

"I kept this one."

From the way she fidgeted, it was nothing but the speed of the car keeping her from gawking at him. "But you told her everything."

Swallowing hard, he lowered his eyes some more. "I didn't want her to see the damage. I'd planned to fix it, but I just didn't know how. I didn't feel right to use mana. As time went on, it just got harder. Eventually I stopped thinking of it. She never brought it up and honestly believed the wood was my real icon. She died thinking that. Thinking that the coin she'd made me was still rusting away somewhere in Koros. Thinking I'd hated the one thing she ever gave me. And that is a truth too horrible to accept."

Tears filled his eyes as that same old city skyline appeared on the horizon. Soon Katife slowed the car to a hundred kilometres as the traffic started to appear. There was no sense getting pulled over by police before they got there.

The city grew closer and closer, going from a skyline to dominating the view before them. Just as they seemed ready to enter it, they dived underground and into a tunnel. The last time he'd been in it was when Rebecca took them home from Koros. For the first time he wondered what it was like for her, having three siblings, six people she considered immediate family, and not one of them shared her pedigree. One had a common mother, two had a common father, and yet every day she greeted him and Allison with a cheerful smile, a strength of her own. And now, that ball of sunshine and judgment was the only family he had left.

"Hey, there's something that's been bugging me since Nikita's spells died," Katife said. He raised an eyebrow at her. It was stupid, her vision focused on the road, but she still knew to go on. "Seems like she used her telepathy to copy all our emotions and memories towards Allison, right? Instead of fabricating a whole new set of memories towards her, she just piggybacked off our past with

353

Allison. It would be less work for her that way, and creates a longstanding bond. Plus, it explains why I thought she was my best friend and you wanted to protect her."

"For the most part. It's also possible she simply couldn't insert a whole new person into our history without manipulating a pre-existing one. Or maybe she figured using Allison as a template would make the bonds between us stronger. But I thought I was *in* love with her, so there was something else mixed in as well." He knew where she was going, but he let her get there herself, just in case he was wrong and she saw something he hadn't.

"Really? Who?" He didn't say, and when that became clear she went on. "Then maybe that's why . . ." she began, her voice quiet.

"No. I doubt Nikita copied anyone else's mind when creating Allison's thoughts of her."

"Why?"

"It's hard to explain. Patterns, I guess."

She mulled it over. "So if the way Allison thought about Nicky was copied from her feelings towards herself . . ." She paused, waiting for his confirming nod. "Then I don't understand. Why did Allison hate her so much?"

Letting her trail off, he waited until it was clear she had no answer. "Is it not obvious?"

Bursting from the tunnel, they emerged into full night. Katife changed lanes, ready for the next off-ramp. She slowed the car, taking the tight circle into the near gridlocked city. "Then . . . Alley really hated herself?"

Nodding, he spoke slowly, taking the time to pick each word carefully. "For as long as I've known her. Sensei seemed to foster any negative emotion he could find.

354

Especially how she felt towards me. When Nikita gave us fake memories with her, she unwittingly copied all that onto herself. But for all her prying, she never looked hard enough into Allison's own memories to realise how she felt about herself, or what it would mean to create a history intertwined with them. At least, that's my guess."

Without the task of driving, Dakota had the luxury of looking straight at Katife to see how she was reacting. He saw her throat bob with a swallow. "I never knew. I mean I guessed, but never seriously."

He only nodded in silence as the traffic backed up. Minutes ticked by as they crawled through the inner city. It took eleven minutes just to pass two blocks. Frowning, Katife said, "Something's not right. City traffic's slow, but this is absurd."

Looking out the windows, he saw some pedestrians running in both directions. Buzzing down the window, he stuck his head out. "This doesn't end."

"What should we do?"

Scanning the buildings, he searched until he found it. "There's a carpark ahead. Might as well walk the rest." She nodded, waiting minutes to spy the sign. As close as it was, it still took another five minutes of stop-starting until she hit the indicator and turned in.

It would have been so easy for Dakota to jump out of the car then and there, but that would mean leaving Katife alone with a stolen vehicle. Forcing his legs not to shake, he waited until she had parked on the third floor. It was one of the types where you take a ticket and punch it out before you leave. She left that ticket on the dash and opened her door. The moment their bags were out, they closed it up again, leaving the car hundreds of kilometres from where they found it. Unsure what to do with the keys, she pocketed them.

Outside, the streets were only packed tighter. At some point, the crowd just stopped altogether, lights flashing beyond. Turning to a passing pedestrian, Katife asked what was going on. "Didn't you hear? Tooth and Claw laid siege to a nightclub."

He felt his blood run cold, saw the same happening to Katife. They both knew Club Lunar was the only one in that block. Worse, another faction had somehow become involved. "You need to go."

"I already told you we're in this together."

"Please. You can't help in there; it's too close quarters. And . . . I can't have you in danger."

"I'm not leaving you. Theta entrusted me with you."

"And he trusted me to keep you safe. Please, Katife. Think about everything we've done, down to that car. If you stay, that will all come back for you."

"He'll get it back."

"That's not the point. Please listen."

"No, you listen. I'm not leaving you."

"And I'm not going to let you throw your life away!" Despite shouting in public, the city noise and fear were so high no one even noticed. "After everything that's happened, everything I've lost, I can't risk you. Over and over, I've lost people important to me. I won't let the last good thing in my life get destroyed."

In her face, he saw something for the first time. He saw her freeze, not in anger or shock or confusion, but something much more akin to a bittersweet joy. In a quick movement, she closed the distance and wrapped him in her arms, her tears falling onto his shirt. He knew if they stayed too long, his would fall as well. "Dakota, about what I said in Inngey . . . I meant it."

He couldn't meet her gaze. He wanted to, he *ought* to. But he couldn't. "I know."

"You know?"

He gave a slow nod. "I'm a fool, but I'm not blind."

Uncertain for a second, she broke into laughing tears, resting her head against his chest. A million thoughts rushed into his head, but he couldn't think of a single word to say. All he could do was close his eyes and reciprocate her embrace. "You really are the best friend I could have ever asked for."

"And you really are the worst boy I ever could have fallen for." He laughed a little, whether in happiness or sadness he didn't know. He didn't want the moment to end. He didn't want her to pull away, didn't want to go to the police line, didn't want to find out if he was too late yet again. He just wanted to stay like that, with her, forever.

If only it were so easy.

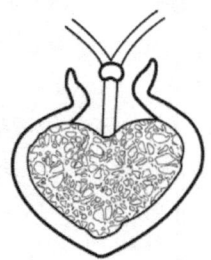

Even as the heat evaporated with the sun, she didn't stop burning. Dakota's promise felt impossible, as if she would still be alive by sunrise, let alone two days' time.

Between the pain, the heat, and being chained to the ground, she felt that old memory knocking. Something older than the twins. Seeking them was a mistake. She cursed herself for trusting them when the old man said only to use them.

Through her dim vision, she swore she could see a doorway, and framed within it, a silhouette. Not Dakota, nor Soul. Someone smaller, with longer hair. A woman. Features she once called homely—the creased forehead, hard cheeks, and tied-back hair. She stepped towards her carrying a tray of food. With her free hand, Nikita rubbed her eyes. "Mother? How can you be here?"

Unheeding of Nikita's protest, she came closer, down the stairs that hadn't been there before. The world changed whenever she wasn't looking, slowly turning the underside of the house into an old basement, the concrete floor beneath her. "No. Get away from here!" Nikita closed her eyes and turned, pulling away on instinct, forgetting her shattered arm. It didn't stop the image, and she saw her mother step even closer. She tensed, clenching every muscle. Her mother kept walking, passing right through her.

Turning where she lay, every movement sent pain down her arm. It was enough to have her near tears when she turned around and saw her mother, now kneeling before someone on the floor. Someone obstructed from view, showing only a pigtail of blond hair. Enough for her to know, even if she couldn't understand how. Ghosts that couldn't hear her scream.

Over a third of her life had passed, yet she could still feel it thicker than the sweat covering her body. No baths or pools, not even the ocean, could wash away the feeling of the pouring blood.

She was no longer chained to the house. She was free to walk and listen and hear, only she couldn't choose what. Her body moved on its own, repeating its actions from all those years ago. How she'd come home with her tutor after finally becoming a mage. He walked her to the door and collected his pay. The next time she saw him was on the news. Wearing her favourite hat, she retreated to her room, and she rewatched the last hours of her normal life. Yet this time she felt the constant dread, knowing how it would end.

She saw the mirror in the morning. The maid, a sweet old woman named Erina, sat her down and started brushing her hair. It was the first time she took her hat off since her last lesson. "Dear me, something seems wrong with your hair."

"What is it, Erina?"

"I don't know, dear. It's like there's a bubble." She'd said it with a smile, a joke, a light-hearted mystery. Then in the mirror, a young Nikita watched as the maid parted her hair, finding the patch that had been carefully cut out so that her tutor could draw the symbols there. He'd done it in such a way that the rest of her hair fell over it, making it look almost normal.

It was her final moment of peace.

Erina told her to sit still, rushing out to find her parents. They came in, and she saw in the mirror her father's horror. "What the hell is that?"

She had turned to look at her parents, their faces white with shock. "I wanted to surprise you, Daddy. Pedro made me a full mage."

Excitement, joy, happiness—none of the things she expected came. Her tutor Pedro had called her incredible, a prodigy, said her parents were sure to be proud. In that moment, she thought he had been wrong. It was only later she realised it was all a lie. Back then, all she knew was that her father was shaking his head. "What has that bastard done to my daughter?"

Her parents, adoptive though they may have been, had ensured every day felt like a dream, from her first moment with them to that one. Her peaceful days were quickly replaced with police and investigations and all other sorts, all examining the runes on her scalp. Every day they tested her mana. They kept saying she was progressing so quickly, her reserves growing at an insane rate. Every time her parents shared worried glances. Not long after, they stopped taking her to school, and her isolation began.

Isolation. What a funny thought, as if I was ever really

alone. As if I ever will be again.

The images changed, the fever dream flashing forward a few months. In some corner of her mind, she swore that if Dakota did come back, she would make him relive his worst days over and over so that he too would know her pain. But that part was small, dull, and muted.

She saw the dinner table. No maids were allowed in the house; no guests came in at all. Just her and her parents, eating in silence. The new normal. *May I please have the peas, Father?* He'd smiled to her and passed them over. "Of course, dear."

But her mother looked different, her tone sharp and harsh. "Nikita! How many times must we say no telepathy! You're going to make yourself sick."

She could only frown, not realising she had done so at all. She'd thought she'd spoken it. She hadn't even tried to use her mana. But her mouth was full, and she realised what she'd done.

Her last fragment of peace slipped away.

Her mother's thoughts began leaking into her head. Her wish for a normal child. Her disgust. She saw her memories without even trying to. "How could you say that?" It only made her scream, demanding Nikita to stay out of her mind.

It only got louder, those leaked thoughts becoming a fountain. No matter where she went in their large home, there was no escape. Soon it was no longer just her parents but her neighbours, and then their neighbours too.

Voices colliding over one another, she ran into the basement, sitting alone on the cold, concrete floor, never daring to go near the stairs leading back out. Soon she was hearing the whole street screaming in her mind.

Every thought, every argument, every passion, every show or movie they watched or music they listen to, every thought both joyful and depraved. All happening at once, crammed within her head. She heard her father work, calling and slowly becoming more and more tired. He stopped sleeping. His quest, a search for some cure, overtook his entire life. Curled into a ball with her hands to her ears, she cried every moment.

Her mother had come down the stairs with the tray of food. Nikita didn't leave her ball. The closer she got, the louder her mother's thoughts became. "You haven't eaten in days. You're going to starve yourself like this."

Her mother took the fork and knife and cut a piece of meat. But that girl, that younger girl Nikita had once been, only pressed her hands tighter into her ears and screamed, "Get away! Get away get away get away!"

Her mother didn't get away. She'd stayed, desperate to get some food into her daughter. "Oh, Nikita, my beautiful Nikita. I promise to find a cure, not matter what it takes."

She heard them all again, the thoughts of her mother. Those final thoughts as she screamed, "I said get away!"

She felt the swell inside of her, felt the full consciousness of her mother right beside her. Then it all exploded, everything inside her mind. It only took a moment for the light in her mother's eyes to fade, for her to become a blank shell with no mind at all, falling forward onto Nikita. In her fall, that knife had found a way to slit into her. It didn't matter, she was already gone. All it did was make her blood spill over Nikita as she watched in the dim light of the basement.

It wasn't like the first time. Back then she received the greatest gift imaginable. Peace, as a voice faded from her mind. Now she kept hearing it over and over.

There were no sounds left to hear. Not in her mind, not in her ears. Every single person stopped, like they had all run away.

Unfed, her stomach growling, she was forced to ascend the stairs for the first time in so very long. Her legs had become too weak to climb, and she was forced onto all fours. Her hair had grown back, becoming a knotted, tangled mess. Supporting herself against the wall, she searched for the kitchen. It was near empty, but she didn't mind. She used her hands, shovelling what was left into her mouth. When she finally felt full, she went in search of her father's voice. She started downstairs. Next, she tried the bedrooms. Finally, she approached his study. Opening his door, she could only watch in horror as her father slumped lifeless on the floor, his mind well and truly gone.

Venturing out into the street, she saw it over and over, and finally she understood where the voices had gone. Tape crossed at the distant intersection, locking her away from the outside, locking the outside from her. And littered everywhere, in the street and in their homes, were the people who had once been her neighbours, their minds empty and gone.

It was so close—the place they found their first clue and where Allison met Yifei. And now, where Arya was trapped. Just a few buildings away, and an army of police in between.

Reaching into his pockets, Dakota took stock of everything he had. Four canisters including the Milton's Twilight, Allison's last three gems, and his icon.

Held within that army was a seated crowd, presumably all the people who had fled the nightclub. Stepping right up to the tape, in front of a guarding officer, he shouted to her before she had a chance to ask him to stay back. "My friend was inside. I need to know if she made it out."

She was taken aback, eyes fixed on his face covered under filthy bandages. With a calming breath, she spoke quickly and calmly. "A lot of people are asking similar questions. But if you give a name, I can check"

Appreciating the effort, he said, "Arya. She has pink hair, glasses, and darkish skin."

The officer called to her colleague, asking him to look among the escaped hostages. It didn't take too long for him to jog back and shake his head. "I'm sorry, but the best thing you can do for her is to let us do our job." It was a nice idea, leaving it all to Temple. *If only.*

Nodding to himself, not them, he stepped back into the crowd. *One option left.* He disappeared from the intersection, using the pub on the corner to sneak past. It was something Soul wouldn't be able to do. Waiting until no one was looking, he used his snake to step through the back wall of the bathroom and into the adjoining building.

He didn't stop for the cameras. *What would even be the point anymore?* Through another wall, he reached that s-shaped alley. Somewhere in the world there was a list of unsolved cases with his fake scene upon it. He wondered if it was driving someone crazy, or if it had been swept into the dustbin along with every other unsolved murder.

His snake peeked into the final building. It was dim, but not dark. He saw a meeting room of some sort, an oak table at its centre, and a glass wall separating it from the hallway beyond. There, two people patrolled back and forth. Waiting for the right moment where neither were in view, Dakota opened the wall and rolled behind the table.

Tooth and Claw. Their uniform confirmed what the pedestrian had said. He saw their insignia, the sabre tooth forming a cross with a talon. *Not a smart design. Looks almost like it's just two spikes.* Using the full extent of his gun knowledge, he identified what they carried as a submachine gun, something fast firing and mobile.

Lying on the carpet, it would have been so easy to retract the floor and drop down into Lunar. The problem was he didn't know why they were here, and the possibility of them attacking him from behind if he went straight down was too real. There was no choice but to take care of them first.

Straining his ears, he listened for footsteps, for breaths. Six sets of lungs, give or take. And a problem. With Tooth and Claw being a militant faction of Yatrice, probability dictated at least some would have hearing as good as his. It left one choice: to hit them hard and to hit them fast. *And to use as little mana as possible.*

Sending the snake into the ceiling, it crossed into the opposite room. Using a touch of mana, he separated a section of the plaster, letting it fall to the ground and shatter. The effect was instant. "You hear that, Murph?"

"Yeah. I'll check it out."

Through the glass, he saw the first man push open a door with the nozzle of his gun. He moved one of his hands down towards his hip, where a keychain was tied to his belt. The other hung back, gun drawn and alert. The position he chose was directly in front of the glass. "See anything?"

They were his last words. As soon as his throat stopped making a sound, Dakota pulled open the door and wrapped his arm around it. Then, Dakota's other hand gripped his jaw, forcing it shut. He hadn't released that hold when he sent out his snake, leaping for the other and constricting on him just the same. Five seconds in and the two were in his control. An elbow to the head later, they both fell unconscious. Seeing them flop, he wondered how hard they really were. He guessed they were once kids who had been approached similar to what happened at the train station. Then at some point they would have traded the placards for guns. *Doesn't change what they're doing.*

He couldn't bet the others wouldn't have heard.

Using the snake to waste a touch of mana, he reshaped a fragment of the oak leg of the table into cuffs, binding their arms together. Reaching for the keychain, he closed two fingers around it. He felt the soft sensation of mana. Pulling it off the man, Dakota dropped the icon onto the ground and smashed it with his boot.

Behind him, the hallway had a t-shaped intersection. He heard nothing on the right, and someone alert on the left. Both sides had a door before the turn. Taking the one on the left, he entered into a records room of some sort, filled with the scent of settled dust. Light revealed filing cabinets and shelves holding junk stacked to the ceiling. He walked until his ears told him he was in line with the next person.

It was the same as all the walls he passed through, starting with a small peephole. This gunner was a woman, slimmer, with a tail as a clear Yatrice trait. And right where he wanted her. He steadied his breath as the snake coiled along the wall. He took in his breaths fast and hard, forcing his adrenaline to kick in. In an instant, the snake dissolved the wall, allowing him to burst through and take her just like the first. But she was not alone in the room. Hands wrapping around her, he had a second to think. Digging in his feet, Dakota backpedalled, dragging her back into the records room and undoing his spell. The wall reappeared just as bullets peppered in. Ducking immediately, he and his captive only just avoided a fatal shot.

She was younger than the others. He almost couldn't believe it. A nice face, the type that would have been pretty once, now covered in lines set from stress and hate. Holding her tight, he whispered his question into her ear. "How many of you are there?"

At first she didn't answer, instead squirming and

367

trying to break out. When it was clear he wasn't budging, she sagged in his arms. He tightened his grip, putting pressure on her neck and cutting off her air. He held it for a few seconds. "How many?" he repeated.

Clawing for oxygen she gasped, "Five. God."

He believed her. Not because she said it, but because it backed up what his ears now told him: that there were only two more left outside. "Thanks."

"Where's Murphy and Lance?"

"Out," he said, assuming they were the first two.

She cursed, loudly and repeatedly. "They were our ticket out."

His eyes narrowed, and in his arms, he turned her around to see her face. "What do you mean?"

Realising what she'd let slip out, she clamped her mouth shut. Dakota ordered his snake to do the same, only with her heel in the way. She tried not to scream, and was pretty good at it for a little while, until finally she broke. "Argh! Murph was a teleporter. He was going to get us out of here!"

"Jayda! Don't tell him anything." The voice was soft, muffled, and cautious. The member who saw her dragged away.

Dakota tilted his head. "If you have a teleporter, you should have left already. Why are you still here?" Taking her partner's advice or warning, she said nothing. She didn't need to. "Temple. They were waiting for you. They put up a barrier before you even knew what was happening." She scowled in a way that told him he was right. "Cheers." As he moved his grip into a blood choke, her eyes quickly rolled back.

Not wasting a second, he fashioned another set of handcuffs. They were barely on when she woke up in time to feel herself being dragged towards the others.

Digging into the first poison he had prepared for Soul, he stepped right up to the entrance of the room he pulled the girl from. He risked a quick peek, bullets hurtling towards him a second later. But it was enough for him to know where his opponent stood, enough to toss the container underhanded into the room and leak the chemical into the air. He heard coughing a few seconds later.

Dakota waltzed right in, holding his breath as he stepped into the haze. There was nothing lethal about the gas, but it acted fast and did its job, bringing his opponent to his knees. Teargas, little more. He used another set of cuffs and gave an elbow to his head. One left.

This one had a whole room to look down, with a gun facing the door. Worst of all, they knew what the room looked like. And as long as he didn't know what weapons or powers this person had, he couldn't just seal the exit.

Using his familiar again, he spied into the room from near the roof. There was a glass divider at the far side of the room, and beyond that the exit, a staircase, and an elevator. The lack of open windows made it clear why the police weren't doing much, but the sounds of gunfire had probably accelerated what plans they had. He released a breath, seeing only the one person. It was a bittersweet feeling. Had Arya been there, it would be tense, but soon over. Same if it had been Soul. Instead, it was a fifth member of Tooth and Claw.

The snake descended behind her, giving him a good look. She had her back to the wall, gun pointing to the only possible entrance. Sound tactical move, but not for mage combat. She was the youngest of all, about his own age. The gun looked too large in her small hands, but he knew how little it would take to tear a body apart. *If it can kill, then it can take a hostage. If it can take a hostage, it can bring a city to its knees.* It was one thing Koros had taught him: that to point a weapon is to intend to use it, and to intend violence is to invite it upon oneself. It made no difference if she was some dumb, misguided kid or a psycho looking for an excuse.

Still, he couldn't help but wonder, as the cold scales of his familiar reached her neck, why she did it. She was still so young, and in all likelihood, still had her whole life ahead. In one quick movement, the snake swung forward, wrappings its body around her throat.

She was quick to drop the gun, reaching instead to tear the snake away even as it dragged her into the air. Her feet kicked and she tried to scream, stopped by the lack of oxygen in her lungs. Her face began turning red. Returning to his own eyes, Dakota walked out in front, taking the path she had so recently been guarding. Her eyes looked down to him, going wild and wide. For a second, he thought it must have been the bandages, but the truth was simpler still. *She can't believe I'm a Yatrice. That one of* her own *could do this to her comrades.*

The snake shifted its body, giving her a straw of air to inhale. He walked right before her, just outside of the reach of her kicking legs. "Since when does Tooth and Claw work with humans?"

She tried to spit, but the constriction on her throat made it nothing more than a dribble. "Never."

The snake squeezed. "I know Soul is here. I know why he's here. I know who he wants. And there is no way you lot just happened to choose the same place on the same day. So why are you helping him, and how many of you are down there?" 370

He gave her the room to breathe right as her face started to resemble a ripe tomato. "None of us are down there. The human's all alone, just as our leader agreed."

Nodding his approval of her answer, the snake lowered her enough so her toes reached the ground. She used it as best she could, which was little more than like having an ant holding her up. "And Soul? Why are you helping him?"

She moved her mouth, ready to speak. But she didn't, instead turning away, or at least trying to. But she answered. "Our leader owed him."

A part of him wanted to know what for, but it was irrelevant. "Thanks, I guess. You can wait here while I go kill that bastard."

Her lip twitching, her face managed to somehow grow even redder. "Screw you. I hope he makes that girl suffer. You're a disgusting traitor . . ."

He didn't hear what she said, his mind filling with rage. His fist tightened as he moved his arm into a swing. It would be well aimed, busting her nose and letting her beg the police for help to stop the flow.

It didn't connect. His snake acted first. He never sent the order, never used the mana. It was a familiar, something deeply connected to his own desires, his own soul. Of all the faults Allison complained of, that was one she never understood. He hadn't either, not really. Not until he watched it sink its teeth deep into her throat, blood erupting as it tore it out. Her eyes widened and her legs kicked away the last of her life.

Not a target. The thought screamed inside his mind. *Not my real enemy.*

Not someone Sensei sent him after, not Soul who he

wanted dead for his own reasons. Just a girl—a pathetic, misguided brat, someone no longer even a threat. She was nothing, just shouting and screaming her profanities, a waste of breath. *Not a target.* But his snake had just killed her. And his snake was his familiar, his mana manifested in a lifelike form. He had just killed a girl who was not a target. He'd just killed a girl he didn't need to. He killed her for no reason at all. And a part of him couldn't believe it, couldn't comprehend it, couldn't understand why, to kill without so much as a cause. Something he'd never, ever done before.

There was always a cause.

He couldn't stop staring as her body swung limp in the centre of the room.

Not a target.

Not my enemy.

Not a threat.

The navigator led him to an airport. The flight logs took him off the continent. From there, the trail faded to nothing. A wild goose chase, time and time again. There were others he found, pursuant to the same goal. A young band of Yatrice had discovered a forward operating base, and together they stormed the barracks. They found their kidnapped member. He found another clue: documents telling him where she was.

Half a week later, Soul parked the hired car before the building in the middle of the forest. It was a surprisingly beautiful location, on the shoulder of the road. He was two months late. With both deicide arms at the ready, their voices whispering in his mind, he stepped through the front doors.

***

Wading through the pool of blood, he entered the darkly lit hallway. Glass cages spanned from floor to ceiling. Looking into each one as he passed, he held his breath until he could see who was in it. Some were empty, some had people hiding in the darkness. The seventh had the person he was looking for. Wasting fading seconds on shock, he rallied his remaining strength, arcing the axe into the glass. It didn't budge. It didn't break. "You won't do anything like that." The voice sounded even more tired than he felt as it drifted from the neighbouring cell. The only thing he could see of the speaker were her skeletal legs wrapped in bandages.

She hadn't spoken for a long time, her voice scratched and croaky in a way that almost didn't sound like speech anymore. An aged voice of someone far younger. "There has to be a way," he pleaded.

"Sure. Get the key. And press the release switch from the control room. At the same time."

Pacing, he looked between his two god-killing weapons, wondering how they might shatter the glass. Coming to an idea, he made the axe permeable and held the blade between the cell's wall, so that when it returned to solid, the glass was left with a neat slit running through. It was slow work, doing it over and over until the glass had lost so much integrity he could ram it with his shoulder, shards shattering down around him. Dropping down beside her, he reached for an embrace. "Fraya," he breathed.

The moment their skin touched she recoiled, kicking out wildly, one foot digging into his stomach. She screamed. Nothing coherent, but loud. "Fraya, it's me. Soul. I'm sorry it took so long. I'm sorry I let them take you, but I'm here now."

He tried extending his hands slowly this time. It made no difference. She kicked out again.

"You're making me jealous here that someone

would actually come for one of us."

Looking through the glass, he was offered a slightly better silhouette of Fraya's neighbour. "What did they do to her?" he demanded.

"Some new test, I'd imagine."

"What test? What are they doing here?"

She paused a moment. "Do you . . . know what we all did?"

"The taboo you mean?"

"Yeah. Well, this place is for experimenting on people like us. It always ends the same. Either they die or they break."

"I won't let that happen."

"Sorry, but she's already broken."

"You're wrong." She didn't respond.

The dim light made it hard to see, but up close he began to realise how much was wrong with Fraya. Her body was so much skinnier, with scars crossing over her pale skin. "What did they do to you?" he mused. Fraya pushed herself into the corner.

"Listen, me and her have been crammed here for a while, so maybe I talk to her. If you get me out, I'll do what I can to help."

The neighbour had crawled outside of the shadow's reach. Her hair was a long and dark mess mopping the floor. He could imagine using her face for a pirate flag. And every inch of her body was covered in bandages, making her look like she belonged in an Egyptian tomb. "Why would you help me?"

"Hello, to get out of here."

Looking her over again, he heard the voices whisper in his mind. "What's with the bandages?"

"Oh, these things? They're the reason why I'm the

only one they could never kill. You see, if my blood mixes with air, it turns into a deadly mist."

"Like a poison?"

She tried giving a shrug. "It's something called white phosphorous. It burns organic things. And it's why this cage is airtight. So, what's it going to be?"

He glanced to his cousin as she lay curled up in the corner. "I'm not leaving them a single soul."

He repeated the process, slowly shattering the wall around her, the shards scattering across the floor. "Have any shoes?" she asked. "Sorry, but if I walk over that, it may kill you."

Looking down, he saw that her feet were bare. Returning to the last room, he found someone dead on the floor, but not yet cold. He pulled off his boots and returned, setting them down before the girl, blood still clinging to their soles. They were big, wobbling on her feet with every step. The glass cracked under foot as she staggered out. He wondered how long it had been since she'd last walked. She entered Fraya's cell, her voice soft and cooing. She moved slowly, and when she was finally close enough to reach out her hand, Fraya took it. She didn't pull her up. Soul doubted she would have the strength to do so. It was an invitation, nothing more.

Hobbling to the control room, together they opened every last cage in the building.

It seemed strange, seeing just how much carnage he'd left in his wake. He hadn't even remembered there being that many people. Yet he couldn't help but not care, not after what they'd done.

Dawn was rising as they at last stepped outside. Bloody footprints traced them all the way to the hire car. Opening the back and passenger door, he let them take seats. He hadn't asked if she was coming, although he supposed the door was the offer. She took it, sliding into the passenger seat. He got behind the wheel, bringing the car to life and leaving the factory of horrors behind.

"So, ah, do you mind telling me the name of my saviour?"

She said it with a sort of crooked smile, the type that was probably pretty once. He returned it as best he could. "Soul. You?"

"Lucina." They didn't share another word.

He had to peel himself away, not taking his eyes off the swinging girl until she was blocked from view. *Arya is waiting.* The thought was the only thing keeping him moving, ending up where he left the first three gunmen. It was where his memory told him the office would be, making it the best place to descend. All three were awake again, turning to see him stagger towards them. "Whose blood is that?" they demanded.

Instead of answering, he made a hole in the floor, looking at a desk beneath. It was all the evidence he needed, expanding it until he was able to drop down. Two of the Tooth and Claw members were wasting breath yelling, but the girl rolled a little, toppling down with him. He ignored her, sparing only the time to confirm she was still bound. A gun had fallen in with her, which he kicked away.

Stepping to the window, hell stared back at him.

The dance floor had transformed, the lighting's blue hue competing with the red blood of the corpses scattered like discarded packets of chips. From the edge of the stage where he sat, Soul looked up to him. There was something different about him. His skin gleamed from hundreds of scars over his face. They were everywhere—the cuts Allison gave that had never fully healed. Soul frowned, but changed to adopt a half smile. Amidst the carnage of broken bodies, Dakota saw police officers, Temple mages, and Arya alike.

Five Temple officers managed to fail. It seemed ridiculous, an impossibility. But then, it wasn't just Soul who had attacked in the end. Some had been stabbed, most were riddled with bullets. One hadn't even made it down the stairs. The regular police, now missing limbs, were the biggest contributors to the pool of blood, flanking both sides of Arya. Pressing his head to the window, Dakota breathed her name. "Arya." Snake coiling like a spring around his arm, Dakota snatched the fallen gun and ran down the stairs.

It wasn't the axe. The precise incision piercing through her shoulder was too thin to be from anything but a knife. Closing his eyes, he sunk to his knees. His snake bit into her arm, trying to sew her back together, but his power refused to activate. "Her soul is no longer in that shell. It's time you moved on."

Soul's voice roused him, dragging his eyes' gaze away. They crossed right past the two officers, and for a moment his eye caught. They were the exact pair who responded to his fake crime report. "I was going to trade. I finally had something to offer you, and you just . . ." His voice lowered, and for a long moment he just stood and stared.

Soul's lip twitched. "I've had enough of trades for a lifetime."

It was like his foot itself didn't want to move, didn't want to leave Arya behind. "You killed her."

"I made sure she felt no pain. These children deserve no undue suffering."

Finally, his voice started to rise. "You're the reason she suffered."

For all the ambivalence he had been showing, Soul seemed to physically recoil at that, his voice dropping to a snarl. "I did not curse her. I did not torture them. That was Pedro and those hunter pigs." He didn't just say the name but spat it, a drop into the ocean of blood. "I saw what they do to the people they capture. Understand it or not, I am saving them from a fate too horrible to accept. Why will you not understand this? Did Nikita not tell you why she spent years running? Or what happened to her hometown? These children need a place to rest."

Getting closer, Dakota took his first step into where the blood truly pooled. "They were running from you."

"She was running from them. When Nikita took police protection, the hunters came for her, and who was it who saved her? Who was it who let her get away? I do not regret that decision for a second, for it is better she suffers a little longer than be put through their hell."

Dakota scoffed. "I don't care if the hunters are monsters. Or Nikita. It doesn't change that you're one too."

"And you? Orphan from Koros, child assassin. Are you not a monster too?" It was deep within Soul's voice, an anger that not even the most skilled liar from the orphanage could fake.

Taking another step forward, Dakota felt the blood cling to his shoes. "I gave protection."

"And I gave mercy!"

Dakota's knuckles were so tight they began turning white. "And who decided that?"

From the look on his face, Soul seemed ready to shout back. But he didn't, biting it down. "I understand how you feel. I lost someone too. I did everything to try and save them all. But I failed. This curse of theirs is all consuming. It is one horror or the next. Sometimes it drives them mad; others lose control. Like Lucina Aries did. She was such a good girl. I thought setting her free was for the best, but I learned how wrong I was. A city burned for my mistake, and now she lives in regret, while my own cousin was driven to madness.

"I saw then what needed to be done. I needed to protect them from what fate will force upon them. To spare them from what happened to Lucina, forever lost to regret. To save them from losing control and committing a mass murder, just like your precious Nikita did. I am truly sorry you have to bear the pain of losing someone dear, but if you cared for them at all, you would understand that what I did was for their own good, even though it hurts. So turn away, Zero. Tend to your girl. Let us end the pain here."

He sounded like a preacher, like someone utterly convinced of his own story. Dakota froze where he stood, standing in the middle of the pool of blood. His voice became as quiet and venomous as a real snake. "You killed my sister, you bastard. There's nothing left for me to tend to because of you."

In that moment, Soul stopped moving. Stopped reaching under his vest, stopped shifting his weight where he sat, stopped even breathing. "No. That cannot be. I brought her to the hospital, she should be saved."

"Screw you," Dakota snarled, and pulled the trigger.

The shots echoed in the empty hall. On instinct, Soul protected himself with his arm, not that it did anything as the bullets ripped all the way through to the back of the room. Only two actually hit Soul. Stepping closer, Dakota adjusted his aim slightly, returning it to the centre, and pulled it again, not letting go until there were no more bullets to fire. His hands were shaking with the vibration long after the clip went dry.

Lowering his arms, Soul looked at himself. He spoke with a dying voice as he crumbled forward. "You have never held a gun before, have you?" Fifteen seconds: the length of Soul's spell. That was what Allison discovered before her defeat, and what Arya had confirmed from her studies. He dropped the gun, charging forward. "You should hold it like this."

Delaying the second when he would crumble forward, Soul took a gun from behind him and pointed it at Dakota. It fit so neatly into his one hand, yet still he used both to keep it stable. He shot, and Dakota felt the bullet split his head.

Oblivion, a feeling of abject nothingness, just a soul-ripping torment beyond the capacity of any words. It didn't last long, but long enough to make him feel sick. The wound undoing, Dakota pushed himself up from the blood he was lying in. "Please, end this violence. I do not want to kill you."

"I wouldn't worry about that," Dakota muttered as he broke into another sprint.

The snake uncoiled like a spring, hurling towards Soul. He dived away as the snake's jaws crashed into the wooden stage. Sending in his mana, the wood changed shape, growing into spikes that chased after Soul. It left him only one way to escape—straight through Dakota. Soul pulled out a knife, one he shouldn't have had. The missing blade of Allison's, a relic from Koros, its fire gem spent.

Pulling the snake back, Dakota had to dodge left fast to avoid Soul's running slash. The bloody floor lacked friction, making it impossible for Soul to stop, instead sliding forward and showing Dakota his back. It took an instant, Dakota's snake swinging for him and biting into his jacket. Connecting his mana, the fabric turned sharp, forming spikes to piece inward, reaching for Soul's insides. "It's over," Dakota said through gritted teeth.

Soul fell, landing on his knees. "I've still . . . got fifteen seconds . . ."

Feeling mocking words on his lips, Dakota clamped his mouth shut to focus just in time to feel another bullet ripping through him, taking his control over his mana and snake in one go. Another bullet tore at him, and then another, and before the spell wore out, he was back in that abyss.

When the feeling finally subsided, his snake was gone, and it would take time to summon it again. Another problem with familiars. When Soul spoke, he couldn't immediately place where it was coming from. "Child of Koros, do not make me defy my cousin's final wish."

Speech in combat, a tactical error. Yet with his familiar gone, Dakota needed to buy time until it returned. He found the voice quickly behind the glass of the upper floor. It was a smart enough move, if he wanted to defend. "You know something about Koros?"

"No. News of your condition broke just as Fraya was stolen from me. It was the last thing she said: her wish to help your kin."

Counting down the seconds, Dakota said, "We don't need your pity."

"Pity? Fraya didn't know the word. And neither did I, until I met you."

"What?" Dakota growled.

"I was born to a village of forlorn beings, where people were dead while they still breathed. You . . . you have their same air."

Dakota felt the snake again, its presence building within his coin. Already it was twisting through his clothes to his arm. "You stole my purpose when you stole my sister."

Shooting from his sleeve, the snake sprung for the glass, gripping it and pulling Dakota up. Soul stepped back and out of sight. While the snake worked like a grapple hook, Dakota kicked the wall, pushing him to the side and arriving at a different pane than the snake. Soul fired, his bullet hitting where Dakota would have appeared. Using his mana to split the glass, Dakota slammed through it and rolled into the room.

The Tooth and Claw member was still there, pushing herself against the far wall. Reaching down, the snake bit into a piece of shattered glass and turned it to metal. Then he saw it.

Soul's vest was in tatters, discarded on the floor. Left wearing just a shirt, torn and filled with holes, a gold-plated brooch of a two-faced leaf was pinned to his chest. Dakota didn't hesitate, seeing no better candidate for the deicide arm. Like a whip, his snake swung forward, reaching for that broach with every swing. Soul was fast on his feet, dodging around and using Allison's knife to keep it away. It found a home, ripping into the belly of the snake. It was made of metal; it had no blood, no sense of pain. But it was a familiar, Dakota's familiar, and so the pain was inflicted unto him. With the pain erupting, he faltered, all but dropping. "Come on, Zero. No one wins likes this."

Through gritted teeth Dakota spat, "I win when you die."

Soul only shook his head as Dakota began pushing himself up yet again, running back for Soul. The gems in the broach started to glow, and Dakota almost smiled, its meaning clear.

They connected again, this time Dakota staying on the outside, not going in too hard. Waiting, Dakota counted the seconds. Fifteen for the spell to undo, which meant he would press in on ten. The moment it came he changed, ducking low and driving forward. The snake came for his left side, the metallic shard for his right. The makeshift blade pieced into Soul's gun arm, holding it in place. He smiled, just waiting for the gem to stop glowing.

Shots. Three of them, loud in the room. Soul's pistol, but not from his hand. Blood rising in his mouth, Dakota picked out the shooter at the corner of the room. The Tooth and Claw girl. The bullets pierced him, Soul, and even his snake. Screeching and flailing, his familiar lost its grip. Dakota could barely breathe, and even when the gem stopped glowing, the pain didn't subside, the attack not made by its wielder.

As Dakota struggled to breathe on the floor, Soul pushed himself up. Pulling the shard out of his arm opened the wound for blood to spill. Not that it mattered, not when compared to the shot that reached into Dakota's side. The bullet hadn't gone through, becoming lodged in his guts. "Let this go. I do not want to fight you."

And then he stumbled away, leaving Dakota on the floor. His snake was barely functioning, his body torn. He knew that only urgent medical attention could spare him. Approaching the Tooth and Claw girl, Soul undid the wires holding her together, setting her free. *I should have cuffed her hands behind.*

Feeling his very life fading, Dakota used everything he had to reach into his pocket, taking out the gems from Allison's gauntlet. They fell to the floor. He grasped for them. With the tips of his fingers, he managed to reach them, crushing all three. His voice was a croak, but it made Soul pause. "I don't care if chaos will be the price. My revenge will be sweet."

Mana exploded inside him, more than he could even handle. There was so much that it began leaking out of the snake, enough to patch the damage with nothing but raw mana. Then he commanded the snake to do something he'd never done before. Turning its gaze on him, it bit right into Dakota's shoulder. He hissed but bore the pain as it began its mockery of Allison's spell, refusing to let Soul escape his grasp, dying though it might be.

He remembered an old expression, that mana is like a plastic bottle. Limitation spells seem counterproductive, but by squeezing the bottle, they compress the space until the pressure makes the cap explode. Having a familiar crumpled the bottom. Confining his power to within ten meters of the familiar was a second hand crushing above that. Being unable to manipulate living things burst the lid.

The workaround was like stepping into hell.

Allison had mana wires; he used the threads from his shirt, making them dig under his skin to wrap around his arms and legs, his torso and neck. It took all his focus to tie them inside his body, which was becoming harder with every second as he had to stitch up the damage that was already done. The pain was so excruciating he couldn't even feel the gunshot anymore.

It hurt just to turn, to stand up. He couldn't even make his back straight. The effort spent trying left him hunched over and panting. Holding back from screaming with the effort, he ran. His feet carried him faster than he ever had run before. It seemed impossible that as a child Allison had constructed something so clever to skyrocket her physical strength for just a sliver of mana. His fist crashed into Soul before giving him a chance to respond, sending him flying into the wall.

Even the technically proficient punch could not stop his knuckles from tearing. He had to fight the wires just to keep them in place. When they finally settled under his broken skin, Soul was back on his feet. Focusing on the wires in his legs, Dakota readied for his next lunge. It turned him into a missile, laser focused on the tip of Soul's nose. In that fraction of a second, Soul managed to twist a hair out of reach while activating his icon. Using the wall as a springboard, Dakota launched himself back after him.

There was nothing Soul could do against Dakota's barrage, blocking only a quarter of the hits he sent. Just as the glow faded, Dakota aimed a strong right at centre mass. It took both of Soul's hands clamping Dakota's fist to halt the strike millimetres from his chest. His momentum killed, Dakota used his newfound force to tear his arm free.

In the ring, he'd seen Allison use leg kicks to wear down her opponent over the rounds. It was something he hadn't practiced, but he knew how to fight and gave it a try. His shin landed, but it did more than just redden Soul's leg. The added strength made it different, forcing Soul to collapse and drop from view. For a second, he even thought that he'd snapped through bone. Wasting a second for confusion, Dakota redirected his next strike, sending Soul flying through the air.

Charging back at Soul, he was rewarded for his speed with a rising knee, ascending through Dakota's unprepared face.

The shock rocked him, and for a brief moment he

was paralysed, the wires going haywire within him. In that moment of regaining control, Soul hit him with a hard fist to his left shoulder, right where the snake was latched in. Dakota felt the pain like it had been his own jaw rocked, dragging a retreating step from his assault. Before Soul could manage another blow, Dakota sidestepped around him, sending in a low-swept kick to his ankles, following up with a hail of elbows. The defence Soul raised was so incapable any ref would rule a technical knockout.

Then something unexpected happened. Something he'd forgotten to even consider. Some*one* he forgot to take care of. Taking a running start, the Tooth and Claw girl named Jayda barrelled into both of them, throwing Dakota off his mounted assault.

Soul wasn't able to push himself up this time. He backed away, crab-walking until his back was against the window. Dakota looked back, his eyes an industrial drilling machine boring into the girl. Tensing his muscles, he stepped forward, ramming his open palm into her face and pushing her to the floor. Before she could recover her breath, he raised his leg and slammed it back down. Her pelvis gave way and morphed around his foot as it almost hit the floor. She screamed, and it rung in his ears. It was enough to make him confident she would not be interfering for a third time.

Soul stared wide-eyed at the display, his horror eliciting an unparalleled disgust within Dakota. Surging forward, Dakota's fist slammed into the glass, making a spiderweb crack, Soul caught in its centre. Soul was fast and agile, but his spiralling exhaustion set both those traits fading. Dakota struck fast. The broach began to glow. His fist landed, crushing into Soul's face, making a ragdoll of his past pursuer. He was sent flying around the room and was barely offered a moment to scramble away before the glow died.

Hurled from wall to wall, every toss made Soul resemble his victims downstairs more. He was slower every time. Landing by the wall, right where Dakota had been shot, Soul grasped for the makeshift knife. Still adjusting it into his palm, Dakota made a final charge with everything he had.

The glow began again, and Dakota lessened his force, counting the seconds until it died once more. *No more. This will be his last spell.*

Three seconds left, and his lessened force allowed that metal shard a pathway into his chest. He cursed himself, realising that by relenting the pressure he had given Soul the opportunity. It pressed in hard, and it certainly felt like it would kill him. Not waiting to see what would happen, Dakota reached forward.

The glow died.

The pain went with it. He felt something cold in his hand. The broach, nearly crushed by his fingers. Pushing away, Soul had to use the wall itself to hold himself up. Running low on oxygen, his words became staggered and slow. "Give that back. I need it . . . to protect . . . my promise."

Not heeding, barely listening, Dakota refused to lessen the pressure again. Every strike sent the wires chafing deeper into his very bones. He knew he was on his own countdown. Ducking a strike, Soul made a desperate grasp for Dakota's shoulders, bringing them into a grapple. They circled around the office's centre, edging closer and closer to the window, right until Soul shifted his weight, pushing Dakota against it. His breath left with the impact, and in that moment, Soul backed away to slam his shoulder hard into him, shattering the glass and sending them both tumbling down to the blood-soaked floor below.

Together they landed, and together they lost their grip, rolling apart through the crimson pool. The wind was gone from Dakota's lungs, and now he was unable to stand. Out of the corner of his eye, he could see Soul fumbling his way up, same as him. "Why won't you just die?" he howled.

In heavy pants, Soul answered, "Only Lucina will kill me. We will die together when I complete my task and erase the threat."

Dakota's neck tensed, his veins begging to pop through his skin. "You're the threat. Arya found a cure, was happy, but you . . . you brought back all the pain."

Both were in a desperate struggle to be the first to rise. Both had managed to get only so far as their hands and knees. "That's not possible."

"Shut up!" Dakota screamed as he made it upright.

One last surge, that was all he had left. It was all he needed. Focusing on all the wires, he used the ones in his legs to propel him forward like a rocket while moving the ones in his arms to create the most powerful strike he'd ever seen. He started five meters away. He brought it to four. Soul got one leg under him and looked up, just in time for Dakota to make it down to three. Two, and he was almost there.

It happened so fast it was almost impossible to even understand. He controlled the wires to pull his arm through the arc of the punch. It extended all the way. Then kept extending, pulling his arm and bone until it snapped. Pain consumed his arm. He couldn't deliver the punch, couldn't even see Soul straight. He tried to undo the wires around the break. His control tainted, his wrist was dragged too, bending into an unnatural angle.

Hotter and harder than anything even Sensei had inflicted, the pain controlled his entire attention. With all his focus directed to his legs, the wires in his legs took an automatic step, pulling him forward and tearing into his thighs. Unable to stand, Dakota fell to the floor, just a hair in front of Soul.

Looking down as Dakota wrestled with his own wires for even just a semblance of control, Soul panted deeply. Every time Dakota tried to focus on one part, the rest of his body went haywire. Wherever the pain went, his mind followed, the wires tearing him further apart. They started constricting around his body so firmly it was hard to even breathe. The pool of blood, the floor, even Soul himself—all of it faded as every cell in his body screamed in agony, his own mana ripping him apart from the inside out.

Until, with the distorted words of his foe, he was delivered into a blissful nothingness. "Sorry, kid. This is for your own good."

Wood creaking underfoot, Soul stepped out of the store and back onto the road. The township was small, and the whispers of a visiting boy with a bandaged face rung loud. Walking through the canopy, he counted the number of children left, leaving him with the inescapable wistfulness of a quest near completed. Only seven more, and he would finally be able to return to Lucina and let it all end.

That name brought him back to a memory not dulled by age. Of returning home, Fraya in the back seat. There were some good moments after that, seeing his friends for the first time in months. They had come with well wishes and cheery greetings, hoping Fraya would feel better and asking for stories of what happened. He never begrudged their response. Not the rage, or shouting, or even Darcy's quiet comments that he had changed. He was a little frustrated, annoyed that she couldn't understand he only did what he had to do. Annoyed she didn't want to be with him anymore, and after months of letters being sent back and forth, leaving him at the funeral of all places. But looking back, he could understand. He was even grateful. If they were still together, he wasn't sure he would have stayed on his path. He could only hope she found happiness wherever she was.

Reaching his rented car, he turned around to the creaking sound coming from the porch. An aging woman, the one he just asked, had stepped out after him. There was something about her that reminded him of Fraya's mother, another person he hadn't seen in years. She had been furious last time they'd met. If there was a single person to be happy about him leaving, he'd guessed it was her. She just kept calling him an idiot over and over, screaming that she was losing another child. He never knew what she meant. Fraya had no siblings.

The closer the woman stepped, the more he saw that something was off in her eyes. The tiny movements, the expression. Inside, she had seemed exhausted; now she looked scared. But it had only been a few seconds, a minute at most. She'd already told him about the bandaged boy. He couldn't think what she had left to say. The changes weren't just in her eyes but her whole body. The way she brushed back her hair, her posture. It was like looking at a wholly different person. "Soul."

Immediately, he reached for his broach. He'd never told her his name. "Nikita? You are here too?"

Her lips tightened. It really threw off her attempt at looking offended. He guessed it should have come as no surprise that someone who relied on telepathy would be a terrible liar. It was cruel of her to use her telepathy to possess the old woman. No matter what she did, he could only retaliate against the innocent woman. Finally, the mockery of fake offence fell. "You got me."

"Would you be so kind as to show up in person? To be honest, I am becoming tired of our dance."

Through the woman's face, Nikita smirked. "I'm hardly ready to give up so easily."

He sighed. "Then why are you here?"

"Why, to bargain of course." She said it with such a chipper smile he had to furrow his brows.

"*You* came to bargain?"

He couldn't stand that smile, how she was twisting someone else into making it for her. "Well, Dakota did keep saying it was the best way. Or was it Allison? Oh, it's just so hard to tell with those two. They're just so . . . well, whatever. Anyway, I now have a way to make us both happy."

The minx. Every interaction was proving that rumour more and more true. "And where are those two children of Koros now?" he said. "Did you set them free, or are you still using them for your own ends? That boy seemed to think you love him. You really found the best way to use others."

"Why, thank you."

He had to hold himself back from cursing at her, instead speaking flatly. "That was not a compliment."

For her part, she just twisted the woman's body to shrug. "Whatever. I came with an offer. That's all that matters, right? See, you want the taboo users, and I want to live. Well, I'm willing to give you the barbie if you let me walk away and never come after me again. Whatcha say?"

When the twins had offered, he was so ready to accept. But in their answers, he knew they lacked his conviction. But Nikita, whom he had lowered all expectations for, still managed to limbo beneath them. "What?"

"Come on, think about it. A life for a life. I give you Arya, and you leave me alone."

He didn't even need to think before shaking his head. "You are disgusting."

"Ever heard of something called a mirror?"

"At least I am not selling someone for my own life."

"Yeah, you're right. Maybe I should start killing folks. Would that make you happy? Listen, Soul. You're not getting in. Dakota built a fortress, and it'll be safeguarded better than you can imagine. In all likelihood you'll die just trying to get through. And then who will murder all the other people if you're not there to do it?"

If it wasn't for the fact that the girl possessing the woman before him was so dangerous, he may well have just rolled his eyes at her. "If you believed any of that, you would not be out here trying to bargain."

She shrugged, playing with her nails. It was so unnatural, Nikita clearly not used to the size and proportions of the woman she was possessing. "For now, sure. But once we finish you may as well give up."

"So this is just you stalling me?"

"What? No." Lowering the hand, she looked straight at him. "You *will* die if you come. But I can't risk the chance you get to me before that happens. I'm just doing what I have to do to survive. How is there anything wrong with that?"

There were so many things he wanted to do right then, but none of them would matter, not against Nikita. "Not if it means living like this."

She sighed. "Spare me. I'll take lectures from politicians and actors before I take any from you. Now, do you want the pink head or not?"

"Her name is Arya Deharak, not 'pink head.'"

"Oh my God, I don't care."

He could only shake his head, utterly at a loss from her display. "You really are unlike all the other children. You are the only one I dislike. They were unfortunate enough to have this atrocity thrust upon them. You seem to relish in it."

"Oh, wow. So you're basically just admitting that you're victim blaming me? If you really thought this was an atrocity, you wouldn't be doing it."

"I am doing this because it *is* an atrocity! What Pedro did to you was truly awful. I want to spare you from the pain it will cause."

"Wow. You know, you really do sound just like those hunters."

He didn't even think about what he was doing, his hand reacting on its own to lift the woman off her feet. Nikita didn't even try to fight it. She was so light. He snarled to her. "I am nothing like them."

The woman's face was turning red and her veins were becoming visible. It was only then he realised what he was doing. He let go, stepping away and turning his back, unable to look into those eyes. "Can't you see I'm trying to save you? That I'm doing *all* of this for you? You have no idea what they do to people like you. It is so much worse than death."

He couldn't help it, he saw that day, recalled what he had seen walking behind Helena. She had a tray of food with her, finally excited to have a psychologist come down to their little house in the middle of nowhere and try talking to her little girl. *The girl who now screamed whenever someone got too close. The girl who always had that fearful look in her eye. The girl who only allowed one person to come near her, who was by all means a stranger.* It was only in defeat that Helena begrudgingly came to accept Lucina's aid. And then that day came when they walked in to see her swinging in the centre of the room, her bed sheets tying her to the lights.

"What gives you the right to decide for me what's a fate worse than death? That's my decision, not yours."

Her words, of all the possible things to do so, brought him back to the present. "You do not understand. People like you are fated to suffer. If they do not get to you first, then you will lose control and go mad."

"Bull. I won't lose control."

"Everyone loses control. It is a curse for a reason."

"Well, hey, seems I'm the exception. Ten years and still going strong."

"Your hometown is dead because of your power."

"I was a child. I'm stronger now."

"You cannot be serious."

"Me? Look who's talking!"

He couldn't look back to her. If he did, he knew he might just snap. "You are the very definition of narcissism." Closing his eyes, he paused, seeing the faces of them all before his eyes. His shoulders sunk. "Fine. Have it your way. Perhaps you are the exception. But not from strength. Because you are so self-centred that even if next time it's a whole city you destroy, you still will not care. Not like how it eats away at Lucina's very soul. Congratulations, I suppose."

"I don't want your congratulations. Just give me my life and let's never see each other again."

Shaking his head, he sighed. "Fine. Give me Arya and I promise not to come after you. But the orphans must not be there. They have suffered enough."

"No, no, no. Call me crazy, but I somehow don't exactly trust you. First I need some insurance."

Taking a deep breath, he half-looked back her way. "What do you want?"

"I want your axe."

"What?"

She repeated herself, stressing every word. "I want. Your. Axe."

He shook his head. "It's been with me since I was a child."

"Do I look like I give a rat's ass? I need insurance, some way to make sure you won't turn around and use it on me."

Unclipping it from under his shirt, he held it before his eyes. The voice of the liquid silver man in his internal world screamed and protested, crying for him to not give it to her. He had to push it back as hard as he could. "I give you this, and you will give me Arya?"

"I'll tell you where she is and let you have her. No Temple, no child assassins. Just you and her."

He had to lower it from his sight, unable to look at it properly. "You realise since you are a mage you cannot use it?"

"Why the hell would I want such an outdated arm? I just don't want you to have it."

There was no doubt at all that taking the deal would mean never finding her again. Not with her having a head start, not with her power. Not with the knowledge she extracted from two orphans of Koros. He could only pray she was right.

Squeezing the handle one last time, he let the old

woman take it. He couldn't bear to look. The moment it left his hand the voice disappeared for the last time. "She'll be in Club Lunar tonight. It's a place over in Isoval. You might want to hurry."

Opening the car door, he looked back to her for the last time. "Sooner or later, this will all come back for you."

"Yeah well, I'll take my chances with life."

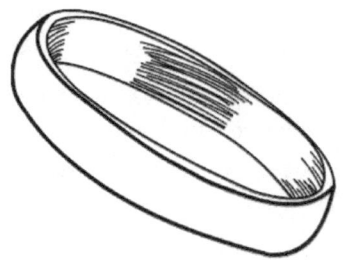

Her mind took a back seat from the moment she read the message. She had no control as her body boarded a train to a different city and wandered into a nightclub. Riley sat there, still as a statue, the manager equally as dazed. Then, without any warning, they both blinked back into awareness. The police were there, arriving along with Arya. *A telepath was involved.* That was the only explanation she was given.

Then the nightclub turned to a hellscape before her eyes.

She'd run at full speed, desperately doing as her sister told her, looking only forward as six people melted from the crowd and began their attack. Escaping into the bathroom, she shut her eyes, other terrified guests crowded around her.

The bathroom should have been considered big, at least, it was by any normal standard. But filled with people hugging their knees, it felt cramped. The door had a lock, and while she would bet that he didn't have a key, nothing would stop a bullet ripping it off.

The outside sounds came in bursts. First the screams during the initial attack, then the rush as Temple stormed in, only for that too to fall silent. She heard a familiar voice sending the others upstairs. Then came the crash. There was muffled speech, bullets, and grunts. She knew that voice, just as she knew the first. One was the burglar she had been warned of, and the other was the boy who gave the warning. Glass shattered, followed by the howls of hell, cut off after a moment.

From there, she couldn't stop herself. The others gasped at her in horror as she reached for the door, some even trying to stop her. "You're going to get us all killed," someone cried. Swallowing, she opened the door a crack.

People littered the floor, all of them bleeding, and only two of them moving. One lay writhing around in the blood; the other stood over him in a state of exhaustion. There was a snake, clearly the familiar of the one on the ground, which she watched fade away. From their positions, she guessed the man punched the boy, rendering him unconscious.

By the side of the wall, lying unmoving, she saw her older sister. The man spoke to the boy, regardless of his capacity to hear him. "I am truly sorry it came to this, but it was the only way. If I didn't do this, then the day would have come where Arya Deharak lost control, same as all the rest. And I know you would have blamed yourself for that destruction, as I do for Lucina."

"You're wrong."

She wished she said it quieter, or even not at all. But it came out, and the man turned, his eyes finding hers through the gap. Swallowing, she stepped forward, out the door and into the room. She took a breath, steadying her voice. "She was the human trial. They were looking for long-term effects. My sister's taboo was already cured."

Soul couldn't stop staring, like he was faced with some ghost. "The curse cannot be controlled. We looked."

Her voice was quiet—she could barely stand—and yet, she refused to look anywhere but into his eyes. "It could. You just killed the only proof."

Soul raised the corner of his lip, almost like a snarl. "They cannot be saved. They have to lose control; that is the way it is. That is why I had to do this, to protect them . . ."

She didn't know if her voice would be considered strong or absent. At that point, she didn't know anything. But she was out there now, in the open, and she couldn't leave anymore. And she had a duty to the truth, for Arya's sake. "She was already safe. Until you came."

"But the hunters—"

"Lost interest."

"That's a lie!" he roared. "I heard the hunters say that, but her power was far from gone. She released that cloud. Mana was still seeped into her. The hunters would have come back. I know how they think. They were just shifting priorities."

Shaking her head, Riley closed her eyes. "She was limited to the dregs of mana. Her sigils were gone. She wasn't worth anything as a subject. They let her be. God knows they had the chance to take her."

That was the line. Battered, bruised, on the verge of collapse, it didn't matter. He rose up, nearly snarling. "If that were true, it would mean Fraya didn't need to die. It would mean everything I did was worse than nothing.

You have to be lying."

She stood still, watching the man unravel.

He came for her. *Perhaps he thinks without me he won't have to bear the truth of what he did. Pathetic.*

Refusing to go quietly, she released a shadow cloud from the ring that was her hallowed icon. An imitation of her sister's. It was smaller and weaker, but in his state, she hoped it would be enough.

He charged with reckless abandon, his feet tangling as he made wild swipes with his arm holding a dark shard of glass. She skirted back, not letting him get close, holding her mana between them. Then came the sound of a door bursting open, of people charging in. His gaze swapped to those intruding upon his frenzy. Temple officers. Both sides saw each other's threat, and the man made a beeline for the stairs. Not that he got close. Although he survived the previous officers, he crumpled in an instant this time, collapsing face-first into the pool of blood.

Rushing down the stairs, the officers put Soul into a restraint while the others checked every corner of the room. They shouted to each other, taking and making orders, until they were confident the threat was over. They found the crowd hidden in the bathroom, and along with Riley, they were all led upstairs. As she passed the door, she looked back to the man, a knee on his back to hold him in place.

Such a shell, such a nobody, such a nothing. He took my sister away because of a fantasy. A fool who used her life to pave a path of good intentions, but all he made was hell. It would have been funny if it didn't make her want to suffocate him right there. It would have felt good, she knew it would. But only for a moment. Then she'd be left with yet another body in a corpse-filled room.

She was taken to the back of an ambulance where a paramedic asked her questions she didn't hear, held up fingers she didn't focus on, and shined a light into her eyes that made her flinch. She vaguely heard him use the word "shock," but nothing else got through.

A stretcher came out carrying the boy. *Dakota.* They pulled him into the ambulance she sat in, right beside her. His eyes had opened, ever so slightly. As the medics rearranged themselves, she heard him whisper in a voice so quiet it was almost inaudible, "In my pocket. There's something . . . you should have."

He was insistent, reaching even when the paramedics tried restraining him. After a brief struggle, one did it for him, dipping her hand into his pocket and removing a pendant of shining golden resin wrapped into a heart. It had silver twisted around the edge like vines. He nodded his head to the medic, and hesitantly it was handed to her.

Dakota didn't say another word.

She didn't want to think about what would happen to him, whether he would live or not as they rushed him to whatever hospital was closest. She didn't want to think about what she had seen. She just sat there, waiting with the police as they questioned every person they found inside. She watched as Soul was led out in handcuffs, his head dropped as he was shoved into a Temple van and taken away.

At some point she fell asleep. It was the most uncomfortable sleep of her life. When she woke, her back was stiff and her body was cold. The only thing she could think was that whatever she'd dreamt, she was glad it was already forgotten. Whatever nightmare it had been, she didn't need it. She'd just seen a real one.

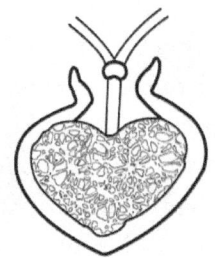

Eye's fluttering open, Nikita found herself in an unfamiliar room, somewhere that definitely was not Inngey. There was a solid roof above her, walls beside her, and a window overlooking a cityscape. She tried moving, finding her arm utterly numb and wrapped in plaster, although no longer bound.

Through the fog of an endless nightmare, she had only been vaguely aware of being transported onto a helicopter. Aside from her arm and the overall stiffness in her body, she felt fine, finally free from Dakota's drug. *A bluff.*

She twirled her arm in a large windmill, twisting over the side of the bed and shaking her legs. At some point she had been changed into a hospital gown. Feet on the floor, she immediately crumbled. It took all her effort, clawing at the bed sheets, just to attempt to stay upright. The door opened before she made it, not that she ever would have. A set of strong hands gripped her sides and pulled her up onto the bed. "Hey, there. You were out a long time. It's probably best you don't rush yourself, okay?"

She heard the voice out loud, completely unaccompanied by thought. Neither could she make out the internal voices of anyone in any other room. "Search and Rescue brought you in four days ago. They said you got caught up in an explosion."

Nikita looked up and matched her gaze. She tried taking in the woman to the fullest extent. She was large, tall, and sported a friendly smile. She had dark eyes and skin, and her nails were trimmed short, as was her hair. It was like someone had gone out of their way to find the person most opposite to Allison in the whole world. "Do you have a name, dear?"

It happened every time. With the twin's sensei, with Arya; every time she broke her rule, misery ensued. Keeping her mouth shut, she promised herself not to speak until her power returned. *Let her assume what she wants.* "Cat got your tongue, huh? Well, hopefully that's just temporary. But you can understand me, can't you? We need to run some tests, is that okay?"

She guessed it technically wasn't breaking her rule to nod. For a short while she complied with the temperature check, blood pressure, and other basic health checks she was well familiar with. After some time, the nurse seemed satisfied and went out, saying the doctor would be in soon.

Left alone, she looked out the window and tried to piece together where she was. With Inngey on the border, she couldn't even be certain of the nation she was in.

A part of her wondered what happened to Dakota, and Soul, and the rest of them. She hoped they took each other out. Soul at least was a goner. In a place like Lunar, an inner-city basement, there was no way he would escape. Not with police close by, Temple on hand, and even the military to be called in if things were looking bad. Even if he somehow made it out, it would be a national manhunt with his face all over the news. Regardless of what happened, she knew that threat had finally been taken care of. Once she slipped away from the hospital, it would be the first time in a long while she could stop looking over her shoulder every other second. *No more Soul, no more orphans. Now I just need to stay away from the hunters.*

It didn't take long for the doctor to come in. There was something vaguely familiar about the aging man clearly in his final years of medicine. He started with the chart at the end of her bed, scanning over it. "Nurse Vihlma tells me you're not speaking. Is that right?" He paused, giving her a moment to correct him. "Well, that is a shame. Now, I've unfortunately got a mixture of news for you—one good, one bad. Which do you prefer? Oh, sorry. And I just asked about your speech too.

"Oh well, I guess we should start with the bad news. Unfortunately, you've sustained some serious burns to your back and arms. There was even some shrapnel lodged there, not to mention whatever happened to your left arm. Now the good news is that we were able to undo most of the damage, so there shouldn't be any pain, but you will have some lingering injuries. Well, with time most of the scarring should disappear. And in the meanwhile, the painkillers should stop the burns from hurting. Well, anyway, there's something I'd really love to ask you. If you can't speak, that's fine by the way. Well, we found some markings on your head. They looked a lot like the runes for hallowed icons, but . . . they couldn't be, could they?"

A sweeping panic drenched her, the defences she put

up whenever this happened stripped away. She shook her head and tried miming a necklace. "Oh, you're saying you have a necklace as an icon?" She nodded, feeling a weight lift from her chest. "How peculiar. Well, I guess stranger things have happened, but nonetheless there are no records of you ever making such an icon, Miss Quinn."

All the weight that had just disappeared returned with a vengeance. Her blood turned to ice in her veins as she tried pushing away. Falling off the edge of the bed, she tumbled onto the floor, unable to press herself back up to even attempt an escape. "Now, now. No need to rush. There's nowhere for you to go anyway, not with all those numbing agents in your body. And we have plenty of Milton's Twilight, so don't think you'll be manipulating any minds any time soon, young lady."

Now on the floor, she tried forcing herself to move, crawling away, but there was nowhere for her to go. Worse, every time she put pressure on her broken arm, she fell again and had to bite her lip to stop herself from screaming. "My, my, such energy. I am impressed. You really are a lovely specimen, aren't you? Well, I guess having to run from *that man* for so long would do that to a person. And I must say, I am truly impressed by how you managed to avoid us for almost ten years. Even when we got through your police blockade, you still managed to slip away. I do hope you thanked him properly for helping you get away so many times."

Even with her mouth dry, she found the words to speak, her charade feeling pointless. "Soul didn't help me."

"She speaks! Oh, and he most certainly did. The way he stayed back to fight our men to let you get away time and time again . . . If I didn't know better, I'd almost guess you two were an item. But alas, he has been a thorn in our side for such a very long time. I must thank you for taking care of him for us. It really was ingenious, although I wish you didn't sacrifice another subject to do so. But considering she's damaged goods, we can let that one slide. Now, what's done is done, and since he will face the justice system with the full force of the law, he will no longer be getting in our way.

"And so I repeat: thank you, Miss Nikita Quinn. You have been quite an asset, and our relationship is just beginning. Of course, those twins were quite useful as well. Was it their idea to create that first scene at Lunar? Quite brilliant, I must say. It got our attention loud and clear."

She swallowed, not sure how to respond, or if she even should. "What do you mean?"

"Don't you see? By framing Soul for what happened, you were basically calling out to us. After what he did, of course we had his prints on record. And then you went and weaselled into my agents' minds . . ." Shaking his head, he held up a wagging finger. "You may as well have told us it was your doing. Well, we could have taken you there, but enlisting two of the children from Koros to fight him was such a clever idea. We just had to see if you could do it. And between the two of us, I placed a bet you'd win. You really have made me such a happy man. I really cannot thank you enough. But as I said, we will have a long time together, so there really need be no rush."

Her breathing increased as she huddled right into the corner. She was sweating again, hyperventilating again. After all her work, all the sacrifices she had made, it felt like some cruel joke for it to end like this, for the hunters to have found her as she was about to make her great

411

escape. She couldn't believe it, begged to wake from the nightmare. But unlike her memories of killing her own mother, this was no vision, and there was no waking.

The world was dark and silent, but slowly Dakota felt his awareness returning. It was unlike the infinite nothingness of Soul's temporary deaths. This was peaceful, like waking up. He heard the beeping of machines, the rustling of clothes, and someone's breathing. But his body was numb, and all he could move were his eyelids.

A different building, a different city, but a hospital room, nonetheless. He wasn't alone either. A difference to Allison, caused by him being attuned not to dark, but to cold, which allowed healing spells to be cast on his body.

Numbing agents or not, there was no need to question why he couldn't move. His final spell had snapped his bones; he remembered that much. That was on top of the destruction caused to his muscles, the same as what Allison did to hers, but without her capacity to rewind time. That all came before calculating the damage Soul had inflicted. From the neck down, he may as well have been a log for all the movement he had.

Blurring at the corner of his vision, he saw the sway of a golden mound. "Rebecca?"

All it took was that one croaked word and she was almost out of her seat, becoming clear in his eyes. "Thank God you're alright."

The healing mage moved, giving Rebecca the time to hug her brother. Dakota let her, not that he had any way to stop her. "Where am I?" he asked, knowing the answer already.

With a swallow, she pulled back, still in his view. "You're in the Royal Isoval Hospital. The doctors said it'll take serious work before you can walk again."

He nodded, sinking into the pillow. *This wasn't what I wanted to emulate from her.*

She said nothing, probably unsure even how to respond. Either done or exhausted or simply to give them space, the mage doctor left. Alone, Rebecca let her strength fade. "I can't lose you. Not ever. I'm not planning another funeral."

He wanted to shake his head, but his body wasn't capable of doing so. "I'm not going anywhere."

She looked like she was trying to smile, but it just wouldn't come. "Will you finally tell me what's been happening?"

He sighed, doing his best to nod before closing his eyes. "I did promise." He waited a breath, then two, then three. It wasn't until the fifth that he started, going back to the night Nikita entered their minds. How she had scouted them, recruited them, and made them do so much to try and help her. How he'd met a girl named Arya and fought to protect her, again for the sake of Nikita, and eventually at the cost of Allison. He told her why she

414

forgot about him, and how they had gone to Inngey, and the secret Katife and Theta unravelled, although he skimmed over what she actually did. He told her all about Arya, how he rushed back to make a bargain that would protect them all. And how Nikita had thrown it all away.

Rebecca's voice was soft and tender. "I should have listened more."

He tried shaking his head. He failed, but it was enough that she saw it. "I'm the one who should have listened. I never even tried to move on, to . . . live with the past. I just acted like it was a choice. Then or now, Koros or you." With nothing to say, she just stayed there, her hands on his. He was tired. He had just woken up and yet he was so tired. Just as sleep started to overtake him, he whispered, "Soul was right. I failed in all the ways he said I would. I couldn't protect anyone. I tried, but it all fell to calamity."

***

As the days passed, the people changed. Theta came in early, greeting him and talking about a whole bunch of nothing. He could see the tinge of judgement, but Theta didn't bring it up. There was Connie, who said little but was covered in grief. And Katife, who he kept missing through sleep. After three days, she left a note, announcing a time and warning him to be awake for her.

He held that note as he was transferred out of intensive care. The time it gave was so very close now. He still couldn't walk but was no longer aided by twenty-four-seven healing spells. They brought in a wheelchair, and he was almost capable of wiggling himself into it were his limbs not all encased in plaster.

415

The door to his new room opened. Blinking at the arrival, he made a double take. It was someone who hadn't visited before, someone he hadn't expected to—someone with sweeping dark locks, refined features, and an utterly grim expression. Yifei. He hadn't seen her since Allison's performance. He said nothing as she walked in. She didn't sit, remaining standing by the foot of his bed. "You seem to be doing better." Mouth dry, he nodded, something he could finally do again. "You're surprised to see me. Why?"

Tilting his head, he said, "We've never met. And I heard you had a fight with my sister."

She nodded, standing there, tall, with great posture. She looked around with eyes brimming with sadness. "A fight? No, I just needed some time. She was sending me photos of your holiday before . . ." He nodded. "I really did like her, you know? I wish our last meeting didn't end how it did."

Dakota nodded again.

"She wasn't well. I don't think she wanted to let herself be happy."

"I know," Dakota replied.

"And she had a weird obsession with her own decadence."

"Yep," Dakota confirmed.

"God . . . I don't even know anyone else who even uses that word."

"Yep. She loved that word. *Decadence*."

Shaking her head, Yifei asked, "Do you know why?"

"Yep," Dakota replied.

"Well?" He turned his gaze a little to look at her fully. "Will you tell me?" Dakota shook his head. "Why not?"

"Because. You don't want to know."

Closing her eyes, frustration rippled across her face. "Look, Dakota. I know this isn't a great forum for a first meeting."

"Really?" he replied, with more than a hint of sarcasm.

Pushing through, she continued, "And I know it must be weird for you, not knowing me and everything, but I have to know, and you're the only one I can ask." She paused, readying herself. "I know it wasn't a car crash. Tell me how she died. And I want to know why."

Seeing the night on the beach, what they had done, he didn't even know if he should answer her, let alone how to do so. It was only thinking of Sydney, of the not knowing he went through, that he found sympathy and wanted her to be spared from that fate. "I wasn't there when it happened."

"But you know." Searching for an answer, he stayed quiet while he thought. "I know what she was; you don't need to hide anything from me."

Suddenly it was easy to know what to say. "Everyone thinks that, but nobody knows. Koros was more than something an article could explain."

"I know that. She told what they made her do."

He shook his head. "There's no way she told you everything."

Speaking louder, frustration was clearly edging into her tone. "She told me enough. Don't bother trying to protect some image you think I have, because you can't. I know she had blood on her hands. And I know that includes her own best friend. She insisted I know, like she was trying to drive me off."

Dakota froze, unable to move even if he wasn't covered

in plaster and injuries. "She told you about the train?"

"She told me how her best friend died. Look, Dakota, I know how broken she was. How far she was from perfect. But I wasn't after perfect. I never asked her to be a fantasy. I want reality, no matter how harsh it may be. And sometimes, that means being open to having everything I know thrown out the window. So please, just tell me."

He could feel the honesty in her voice, a sincere desire to know. "The reality is more than harsh. It's a whole different world."

"I would rather know both worlds than be blind to either," she countered.

Struck by her words, he sat staring. Then he nodded. "She was hit by a car."

"Don't . . ."

"I'm not. I promise. I just . . . don't know the details. I don't know how he did it. We were fighting, me and her against this guy. But we got separated. I don't know how it happened, but somehow, he had her run over."

Nodding, she asked, "Why were you fighting?"

"Does it matter?"

"It does to me."

Looking to her, the way she stood, the determination of her face, he caved. "You know the curse? Using yourself as an icon? He wanted to kill someone over it. We were trying to protect her. Those goals don't exactly align."

Nodding slowly, Yifei asked, "Who was he?"

"Soul," he said, knowing the name meant nothing. Dakota deflated, unsure what else to say. There was so much about Soul that made it impossible to know where to even begin, from the things he'd said to the simple fact he was the one who brought her into hospital. Wanting to add something, he said, "He's been arrested."

Looking for more, she asked, "I take it he is the one who did this to you? Who held up Lunar?" He nodded. "Why?"

Sighing, he watched the ceiling as if it held some answer. "I told you, it was about the taboo. That's what it all came down to."

"I've never even heard of the taboo outside of school."

Unsure what to say to that, he shrugged. "He believed that by killing people who'd done it, he could keep the world safe. And them, too, in a way. I think that was actually more important to him. *Protecting* them from a cruel fate. So, he killed them, and apparently anyone in his way. But . . ." He cut himself off, finding it hard to say the next part. With a swallow, he forced himself to continue. "I think he truly wanted to do the right thing."

Closing her eyes, Yifei looked out the window. "Psycho."

Exhaling his breath, Dakota shook his head. "I don't think so. I truly believe he thought he was doing good in his own messed up way."

Looking back to him, her tone turned sharp. "Do you think I care? He killed Alley. I don't give a damn what he wanted or believed. I don't care if she was killed with good intentions or bad. She died because of him. And no amount of wishful thinking will bring her back."

Unable to move, unsure what to say, he froze for a long moment. But she was patient and waited for an answer. "I can't pretend he was some demon. At the end of the day, he was trying to help."

"No. No. I don't accept that. Good intentions? Screw that. If his intentions were so pure, he wouldn't *accept* killing someone innocent in the crossfire. He wouldn't accept killing people, period. That wouldn't even be an option. You can't commit evil to achieve good. That's just called evil in a fancy dress."

Yifei's words left a gnawing sickness in his head. About the things he had done for his own just cause. And the girl he killed in the process. He was sure that face, that screaming face as her throat was torn out, would stay with him forever.

"Tell me what happened to her in Koros." Yifei's words shifted his mind away from the girl, at least for the moment.

"You said you knew."

Shaking her head, she persisted, "I know what she did. But she refused to say what they did to her."

Biting his lip, Dakota nodded. "I see."

She waited, and after a moment, added, "So?"

Closing his eyes and taking the deepest breath, Dakota replied, "She was abused. We all were but . . . Sensei had a special thing for punishing her."

"How?" Yifei insisted, her words becoming more forceful.

He didn't want to say, didn't want to relive those days. But he wanted her to know. That felt important somehow. "Mentally. And Physically. And . . ." he took the longest of pauses, delaying the final part as if it might change the past. In the end, all he managed was to say, "in other ways."

"What other ways?" Yifei pleaded.

Dakota swallowed, looked at her, but couldn't bring himself to say the words. All he could do was shake his head. Finally, Yifei said, "I see." She took a deep breath, standing for a little in silence before adding, "Thanks for giving me the truth. Hope you get better. See you later.

Or not. Whatever."

Not rushed, not slow, she walked out.

She would have crossed Katife in the hallway, considering how soon after she knocked on his door.

Seeing her again—cleaned up with her hair tied back and wearing a hairband again, dressed in new, fresh clothes, and smelling clean—a smile was dragged out from him. She smiled back. "Hey."

"Hey."

"Wanna go outside?" she asked, indicating the wheelchair.

"Sure."

She tried helping him move, but even without all the plaster, he was too heavy for her. A nurse had to help, seating him on the chair and allowing Katife to wheel him out of the room. On the ground floor, she followed the signs to reach the garden. It was in the centre of the hospital, surrounded on all sides by the building, but even so there were enough trees and plants to make it all look beautiful. All greenery along with the brown tree trunks and benches. There was even a small pond, artificial of course. She stopped, facing it, sitting herself on the bench right beside him. "So how are you?"

He shrugged. "Alright, I guess."

"There is no way that's true."

Exhaling, he leant back as far as he could. "I don't know. I keep telling myself I should be fine. I mean, I've lost people before. I've lost so many people before. But it doesn't change that I feel like crap."

Laying her hand on his shoulder, she spoke with soft words. "She was your sister and your twin. There is no world where this should be easy. If it hurts, it just means you're human." He tried looking at her with a harsh stare, but her grim smile was nothing if not disarming. "So, how are you really?"

His mouth felt dry, and in that moment the pond's water looked so alluring, he was tempted to ask her to tip his chair into it. "Is it okay if I say I don't know?"

"Probably. Better than saying fine at least." He could hear others in the garden, all talking in quiet voices. "I spoke with the police. They wanted to know what happened." He raised an eyebrow, waiting for her to continue. "I didn't tell them anything. Not really. Just that we'd left Salbador to get some fresh air together."

He nodded. "They spoke to me as well. There's a reckoning on its way for what we did."

She paused, turning full towards him and speaking with slow words. "What do you mean?"

Closing his eyes, he looked away. "Katife, we broke the law. A fake mugging, kicking a guy out of his house. Hell, even squatting. The walls, the bombs. Stealing the car. Vigilantism. We can't escape the consequences of what we did."

From the look on her face, he wondered if her mouth had gone dry. "Oh my God. What will we—"

"Don't worry. I swore you weren't involved in any of it. It'll keep it all on me and Nikita, wherever she is."

Reacting with a sudden burst of anger, her face went red. "Why do you keep doing this? Why do you keep trying to cut me out?!"

"Because I refuse to be like Dylan," he said.

"What?"

Looking to her, he explained, "My father didn't look out for his own family. He refused to be a man and take care of those precious to him. Because of that, he lost us all. I have to be a man, Katife. I have to do my duty. I have to protect those precious to me. I refuse to wind up like him." Swallowing, he shifted his arms as much as he could until she saw the invitation that it was. Standing up, she took his hands, facing him. Her breathing was heavy as she waited for his explanation. Her hands were soft and warm, with a roughness that made them real. "Meeting you has been one of the best things to happen in my life. I lost my sister, then failed to protect Arya. At this point, I will do anything for you. But I won't let you suffer. Not for me. I won't do that."

There were tears forming in her eyes. Light was falling, and in that space of time where the sky was dim but the lights were still off, she was like a dark angel standing before him. Collapsing onto a knee, Katife leant forward, resting her head on his chest. "You are such a fool," she said, and he could only smile.

In that moment, there was nothing he wanted more than to slowly stroke her hair, but with his arm in a cast, there was nothing he could do. "You really are the best friend I ever could have asked for."

He felt her nod a little. "And you were the worst boy I ever could have fallen for. But I wouldn't trade it for the world."

"I wouldn't trade you for two."

"I'm sure," she said, burrowing her head in more. "Okay. Do it your way. But don't you dare ditch me." With nothing else to say, he could only nod. Sighing, she added, "I get it. God, you're right. I know we had our reasons, but I just wish we didn't do it."

He only nodded. "I know. But what's done is done. I can't make that same mistake, not after watching it kill Allison."

"What mistake? You already chased Soul."

He had to look down to see her, but her hair was in the way of her face. He didn't mind. It was beautiful hair. "Not that. It was . . . something else." Taking a breath, he looked to the pond, its water rippling in the fading light. "Did you know she never wanted to leave Koros? Rebecca wanted us to go back with her, but I was the one who pushed Allison into accepting her offer. I still believe leaving was the right thing to do, but in the end, I just made her feel ashamed. We never dealt with the cravings that place left us with. That's why when Soul appeared, it was almost a relief. It was like we could finally live out what we desperately wanted to. All because I was too stupid to assimilate our past into the present. I killed my sister."

Pushing herself up, Katife looked right into his eyes, and he looked into hers. "I won't ever accept that. Soul killed Allison. Nobody else." She paused, but finally added, "But I also won't pretend there's no truth there. I know what you mean, because it's the same for everyone. Some dark part of yourself you want to hide. If this nightmare made you realise it's smarter to make peace with those parts than sweep them under the rug, then at least there was some good to come of it."

Caught in her words, he could only nod. She really was beautiful. It made him wish all the more for Nikita to never have been involved. "Sydney was wrong."

"How's that relevant?"

Matching her gaze, he took a breath. "Sydney. She used to say Allison could be an amazing imperfect creature. After Sydney's death, I watched Allison use that as a justification for being broken."

"What . . . I don't get it."

He nodded, slowing down. "Sydney knew that perfection is impossible, but even were it achievable, it would be undesirable. I mean, what is perfection?"

She shrugged. "Something as good as it can be, I guess."

"And what person is ever so good they have nothing left to improve or learn? That is why she said 'imperfect'. But she never said broken. Someone shattered, struggling to breathe, the person Allison became . . . Sydney would never praise that. She wanted her to be imperfect. As good as she could be, but always trying to be better, always aware of her faults and limitations, desperate to overcome them. Because to be perfect is to have no room left to grow. Sydney's idea of an imperfect creature wasn't someone broken like us. It was someone vibrant like you."

He could see the confusion on her face, as if she wasn't sure if she should be offended or not. "Katife, you are the most brilliant, beautiful, thoughtful person I've ever known. You are *my* imperfect creature, an amazing work of art. I've been such a fool to not see that."

She shook her head. She had never looked so sad. "I've told you. I know your tells. You fell for Arya. Don't try to deny it."

Taking his own turn to shake his head, he answered, "It's as Nikita said. It was the one thing she got right. That I used Arya to fill the hole Allison left. But that's not love. It's a crutch."

Hesitating, not willing to say what she desperately wanted to, she managed to croak, "I know how I see you. And I know you don't see me the same way."

"There're tears in your eyes. You've mixed up my tells. I know how I feel, Katife. I just wish I told you a year ago."

She shook her head, pulling back a little. "Don't make me repeat it. You can't lie to me."

With the slightest hint of frustration, he cried, "If you're so good at reading my tells, then explain this one."

Using all his flexibility, he leant forward, pulling her arms toward him as much as he could. She was too far, and it hurt so much, but he couldn't bring himself to stop, not until their lips met.

Any fighting, resistance, or hesitation she had died as she pressed forward, pushing him back deep into the chair. There was no describing the feeling of her warmth, her breath, her skin, hair, and even just her raw presence. She was passionate and wild and fierce. When she pulled away, he could see her face, a mirror of his own. He started to laugh and to cry, both at the same time, and not really sure why.

For more, visit
www.thomasjmaine.com

NEON RAINBOW

Ariamendle is more than just a boarding school. It is one of the highest ranked schools in the nation, attracting young magi from around the country. Classes are hard, attendance is strict, and expulsion threatens around every. It is, in every way, a school for the elite of the magi community.

Daughter of a successful fashion designer, Neo dreams of following in her fathers' footsteps, but fate has other plans for her. Enrolled into Ariamendle, she struggles to meet the school's demands while finding the time to train for her future. A future that is deemed unfit for a magus, especially one of Ariamendle's calibre.

Meanwhile, Kona Haruka claims one of the two scholarships to enter the school. Thrilled for the opportunity to advance her life out of poverty, she quickly realises the poisoned fruit she was given with one simple realisation; no scholarship student has ever graduated.

Their daily lives quickly become a mixture of façades, training, and surviving the brutal curriculum. All the while fighting to stop the school leaving permanent scars upon them.

Dropping out is not an option. Failing is not an option. Revealing the truth is less than not an option. So begins their four year journey of lies and deceit. Will they make it to graduation while keeping their souls intact, or will the school consume them whole?

www.ingramcontent.com/pod-product-compliance
Lightning Source LLC
Chambersburg PA
CBHW050107120726
47904CB00004B/1250